THE FAMILY—
RICH, FLAMBOYANT,
UNFORGETTABLE

BEA. She was their mother. She wanted to keep them close to her, but all she knew how to give was money.

SAM. Brash and big as life, he gave the most, and expected the most. When the family let him down, he never forgave.

JONNY. The golden boy who charmed his way into a staggering fortune. And paid for pleasures the world never suspected.

DIANA. She threw her love at too many men, and too many women. But never loved herself, until she loved George Sloate.

GEORGE. Like one of the family, he loved them, served them, fought their battles . . . and waited for Diana.

"*MIAMI MILLIONS* has it all . . .
"Real people to love, to disturb, to engross, the urgent heat of sex and love, and the rush of a big grand story."

—Jill Robinson
Author of *Bedtime Story*

ABOUT THE AUTHOR

John Maccabee is at work on a novel about rich boys who are trying to become men. His first novel, *Day One*, was also published by Bantam.

Miami Millions

■

John Maccabee

MIAMI MILLIONS
A Bantam Book / July 1980

ISBN 0-553-13313-6

Published simultaneously in the United States and Canada

Bantam Books are published by Bantam Books, Inc. Its trademark, consisting of the words "Bantam Books" and the portrayal of a bantam, is Registered in U.S. Patent and Trademark Office and in other countries. Marca Registrada. Bantam Books, Inc., 666 Fifth Avenue, New York, New York 10019.

PRINTED IN THE UNITED STATES OF AMERICA

0 9 8 7 6 5 4 3 2

for Sidney and Ruth Greenberger

No one could ever stop the water's flowing;
nor thought nor love has ever held it back.

Pablo Neruda

Contents

I

Magic City

1

The first time I met Sam Willig was in Miami in January, 1925. He was sitting at the bar in the Ponce de Leon Hotel, cursing something or someone under his breath.

It was my first day in town. I slipped inside the bar to get my bearings, and that was not going to be easy. Outside, the street was a madhouse. The noise alone was enough to split my head open. Jackhammers were pounding at ten different construction sites up and down Flagler Street. Marimba bands were playing on street corners, and car horns bellowed *ah-ooo-ga, ah-ooo-ga* at pedestrians who were spilling off sidewalks, darting in and out of traffic. A million people a year were coming down during the twenties, and in '25 alone, two and a half million of us made the trip. The rich were there playing, buying, flaunting their cars and clothes while speculators were grabbing what they could out of what all the northern newspapers were calling, "The Land Boom of the Century!"

All the action was crammed into the bar at the Ponce de Leon. Talk there was wild—men milled around in groups exchanging stories about killings made on prime lots in Hialeah and Allapattah. Half the time it sounded like some Seminole dialect was being spoken, but it was just the jungle drum of land fever. Money, sunshine, beaches, there for the taking.

In the midst of it all, Sam Willig sat alone, staring out at Flagler Street, banging his chubby fist against the cypress wood bar.

Sweat was seeping through my one and only seersucker suit. I leaned over the bar and ordered a beer.

"Damn," Sam said.

I followed his gaze. Outside, a group of men wearing knickers were surrounding an elderly lady who seemed to be as dazed as I was. The men were shoving pieces of paper in her face.

Sam shrugged, downing a glass of root beer.

"Hey, friend," I said, pulling my flask out of my jacket. "Want a chaser?"

He smiled, took a slug, then I pocketed the flask.

"No need to conceal it in here," he said.

I figured he was about my age—twenty-two or twenty-three—but he had the look of a harried, middle aged, door-to-door salesman with a squat little body and short spindly legs that dangled from the bar stool. His face was perfectly round. He had fair skin, red cheeks and lips, and round blue eyes that followed the frantic action at the bar.

"You're cursing like you lost money today," I said.

"Lost money? Hell, no one's losin' money. I'm just not makin' any. Those binder boys are makin' it. Everyone of 'em will walk home with a couple of thousand in their pockets. That is, if they have homes." He looked over at the window again.

The elderly lady was going through her purse as the men in knickers beamed Cheshire-cat grins and slapped each other's backs. When she brought out her cash, another group of men wearing knickers circled around her.

"They say they wear those damn knickers 'cause they don't need pressin'," Sam said. "Fast bunch. All a binder boy knows is land and paper."

"Binder boy?"

The question gave me away. Sam looked at me with more interest. Instinct, I guess. Newcomers were unloading so much of their money on residents at the time. Whatever he had been cursing at took a back seat to some friendly advice laced with a not-too-subtle interest in my prospects for dealing land.

"Binder boys come down here from up north for a killing. Most stubborn bunch around. You know some of 'em were camping on our front lawn last week. A gun barrel's the only thing that got 'em off it. Watch out around them. You down here investing?"

Before I had a chance to answer, one of the boys from the street gave a whooping war cry and kicked open the bar door. Sam leaned over to get a better look at him. The boy rushed to the bar, ordering drinks for the house.

"You got money or paper to pay for that?" Sam called out.

The man downed his drink, then winked at us.

"All they got is the paper you see," Sam said out of the corner of his mouth, "nothin' but paper."

"How's that work?"

"You'll see in a minute."

The binder boy ordered another shot, and headed toward us, planting a wide grin on his face, and staring me right in the eye.

"You gentlemen interested in some Miamiland acreage?" he asked. "Got two or three fine lots."

Other men near us at the bar craned their necks, trying to listen.

"What went on at Miamiland?" Sam asked.

"It's still going on. Never seen anything like it. Fastest land sale in history."

No sooner were the words out of his mouth, when three men hopped off their bar stools and headed for the door.

The binder boy gave me the once-over. "Got binders on choice lots. Prime Miamiland."

"What's Miamiland?" I asked. His smile became hungrier.

"Housing development north of here—went on sale today." Sam shushed me up. "How much they takin' in over there?"

"Some say it's close to six."

"Thousand?" I asked.

"Millions, boy, millions," Sam said impatiently. "What you got on you?" he asked the man.

"Two lots—750 apiece. Sell you the binder—ten percent down."

Another group of men in soiled white knickers came charging through the door; activity in the street behind them looked frenzied.

"Miamiland's closing down!" one of them shouted. "They got to—it's too much to handle!"

All heads turned toward the windows. People were racing up Flagler, waving their wallets. Before I knew what had happened, Sam and I were racing along with them into the middle of a mob scene around a storefront land sale office that had a marimba band playing in front of it. Crowds were trying to force their way inside as an officious, pink-faced man in a pin-striped suit barred the way.

"It's all over," he was shouting at them. "There's nothing left to sell."

A well-dressed woman hopped onto someone's shoulders and railed at him, "I want two lots!"

"There's nothing left!"

She opened her purse, took out a wad of bills, and threw it at him. "I don't care where they are!" she screamed. "I want two of them."

Surging forward, the crowd went wild to the accompaniment of the marimba band's rinky-tink music. Suddenly instruments went flying. A lone conga drum rolled into the street. More money appeared; bundles of it went sailing through the air. Checks were thrown like confetti, forcing the sales official to retreat inside. People up front were pressed against the store windows, which looked as if they were about to shatter. Fights started breaking out.

"That's Miamiland," Sam said. "Damn 'em, I want in."

It was the craziest thing I'd ever seen. Right next to a couple of guys punching each other fast and furiously were another couple of guys trading deeds, signing papers, and exchanging cash.

"Let's get back inside," Sam said, "or we'll wind up on the wrong end of somebody's fist."

We headed back to the bar and ordered beers. Sam sat there sullenly.

"Sure looks like one of those boys took you over the coals," I offered.

"Hell, no, I could've taken them for plenty. The ones I had to shoo off the lawn? When I finally brought the gun out, they up and offered to buy the house. No For Sale sign on it, but they wouldn't take no for an answer. I had to persuade my mother to go out and buy a Not For Sale sign just to keep them from comin' back."

I found that a little hard to believe. "Is that why you're so angry?"

"What you say your name was?"

"George Sloate."

"This your first week in Miami?"

"First day."

"You got a lot to learn."

It wasn't as if he said it nastily, it just shut me up for a while.

We saw there staring down into our beers until Sam finally

grinned and slapped me on the back. "Don't mind me. I'm just edgy, that's all."

"You're right. I do have a lot to learn. I thought you could help."

"Maybe I can. What do you want to know?"

"What's this binder boy nonsense for starters—this ten-percent-down business?"

"Boys ask you to put that down as a binder on a lot—that's how they got their name. While deeds and titles are being searched at the courthouse, you can go out and sell binders on your binder—trade 'em like stocks. Prices rise so quick, you make more money that way. A single piece of property winds up with dozens of owners. But all you really got is the paper, no land at all. What you saw today is just the beginning of it. You mark my words."

"When did you get to town?"

"Me? Me and my family have been here since 1919."

"You were in early, then."

"Hell, early's not the word for it. I could've had an acre on the ocean for one fifty, but no go. Where'd you come down from?"

"Columbus, Ohio."

"That's where we're from. High Street, Columbus. Those palm trees out there are a far cry from hillbilly Ohio."

"Are you speculating on land?"

"Money's all tied up," he said. "Can't get my hands on a penny. All tied up in a business down here."

He eyed me again. Again, I felt as if I were a prospective customer. "My name's Willig. Sam Willig," he said, extending his hand.

"Willig? I know the name. You've got that store up on Flagler. I bought this skimmer there this morning."

He reached up, pulled the hat from my head, and inspected the hatband.

"Good purchase. My brother-in-law brought that line in here last year. It's a good seller. Who waited on you?"

"A blonde girl."

I was about to say a slightly drunk blonde girl, which is what she had been, and at a very early hour of the morning to boot, but something stopped me. I was glad it had.

"That's my sister." He replaced the hat on my head. "So, you gettin' into land?"

I paused, thinking the question over more seriously than he

expected. I'd just gotten out of college. My father wanted me to rush right into law school, and then into a partnership with him. I was feeling ripe for something, I just wasn't sure what it was. The fact that my granddad had died recently, leaving me a couple of thousand dollars, was what got me on the train to Florida.

"I'm just looking around," I said.

"This ain't no time for that. This is the time for action. I tell you if you got any money on you at all, you can make a fortune down here."

"You must be doing well, serving the likes of me."

"Shoot! Shoes, hats and birdseed's okay, but land is where the action is. Been out to the beach yet?"

"I haven't been anywhere except your store, my room, and here."

"Where you stayin'?"

"The Elysium Gardens."

"Hell of a name, but you better carry a gun in that place." He yelled to a passing waiter. "Hey, Sidney, wasn't that Percy boy cut up real bad at the Elysium?"

Sid nodded.

"I thought so. Someone sliced that kid up real bad over there. Rough times." He lowered his voice. "We had so many murders last year the damn Ku Klux Klan offered its services, wanted to come in here and clean everything up. No thanks, the city fathers said. No thanks, indeed. What line you in?"

"I just got out of college."

"Just what we need—another educated man. You ever read a land contract?"

"No."

"If you can write a good one, you got it made. Got any money on you?"

I was not about to answer that question, but that didn't stop him.

"You better get yourself a good look at what's goin' on down here. You can make a bundle on it."

"That's tellin' him," a drunk at the bar called out.

Sam smirked. "What a dive. You wanna go watch the best show in all Miami?"

"What's that?"

"What time is it?"

I pulled out my watch. "One-thirty."

"Nice watch. We drive fast enough, we'll make it."

"Make what?"

"The Great Commoner himself, preachin' fear o' God and Coral Gables, Florida."

"Bryan?"

"William J., boy orator."

Two men in white flannels turned around, staring indignantly as Sam hopped off his stool. "They don't like me callin' him William J. like that, but of course they are in here getting boozed up all day. I tell you there's a wealth of hypocrisy in our midst. Come on, I'll show you around. Hey, Sid, put this young man's drinks on my chit."

"What chit?" Sid shot back.

Sam cocked his skimmer, and then wheeled around, his voice sounding as dry as gravel. "I'll pay you later, you dumb bastard."

My legs were twice the length of Sam's, but I was panting just trying to keep up with him once we hit the streets. We headed toward a landfill area that fronted Biscayne Bay. Wreckers were taking apart a wooden pier that stretched out into the water.

"That was old Elser's Pier," Sam said. "Met my damn wife there. You married?"

"No."

"Old Elser's. It's progress. We're puttin' in a park here. Gonna plant royal palm trees everywhere. Nothin' but the best for this town from now on."

A binder boy came running up behind us, draping his arm around Sam's shoulder. "Mr. Willig, someone in the Ponce de Leon told me to talk with you. Got a great deal on some prime Miamiland."

Sam winked at me.

"How much?"

The boy waved his piece of paper around, shouting over the pounding of yet another marimba band's conga drum.

"Prime acreage. Two lots, three thousand."

Sam turned to me. "See what I tell you—up thousands in less than an hour." He waved the boy off. "Not interested."

"You sure you have time to take me around this afternoon?"

"My wife and sister are in the store. They don't need me. There's too much action downtown what with the Miamiland sale and all."

"Well, it's awfully nice of you."

He stopped dead in his tracks, pointing a stubby finger at my chest. "You're right about that. I collect strays, George Sloate. Always have, and you seem like a nice enough one. Fellow boozer—fellow Ohioan—though there's no lacking them down here. But you do seem nice, and you didn't answer me when I asked if you had any money on you, which leads me to believe that you do. Now, I'll take you for a ride around this fair city, but I won't take you for any ride, if you get my meaning. And just maybe with your clean young face and my mouthpiece, we can do some business."

He turned, took off again, and I raced after him. I suppose I was as intrigued with his honesty as anything else. He seemed so sure of himself, but I kept wondering why he had been cursing under his breath at anything and why he thought he needed me.

When we turned the corner, he started running.

"Hey, Charley! Don't do it to me. That's my car," he shouted.

The street had two or three rows of parked cars on it; some up on the sidewalk, most jammed in end to end. A policeman was bending over a black Model T, unhinging its front seat. A pile of car seats lay beside him.

"Charley, please, I was only inside for a minute."

"Don't give me that crap, Sam. I been working this street for almost an hour. You can't park here, and you know it." Charley straightened up, spit into his hands, and with one final tug, ripped the seat out and threw it on the ground.

"That's just great. Perfect," Sam said, taking off his skimmer and fanning himself with it.

"You guys park here anytime you want. Can't do it no more, Sam. This ain't a small town no more. You guys rip up your parking citations. Chief says this is the only way to stop it. I gotta haul these seats down to the police lot. You can pay when you collect. That's the way it's gonna be done. You think this is easy work?"

"Don't expect me to feel sorry for you. You ruined my car."

"I don't care, Sam. I like you okay, but this street's too crowded. Come on down and collect when you're ready."

"Now wait a minute, Charley. I'm here. I'll pay you the money."

"Against the rules. Come down to the lot."

Charley began carrying car seats over to a police truck as I stood under a store's awning out of the sun's glare. Sam waved to me.

"Have you met Mr. Sloate yet? He's a businessman come down here from Ohio."

Charley looked up and grunted. "Who ain't a businessman from Ohio." He started dumping car seats into the truck.

"You're working up quite a sweat hauling those seats. Mr. Sloate here had some nifty bourbon, if you'd care to take a snort. Real stuff."

Charley looked interested. "What you pullin', Sam?"

Sam nudged me. "Pass him your flask, George, and don't be stingy."

I reached into my pocket and brought it out. Charley grabbed it, downing half of it before Sam tapped him on his shoulder.

"Yes, sir, quite a thirst. Now let my have my seat. I'll give you the five bucks, and you can go have yourself a nice dinner somewhere. We're in a hurry."

We got the seat bolted down in the car, finishing off the flask in the process. Both of us were half-bagged by the time we took off. Sam kept waving his hand around, pointing things out to me. The place looked like someone had dreamed it into existence. Anchored off the bayfront were a dozen schooners whose masts looked like shadows of trees cast against the blazing sun and vapor rising from the bay.

"Ships unloadin' buildin' supplies. The rail lines are gettin' all tied up tryin' to get that stuff in here," Sam said, pulling off the road for a minute to show me a mound of sand in the middle of the bay.

"See, they dredged the channel to make more room for the ships to get in. When they did that, they created an island out there. Then they come up with this grand notion of selling lots on it. They want to put five hundred people out there, place is going up for sale next week. You mark my words, the suckers'll buy it, too."

"But there's no bridge going out there."

He gave a high-pitched wheeze of a laugh. "This is Miami, boy, don't need bridges. And, damn it, I won't own an inch of it."

He kicked the car into first. We turned the corner and ran into downtown traffic.

"Sam, let me ask you something. You got yourself a nice store there on Flagler. Looks like it's doing pretty well. Why can't you get up any money on it to buy land?"

"I don't got nothing myself. My mother's got it all. She's a conservative woman. She's not ready to move on this land business."

"What about your brother-in-law?"

"He's dabblin' in other things. He's gettin' ready to move. Stop askin' me so many questions. You're makin' me nervous. Just look around, keep your eyes open, and think of some way to make your fortune. That's all you should be doin'."

On we went past storefronts, hotels, and land sales offices. Above us loomed building cranes and scaffolding for skyscrapers, each with a sign bolted onto it advertising it as the tallest building in the South. Mammoth billboards with long-legged girls in bathing suits posed next to elephants on the beach—all of them promoting Miami, the Magic City; Miami, America's Winter Playground. Charley the cop was right: all the promoters in Ohio had wound up here, and they seemed intent on turning it into Akron by the sea.

Outside the city the land was as flat as a table top. Engineers in sweat-soaked shirts were surveying it, Negro workers clearing it. We drove west, then south, and finally came upon a caravan of pink buses with the words Coral Gables, Florida, painted on the side of them. Each had a man with a megaphone standing in front of it, pointing out the same sights Sam was showing me.

"That's Mr. Merrick's sales fleet," Sam said. "He brings the buyers out here for lunch and throws in William Jennings Bryan for dessert. You're gonna love this."

"Merrick's a developer?"

"Poet, farmer, dreamer—he's got it all. Owns almost a thousand acres out here."

He drove up the Tamiami Trail to Douglas Road, parking at Coral Gables's Douglas Entrance, which looked like the outpost of a Mediterranean walled city. Someone with a flair for the outrageous had designed a Moorish guard tower and battlements above it. Inside were balconies, trellises, palms, palms, and more palms.

"Guys like Merrick are the modern Medici," Sam explained. "There are more European iron and marble workers here than anywhere in the world at the moment."

"You do have quite a mouthpiece, Sam. You should be selling for Merrick."

"That's a thought. Now mind your manners. High-class clientele. Don't go droppin' your final *t*'s and consonants." Two women wearing cloche hats sauntered by. Sam tipped his hat. "Good afternoon, ladies." All consonants intact.

We made our way to a place called the Venetian Pool. This *was* an affluent crowd; about three hundred of them were milling around on marble walks. Black and gold gondolas floated in the biggest swimming pool I'd ever seen. They were manned by Negroes wearing red silk scarves on their heads and gold earrings looped through their ears.

The surrounding buildings were pale pink stucco and terra cotta with red-tiled roofs. Surrounding them were elaborate gardens—bursts of magenta and lavender blossoms. Jan Garber's Society Orchestra was playing on the lawn. The lead singer kept repeating a lyric—something about falling in love in Coral Gables. People were dancing, and jamming food into their mouths.

"No hooch?" I asked.

Sam was properly startled. "Saints preserve you, sinner, Mr. Bryan's here. It's all very moral."

A group of ladies started squealing as a fully dressed, sun-tanned man jumped into the pool dragging a twelve-foot-long alligator in with him. The gator's tail snapped around as it hit the water, missing the man by an inch. He dove under it, hoisting it up on his shoulders, parading it around the shallow end. The gator wiggled free, hit the water again, then surfaced and floated silently. The man pounced, forcing its jaws open with his bare hands. The crowd gasped but inched forward, peering into the undulating throat.

"How many arms has it chewed in its lifetime?" someone called out.

The man merely laughed as one of his helpers threw him a rope. He tied it around the gator's neck, then jumped out of the pool and walked the gator back into the foliage.

"Does that like clockwork," Sam said. "The real show'll start soon." He pointed to a concrete island in the middle of the pool. A wood slat chair and striped beach umbrella had been set up on it. "That's where Bryan sits. Merrick pays him a hundred thousand a year; fifty thousand in cash and fifty thousand in land. William J. wasn't ever just anybody's dumb preacher."

"My father idolized him."

"Sure. he went over big in Ohio. Wanted to kick out all the corrupt Republicans. Silver coinage! Freedom from London banks!" Sam's eyes rolled back in his head. " 'You shall not crucify mankind upon a cross of gold.' " He laughed. "Heady stuff. Tell you the truth. George. I don't trust in anything that heady. but I believe in what he's doing now in his old age. There he is."

I turned my head and saw Bryan sitting on the concrete island. It was as if I'd conjured up this vision from my childhood: the bald dome, the tight. thin lips. the black cloth coat. I rubbed my eyes in disbelief. What a convenient smile he suddenly flashed to one and all. He looked like a ringmaster.

"How do you like Mr. Merrick's paradise?" he asked.

Someone tried handing him a megaphone. "I've never needed that." The crowd roared. "You all know who I am. That's something God has been very kind about. You know my words and my deeds. I bless all of you for coming out here today, out here to Mr. Merrick's Master Suburb—that's what they call it, new one on me." The crowd laughed again. "God has produced a bountiful harvest here, and men like George Merrick have worked the harvest with all their skill, all their heart—for you." He sat forward, distracted, staring down into the pool. "My life is the best record I leave. Mrs. Bryan and I came here years ago. We love this spot. I transferred my citizenship here from Nebraska in '22."

He rubbed his eyes, looked up, and smiled again, but he seemed confused and. hard as it was to believe, he appeared to be tired of talking. "That was a good lunch. I want to talk with you about this wonderful town and its builder and designer, George Merrick. For it is the men of vision of our great land who will hand you the harvest of God's work. . . ."

I wanted to run. The man my father had brought me up to think of as a firebrand, a saint, was sitting there stumbling through a half-baked sales pitch. I tried blocking out the sound of his voice with a poem I'd memorized as a child.

> The bard and the prophet of them all
> Prairie avenger, mountain lion
> Bryan, Bryan, Bryan, Bryan
> Gigantic troubador, speaking like a siege gun . . .

"You're talking to yourself, George," Sam whispered, "and I believe the last line goes, 'Smashing Plymouth Rock with his boulders from the West.' "

I shook my head, feeling sorely disillusioned.

"Don't pay it any mind, George. Consider this your rite of passage. See him for what he is."

"But the Stock Exchange threatened the succession of New York City over the candidacy of that man."

Someone shushed me. Sam lowered his voice.

"They should have put him to work sellin' bonds. Have you seen enough?"

I stared at Sam who was smiling so enthusiastically.

"Is it in your blood, George?"

I must have looked dumbfounded.

"What's goin' on down here, I mean. Has it hit you yet?"

"Well—it's got religious portent, all right."

"Now, what does that mean?"

"I see the temptation coming. I pass through the baptism with that alligator in the pool and Bryan himself blesses me on my way."

Sam giggled. "That's a good one. Bryan blesses you. That's a rare one. You've got a good head, but you've got to feel the land fever. Hasn't it hit?"

"Damn," I muttered under my breath.

I had eyes. The future was rearing its palm-laden, cash-laden, terra cotta-and-marble head. It had hit all right—I wanted in as well.

2

Once we got back to town, Sam asked me to walk over to the store with him. Two men in matching gray linen suits were standing in front of it.

"Are you Mr. Willig?" the older one asked.

Sam tipped his hat. "I am."

"My name is Colonel James Paley. This is my son, Jimmy."

Jimmy smiled wanly.

"We're down here on vacation from Savannah."

"Lovely city, Savannah," Sam said.

"Yes, sir, Mr. Willig. I'm interested in your store."

"Didn't anybody wait on you inside?"

"No, sir, it isn't a matter of that. Does this lot next to your store belong to you?"

There was a scrubby clump of brambles adjacent to the building.

"Yes."

"What's the front footage on Flagler?"

"Beg pardon?"

"What's the total footage?"

"Well. the store's fifty or seventy feet wide. I don't know about the lot."

With that, the colonel marched young Jimmy over there. The two of them paced it off.

"Fifty as well," the colonel said. "I'm interested in the store and the lot."

"You want to get into the dry goods business?"

"No, sir, I'm interested in real estate. Flagler Street lots, to be exact."

"I'll be damned."

"You interested?"

I found it too difficult to follow this pace of business, so I occupied my time browsing in one of the rectangular display windows that jutted out into the street. A woman's hand was adjusting the price tag on a pair of flashy white and tan wing tips. As I looked over the curtain that hung behind the case, the woman drew back her hand. She patted her hair and smiled coquettishly. From the looks of her, I thought, it had been years since she had any right to do that. Her hair was too black, her mouth rouged ruby red, and there were flecks of mascara in the lines around her eyes. I thought she was Sam's mother.

"George." Sam was saying, "listen to this. Repeat your offer, Mr. Paley."

"Colonel Paley," Paley the younger said.

Paley the elder was staring up at the sun. "I think that six hundred dollars a front foot is not out of the question."

"What did you pay for it originally, Sam?" I offered, but his eyes flashed, warning me not to utter another word.

"Colonel Paley, I'll have to take this up with my family."

Paley took a card out of his vest pocket.

"Jimmy and I are staying at the McAllister. Anytime you

want to talk, drop by. I want you to know that I was here first if anybody else starts coming around. Good day, gentlemen."

The Paleys took off. Sam whipped his skimmer off and fanned himself.

"George, you're gonna learn a rule of thumb in the real estate business right now. Don't ever remind 'em of what prices were way back when. That'll only make 'em feel stupid for missin' out when the goin' was good. You gotta sell 'em on the chance of a lifetime."

"Well, what did you pay for it?"

"Hell, I think the whole hundred foot went for five grand. Do you know what that means? That goddamn crazy southerner wants to fork over sixty grand for it!"

"That's a deal your mother won't want to pass up."

"You're readin' my mind."

Brass bells clanked as he opened the front door. "Tildy! Tildy, where are you?"

The store was cool and dark and had that rich, musty smell of leather. Rows of saddles were lined up on one wall. In front were five counters with merchandise piled neatly on them. Shirts, bolts of fabric, hats, tools, buckets—everything you could think of. The black-haired woman strolled out of a back room; she was about five feet two or three, buxom, and gap toothed.

"Tildy, you're not going to believe this." Sam rushed over to her and kissed her. She turned her cheek to him but stared at me.

"You better have a good story worked up. Left the poor women to fend for themselves in this heat. Been no one here all day except Diana and me."

"Where's Jack?"

"You tell me. You boys been hatchin' some great scheme?"

She had the most irritating voice: shrill southern, with a dash of nasal whine and a deep breath after each sentence as if she'd pass out before she'd have a chance to complete her next one.

"Who's your friend?"

"George, come over here and meet my wife. This is George Sloate. George, Tildy Willig."

Well, she looked old enough to have been his mother. Her hand floated up at me, and I had the distinct impression that she was waiting for me to click my heels together and kiss it. I took her hand and shook it lightly.

"Two men just made me the most unbelievable offer for the store."

"You a friend of Sam's?" Tildy asked.

"You aren't listenin' to me."

"Of course I'm listening. Two men just made you an offer for the store. That and a dime'll buy me a ham sandwich at the lunch counter at Woolworth's."

"Where's Diana?"

"She's in back. Got herself another headache. There's been no one helping me all day."

"I've got to talk with her about this. Plan strategy for mama."

He walked to the back of the store. "Where's Albert?"

"He should be right under your feet."

A squeal of delight rang out as Sam scooped up a little boy who'd been hiding in the cardboard boxes.

"George, this is my son, Albert. Wave at the man." The boy had Sam's round face and Tildy's full, sullen mouth. "He was four just last month—weren't you? You been hiding from me?" He took him into the back room.

Tildy sighed heavily, then began straightening the counters.

"You movin' in?" she asked.

"I beg your pardon."

"Very polite," she said. "Has Sam offered you a room at the house yet?"

"Why no."

"That's surprising. Where'd you two meet?"

"Over at the Ponce de Leon."

"That naughty boy."

"There was a lot of activity down there today. Miamiland went up for sale."

"Don't I know it. That's all anyone's been talkin' about. Sam take you out to hear Mr. Bryan?"

That voice. The questions. I nodded but felt like lying or rushing to Sam's defense. What I'd seen in this short time convinced me that marriage to her was more than any man would have bargained for.

"Sam's such a congenial man, don't you think?" She sighed again. "I think business is wasted on him. He'd do better teaching somewhere. Chalk and all. Where do you come from?"

"Columbus, Ohio."

Her eyes narrowed. "You're not a relative, are you?"

"No."

Her hands fluttered up to her bosom. "Thank God for that. There's enough Willigs in Miami for me to contend with. You met the mother yet?"

I looked down at the shirts, praying she'd go away.

"Weren't you in here this morning?"

"I bought this hat."

"I thought you looked familiar."

The blonde girl who'd waited on me earlier walked out of the back room, still wobbling drunkenly. She was even lovelier than I remembered.

"I'm trying to concentrate," she was saying to Sam, "but you're running on so fast. I've got this headache." She looked up without recognizing me. "Can I help you?"

Sam walked between us. "George here heard the offer, didn't you? Tell her about it."

She smiled faintly, but said nothing. I wish I knew how to describe her smile; it looked out of place in that musty, poorly lit store. What on earth did she have to smile about, being locked up all day with the likes of Tildy Willig?

Tildy, obviously miffed by the attention Diana was getting from me, sighed more loudly. "Whatever are you running off at the mouth about, Sam?"

"Tell them, George."

Diana studied my face. Then, almost as if it were an afterthought, she placed me. "That hat does look well on you."

"Tell them, George," Sam said impatiently.

All three were staring at me. I hadn't known Sam long enough to tell him that I didn't possess his ability to register enthusiasm in front of total strangers, but he kept egging me on.

"There were two men here who offered your brother about sixty thousand for this building and the lot next to it."

"Sixty thousand!"

Two or three boxes came crashing down in the back of the room as Albert started screaming.

"Tildy—go mind that child," Sam shouted. Tildy took off. He started pacing. "Now there's no way in hell that mama is going to be able to resist that."

"She'll find her own way in hell," Diana said.

The statement made her sound older than her years. I think

she knew that, too, because she gave me an embarrassed smile. Her hands brushed through the honey-colored curls that framed her face.

"What's your name?" she asked, tossing a ringlet behind her.

"George Sloate."

"Sam says you've come down from Columbus," she said, smiling again.

The smile started in her eyes; it was slow, appealing, and very private, inviting me to ask her questions about herself. But Sam stepped between us again.

"I took George around today, showed him everything. He knows a good thing when he sees it."

"We all see it," Diana said. "I know it. Jack knows it, but you make headway with mother. I won't."

"What would she object to?"

"For one thing, you'd be taking away her store."

"With sixty grand we'd be able to build and stock three stores."

"And she'll tell you that she doesn't want it to get that big. She'll say that the lot is being saved for the future, for expansion, or whatever she needs for her future. Meantime, she hasn't set foot in here in weeks."

"Maybe Jack should pitch it to her."

"Jack wants to stay clear of her for a while."

"Where is he, anyway?"

She walked over to the window and stared at the street. A two-car parade was passing by—cymbals crashed, trumpets blared, bunting and confetti were flying in the breeze. Diana came alive, looking as if she wanted to run out there and join them, but she stayed put, her finger tapping the trumpet beat on the window as sunlight caught her reflection in the glass. That smile again. It looked as if it haunted her as well as me.

"Got themselves a damned good excuse for a parade today," Sam said. "Fastest land sale in history. Where is Jack?"

"You're not the only one trying to make some money in this town. Jack's setting up another delivery. I could sure use some of it right about now."

Sam pointed to me and shushed her. "Okay, there's time to talk about that some other time. You know, Jonny could sell her on it."

Diana's eyes flashed mischievously. "That's a good one. She

wouldn't take him seriously, and if she only knew about the dirt he was playing with, she'd send him away."

Tildy stuck her head out of the back room. "Sam, you have not spent more than two minutes with your son. I'm getting a little tired of this."

Sam put on his skimmer and grabbed the doorknob. "I will later. We got work to do. I'll see you at dinner. Come on, George."

"I expect I'll see you at dinner as well," Diana said to me. She was staring at Sam pacing up and back in front of the store. "My brother is a lunatic, but he's a nice one."

"He makes quite a case for investing in this city."

Tildy's head reappeared. "He makes a case for anything involving lots of running around and no work."

Diana shuddered at the sound of her sister-in-law's voice. "Do come for dinner. He can use the support."

"Now what does that mean?" Tildy yelled.

I slammed the door, missing the rest of her barrage.

We drove over to a residential district near Fifteenth Street.

"They call this development the Garden of Eden. That's our place over there."

He was pointing to a wood house that had a long porch trimmed with craggy rock. There were a great many houses like it built before air conditioning came into being. They were called Belvederes. My dad had one like it on a lake up in Michigan. Each had bedrooms on the second floor with windows on four walls for cross ventilation. Roof lines and porches had large overhangs so that you didn't have to close the windows during the rainy summer months. Inside, the rooms were always cool but damp and dark.

There was a large tree beside Sam's house that had a pale gray trunk and clusters of lavender blossoms on its branches; bunches of them had blown onto the lawn.

"It's called a jacaranda," Sam said when he saw me staring at it. He pulled a low-hanging branch to his nose and breathed deeply. "This is my mother's favorite. My favorite's that one just starting to blossom over there. Called a royal poinsettia. In the late spring or early summer after the flowers blow down, it spreads a blood-red carpet out here on the lawn."

I couldn't help but notice that Sam's demeanor changed the minute we walked up to that house.

"Tildy, the boy, and me live in a little apartment over the

garage. Jack, Diana, and Jon live in the house with her. I'm surprised she's not out in her garden."

He walked up on the porch. There actually was a sign saying Not For Sale tacked up on the front door. He cupped his eyes, staring in through a screen window.

"Don't see her." He tried the front door, but it was locked. He knocked. "Mama? She should be inside. Mama?" No answer. He looked up meekly. "George, why don't you walk around back and see if she's working in her garden. Mama? You in there?"

Walking on the grass was more like walking on rusted blades, as if it were more of a weed than a grass. It was boxed in by a low hedge of crotons. As I turned the corner, a breeze carrying the sweet odor of jasmine hit me. Hibiscus bushes, overcrowded and overgrown, momentarily blocked my view of the star jasmine which were neatly trimmed below a window ledge at the rear of the house.

I heard Sam call out, "Mama?" again, and then a woman mimicked his voice:

"Mama, mama, mama. Sounds like a damn fool."

She was inside staring intently at something she seemed very interested in on the back lawn. I walked a step closer. She didn't hear me, and I had the strangest feeling that I was intruding on one of her most intimate moments.

Sam shouted again, "Mama!"

"If I keep very still," she said to herself, "he'll up and go away."

There was a fat black rubber hose coiled on the ground below her window. She was staring at a single ripple of water that pulsed out of it, glimmering like a silver ribbon on the baked-out grass.

"Sail away," she whispered.

"Mama!" Sam walked past me and stood below her window. "Don't you answer when I call you?"

She kept her back to me.

"Don't you think I hear you? That everyone down the block doesn't hear you yelling 'mama, mama, mama'? Have you no manners?"

"I came to talk with you."

"Who'd you leave in the store?"

He coughed nervously. "You're not having a very good day."

"Never mind about my day. Who'd you leave there?"

"Tildy and Diana."

"You're a very trusting soul, aren't you? What were you doing all day?"

"Miamiland went on sale this morning. The town's goin' wild. I sold out in four hours."

She shook her head wearily. "And how many lots did you buy?"

"Very funny," he said, staring down at his shoes.

"Why? You can buy land with the money you've saved from the store."

"I haven't saved any money."

"What happened to all of it?" she asked, as if she already knew.

Sam put his hand on the house, resting his head on his forearm. "I don't make that much, you know."

"Tell that to your wife if you want to, but not to me. You make enough. You pay no rent. You eat over here every night. What did you do with your money?"

"Everything's getting very expensive down here now."

"Sure, gambling is a rich man's sport."

"Who told you about that?"

"I know all about you. You were talking up a storm when you were winning. What happened to all of it?"

"There wasn't that much."

"Enough to get you into another game. You lost it, didn't you?"

Sam noticed the hose. "You left the water running out here."

"I know I did. How much did they sell Miamiland for?"

"Six million."

"Insanity."

"Those binder boys got involved in it. The one I met doubled the price of one lot in an hour."

"And you're thinking you'd like to do the same. Well, you could have if you'd held on to your money. Or is that why you've come here to talk with me today?"

"Well, something is up—"

"Where's Albert?"

"Tildy's got him at the store."

"That poor child, spending so much time in that place while the sun's out. The last time I was in there, she was letting him crawl over the dusty floor."

"You could have taken him today."

"I'm just about finished raising children. He's your responsibility."

Sam shrugged his shoulders, turned to me, and winked. "It's a losing battle, George."

"Who's here? Who's that?" she said.

"This is George Sloate. He's from Columbus."

Her head darted nervously, trying to get a better look at me.

"Hello, Mrs. Willig."

"Sam, why didn't you tell me someone was here? That's very rude."

"This is his first day in town. Bought that hat he's wearing from Diana this morning."

I took my hat off and held it self-consciously.

"From Columbus? Not one of those binder boys."

"No, George is a businessman."

I couldn't see her face. The sun was behind the house, and the overhang threw shadows on the screen.

"What's your name?"

"George Sloate, ma'am."

"Sloate. I knew a Dr. Sloate in Columbus."

"That's my Uncle Bill."

"He lived in Bexley. Is that where you're from?"

She wanted to peg me as soon as she could; Bexley was the richest suburb in Columbus.

"Yes," I said, although we actually lived a block or two from it. I just thought I'd give her what she wanted to hear.

"We lived near there," she said quickly.

High Street was hardly a stone's throw from Bexley.

"Your uncle is a fine doctor. He treated my youngest boy once. Tell him you met Bea Willig—he'll remember me."

Car horns honked in front of the house.

"What time is it?" she asked.

I pulled out my watch. "Four o'clock."

"Banks are closed. They've got pockets filled with cash, and they're cruising the neighborhoods. Get rid of them, Sam." She walked away from the window.

"Come on, George."

"What's going on?"

"Happens every night. Binder boys." He patted my shoulder. "She likes you. That Bexley stuff didn't hurt matters any."

There were two Model T's parked in front with about five or six binder boys in them.

"Good afternoon," the fattest of them said. "Beautiful afternoon, isn't it?"

Sam and I remained on the lawn.

"See that sign?" Sam pointed up at the front door. "We got no rooms to let, and this place is not for sale."

They giggled drunkenly.

"This is a day to do Miami proud. Did you hear the news about Miamiland?"

"We heard all about it. You're wastin' your time here."

I looked back at the house and saw Mrs. Willig's silhouette in one of the front windows.

"You couldn't have heard the latest on it. We just come up from there. They oversold the place."

Sam walked down to the street. "What do you mean?"

"What I said. Miamiland was oversold. You must have heard that those people went crazy buyin' today. It's gonna take days for the management boys to count it all, but they're sure they oversold it. Now they got to refund about a million dollars. Isn't that the damnedest thing you ever heard?"

Mrs. Willig called out, "Sam, what are you doing? I told you to get rid of them."

"Mama, did you hear that? They oversold a million bucks' worth!"

"Do I have to come out there to get rid of them my-self?"

The fat one reached into his pocket and brought out a wad of bills. "Beautiful house you've got here. We're interested in talkin' business with you if you'd like."

"I'm calling the police," Bea said.

"She's a tough woman, but I'll make her a good deal."

Sam scratched his head. "She's not in a talkin' mood."

"Maybe I should show her what I've got on me. No checks here. Solid cash and binders on beach property."

He waved his billfold under my nose.

"I don't think the woman is interested," I said. "And I suggest that you and your merry band leave immediately."

The fat one backed off with a shrug as one of the others yelled out, "Let's go, Willy. There's plenty other places for sale."

They piled into their cars and took off.

"You handle yourself real well, Mr. Sloate," Bea said. "You have plans for dinner?"

"No."

"You do now."

Sam patted my shoulder again. "I told you she liked you."

I looked back at the house, but she'd walked away from the window. I still had not gotten a good look at Bea Willig.

Sam sank into the grass, staring up at the jacaranda tree. "We gotta get to her on this Paley offer."

"She's probably listening to us right now. Why don't you whisper the offer to me, she'll hear it."

His head snapped around, then he giggled. "Naw, she's gonna fix you a good meal. Jonny's the one to pitch her."

"Who's that?"

"My youngest brother. You'll meet him tonight. She wants him to go to college. That's why she'll want you to stick around."

"Listen, Sam, I've got a place."

"Hell, George, this is a nice setup over here. She cooks real good. Clean sheets. Don't turn her down if she offers. She likes to keep a decent influence around Jonny. If she only knew. You better watch your step around him."

"He sounds lethal."

"No, no such thing. He's just a charmer and a troublemaker. Hell, he's only eighteen. He's got more schemes runnin' around his head . . ."

That seemed to run in the family.

Mrs. Willig did not invite us in while she prepared the meal, so Sam and I stayed out on the front lawn swapping stories.

"Abe Willig was my father's name."

"Where is he?"

"We haven't seen him since 1918. Remember the bad influenza that year? We think that got him."

"You mean you aren't sure?"

"I suppose I should tell you the whole story; you're bound to hear the gossip anyway. My dad set out from Columbus in the winter of 1918 to scout business opportunities down here. A picture postcard of two Seminole Indians 'wrastlin' an alligator, bearin' the message, 'Bea Dear—Have stumbled upon the land of Milk and Honey. Love to the children. Your husband, Abe,' was the last my mother heard from him. He didn't turn up after a year, so she came down here lookin' for him. She didn't leave a stone unturned either . . . she talked to the police, hotel clerks, even photograpers who'd taken pictures of Seminoles 'wraslin' alligators, but he'd disappeared completely."

A door inside the house slammed. Sam flinched and lowered his voice.

"Like I said, there's been a lot of 'neighborly' conjecture."

"What do you mean?"

"Some people say he never existed, which is a bold faced lie. Others say he ran out on her the first chance he had. Mama says he's dead."

"And you?"

"I back mama up a hundred percent. She hasn't had an easy time of it."

Another door slammed.

"Why'd she stay down here if she couldn't find him?"

"She's no fool, George. Abe was right. Mama got a good whiff of the 'milk and honey,' and relocated the dry goods store we had up in Ohio. I help her run it."

"Diana seems to do her share."

Sam laughed. "Those two women are at war."

"What about?"

"Who knows? They don't." He stretched out on the grass. "What about you, George? What sort of people hatched you?"

"Not very interesting ones."

"What do you mean? What's your old man do?"

"Lawyer."

"Sounds serious."

"He's serious all right."

"And rich?"

"More respected than rich."

"You take after him?"

"I take after my granddad."

"Your granddad, huh? What about your mother? What's she like?"

"I never really knew her. She died when I was three years old. I was raised by my father's sister."

"Spinster aunt?"

"Aunt Clara."

"And the one you like the most is your granddad."

"My father's father. He was a great one."

"He's dead?"

"Died about a month ago."

"What was so great about him?"

"He had a sense of adventure—that is if you can have one and still be a lawyer in Columbus, Ohio."

"But he did."

"He once defended a murderer. Got him off too—a bartender who'd slapped around his girlfriend, killed her by accident . . . he claimed she threw the first punch. My granddad took him on because no one else in town would—my father was much too Rotarian for that—but granddad built a case for this guy. I think it had something to do with the bartender being driven mad by the booze he sold. Of course granddad wasn't pious or anything. He just knew what it would take to get this bartender off, and he did it."

"Your father and aunt must have been scandalized."

I laughed. "Granddad loved getting to those two."

"Mama's like that. Straight-laced. I got to figure out a way to get to her with this Paley offer." Sam turned and stared up at the house. As he continued plotting his strategy, I studied him.

I've always been attracted to people like Sam. And that spinster aunt of mine may be the reason why. Although she was a good substitute mother, I think she lavished too much attention on me, and that set me apart from the rest of my friends. It made *me* a little spinsterish. Aunt Clara was always telling me what a joy I was to look at, so I often sat back and let everyone do just that . . . watch me, walk around me, poke at me to find a chink in my armor. I became such a passive child that my only relief came from my collection of outrageous friends. In second grade, for instance, Fred Batish and I were great chums—he ate toads. Marabelle Davis used to take off and put on her clothes in less than a minute for a nickel, and I was hopelessly in love with her.

And now there was Sam Willig, consummate dreamer and schemer, his drunk and beautiful sister, and Bea Willig. I stared up at the house too, hearing more doors opened and slammed. I had this vision of her whirling around in there like a dervish. What was she doing?

"You think your mother needs any help in there?"

"George, that woman needs all the help she can get, but she'd rather be damned than ask for it."

"That so."

"Sometimes." He sighed. "Sometimes it's that way, then other times all she does is ask. I tell you, I'll never figure her out."

Another Model T pulled up. The curb-side door flew open as Albert ran out and pounced on Sam. Tildy saw me, then started straightening her hair. "Albert, don't you get grass stains on those pants," she squealed.

Diana was in the car, too, talking with a man who had a long, mournful face. She pointed to me, and the man, who must have been in his middle twenties, nodded a quick hello. Diana got out, walking a little more unsteadily than before.

"Hello, George. You are staying. Good. This is my husband, Jack Chason." She slurred her words.

He came loping up the lawn in long, awkward strides, and shook my hand. "Hey, Sam, you see all the excitement today?" he asked in a thick New York accent.

"What you been up to?"

"Up to no good."

Diana grinned. "He's got a taste of something real good. Don't you, Jack?" She threw her arms around him, hugged him, then toppled off his shoulder. He looked embarrassed.

"Don't you see children around here?" Tildy asked. "Good evening, George. Sam, don't roll around on the grass with him like that." She pulled on the boy's arm and carted him off with her.

"Diana tell you about the offer these Paley people made me?"

"That's big money. You told *her* yet?" Jack nodded in the direction of the house.

"Haven't had the chance. I don't know how to handle it."

"Who would?" Diana asked.

Jack interrupted. "Diana and me been talking about it. We think you should have those people come right over here and ask her about it themselves."

"No way. She'll get madder 'en hell and ruin it. No, we've got to handle it ourselves."

"She won't let you do that," Diana said.

"Damn, I don't want her takin' all the money if I put this deal together. I gotta make something on it."

Diana put her hands over her ears. "Jack, take me to that place out on the beach. I don't want to eat here tonight. I smell trouble. I shouldn't have had any of that booze if this is the way it's going to be. I can't face her tonight."

"That's very mature thinking," he said. "Sam's right. We've got to protect our interests."

"We've got no interest. I don't want her yelling at me."

"We help her run that place, and we deserve a share of whatever she gets for it," Sam said adamantly.

"Daddy wouldn't want you talking like that."

"He ain't here. Anyway, it's not as if we'd be stealing anything from her."

"Why don't you ever learn the facts of life?"

"It's worth a try."

I never saw a more conspiratorial atmosphere in a family. All conversation stopped as the front door swung open. Beatrice Willig stood on the porch with a tray in her hands. She must have been about forty-five that first day we met, but she didn't look it. Sheer will probably kept her from aging. She was short and thin, and her clothes were stylish in that loose, shapeless way they were back then. Narrow, half-moon blue eyes passed a stern expression over all the family. I was the only one she smiled at, and her smile was not as forbidding as I expected.

"Mr. Sloate, would you help me with this tray? Some iced tea."

"Good evening, mother," Diana said.

"Get yourself cleaned up inside. Then come help me with dinner. Where's Albert?"

"Tildy has him in the apartment."

"Maybe she'll feed him for once. How are you, Jack?"

As I walked up to the porch and took the tray, I heard Sam whisper, "I'm gonna do it now."

"Mama," he said. She turned, glowering at him. "Mama, someone made me an offer for the building and the lot today."

"Our building?"

"Yes. It's an incredible offer."

There was dead silence. Sam looked as if he couldn't believe he was holding her attention, but she stood there staring him down.

"Well?"

"This Colonel Paley from Savannah is here with his son scouting real estate investments. Lots of money on them. . . ."

Diana turned away, avoiding her mother's eyes and the scene she knew would follow.

"They're looking at Flagler Street lots for a hotel or something. Seems that Flagler lots are getting hard to come by."

Jack interrupted. "I heard about these Paley people, Bea. Bought some Palm Beach property last week."

"What did they offer?"
"They're talkin' about six hundred dollars a front foot—six hundred, mama. That's sixty thousand for the whole deal."
She looked at me. "You were there?"
"Yes."
"He heard it, didn't you, George? Sixty thousand. I got his card right here." Sam fumbled through his pockets.
"Don't go getting lightheaded at your prospects." She reached for the doorknob. "He's a banker?"
Jack nodded.
"If he's offering me sixty thousand today, we'll get over a hundred thousand next week. I'm not taking a cent under a hundred thousand. And cash—you hear me!"
She walked into the house, slamming the door behind her.
Sam rushed to the front door.
"Mama, you serious?"
"I hate that damn store. Always have. But I won't give it away for nothing!"

3

Bea Willig was my archetype for a group of women performing what I've come to call the "woman alone" song and dance. With some, it's a vamp leading to a carefully orchestrated bump and grind. They're the hungry ones fresh from widowhood or divorce, wearing their furs and jewelry as if these were bounty unearthed from some old pirate's chest.

The less willful "women alone" slink off into an early sexual retirement, rechanneling those energies into jobs as personal secretaries, teachers, charity workers, or librarians. Their dreams of glory have all been dreamed and laid out in the shroud with the "mister." Woman alone as dirge.

Bea fell somewhere between these two. She whistled her version as if it were a battle hymn protecting her from ever becoming intimately involved with anyone but her family. Perhaps she'd been hurt or suspected that old Abe's disappearance did not involve something as clear-cut and final as influenza death. I don't know. All I do know is that she was a woman with one personality reserved for the family and another for dealing with male strangers like me. I got to see the part her children never saw. She was as strong-willed and playful as a girl of eighteen, although I know if I'd suggested that to her she would have lost her dinner right then and there.

Dinner was a series of stops and starts, no one sitting at the table at the same time. Albert had to be fed. Tildy looked disinterested. Diana offered, but then Tildy pouted. Bea had to step in, swooping down, grabbing the fork from Diana's hand, delivering it into Albert's mouth. She was uninhibited in her display of affection for him, and he giggled, relishing the attention.

Sam could hardly contain his excitement, although Bea refused to discuss the Paley offer again.

"When you see their money, you come talk to me," she said, as a fork full of vegetables hit Albert mid-face.

"But we need a strategy for them."

Bea turned to a dour-looking Jack Chason, apparently her last resort. "Will you take him out of here? All of you get out of here until Jonny gets home. I will not eat without him."

We began to file out of the room.

"Mr. Sloate," she called out.

"Please call me George."

"You are a very polite young man, George. Tell me, what line is your father in?"

"He's an attorney."

"How nice. . . . Damn. That woman cannot even feed her own child." She looked up and signaled me to come closer. "I tell you she will be the death of me."

"Who's that?"

"Close the glass doors there, will you?"

I did as I was told.

"That Tildy Schultz."

"Sam's wife?"

"What other Tildy is there? Don't you see how she treats me?"

"Mrs. Willig, I'm a stranger here, and I don't—"

"Don't be silly. You have eyes, haven't you? She wants everything I have. You know when I wear my garnet necklace, she always walks up to me, rolling those cow eyes around, sighing . . . 'Oh, you have such lovely things.' "

She paused, waiting for my confirmation of Tildy's terrible deed.

"'Oh, you have such lovely things.' How do you like that? It isn't as if I was ever anything but wonderful to that girl. Some girl, she looks older than me. I treated her like my own daughter, but never once has she called me Mother. Just, 'Oh, you . . . oh, you have such lovely things.' Well, that's all right. I've learned my lesson. When I make up my will, you know what it's going to say?"

I could hardly suppress the smile creeping across my mouth.

"You think I'm joking? It's going to say, 'To my daughter-in-law, Tildy Schultz, I, Oh, you!' "

Laughter poured out of me, and she roared.

"You wait and see."

When Tildy opened the glass doors, Bea dropped her smile.

"Tell me, George, are you a lawyer as well?"

"No, I've just gotten out of undergraduate school."

"Back East?"

"Ohio State."

"Oh, you can give him to me now," Tildy purred.

Bea leaned over. "What did I tell you?"

I giggled. Tildy sensed the laughter was aimed at her, and she grabbed for Albert.

"I said I'll take him now!"

"Don't pull him like that. You'll hurt his arm."

"Don't tell me what to do with him. He's too old to be fed anyway."

Sam came rushing in. "What's going on?"

Bea started cleaning up the child's mess. "I think it's very nice of me to feed your child."

Sam turned on Tildy. "What are you gettin' yourself into?"

She slammed out of the room.

"May I suggest that you teach that woman manners?"

"She's not my child."

"No, but she's raising your child."

"You don't have to start in on her."

"Tell me, George," Bea said turning her back to him, "are you a lawyer like your father?"

"What? Well, I told you . . . No, I've just grad—"

"That's nice," she said, sailing into the kitchen.

Sam and I stared at the kitchen door swinging in her wake.

"Powerful woman, George. Don't get mixed up with powerful women. You and me have got to make plans. How much money you have on you? You never did tell me."

"I've got enough to get by on."

"I'm gonna put this Paley thing together all right, but I thought you'd be interested in speculating with me before we get started on that. Nothin' too big, just some binders for a bankroll so we can play big when the deal goes through."

"Let me think about it."

"You college guys. I'm talkin' pure gold. We could get binders on two lots worth four thousand. Only have to come up with four hundred down. You got four hundred in cash?"

Diana rescued me. "Psst, George. Sam. Jack's got some fine hooch. You want a taste before dinner? Come around back."

"In a minute," he said, waving her off. "Okay, George, you think about it. But I swear on all that's holy that if we go out lookin' for binders in the morning, by the time the banks close, you'll have doubled your money."

"What's in it for you?"

"I just want a small commission on it—for puttin' you in touch with the buyers and sellers."

"How small?"

"Ten percent."

I must have looked perplexed. I know I felt it.

"It's negotiable," he said. "Everything's negotiable in Miami."

We walked out of the house, and Sam draped his arm around my shoulder. "Listen, Jack's involved with some of them rum runners."

"Running booze?"

"Small-time stuff. But don't let him lean on you for any money. You got better prospects than that."

There was a small forest of pine trees behind the garage. In a clearing were the binder boys we'd seen earlier. Their cars were parked alongside each other, and the boys sat on the running boards, swapping drinks. A girl with bobbed hair and a red hat had joined them.

Diana stood at the edge of the forest sipping gin, staring at them. "Is that our land?" she asked Jack.

"I don't know whose it is."

"We should get them outta there. I don't like them poaching right near us."

"I sold them that booze they're drinking." Jack reached up for the bottle.

She scowled. "Well, I don't like them there. They picked up a bird dog. Women like that are parasites."

She studied the woman and then ran her hands through her long hair. "I'm cutting all my hair off this week."

"Flaming youth." Jack sighed as he passed the bottle to me.

The woman hopped up on one of the running boards and began to shimmy. The men clapped in time as she threw her head back and laughed. Her eyes looked dazed.

"She's trapped," Diana suddenly said as she began to dance, mirroring the woman's movements. "I know it all too well. That's what a haircut buys you." She tried making a song out of her words. "Oooooh, that's rhythm. That's jazz, baby. So much jazz, baby."

Sam took a swig. "Better keep it down, Diana. Mama'll be out here in a minute."

"You're a brave one." The woman in red looked at us and froze. "She's seen me dancing," Diana said. "She thinks I'm making fun of her. I'm not doing that." She grabbed the bottle from Sam's hand, raising it to the woman in a toast. "Woman's suffrage," she yelled. "Let's drink to the vote!"

The bottle went up to hr lips, and she downed a shot. The woman in the clearing laughed, grabbed a bottle, and did the same.

"I don't want any trouble with your mother tonight," Jack said gruffly, taking the bottle away from Diana.

She flopped to the ground, hitting something hard buried under the pine needles and moss.

"What the hell?" She scraped the needles away; underneath was a wooden case with the words Haig Smooth written on it. "Will you look at that!"

Sam and Jack scurried over, prying the lid open. All of us heard footsteps coming from the other side of the garage.

"Don't touch that," a deep voice behind me said.

A young man came straight at us, sinking to his knees in front of the box.

"Jonny, this yours?" Diana asked.

"Don't go near it." He lifted the lid. Inside were twelve green fifth-bottles of Scotch. "You been rifling through this?"

"Oh, Jonny, so suspicious."

His body arched forward defiantly, but the deep voice and aggressive display seemed more for his benefit than ours.

"Suspicious? Damn right. The whole lot of you were going to turn me in last year. How'd I know you'd all wind up a bunch of lushes." He saw me for the first time. "Who's this?"

"He's a friend of mine. From Columbus. George Sloate, my brother Jonny."

He looked like Diana, had her fine bones and deep-set blue eyes. He was taller than any of them and was wearing a spotless white shirt and sailor's pants.

"How'd you get your hands on stuff like this?" Diana purred.

"It's mine, and if you want a taste, you'll have to wait for me to offer it to you." He had more Southern in his voice than the rest of them.

"A good friend of yours, huh. There's a lot of federal agents around here."

"Jonny, mind your manners."

"You're a damn fool. George here is gonna do some business with us."

Bea called to us. "Is he home yet?"

Jonny walked into the garden, smiling at her. "I'm here. How are you, mother?"

"Hungry. Get yourself cleaned up. We're all hungry." She went back inside.

"You better stash that bottle," Jon said to Diana.

Jack patted him on the back. "You haven't heard the good news."

"What's that?"

"Tell him, Sam. Tell him how he's gonna get his wish and wind up in a rich family."

Sam told him about the Paley offer, but Jon merely shrugged. "I've got better ways to make money." He covered the box of Scotch with moss.

Jack laughed. "Sure. Running booze for the likes of Reno Devane will make you a heap of money."

"You work for him, too."

"But you'll get yourself killed doing it."

"It isn't as safe as delivering the stuff to those mansions, but we all know that nothing cheap is ever safe. You're going real cheap, Jack."

"Quit it, you two," Sam said.

"You can make more money on the water, that's all."

"This is going to be your life's work?" Diana asked Jon.
"It's a start," he said.
He took off. We followed him inside.

Dinner finally did get under way. Tildy made a late appearance, which was ignored. Bea had turned her guns on Diana.
"You keep drinking," she was saying, "we'll see what you wind up looking like."
"I don't know why I have to sit here and take this," Diana snapped.
Bea hopped up and went into the kitchen to get more food.
"Don't pay any attention to her," Jack said.
"That's easy for you to say—she's not yelling at you."
"Just learn to shut up and take it."
But Diana wouldn't give up. "You know I work my head off in that store, mother. I'd like to come home to some peace and quiet."
"You're drinking yourself out of your youth."
"What is that supposed to mean?"
"I have a good notion to call the police on the whole lot of you." She passed a furious eye over Jack and Sam but smiled politely when she came to me. "Some potatoes, George?"
I nodded. She served me. Diana picked at her food. Sam ate as if this were his last meal.
"Your family been in Columbus long, George?" Tildy asked, a heaping forkful of food disappearing through her ruby lips.
"I guess."
"My people have been in Tallahassee forever," she said.
Jon snickered. "You must have heard of the Schultzes of Tallahassee, George. What part of Columbus are you from?"
"He's Dr. Sloate's nephew," Bea said. "From Bexley."
Jon took a new interest in me. "You must know my friend James Harris. His father is King Harris, the newspaper man."
"They belong to my father's club."
"I've played tennis at that club."
Diana and Sam looked at him, and then winked at their mother.
"He's got his moments of sanity, too, George," Bea said.
"It's true. I've played there any number of times. We're going to have grass courts down here soon just like theirs.

Mr. Fischer has built this wonderful polo field out at the beach. Do you play polo, George?"

Jonny's youthful show of sophistication would not be stopped either by Bea's gentle chiding or Diana's knowing smiles. He talked on about Bexley, then about Henry Ford's new Model T's, which, he said, would be built in two new colors that year: deep forest green and maroon. He dropped local names I'd never heard, and when the family poked fun at him, he slipped into a sullen silence.

"He'll be a rich man with dreams like that," Bea said softly.

Sam finished one plate and was offered another.

"It seems to me that if those Paleys offered sixty thousand, they'll up it if I can get someone else interested in the property. I'll have to fish around. What'll we do after we make your hundred-thousand-dollar sale, mama? Should we form a real estate corporation?"

"I will positively not engage in business discussion during dinner."

Tildy winked at me. "Sam's got a killer instinct for business. Don't you, darlin'?"

Sam went on eating.

Jon finished his meal by politely dabbing his napkin around his mouth. "I heard old Commander Moss talking about us down at the docks."

"What'd he say?"

"He was with a pal of his. 'There goes that Willig boy. They're a bunch of Jews, aren't they?' "

They sat there stony-faced. I don't know why, but I felt responsible for breaking the silence.

"Well, that is a terrible thing to say."

Their faces turned toward me, and the worst feeling crept up my spine. I wanted to drop to the floor and crawl out of there.

Bea spoke up. "Why, George, we are Jewish."

"I'm awfully sorry for saying that."

"You just thought you'd be polite," Diana said.

"We don't practice it regularly—but we are. Family came from Austria in the late 1880s."

"Sure," Jonny said. "Every Pole or Hungarian who passed through Vienna on the way to Ellis Island considers himself a German Jew. It seems to make it better."

Bea was trying to be polite herself, but she would not have any of that talk. "Now you mind what you say. You know damn well what you've come from, and there's no reason to feel anything but good about it."

"We're not completely offended," Diana said. "Even Mr. Fischer, the big developer around here, has clauses written into his land contracts restricting his sales to members of—how does that go, Jack?"

"Members of the 'Caucasian race.' We've got the south beach—anything goes down there."

"It just shows how little all of you know," Bea said. "If you've got the money like that yeast man, Mr. Fleischmann, they'll sell you anything you want. Where are you staying, George?"

"At the Elysium."

"Oh, my, that's a dreadful place. I wouldn't want any son of mine staying there."

"It was all I could find."

"Why don't you move in with us for a while? We've got plenty of room."

Sam looked up from his plate and winked at me. "Jonny wouldn't mind rooming with a Bexley boy, would you?"

"I don't think I should."

Diana flashed a smile. "Why not? You can come and go as you please, and we'll introduce you to some nice people."

"Well . . ."

"Someone was killed over at the Elysium last year," Jack offered as I started wondering about the safety of my bags.

"You could keep the peace around here, that's for sure," Tildy said. Everyone gave her a look that would have killed.

"It's a very kind offer . . ."

"Do it, George," Jon said. "We can play tennis. I'll bet you probably have nothing but winter clothing with you. I've got a closet filled with suits from the store I never use. We're about the same size."

I suppose a lot of important decisions are made without much thought in the time it takes you to blink. I was ready for a real change in my life, and these people seemed to be as far away from what I'd come from as I wanted to get.

Aside from that, Bea was willing to put me up, Sam was filled with business prospects, Jon was willing to outfit me, and Diana was so damned attractive.

"All right, I'd love to," I finally said.

After dinner, Sam, Tildy, Jon, and I piled into Sam's car to collect my things.

I was able to get my bags, but we did not get out of the Elysium unscathed. The night watchman accused Tildy of loitering in the lobby, insinuating that she was a streetwalker looking for a little action. She went mad. It was all we could do to calm her down and get her back into the car.

Downtown was deserted at night. We circled around Flagler Street a couple of times. Tildy was furious—at the nightman for suspecting her; at Jonny for laughing at her; at Sam who hadn't defended her.

"What kind of a man are you? How could you let that shriveled-up prune say those things to me!"

"Calm down."

"I will not. I've never been so embarrassed in my life."

"It's all over, I'm gonna take you dancing."

She melted as quickly as she froze. "Dancing? Where?"

"Anywhere you want."

"How about old Elser's Pier?"

"They tore it down last week."

She stared in disbelief when we drove past it. "Why on earth did they do that?"

"Progress."

"Head out to the beach," Jonny said. "Let's show George some clubs."

We crossed the bay on the county causeway, passing the landfill island Sam had shown me that afternoon. In the distance were silhouettes of beach houses and a number of big hotels. Near them were the skeletons of at least a dozen more under construction.

The beach stretched north and south as far as I could see. In the bay stood dredges, and cranes, which, with their tiny heads and long necks stretching up to the sky, looked like prehistoric reptiles wading in pools. An orange crescent moon hung over the water above the horizon.

Sam stopped before we reached the land. "This is where the big money is made. This is the real future out here."

"That's Carl Fischer's hotel." Jon pointed off to the right. "He's got a polo field and a golf course. Glenn Curtis has a flying school up north there."

"That's the place I want," Sam said wistfully. "Get me ten or twenty acres up there on the north end, build something just like Merrick's town up there."

"Where we gonna dance?" Tildy asked, applying more rouge to her lips.

We drove south on Collins Avenue, a narrow street in those days, lined with scrawny pines and full-grown palms. All this had been a coconut plantation just ten years before. Now hotels and estates, pools and golf courses dazzled like lights in a holiday pageant by the sea. The beach itself was deserted, but as we drove on I saw a bonfire blazing near the water.

"Those Indian boys drinking hooch again," Jon said.

The ocean was still, dark, and brooding; waves rolled in languorously hushed beats onto the shoreline. The air was thick with brine, jasmine, and a sense of calm, which was suddenly broken by the tinny sound of a Victrola playing in a shack nestled under the palms. Sam parked under a sign that read Jungle Inn Club.

"Good booze," Tildy giggled, running ahead.

The place was dark and smoky; Spanish moss hung from the roof. Two flappers were dancing together on a warped pine floor while a small group of menacing-looking men stood watching them.

Sam stepped up to the bar and ordered drinks. Jon stayed back in the shadows with me.

"Why don't the police crack down on this place?"

Jon squinted, nodding in the direction of a redheaded man standing near the stone fireplace. "Because of him."

"Who's he?"

"Reno Devane. He's the biggest rum runner around these parts."

"They let him go around doing it just like that?"

"They can't afford not to. The local police protect him from the Feds. They break up his operation, the local boys go broke."

The man looked over at us, smiling at Jon.

"He's my chief vice and sole supporter."

"You've really gotten involved with him?"

"Every now and then."

Devane sauntered over to us, walking like a sailor who was used to rolling with the sea. He wore a silk tuxedo and had a taut, handsome face covered with a mass of light freckles.

"Where you been, baby boy?" he asked, rubbing Jonny's shoulders with a massive hand. "This ain't no way to dress down here." His eyes glowed covetously. "Who's your friend?" he asked without looking up at me.

"George Sloate, Reno Devane."

His hand gripped mine, leaving it limp. "You chums from up north?"

"I'm his brother's friend."

He wasn't interested in my conversation.

"I haven't seen you around, baby."

"I've been busy working on a friend's boat."

"The kid is a smart one," Devane said to me. "He's goin' places. You get my present?"

"The Haig is my commission," Jon said indignantly.

"Call it what you like. Use it or sell it. It's yours."

Devane watched the flappers circle the floor. "Figures like boys," he said, winking at Jon.

Sam and Tildy waved as they two-stepped past us.

"Your brother, ain't it? Who's the hog he's with?"

"His wife."

"Oh, you kid!"

"Let's get out of here," Jon said to me irritably.

"Wait a minute." Devane grabbed his arm. "I got work for you."

"I can't. My family is here. I don't want to talk."

"Make a pretty penny on it. Make close to five hundred. Very little moon tonight. Just your cup of tea."

"Five hundred? You said my share was going up."

"In time. Some kid. You gotta be patient. We gotta go at two. Go talk with the Seminoles. They're down on the beach."

"I'll think about it."

"Better think quick."

"You won't get me for five hundred again. Tonight's the end of that."

Devane turned back to the flappers again. "Figures like boys—huh, Jonny? Just like boys."

Jon didn't respond. He walked out of the bar, and I followed.

"Devane sounds tough because he is," Jon said when we walked down to the beach.

"How'd you get involved with someone like that?"

"I got a taste for adventure and a fair amount of brains. Want you to meet some of these Indians over here—they're good people."

A group of four of them were sitting around the bonfire, laughing, taking slugs out of a gin bottle. We stood behind them, watching for a minute.

"You ever met Seminoles?" Jon whispered.

"No."

"The word means wild horse, but the white men changed it to mean runaway—sorrowful meaning for those boys," he said. "Hey, Homer," he called out. "Want you to meet a friend of mine named George Sloate."

The oldest of them stood and smiled. "I know another George. He your wife, Jonny? Or you his?"

They laughed again. Jon shook his head. "He's a new friend, Homer. You be on your best behavior."

"You dress real white, George. This other George I know dresses white, too."

"Devane has some work for you," Jon said. "Wants to know if you'll be around later tonight."

"Drink with us."

"Just one."

They passed the bottle to me and applauded the amount I got down.

"Good drinker, George. You share my booze."

"We're all good drinkers," Jon said as he eagerly drank the gin, playing his part, a man among men.

"Like a taste for the booze, right?" Homer asked. "And a taste for the wet grass. You been down to the Everglades, George?"

I shook my head.

"Wide open land—trees all over. Take you there. Five bucks. Best damn guide around." The bottle was passed to him. He drank and passed it on. "Taste for the booze, all right. Taste for stories, too, George? You got white stories to tell?"

"He's got no mind for storytelling tonight," Jonny said.

The gin hit me like a sledgehammer, while Homer's face danced in and out of the shadows cast by the flames. In the distance I heard Sam calling Jon's name.

"That your brother?" Homer asked.

"He's ready to leave. Thanks for the drink, Homer. Remember, same place as always. Two o'clock. You boys can get sober by then, can't you?"

They laughed again. Then we said good night and headed back up the beach.

When we got home, everyone was asleep. Jon got me settled in his room where there were two beds facing a screened window. He gave me the one next to an old oak bureau. I was dog tired, but I unpacked and washed up before getting into bed.

Jon was asleep as soon as he hit the pillow.

Something awakened me that first night. My eyes opened a crack. I saw Jon sitting in his shorts rubbing some acrid-smelling stuff all over his body. I studied him for a moment before turning over. The first rough lines of manhood were making their mark on him, but he looked as if he would retain his boyish defiance longer than most. His fingers kneaded the long, slender muscles of his arms and thighs. His mouth was open in a pouty half-smile.

"What are you doing?" I asked.

"Witch hazel for the bugs."

"What time is it?"

"One-thirty."

"You're going to do it?"

"Going out on the water."

"What for?"

"I'll take you sometime so you can see for yourself."

"No, thank you." I stared up at the ceiling.

"Spoken like a true Bexley boy."

"Are you really helping that Devane character?"

"Yes."

"The money is that good?"

"It's that good, and there's nothing like being on the water running the stuff in on nights like this. The night sky's like velvet."

"Sounds like madness to me."

"That's right, too, madness is what it is. You owe yourself a little of that every now and then. Don't you ever blow off steam?"

"I'm usually content watching crazy people like you."

"That doesn't seem too interesting."

"I'm an observer."

"Don't you ever want to jump in there with the rest of us?"

"I don't know what you mean."

"Jump into life, not just walk along the edge."

"I've never thought about it."

"That's too bad, but don't worry, I'll take care of that for you."

The little squirt. Who did he think he was? I was about to

tell him he was acting a little too big for his britches, but he opened the window.

"Sleep tight, George. Cover for me if I'm not back by morning."

With that, he picked up his clothes and crawled out into the night.

4

Jon was in his bed sleeping when Sam came in to awaken me in the morning.

"Get your best duds on, George. We got work to do. You thought over my offer yet?"

"About the binders? I'll do it on one condition. I want to take a look at anything I buy before I buy it."

He laughed. "You're crazy, but if that's what you want, that's what you'll get."

Bea was passing by in the hall outside the room. "He's not crazy. You're a smart boy, George. See what you pay for," she said.

Sam said our best bet was to look around for bargains on Miamiland property, so we drove out there.

"This is what oversold in four hours?" I asked.

"Sixty acres of it."

I couldn't believe my eyes. We were standing in the middle of an abandoned orange grove where a warped sign tacked onto a tree read: These Investments are Fruitful—Make a Fruitful Investment in Miamiland.

"What's a bunch of oranges compared to land," Sam said.

At one corner of the property, someone had laid out a series of sidewalks and put up street lamps. The walks crossed each other at perfect right angles, but they were surrounding nothing but scrub brush. What made the scene thoroughly ridiculous was the presence of street signs: Victoria Parkway, Jane Street, Louise Drive.

"I guess you'd want to know if your poison ivy abutted

Jane or Louise," I said, scratching my head. Sam wasn't listening. He seemed interested in a field adjacent to Miamiland.

Puffs of smoke accompanied the clang of hammers in some mangrove swamps and wetlands about a mile from where we were standing.

"That's a new one," Sam said, walking in that direction.

Groups of Negroes wielding axes and machetes were hacking their way through the swamp. Some of the mangroves were fifty feet tall, and axemen chopped away at the trunks while others set small fires around the gnarled roots.

"What's goin' on here?" Sam asked one of the workers.

"Boss back 'dere," he said, without missing a stroke.

We made our way through the underbrush but were stopped by a large, shallow pond. Mosquitoes swarmed in thick, gray clouds. Across the pond was a machine that looked like a miniature riverboat. A white foreman was overseeing two Negroes who were operating it.

"What's goin' on here?" Sam asked the foreman.

"This here's Sun Estates. We're not open for sales."

"How many acres you workin'?"

"Two hundred. You better get outta here. These fires'll burn fast once they get started."

"Let's leave, Sam. If the fires don't get us, the bugs will."

"I wanna look around. We might be able to get in on the ground floor with this one."

"I'm heading back to the car."

I spotted the road in the distance and tried making my way to it. I'd lost sight of what Florida was built on to begin with, but out here there was no mistaking it. I could have been in the wilds of Africa for all I knew. As I cut through the jungle, my foot hit loose sand, and my immaculately polished wing tips disappeared into a bog. I bent over to retrieve them and heard a thrashing sound behind me, then what I thought was a donkey's braying. It seemed to be quite close. Suddenly an elephant's trunk came out of nowhere and swatted me on the rear.

A man called, "Hup, hup!"

"My God!" I screamed, dropping the shoes and breaking into a sprint.

"Hup! Hup!"

The elephant was on my track; its trunk flipped up and struck my head.

"Hup, hup!"

"Help!"

An East Indian in a loincloth and a soiled turban ran out of the brush, boxing the elephant.

"What the hell is this?"

"She hurt you?"

Another elephant sauntered out behind him.

"Where am I?"

"You hurt?"

The elephants nudged me with their trunks.

"Will you get them away from me!"

"She easy as cream. Rosie. She's sweet." He smashed them both this time with a whack that would have brought down a building. They nodded and ambled away. "They pull logs out. Got out of their harness. You hurt?"

"I'm all right. I lost my shoes."

"Come, we'll find them."

"I'm not moving."

"I find them."

He retraced my steps, found them, and came running back. "You one of the owners?" he asked.

"No. How do I get back to the road?"

The bull elephant reared its mammoth head, and its ears spread out like flags in the wind. I grabbed my shoes and took off without asking more questions.

When I got back on the road, Sam was standing there surveying the property. "I wonder if they'd sell binders on it this early on," he was saying.

"Binders? This is insanity. I'm getting out of here."

He looked at me and laughed. "What did you fall into?"

"Elephants. Elephants and Indians. This is no man's land and no place to live."

"Exotic, ain't it?"

I pulled my shoes on and walked off in a huff.

"Now come on, George, no one's asking you to live here. Just to buy and sell it. Where's your sense of humor?"

It was gone with the pride that had just been swatted down by an elephant's trunk. Enough was enough!

As I walked toward the car, I heard what I thought were screams coming from a tiny stucco shed by the side of the road. Sam came running up, grabbing my arm as I was about to unfasten the bolt lock on it.

"Keep movin', George."

"But that's a man's voice—there's someone locked up in there."

"I know all about it."

The screaming became louder, more desperate.

"Just keep movin'. You may think you've wound up in a jungle they're makin' into another suburb of Ohio, but don't you forget this is still the South."

"What's going on in there?"

Sam looked over his shoulder. "Listen, George, they got their way of doin' things down here. If one of them niggers gets to doin' what he's not supposed to be doin'. . . . Well, they been treatin' them this way for a long time."

I pulled the bolt. As the wood door swung open, a foul odor hung in the air. Inside was a sweat-slicked young Negro huddled in a corner crying.

"Now you've done it. Let's get a move on." Sam ran toward the car. I heard the white foreman yelling in the mangrove swamp as the Negro shook convulsively.

"Get out of there," I said. The Negro just stared at me.

Sam started the car.

"You got yo' moto' ca'?" the Negro asked.

"Come on, we'll take you into town."

"Where?"

"Into town, come on."

Sam pulled up alongside us. "Get in, George. Don't you mess with him."

The foreman started running toward us with a shotgun raised above his head.

"Let's take him into town."

Sam reached over, grabbed me from behind by the shoulders, pulled me into the Ford, then kicked it into first, and we sped away. I turned and saw the Negro bolt from the shack and head out into the field.

"Why'd you do that?" I screamed.

"You don't mess with that. You'll get yourself killed."

Road dust flew up in my face as I saw the foreman take off after the Negro

"They put 'em in that sweatbox to get 'em to work. You take him into Miami, you get yourself killed, get that Negro killed, too."

"That guy looked as good as dead to me."

"Sounds verv noble, George. Very high-minded."

"You don't believe in anything."

"I can't afford to."

We were not what you'd call civil companions by the time we got back into town. Sam parked in front of the store but remained in the car. "Voiceless, huh? If this is the way you want it to be, it's okay with me, George. We can sever our business relationship anytime you want."

"What business relationship?"

"College men." He took off his skimmer and fanned himself. "When was the last time you was with a woman?"

"What does that have to do with anything?"

"Pardon me for sayin' this, but you have got a bug up your ass." He stepped down from the car. "I'm gonna fix you up. Just give me a little time."

"I'm talking morals."

"Me, too. Yours could stand getting loosened up in the sack." He giggled, then walked into the store.

What could I say? He had no idea what I was talking about. We were witnesses to the torture of some fellow human being, and all he could think about was getting me a little action on the side. I slammed out of the car and slammed into the store to confront him, but a middle-aged, well-dressed couple was inside talking with Diana and Tildy. Sam was trying to make sense out of what was being said.

"Hold on. One at a time."

"I been telling these people, the Jaystones—that's it, isn't it, honey?" Tildy said to the man, who nodded. "I been telling these Jaystones here that someone has already made you an offer."

"What Tildy does not understand is that the offer wasn't binding." Diana looked ready to burst. "Sam, these people are interested in the building."

Mr. Jaystone pulled a card out of his suit, as Mrs. Jaystone cast a disdainful eye over the merchandise on the counter.

"Mr. Jaystone, sir, the property has not come up for sale."

"That isn't what I heard." His accent was flat and upper crusty. "A group of us were out at the Roman Pools this morning, and one of the young gentlemen there said that the Willig store on Flagler had been bid on. Five hundred a front foot was the figure he mentioned."

"Six hundred," Sam said quickly. "Do you have a counter offer?"

"Darling," Mrs. Jaystone said, "I did not come all the way down to Florida to stand around in a dank store."

"What would you consider to be a fair offer, Mr. Willig?"

Sam twiddled his thumbs. "Seven hundred is something like it."

"Too little," Diana snapped.

"Seven twenty-five."

"Seven fifty."

"Seven seventy-five."

"Seven eighty."

"Eight hundred is my last offer."

"Well, that didn't take too long," Tildy said.

"We'll have to think about it."

"You do that," Mrs. Jaystone said, pushing her way past me.

"Do think about it. My wife and I will be in Miami Beach at the Flamingo for another week. Good day."

They left.

"Tildy, you can spend the money once we get it made, but don't think you can make it yourself. You almost loused this whole thing up. Good goin', Diana."

"I did the best I could. Up twenty thousand in one day. Mother's right. This land business can't last." She looked over and noticed my muddy shoes and pants. "My God, George, what hit you?"

"Did you know they have elephants working in those fields?"

"Some real estate promoter brought them down last year. You meet them?"

Tildy was convulsed with laughter by this time.

"It's not that funny," I assured her. "I don't consider the state of your husband's moral values any laughing matter, either."

"Come off your high horse, George. I told you, I'm gonna take care of your problem."

"Now just wait a minute. Let's see if your wife and sister think what you did had any merit to it."

"What went on out there?"

"We found this Negro locked up in a sweatbox, being tortured out there in the field. I released him, but Sam wouldn't help the poor fellow escape."

Tildy blanched. "You let him out?"

"You've got to let those sorts of things alone down here," Diana said.

I slumped forward, feeling utterly defeated.

Sam leaned over me. "He's a little ticked off at me, but he

doesn't understand that he's gonna love me when the day is over. Snap out of it, George. You got any cash on you?"

"There is no end to your nerve."

"Ain't that the truth. I'll tell you the way the land lays, my boy. We got to get ourselves something to buy and sell so we can get up some scratch. That rich guy, Jaystone, said he heard about our place bein' sold out at the Roman Pools. That must be where all the rich action is goin' on. We got to get up some money to go right in there and play with those Paleys and Jaystones. Come on, George, we're goin' back to the Ponce de Leon to do some buyin'."

"He's got to clean himself up first," Tildy said. "And you've got to help me out here today. Diana has an appointment, and I'll be left alone."

Sam nodded but reached for the doorknob. "Give Tildy your pants, George, but don't get any funny ideas. I'll be right outside." The brass bells clanked as he shut the door.

"Your brother is very disturbed."

"Stick with him, George. He just might make you a rich man."

We walked, half ran, over to the bar.

"What was the last price we heard quoted on Miamiland yesterday?" he asked.

"Who remembers?"

"I think one of those guys said something about lots for fifteen hundred, so you keep that figure in your head and circulate around listening to the numbers when we get there."

The air inside the bar was dense with cigar smoke. Every binder boy was feeling as flush as J.P. Morgan, after yesterday's sale.

"Morning, Sam," Sid the bartender called out. "Want a root beer?"

"Bourbon."

"No booze today. New federal boys in town. Big run-in last night."

Sam leaned over the bar. "Anybody got binders left on Miamiland?"

"Got a roomful of them. You goin' into it?"

"I'm thinkin' about it, but keep it to yourself."

"Hey, Willie," Sid called out. "Buyers for Miamiland."

Every head in the place turned and stared at us. Ah, suckers! was written on every face.

"Great goin', Sid."
Willie, the fat one who had wanted to buy Bea's house yesterday, beat the rest of them to the bar.
"What can I do for you, gentlemen?"
"You got anything left on Miamiland?" Sam pointed to me. "My friend is interested in buys out there."
Out came the sheaf of papers. "Got some beauties for you."
"What price you talkin'?"
"Corner lots, three thousand. Interior locations, two."
"Where in the interior?" I asked.
"What?"
Sam whispered, "Don't go askin' dumb questions. We're doin' business."
"I've got a beauty that's as large as two—I can let you have it for four thousand."
"Where is it?" I asked again.
"Four's a good price for it. If you want a corner, you'll have to pay for it, but that one for four is the beauty."
"Where is it?"
He looked at me as if I were crazy. "I wouldn't know. You want to talk turkey, or you want to do a land survey?"
"You haven't even been out there," I said.
"Who has?" He turned to Sam. "I'll give you the inside one for thirty-five hundred."
Another man pushed his way up to us. "I got an inside for three."
Sam whispered to me. "This'll get 'em goin'."
That it did. They started going wild, bidding each other up, down, in, out—all for a couple of street signs in the middle of nowhere. Finally one of them yelled out, "Twenty-five hundred. And that is the lowest I'll go."
"That's the one for us," Sam said.
"Not for me," I added.
His head jerked around. "What?"
"You do it. I'm not going near it."
I walked past him, heading for the door, but he was hot on my heels. "What are you doin'?"
"I'm obviously not interested." I'd show him whose high horse he was hitched to.
As we hit the street, we almost fell over the Paleys, junior and senior. Sam's hat came off in a gallant swoop as Colonel Paley nodded a polite hello.

"Have you discussed my offer with your family?"
"Tell you the truth, something has come up."
"Another offer?"
"I'm afraid so, colonel. It's a good one."
"Who made it?"
"A man named Jaystone."
"Parvenu," the colonel muttered. "How much was the offer?"
"Eight hundred a front foot."
"Outrageous. Thank you for telling me."
He tipped his hat, and off he went.
"I've ruined it," Sam said watching them leave. "I rode him a little too hard."
The colonel suddenly stopped in his tracks.
"I'll go to eight hundred and fifty, sir, no more." Off they went again.
"Well, you'll get your money without having me buy some scrubland," I said.
"You still don't understand. They're goin' at it now. Now we got to dress ourselves up, hang out with them, and get 'em going higher. I need the cash. What's wrong with Miamiland?"
"It doesn't even exist!"
"Oh, shoot, let's walk," Sam finally said in disgust. "Just give me one sucker who'll offer a thousand a front foot, and we've got it made."
We walked up Flagler past the store, then cut over to First Street, where we came upon a block of modest frame apartment houses. A man was sweeping the street in front of the only brick one.
"Howdy, Sam. Heard you're sellin' the store."
"Who'd you hear that from?"
"Some guy walkin' around here earlier. Said he's offerin' you nine hundred dollars a front foot."
"What?"
"Looked my place over, too."
"Who was he?"
"I'll think of the name in a minute."
"Jaystone?"
"No, big burly fella from Cleveland."
"Nine hundred?"
"What he said."
The brick apartment building was in fine repair. I looked

into one of the ground-floor windows; there was a nice, neat living room with heavy oak furniture.

"You selling this place?" I called out.

"George Sloate, meet Henry Mason," Sam said matter-of-actly.

Henry smiled, toothless as a baby. "I might."

Sam walked over to me, staring up at the place. "Not this one, George. It's not for you."

"It looks rather substantial to me. How old is it?"

"Built in 1918. I keep it up myself."

"How much?"

"George!"

"How much do you want for it?"

Henry scratched his head and drummed his fingers on his broom shaft.

"Twenty-five."

"I'll give you twenty if you'll take a ten-percent-down binder on it."

"George, have you lost your mind?"

"Got some binders inside. You got a deal." Henry ran into the house.

"I thought you were a smart man."

"I am, Sam. Got myself a nice little apartment house. Imagine business being this easy."

Henry came running out with the binder, which we both signed; then I reached down into my sock and pulled out my net worth—two one-thousand-dollar bills. Sam's eyes bulged.

"You are nuts."

I pocketed the binder. "What do we do now?"

"End of the month comes, you give me twenty-five percent more," Henry said, smiling.

My heart sank.

"Take that binder down to the courthouse and get them to file it. It's all yours."

"You should feel as bad as you look," Sam said. "Come on, I'll buy you a drink. Henry, what was the name of that guy from Cleveland?"

"Fuderman or Federman or something like that. Wish ya luck, Sam. Maybe we'll both make sales today."

I was speechless and nervous, couldn't stop my heart from pounding or my palms from sweating.

"Cheer up," Sam said. "You're a land baron, get used to it."

Little did I know I didn't have much to worry about. This was, after all, Miami in 1925, and land was bought and sold in the blink of an eye.

We cut over from First Street to Flagler through the Halcyon Arcade. A frenzied-looking, thin guy waved at Sam, then came rushing up to us.

"Hiya, Stanley, what's shakin'?" Sam asked.

"Fever, boy, got me the fever and a whole shitload of money," the skinny man said, shaking like he had a bad case of the heebie-jeebies.

"Watch your mouth there, Stanley."

"You got anything for sale?"

"No, I don't got anything you'd be interested in."

"Who's your friend?"

Sam's eyes lit up. "George here's got something. I'm brokerin' for him. Aren't I, George?"

I nodded like a mute.

"What ya got?"

"Know Henry Mason's place?"

"Up on First."

"I got a good deal for you on that one. George just took a binder on it. Sweet deal."

"What you pay?"

"He'll take thirty-five for it," Sam chimed in.

Stanley pulled out a wad of bills.

"Give it to me for thirty, with ten down in cash, and you got a deal."

"What?"

"You heard him, give him the damn binder," Sam said, rifling through my pockets.

Stanley stood there in broad daylight for all the world to see, peeling ten thousand dollars cash off his wad, as I stammered through a couple of very grateful remarks. Then Sam offered his back to us, and we signed the binder. Stanley acted as if I were doing him a favor. It was all over before I could catch my breath.

"Lost your virginity, boy," Sam yelped as Stanley walked away, holding the binder as if it were pure gold. "Lost it, just like that. Business, Miami-style. Didn't hurt one bit. Let me look at it. Holy cow. You're rich!"

I grabbed the wad and counted off a thousand dollars and handed it to him. "Commission, partner."

He grabbed my face with both pudgy hands and planted a wet, slobbering kiss on my forehead.

"Cut it out."
"Let 'em all look. Hell, I'm gonna go get you laid."

5

We treated ourselves to twelve-dollar haircuts, manicures, massages—the works. Sam managed to get his hands on a not-too-poisonous bottle of bourbon. We were feeling no pain by the time we pulled out of town.

"Where you taking me?"

"This car's gonna take us, 'cause I'm as drunk as a shithouse rat."

"Are we back in the jungle?" It was all I could see—lush, green ferns and palm fronds slammed into the car window, brushing the hat from my head. Two stone lions stood at the side of a narrow road. "Where the hell are we?"

"This here's the old Brigham Mansion—now it's Gertie Walsh's place."

"Who's she?"

"Best goddamn madame you ever saw. The girls here are not to be believed. I figure we got about an hour to spend in here before the banks close. Remember that. Got to get your money put away in a safe place."

"What the hell am I doing taking it into a whorehouse?"

He slammed on the brakes. "I forgot about that. Okay, sober up."

I laughed, and he roared. "Okay—okay—got to do some serious thinking. Stick it back there in the boot."

"How much do I need for inside?"

"This is on me. Fold it up real good and tuck it in back there."

The road curved around a thicket of bamboo, then the house came into view. It was made of marble and gray stone. Two golden girls with straw hats were chasing ducks, trying to get them back into the small pond on the front lawn. On the long, columned porch stood a woman, the likes of which I'd never seen. She weighed at least two hundred and fifty pounds, and it was all jammed into a pink satin dress with ostrich plumes that stuck all over it and her. Her breasts were propped up like two strawberry ice cream cones.

"Gertie, you got yourself two big suckers for the afternoon."

"I got a house full of 'em, baby. Twenty girls that will, and forty men who'll pay for the pleasure. How you doin', Sam. Long time no see."

"George, say howdy to Gertie Walsh."

She snapped her hand, and a plumed fan swept out of it.

"Hello, Miss Walsh."

"Northern boy?"

"Ohio, ma'am."

"My sister ran a place up in Cleveland. Lots of rich ones up there. She's in Washington now. Old Warren Harding, rest his soul, brought a lot of business to Washington. We had old Warren here once. Come on inside, boys. Got some champagne on ice."

She lead the way past two Negroes in livery to an opulent, albeit sparsely furnished, ballroom. Three girls in peach and apricot silk camisoles and peignoirs were lounging on sofas and chairs. A plump redhead brushed her hair in a shaft of sunlight in front of tall French doors. Glints of blue and green in the mother-of-pearl brush she was using matched her eyes. When Sam walked in, she winked naughtily.

"Susanna's your girl, ain't she?" Gertie asked, pointing to the redhead.

Sam beamed like a schoolboy. "Tons of fun."

"You like 'em big, my friend," Gertie said. "Your wife's a big 'un, too, ain't she?"

The redhead scowled. "Now, don't you make him go all limp thinkin' about her."

Gertie poured us champagne. Sam brought a glass of it over to the redhead as Gertie signaled the other girls to leave.

"Come on, George. I'll show you around."

A fragile-looking blonde girl was sitting on the stairway in the hall buffing her nails. I had the feeling I'd seen her before, but it was just that she evoked all my memories of first loves—those pale, fragrant girls.

"You got nice taste," Gertie whispered. "I'll see what I can do."

We walked out onto an enclosed veranda where two men in whites were sitting puffing foot-long cigars. Other girls were draped at their feet. Crystal ornaments glistened in the sunlight and clinked lightly in the breeze, which was just starting to come up across the lawn.

Gertie pointed to the bigger of the two men. "He's from Ohio. Do you know him?"

I shook my head.

"Down here buying land."

More girls sauntered in, smiling, nibbling grapes and mangoes. Some of the girls were freshly scrubbed, others wickedly painted. Gertie seemed to have someone for any fantasy you could think of.

"Take your time, George. I'll be around if you need help."

I wanted to get back to the girl on the stairs before she was taken, but I overheard one of the two men speak the name Federman and then say something about Cleveland. I walked closer and eavesdropped: they were talking real estate prices and discussing the rising market.

"I still think your money's golden down here. There are a lot of nice buys."

"Federman, like I said, I just don't know."

"But I saw a fine property this morning over on Flagler. Perfect place for a hotel."

"The Willig store?"

"That's the one."

"Paley and his group are bidding on it. They seem very sure of themselves."

"They've offered too little," Federman said.

"Word is they can go as high as they want."

Federman smiled greedily as he reached over and stroked the girl next to him. "Who says I can't?" The girl smiled back at him in the same greedy way. "I'm gonna offer them nine hundred a front foot. Paley won't touch that."

I wondered if business could recall Sam from the heat of the moment with the redhead in the ballroom. It probably could. I went looking for him but was intercepted by the girl on the stairs.

"Are you George?"

"Yes."

"Are you busy?" Her fingers traced a soft line from my temple down my back.

I wasn't that busy. She took my hand and led me upstairs.

"What's your name?"

"Hannah. You're handsome. Can I touch you?"

"Isn't that what we're here to do?"

"I didn't know what you wanted."

She removed her peignoir, then asked me to untie the bows on the front of her camisole. "But slowly, now. Ain't it pretty?"

Her chest was lightly freckled, honey colored. The bows were a light pink, the satin was peach. She had frail arms, large breasts for her size, and pink nipples almost the same color as the bows.

"Let me undress you," she said, tugging my shirt out of my pants. "Where you from?"

"Midwest."

"You're so white." Her fingernails skipped down my back. "The men I been with all have hairy backs. You're so smooth." She stood and dropped her camisole to the floor. I reached up, molding my hand to fit her breast, then rubbed her lightly until her pink nipple puckered. She rubbed her legs together.

"I can make your nipple hard, too," she said, bending over me, nibbling my chest.

I started laughing. "Quit it."

"What for?"

"Come on."

"Why should I?"

"It tickles."

"What's so bad about that? Do you want to do everything seriously?"

"What?"

"What's wrong with having a little fun? Don't you want to watch your nipple get hard? It feels good. Lay back now and relax."

I obeyed. She rubbed her hands roughly over my chest, then lightened her touch. I twitched as her lips grazed my stomach. They traveled up my chest. "Hasn't anyone ever done this to you before?"

"The truth?"

"It'd be nice."

"No."

"You been with a working girl before?"

"Yeah. Older ones."

"Never one as young as me?"

I picked her head up and stared at her eyes. She was innocent and just a touch frightened. She appeared to be sincere.

"What do you think about me?" she asked.

"I was thinking before, when I first saw you sitting on the staircase out there, that you remind me of the girls I never made love to."

She giggled. "You've got a wonderful opportunity in store."

I pulled her up on me and kissed her. Her fingers continued massaging my chest. Her tongue slithered through my lips, licked playfully at my tongue, then moved over my lips again, grazing my chin, my Adam's apple, rolling over and over the veins on my neck. . . .

"Look down," she finally said.

Her head was an inch above my nipple which stood as stiff as hers. Her hand trailed down me until she cupped my penis through my pants. "It's like the horn on a Western saddle." She laughed.

My pants were off in record time.

After about fifteen of the most gently massaged, sensually orchestrated minutes of my life, I heard Sam rumbling around in the hall in front of my bedroom. He was pounding on doors, calling my name. I wrapped myself in a sheet and opened the door. He was in a sheet too, his eyes glowing.

"George, guess what I've just heard."

"I wouldn't begin to speculate on that in this place."

"Federman's here. He wants to bid on the store. We got to meet him."

"He's offering you nine hundred for it."

"How'd you know that?"

"I heard him."

"And you didn't come to get me? That's no way to do business." He bunched his sheet up and stalked down the hall. "Get your duds on. We got business to do."

We searched everywhere for the elusive Mr. Federman, who was even more elusive in a whorehouse. Finally we happened upon the thin man he'd been talking with, who told us that Federman was on his way over to the store to present his bid in person.

We sped back to hear Tildy tell us that Federman had been hanging around getting fresh with her, so she'd sent him packing off to the bank on the corner.

"You got a good look at him, so keep your eyes pealed," Sam said to me as we walked over to the bank.

There was a mob scene in front of it: cameras clicking and lights flashing; bathing beauties parading up and down; newsmen and bank people screaming at each other, as a couple of cops tried restoring order.

"I got a friend inside named Meeker who'll probably know all about Federman," Sam said as we tried pushing our way inside. "You better deposit that money of yours, too."

The crowd surged forward, filling the bank as if it were air flooding into a balloon about to burst. We were carried up with it and finally landed on the marble floor of the main room. Then came the fearful words I'd heard that morning in the mangrove swamp.

"Hup, hup! Hup, hup!"

I looked up and to my utter amazement saw the two elephants; their trunks were hanging over the tellers' cages. I scrambled for safety under a bank officer's desk as a slight man with a tanned, round, pixie face grabbed a radio microphone.

"We've brought Rosie and Nero here because they're gonna make their first deposit with all the money they've made on Miamiland."

The crowd went wild. The elephants looked ready to charge. The little Indian flogged them both back into the depositors' line.

Sam looked down disgustedly at me cowering on the floor. "Get out of there, George. You're making a fool of yourself."

"What is this all about?"

"Publicity stunt. That little guy is Carl Fischer." Sam pushed his way closer to the elephants and called out, "Mr. Fischer, how do you like real estate prices these days?"

"We're not here to discuss real estate—we're here to hawk it. Rosie and Nero have been given their own accounts, and they're gonna make a deposit."

More photo flashes went off and, sorry to say, Rosie and Nero made the only deposit that nature ever intended them to make; both of them reared up, dropping a load of turds the size of beer barrels in front of the cages. Two women near them fainted; then people started running as the odor spread quickly and hung in the congested room.

Sam grabbed my arm, pulling me to my feet. "Do you see Federman anywhere?"

"It's hard to tell."

"Look, man, look!"

"He's big and burly—all done up in whites. Got a head the size of a watermelon."

"See him?"

"Oh, Sam, we got to get out of here, or I'm gonna lose my lunch."

"Don't give up." He spotted someone he knew. "There's Meeker. Come on."

Meeker was a mousy man standing in a corner holding a handkerchief over his nose.

"Meeker, I got to talk with you. Do you know a man from Cleveland named Federman? Does business down here."

Meeker was close to gagging. "Come back later, will you, Sam? I'm not up to talking."

"This is business. You got a back door?" Sam looked around frantically. "You need some air."

Meeker led us through a long corridor. When we got outside, he leaned over and, as the old saying goes, coughed up his cards. I couldn't help it, I followed suit.

Sam looked disgusted. "Grown men! Get yourselves straightened up. I need some information."

Meeker wiped his face. "What is it?"

"Federman—do you know him?"

"Yes, I know him. He's been looking for you. You're a lucky man, Sam Willig."

"Then it's true—he's bidding on it."

"It's true. He and Colonel Paley had a run-in here before all this nonsense started."

"Over my store?"

"Federman claimed that Paley was in league with you people and he was just in it to jack the price up. Paley said that wasn't true, that he wanted the place for a hotel site. Then Federman said he was offering you people ninety thousand and Paley upped that to ninety-five. One of the bank officers overheard them and told them both that a man named Jaystone was offering ninety-eight. They headed out to the Roman Pools to find him and quiet him down."

"Quiet him down? What does that mean?"

"Maybe they'll join forces. All of them buy in together—keep the price down."

"They can't do that. Let's go, George."

"What about my money?"

"Go inside and open yourself an account."
"Not on your life."
"Come on, then, we'll take it to the First National."

I got my money put away, and then we drove out to the beach.

The Roman Pools had a bathing pavilion and a Dutch windmill. Sam told me that at eleven o'clock in the morning every well-heeled pretender to the American aristocracy was there frolicking in the sand. It was four by the time we got there, and the crowd looked just about five hours short of fashionable—a little too overdressed and laughing a little too loudly. Circulating among the ranks was Reno Devane with two menacing-looking henchmen in tow. He winked hello at me.

"There they are," Sam said, looking in another direction.

Federman, Paley, and Jaystone were going at it at a table overlooking the ocean. Sam was a wreck. "Now, how do we do this? How do we get them away from each other?"

"You don't know they're discussing your land."

Their heads were now bobbing up and down in unison.

"I can feel it in my bones. I'm about to get screwed."

Reno Devane parked his goons at a table and began staring at us with more interest.

I nudged Sam. "That guy Devane is here."

"I can't be bothered with him now."

"He looks interested in us. Jaystone just waved at him."

Sam was lost in thought. Suddenly an idea popped into his head. "You do it, George."

"Do what?"

"You go over, and you start bidding against them—get them going against each other."

"I've never done anything like that before. I'll botch it."

"Listen, when we make this sale, there's going to be a lot of money around, and if you have a hand in making some of it, you'll get yours."

"I'll tell them I want to buy it as well?"

"Yeah, say it just like that—all polite and polished. They'll believe you. Hell, you just made yourself ten thousand dollars —you've got experience behind you. Come on, I'll introduce you."

He grabbed my arm, shoving me in their direction. Jaystone was the first to see us.

"Hello, gentlemen," Sam said, "this is quite a coincidence.

I was just telling Mr. Sloate here that he's gonna have to stand in line if he wants to bid on my property as well."

The three of them looked as if they'd devour me in one bite if I messed up their plans.

Federman spoke up. "I don't believe we've been introduced."

"This is Mr. Willig," Jaystone said.

Federman nodded.

Colonel Paley grumbled, "What line are you in, Mr. Sloate?"

"Land."

"That is hardly a rare occupation or, shall I say, preoccupation these days. Mr. Willig, may I ask you why you did not tell me that your young friend here was tendering an offer on your property?"

"He's been thinkin' it over."

"Very interesting."

"But he's finally made up his mind. He's offerin' us eleven hundred a front foot."

Colonel Paley threw down his pearl gray gloves.

Federman fumed. "That's way out of line."

"I've seen you somewhere before, Mr. Sloate, but at the moment I can't recall where," Jaystone said.

Colonel Paley smiled wickedly. "Before we go any further, may I suggest that we are all about to be had. With all respect for your business ability, Mr. Willig, I do not believe this young man has any more intention of buying the Willig land than I do at this moment. Willig here has been squiring his young friend around town all week."

"What do you mean?" Federman demanded.

"Mr. Willig happens to be at the Roman Pools at this unfashionable hour"—this was said in the broadest, nastiest tone imaginable—"happens to see the three of us sitting here smiling benignly at each other, and, I believe, he happened to come up with this idea of having his friend rekindle the bidding on his land."

"That is a direct affront, sir!" Good old Sam. When the situation called for it, he could pour it on with the best of them. "That is an insult I will not tolerate. I have a good notion to withdraw my land from the marketplace."

We were certainly drawing attention by that time, and Sam was getting exactly what he wanted: the bidding resumed. Gentlemen though they were, I could see that this well-mannered banter was heating up, and it would take no time at all for the gracious Colonel Paley to launch a full-scale assault. Oddly enough, it was Reno Devane who stepped in to restore order.

"Good afternoon, gentlemen," he said, pulling up a chair. "A little business on the beach?"

They seemed to know him quite well. They went sulking off into their corner of the table as Devane ushered Sam and me into vacant chairs.

"I know that crime is a problem in Miami, but this is far too civilized a group to come to that."

Everyone but Colonel Paley smiled. "This is hardly any of your concern," he said.

Devane squinted up at the late afternoon sun, popping a Havana cigar into his mouth. "I don't know about that. We are talking land, aren't we?"

Sam was uncomfortable with him, sensing, no doubt, that the rum runner would disturb his plans.

"I didn't know you were into land, Devane," Sam said. "All I do know is what I heard today about your other operations."

Devane licked the blunt end of his cigar and smiled innocently. "What's that?"

"New federal boys are in here because of that big run-in last night. I'd think you'd be makin' yourself pretty scarce."

It suddenly became evident that Sam was out of his league.

"They could be looking for all sorts of criminals. I guess you and Mr. Sloate haven't heard the big news."

He made us wait until he'd lit his cigar to unload the news on us. "Seems two white men freed a nigger from a sweat-box out near Miamiland today."

Federman, Paley, and Jaystone may not have noticed it, but I saw the blood drain from Sam's face, and I was sure I looked as white as the tablecloth.

"That nigger took off into the fields out there, and the foreman went out after him. Seems it was a real crafty nigger. He stalked that foreman, got his rifle away from him, and shot him dead." He stared directly at me. "Big manhunt on for the nigger and the whites that helped him."

Federman flipped open his pocket watch. "I've got to meet my wife."

"Let's get on with it," Devane said, locking eyes with Sam. "We're here to talk land, aren't we, Mr. Willig?"

"Sure," Sam mumbled contritely.

"I'm giving you a bid on the Flagler property," Devane finally said.

I figured he'd go in for the kill; he leaned back in his chair comfortably, savoring the moment.

"Fifteen hundred a front foot is a fair offer."

Sam looked ready to faint. My heart stopped beating for a full minute, and the three others turned beet red.

"That's ridiculous," Jaystone said.

"Preposterous," Colonel Paley muttered.

"Way out of line," Federman added.

"It's the going price at the moment," Devane offered. "I don't know what these boys been telling you, Sam, but the property next to yours went for fifteen hundred this morning, so fifteen hundred seems pretty cheap this afternoon."

What was Devane after? He could have had the land dirt-cheap after telling us in no uncertain terms that he'd found out it was Sam and me who'd been involved with that thing out in the fields. But now he switched tactics, and the three money boys started in again, bidding against each other.

The price went up to seventeen fifty.

"Eighteen fifty," Devane said.

Colonel Paley halted the action, asking Sam if he'd mind a brief interruption while he and Jaystone and Federman conferred privately.

"Not at all. Take your time."

The three of them went off. Sam was a wreck; his land had skyrocketed overnight, but he knew he wasn't in control. Devane held him the way he was holding his cigar, rolling it back and forth playfully between his thick fingers.

"What do you want, Devane?" Sam finally asked.

"I would like to see your family prosper, my friend."

"Come on, what is it?"

"I enjoy doing favors for my friends."

"How do they repay you?"

"They're naturally indebted to me. That's gentlemanly, isn't it?"

"And how do I pay you back?"

Devane leaned over the table. "I need your brother."

"Jonny? What's he got to do with it?"

"He's the only one who can handle a job I got."

"What job?"

"You're no dope, Willig, although you are a loose mouth. The Feds are crawling all over the place waiting for me to make a move, and I've got a boat between here and Bimini with a big shipment on it waiting to get in. I've paid for it and sold it, and it's got to be in by this weekend. Your brother is the only one the cops won't be watching out for. I want him."

Sam was stunned. "I can't promise that. No one's got any control over Jonny."

"Get some control. He's been acting real independent with me. But let me tell you something, pal. I'll foul up this land deal as fast as I made it for you." He stood and smiled. "I got the power to do that, and I also got the names of the guys who helped that nigger. You get Jonny for me." He walked off to a nearby table, watching us, his goons beside him.

Sam grabbed my hand and pressed it against his chest. "Feel my heart, George. Am I dying or what? What am I gonna do?"

"Don't panic, for starters. Jonny will jump at the chance to get himself killed out on some rum-running scheme. I just don't know about this other thing, though. How could he have found out about us being out there this morning?"

"This is bad. Real bad."

Jaystone, Paley, and Federman filed out of the enclosed bathing pavilion and began walking toward us.

"Forget it for the moment, Sam. Those guys coming at you have money written all over them, and they're gonna be handing it to you in about two minutes."

Colonel Paley was now their unofficial spokesman.

"Mr. Willig, we have arrived at what we think is a more than equitable solution. The three of us are joining forces, and we're prepared to offer you two thousand a front foot."

Sam was dazed. "Two hundred thousand dollars for that damn store—that's lunacy," he mumbled.

"He'll take it," I said.

"We would like you to accept a ten percent payment this afternoon as a show of faith. Will a bank check from Savannah be sufficient?"

Sam snapped back to attention. "Sure."

Paley took the check out of his pocket and filled in the amount. "To whom do I make this out?"

"Beatrice Willig. When do I get the rest of it?"

"We'll have you sign a binder now, and we'll get the contracts drawn and have them and the remainder of the money for you by next week."

Sam turned to me with tears in his eyes. "Get the car, will you, George? Chauffeur me around. I'm a rich man."

Devane walked back to our table. "I'm sorry I lost out on your building, but I trust you have nothing to complain about." He smiled maliciously, then took off again.

"You got yourself a chauffeur—I'll be waiting out front for you. Gentlemen, it's been a pleasure."

Not one of them acknowledged my leaving.

Devane was standing in front of the pavilion puffing on his cigar.

"You got yourself some nice new friends," he said as I passed him.

I suppressed an urge to ask him how he'd found out about Sam and me, but as soon as I stepped into the parking lot, I got my answer.

One of Devane's goons was driving up the street in a shiny red Hispano-Suiza Cabriolet. In the back seat, sporting a very expensive dress and newly bobbed hair, sat Diana, who looked as if she were going to faint when she saw me.

Devane opened the door, leaned in, and kissed Diana on the cheek, looking over at me to make sure I'd seen him do it.

"Not a word, George, please. Not a word about this to anyone," she whispered, panic-stricken.

Devane hopped into the car. It sped off down the beach road.

Mixed blessings was what I kept saying to myself as I stood there watching her drive off. The family was afflicted with mixed blessings, used to them in fact.

When we finally got home and told Bea she was now worth two hundred thousand dollars, she mumbled something about "poor Abe" not being there to share it with her. Then she burst into tears and locked herself in her room.

6

The next couple of days were some of the most nerve-racking of my life. Bea stayed locked up in her room, finally emerging to chastise Sam for not having involved her in the deal from the very beginning. When she heard the juicy terms, however, she calmed down somewhat, but she wouldn't let any of them forget it was *her* money they were playing with.

Sam could hardly wait for the chance to begin playing with it. On the second day, however, he still had not gotten up the nerve to tell Jonny what his part in this was going to be.

I studied all of them and tried to get my bearings. Tension was what they thrived on; a single moment of calm would have brought them all down. Through all of this, Bea sustained a genuine liking for me. Whenever the deal was discussed, she brought me into it; even had me sit down with her and go over every step of Sam's negotiations. She seemed particularly interested in the personalities of Paley, Jaystone, and Federmen.

"I'll handle them when the time comes," she mused after I finished. "I've dealt with men like that my whole life. I'll dress myself up. Cloak my dagger in the velvet glove, like they say. All you have to do is butter men up and then go after them. Remember that, George. It's one of life's lessons."

"What are you going to do with all that money?"

"Bank it just like you banked yours. And First National is the place to do it because their president isn't getting into all this land nonsense. Just remember what I've told you. Flatter the men to death to get what you want."

Cogent advice, I suppose, although she did miss one salient point: I was a man!

Diana heated up the place with her new hairdo and jazzy ways. She flitted from mirror to mirror as if she would dissolve without her reflection in front of her. Her style of dress changed, too—loose and shimmery. Her hips swayed with a new ease. It was as if she relished being called loose; it scared and titillated her. In Diana's case it seemed as if she had only two choices: either she'd darn socks like a dutiful *hausfrau* or run around with the likes of Reno Devane.

She had no idea what to make of me. Was I a collaborator or a conspirator? Tell you the truth, I didn't know, either. I was not ready to tell tales, but neither was I ready to embrace what she was doing. I couldn't dismiss her part in Devane's treacherous insinuations, and I was the only one in the house who knew about it.

All of this was taking its toll on taciturn Jack Chason. He looked at his now boyish-looking wife and shrank in disbelief. She was overtly aggressive with him, teasing him, petting him, provoking him. All she had to do was breeze into the room, and he'd start tripping over his feet.

He was a strange one, always playing life fairly close to the vest. Sam filled me in on part of his history. Jack was a poor boy who'd come South seeking his fortune. He married Diana and went to work for Bea, and while Diana thought he'd take her out of her mother's house, Sam said Jack was smarter than that. Bea held the power and the purse strings, and Jack wanted to stay close to both. When he went out on the road selling, he also managed to bring along some of Devane's booze to sell, which must have turned a nice profit for him.

Against my better judgment and because the balmy nights were beginning to get to me, my chilly relationship with Tildy began to thaw somewhat. She seemed to be the only one in the house in touch with what she had an itch to do. Or so I thought.

By the end of the week, Sam went back to work in the store, and Bea was running around town on errands. Tildy paraded around the house like a beer garden wench.

Big, globelike breasts have always been a weakness of mine; Tildy's got me waxing poetic. I fantasized licking them, tracing their pale blue veins. She got me so worked up it was as if I were walking around the house with a cucumber stuffed inside my pants. I finally developed a tic. Every time she brushed by me, my hand flipped into my pocket.

"Sam's coming home for lunch, isn't he?" I asked one day when she pressed in.

"I don't think so." She licked her lips and pouted.

"Is that Albert calling you?"

Her tongue traced over her lips. "He's asleep."

My hand dove into my pocket as if it had a life all its own.

"It's the heat."

"Your undershorts botherin' you?" she asked.

"Mine are a mess by the end of the day." She paused. "I don't think Sam'll be home for lunch today," she said playfully. "Want some lemonade?"

"Sam's a good friend of mine, Tildy."

"He loves lemonade. Wasn't dancing fun the other night?"

"Very nice."

"My gawd, you are polite. Don't ya love that jazz?"

"You do an evil two-step, Tildy."

"Now you're talkin'. Dance my dogs off. Let's jazz it up." She went into her version of the shimmy.

"How do you like Diana's haircut?"

"You're not one of those powder puffs, are you?"

"I beg your pardon?"

"Men with slave bracelets, and shoe polish in their hair."

"Tildy, I've got an eyeful of you, and I like what I see. If you want to feel the way I feel, be my guest." I offered her my pocket.

"I take that back. You aren't very polite."

"I don't feel this way about everybody, honey. I'll have that dance."

"I'll get the lemonade."

"Don't bother."

She made a beeline for the kitchen. "No bother, I want it. I'm dry. About Diana's hair—it's a scandal."

Whoosh, slam, patter, slam, patter. The kitchen door swung shut.

Just as everything was calming down, Jonny came rushing in the front door looking decidedly hot under the collar.

"I want to talk with you," he said, pointing a finger under my nose.

"Sam's told you about the rum run, huh?"

"Come out back with me right now."

I followed him behind the garage where he sank down on the ground and kicked at the pine needles.

"They always get me involved like this," he said.

"Well, then, you can imagine how I feel. I'm not even a member of this happy little brood."

"Don't joke around, George. Sam's sold me down the river."

"Oh, come off it, Jonny. You'd have done it anyway if Devane offered it to you. Where's all your spirit of adventure and madness gone to?"

"Big talker. How'd you let Sam get so stupid?"

"What do you mean?"

"I mean him letting that nigger out of the sweatbox. Why didn't you stop him?"

"Sam didn't do it. I did."

"Jesus Christ. I have to go get myself killed because of some guy who walked into the house a couple of days ago. Why'd you do that?"

I sank down beside him. "It just didn't seem right to me."

"Right or wrong has nothing to do with it. Now I'm going to get my head shot off."

"Come on, you won't get into trouble."

"Not much."

"Listen, what if it had been one of those Indian boys inside that sweatbox—you'd have done the same thing."

"It's different. The Indian boys ain't—aren't niggers."

"This family is as dense as the trees."

"Fine talk coming from a Bexley boy."

"Okay, so it was stupid, and I've gotten you into a mess, but look at the other side of it. Your family is making all this money. You told me yourself you know what you're doing out there on the water."

"There's more to it than that—I wanted to get away from Devane. Now I'm right back in his hands."

He leaped up, kicked the garage wall, then looked down at me.

"You are white, George." He smiled playfully. "White and stiff. I'm going to offer you the chance to lose all that Bexley stiffness."

"What did you have in mind?"

"You got to repay me for getting me into this. It's only fair."

"What are you aiming at?"

"You're gonna come with me."

"On the run?"

"In the dead of night."

"You little maniac. You think I'm as crazy as you are?"

"You owe me, George. It isn't even enough payment, because you're gonna learn something about yourself. I'm gonna give you the chance to get yourself wet and dirty." He laughed.

"You are crazy."

"And you are a man of honor. You'll do it. That's all there is to it."

He got up and sprinted into the woods.

He had me by the short ones, and both of us knew it. Damned if I didn't feel as if the whole thing were my fault. My fault and Diana's, to be exact.

Later that night after dinner, I took a walk around the block and ran into Jack and Diana. She bounced as she walked, nervously stroking the bare back of her neck as Jack and I chatted about the weather and the real estate market.

"I'm going back to the house," Jack finally said. "You coming?"

Diana stared at me. "No, I think I'll walk along with George for a while."

Neither of us spoke for a long time. She suddenly stopped.

"You really have been sweet, George—about everything. And you must think me a horrible tramp."

My eyes swept down from her slim shoulders to the stockings rolled up beneath her knees.

"That's the general effect, isn't it?"

"Oh, yes, be cross, George. That's what I deserve. I really do. But it is the price I'm willing to pay."

"You're willing to pay? Seems like all of us are paying for it."

"What do you mean?"

"Don't you know? It's my neck, too. You told Devane about Sam and me, and he forced Sam to agree to have Jonny go risk his neck on another rum-running scheme."

Diana bit her lip and ran her hands nervously through her hair.

"I didn't know about that part of it."

"Devane said he'd ruin the land deal if Sam didn't cooperate."

"My God."

I started walking away from her, but she ran after me. "Please, George. I didn't know. Stop walking for a minute. Please."

Tears welled up in her eyes. Those soft, blue-velvet eyes. I couldn't take it.

"Oh, calm down. I guess you didn't know. Stop it now. Don't cry. Jazz babies don't cry about anything."

Then the dam burst. She buried her head in my shoulder and sobbed. Was it real? I couldn't tell.

"I want to have some fun, George. You don't know what it's like to be young and pretty and locked away in some dreadful store all day. I want to have some fun."

"You're having your share."

"You just don't know."

"What are you planning to do about your husband?"

Her head snapped away from my shoulder.

"Do you think he sees me when he looks at me? I tell you I'll never know what's going on inside that man. Just like my brother. The two of them, playing at my mother's feet. Are they waiting for crumbs to drop? I don't want to wait. I don't have that much time."

"Devane doesn't look as if he's a man who likes waiting, either."

She smiled. "Oh, he's just a young bull. There's nothing between us. Really. We're just having some fun."

"Well, don't ask me what you're doing. I'm not used to any of this."

She smiled sweetly, then tugged on a lock of my hair. "You're so handsome and noble, George. And you've taken such good care of me. I really do think you're the only one I could have entrusted with my secret."

"I'll tell you one thing, Diana, you can drop that poor southern belle pose you keep lapsing into. It's falling on deaf ears."

She leaned over and quickly kissed my cheek. "Let's share secrets, George."

"What do you mean?"

"You know one about me. Let me know something about you."

"What about me?"

"Oh, you're so evasive."

"That's part of my charm, isn't it?'

"Be serious with me. Tell me something you've never told anyone."

I thought about this for a moment. She was being so attentive, so lovely.

"I can't think of anything."

"Let's see—have you ever been in love?"

"Maybe once, years ago."

"Who was she?"

"Diana, I'm talking about a crush. Maybe eight years ago at age fourteen."

"Those are wonderful. Who was she?"

"A girl named Marabelle Davis."

"What was she like?"

Thinking about Marabelle's disrobing act, I laughed. "She had a wild streak."

"How so?"

"She wasn't scared of anything."

"You like that, don't you?"

"I don't know."

"Sure you do. I'll bet she used to drag you all over her house searching for a secluded spot, just so she could put her arms around you and kiss you."

I laughed again. "Something like that. She had almost no shame, but she was a very proud girl. I kissed her, but it wasn't as if I tricked her into it. She gave me whatever she wanted to."

"And you probably haven't been in love since then. Not many shameless girls like Marabelle around any more, are there? I suppose you had to put up with a lot of guff from your friends. The boys must have thought Marabelle was a terrible tramp. I'll bet you fought for her honor."

"They didn't understand her. She was a wonderful girl. Probably still is, although I think my father told me she'd up and married a dentist."

"Yes, I'm sure of it. She settled for safety in the end. I do like you, George. You're a gentleman, but you're naughty underneath. I like that in a man."

She walked away from me but called out over her shoulder, "I really do like that."

I watched her as she ran down the street. Diana Willig Chason: romantic and tempting, a wild streak as well.

7

The night of the run, Sam was offering me comfort out of a bottle of bourbon behind the garage.

"You don't know how badly I feel about all this, George."

"That seems to be the popular line of conversation in this family."

"No really and truly. First I go get you laid, now I get you screwed. It's all my fault."

"Don't feel so badly, Sam. I was the one who pulled the bolt off the sweatbox. Like Jonny said, I've got to pay my share, too."

"Have another drink."

I had two.

"Tell me, Sam, you ever been out on the water at night with Jonny?"

"You crazy?"

"That's comforting."

"But I hear he knows what he's doin'. You okay?"

"I guess so. I don't know. I'm playing this by ear."

Jonny joined us.

"We better get inside. Mom's wondering what in hell you two are doing out here. You all ready, George?" He was grinning like a fool. "Don't be scared."

"Jon, don't scare me by telling me that you're not. . . . I want you to be as careful as can be."

He laughed. "I guess you've heard the news."

"What's that?"

"Federal boys are crawling all over the place."

"I've heard," I said in disgust.

"Now don't worry. I've done this plenty of times. It's easy, and we'll be in the fastest boat. The Coast Guard boys will never catch up with us."

"Are the Indians coming with us?"

"We'll head out of Bear Cut in a little flotilla formation. The Indian boys will be behind us going out. We'll meet up with Devane's yacht, load up, and head back."

"How much are we going to bring in?"

"Each boat takes on about fifty cases."

"That's not too much."

"Exactly. So if we ever are hauled into court, they won't throw the book at us."

"My God." I shuddered.

Sam and Jon pulled me to my feet.

"You'll be repaid for this—both of you," Sam said as we made our way back to the house.

"Either that or we'll have damned nice funerals," Jon said lightly.

Gallows humor, indeed! My life was in the hands of an eighteen-year-old lunatic.

The family said their good nights, and Jon and I turned in at about eleven. There was ample cloud cover over the full moon before I got into bed.

"That's a good sign," Jon said. "This will be a piece of pie. Try getting some sleep."

He slipped into his bed and went out like a light, but I stood guard over the covered moon.

All my well-intentioned guarding and praying were of no use. A breeze came up from the water at about twelve-thirty, dispersing the clouds, slowly at first, and then breaking the gauzy cover apart. Clouds like puffs of cannon smoke flew through the sky, leaving the moon bare, bone white, as bright as any midday sun.

Jon awoke and joined me at the window.

"It doesn't look good," I insisted.

"Nonsense. Now we'll have no trouble at all on the water."

"We should think about this—it could be serious."

"No doubt about that," he said, reaching under the bed, pulling out the bottle of witch hazel and his clothes. He passed the bottle to me. "Spread a coat of it all over you."

We dressed and crept out of the house.

The streets were deserted, and the moon cast an indifferent eye over the lacelike shadows of the acacia trees silhouetted against the night sky.

When we reached Bayfront Park, we walked to its southern point.

Jon had told me that the only way to live was to jump into the stream of life, and here I was wading in behind him.

"The full moon," I whispered. "It bothers me. Don't you care about it?"

"Hell, yes. We could get caught. Now just you follow me." He pointed to a group of boats tied up to buoys in the middle of the channel. "I'll go first and help you board."

I immersed myself and had to admit that it was a relief to be in that warm water. A veil of salt vapor was rising ever so slowly. This was the adventure Jon had promised me, but I wanted it to be over.

He looked back at me and smiled coyly. "You're pretty brave for a Bexley boy."

"Pretty stupid, you mean. I have some idea of what the punishment could be." I swirled the water around my body. A twinge of excitement hollowed out my stomach.

"It gets deep here," he said. "I hope you can swim."

I tumbled off the shoal and lost my balance for a moment, then kicked my legs. My pants got in the way, and I had to redouble my efforts to remain afloat.

Jon's head bobbed up and down as he took long, measured strokes, cutting through the water like a boy riding a fish. I concentrated on his movement, and my fears disappeared. I kept trying to think: yes, this was all perfectly normal and wholesome, a midnight swim, fully dressed. Jon treaded water, turned and smiled reassuringly, then headed out again.

This boy and I will remain friends, I said to myself. No matter what happens, we'd be bound to each other by this adventure. It did not seem to matter that we had age differences or personalities as different as day and night; we would be just like old army buddies who had shared danger.

He put his hand up on the bow of a twenty-five-foot-long boat that looked sorely in need of repair. Up and over he went. I was exhausted. Tricky channel currents pressed in on me, carried me for a while, then turned against me. His head popped up, then his hand came toward me, finally grasping mine, pulling me over the bow.

"Now the real fun starts." He began tinkering with the motor.

"Maniac," I said as my head hit the bow rail.

There were clumps of mangroves on shore that someone had forgotten to burn. Ahead lay the brooding, moon-tipped Atlantic.

"Where does Devane keep his boat?"

"It's out a mile or so beyond the cut."

"Where're Homer and the others? I don't see them."

He concentrated on the motor while I stared at the water.

The engine sputtered over once, twice, then churned on full force.

"It's too loud."

"Sit down," he said, throwing the throttle into forward.

"Why don't we paddle out?"

He said nothing but kept his eyes trained on the horizon as we passed through the narrowest part of the cut.

The breeze had become a wind. The shoreline was disappearing. The boat was cutting through the dark water, over the waves, flying like a bird on a forgotten mission. The jungle shadows on shore were all I could see. I felt terribly alone with him there.

"We're alone," I said. "Those Indian boys aren't as dumb as we are."

"Look behind."

Creeping out of the mangroves were six boats manned by about eight or nine men. Homer stood in one, waving a lantern; its amber light flooded his chiseled face.

Jon pushed the motor to full power, and we bounced over the water. My stomach double flipped. I must have looked green, because Jon laughed and then tried to distract me.

"Lean out," he was yelling. "Let your hand drag in the water."

My hand floated above it, then sank in. It spread my fingers apart and rushed over my forearm, warm and chilly at the same time. I felt free and unburdened. The moonlight seemed warmer, more accessible, as if I could reach out and scoop it up and hold it to me.

I lost track of time, but I knew Jon had stretched the truth when he said we were only going out a mile or so. All views north, south, west, and east were wide open and blank, although I began to see the flicker of lights in the distance.

"We heading back in?"

"That's Devane's boat," Jon said.

A building in the middle of the Atlantic is what I would have called it. It was huge, pearl white, hugging the water in sloping, graceful lines. Two searchlights blinked on and off twice. Homer raised his lantern again, then extinguished it.

We came alongside, and there was Devane grinning like a demon.

"Any trouble getting out?" he yelled.

"None," Jon said. He turned to me, and for the first time I saw fear creep into his face. "You just keep quiet, George. Don't talk to him unless he asks you questions. The Indian boys do all the loading and unloading. He'll offer us some booze, and then we'll head off again."

Two crewmen from Devane's yacht threw down the lines.

"Who's that with you, Jonny?" Devane asked.

"George Sloate."

"What did you bring him out here for?"
"He needs the experience."
"Damn well isn't too funny, Jon. Not funny at all," Devane said as he helped us board.
The outer decks were teak, but in the staterooms the walls and floors were covered with pegged mahogany. He had a full bar set up in a glass-encased salon that had tapestries hanging from the ceiling. Everything smelled of money—tastefully spent but newly acquired.
"This is fabulous," I said.
"It's my home," Devane said briskly. He went to the bar and poured us drinks.
The crew filed past the windows. Deckhands were hauling up the wooden cases, loading them onto the Indians' backs.
Jon flopped across a red leather couch. Devane studied me suspiciously.
"You should have told me you were bringing Sloate out with you."
"I didn't think you'd mind. We'll be gone in a minute."
"I don't like it. I wanted to talk with you, Jon."
"We've got nothing to talk about."
"I wanted to talk with you alone."
"Talk," Jon said sullenly.
"I'll go out on the deck," I said.
Jon's eyes were filled with fear. "There's no need to do that, George."
"You do that, Sloate," Devane said. He was not a man you argued with—not in the middle of the ocean at any rate.
I took my drink outside and stared down at the boats that were pitching alongside the yacht. Homer came up beside me. "Jonny got himself all well fixed, you think?"
"What are you talking about?"
"He got the whole setup, you think?"
He pointed to the salon. "They play those games, but Jonny look like he don't want to no more. Young boy. He got to find himself some pretty girl. You do that for him, George. You get him some pretty girl."
Devane was leaning over the couch whispering. Jon looked distracted and frightened. They got up and walked behind a wall out of my view.
There was something going inside that room that bothered me, and I wanted to find out what it was. All the lights were

trained on the loading side of the yacht, so I crept past the windows on the other side in the darkness. I stopped as soon as I heard Jon's voice clearly.

"You don't care a damn about me. You'd just as soon ruin my life as save it."

"Look at me, Jonny. Am I any less of a man because of what we did?" Devane's voice was urgent and soft.

"I can't do this any more."

"Come back tonight."

"No."

"No one knows. No one suspects a thing. I got hot and cold running girls all over this boat. I even got the sweet one we had the first night."

I had to see what was going on in there. My head inched forward, one eye trained on the two of them standing against the inner wall. Devane had undone his shirt buttons; a mat of red hair covered his chest.

"One touch for me, baby boy," he said.

I almost dropped my glass.

"Just one."

He grabbed Jon's hand, placing it inside his shirt. Jon froze. His eyes were cold, but he kept his hand there.

"Together, Jonny—just the two of us and the girl."

The two of them and a girl? Was that the way it went? Somehow I didn't think a girl would have anything to do with it.

Devane leaned over, nuzzling Jon's neck as a wind swept across the deck. The boat pitched. I bounced off the salon's windows, then hit the deck railing. My glass dropped overboard, and I cursed. Then Jon called out.

"George? Is that you? You all right?"

I didn't want to face him, but there was nowhere to go. He rushed out onto the deck.

"You all right?" he repeated, touching my shoulder.

"My God, what's he gotten you into?"

His hand dropped.

"You spied on me."

"What's he done to you?"

"You think I'm some innocent?"

"You're no more than a boy."

Jonny stared out at the ocean. "I never would have seen him again if it hadn't been for you and my brother."

"Don't blame this on me, pal. Not a chance."

Devane walked out onto the deck. "Is Sloate here the reason you won't come back and spend the night with me?"

I didn't like the sound of that insinuation. My fist went up, but Jon blocked a punch aimed right at Devane's toothy grin.

"Don't mess with him, George."

"You tell him," Devane snapped.

"He'd just as soon drop you off this boat as talk with you again. I know him."

Devane laughed, then went inside.

"Get me off this boat," I pleaded. "I've had it with the whole lot of you."

It took another fifteen minutes for the Indians to finish loading the booze, then Devane paid everyone, and we shoved off.

Jon and I did not speak at all as we headed back to town.

When I saw the lights of the beach hotels twinkling in the distance. That this episode in my life was drawing to a close.

Suddenly Homer ran to the bow of his boat.

"Trouble!"

"What is it?"

"Big boats in the channel!" He looked back at Bear Cut. "Two, maybe more—one on each side."

"Just anchored there," Jon said. "Forget it. Let's get in there as fast as we can."

As the Indians picked up speed, Jon dropped back. Then searchlights lit up all over the place. The Indians panicked. They raced their engines faster, sprinting toward the narrow part of the cut.

"What's going on?" I called out.

"Coast Guard," Jon said.

As the Indians stormed into the narrows, the first boat hit something; its bow soared out of the water, flipping upside down. Indians, paddles, bottles, and cases went flying. Then the next one hit. And the next. Over and over. Each boat flipped wildly in the air. Indians were screaming, flailing, landing headfirst, feet first, flopping like puppets in the drink as the Coast Guard boats started closing in.

"They strung a cable across the channel," Jon said, measuring the situation and cutting our speed.

"Let's head back out into the ocean."

"They'll follow. We'll surprise them. Ram it, head on," he said.

"You are out of your mind."

"This boat is fast enough to take that damn wire."

"Don't do it!"

"Sit down!"

He spit into his hands, then jammed the throttle full ahead.

"Don't!" I screamed as the boat jolted forward, knocking me on my ass. The other boats looked like broken toys in a tub. Searchlights were flashing, water and land were rushing toward us at incredible speed. My heart was pounding, teeth chattering, my fists pounding on my lap.

"OHHHHHHHHHHHHHHHHH, SHIT!" Jon screamed as we hit the cable.

It swung us back like some giant rubber band, then swung us over, sailing us clear out of the water, undamaged, almost home free.

"Head for the mangrove swamps," I screamed.

He cut over to the right. The water was flying like a pair of wings on the port and starboard. Coast Guard boats were too busy with the Indians to bother with us for the time being, but I knew they'd be on our tails in a minute.

Our motor hit the sand and the mangrove runners. It flew out of control and then ripped off its hinges.

"Jump!" Jon called out.

I leaped into the water but held onto the boat.

"Push her into the swamps," he said, steering her into a thicket of gnarled roots and trunks that stuck out like long, crooked fingers in the channel.

We headed for cover through the water. Tangled vines and creepers tore my clothes and cut my shoulders and forehead. At every bend I thought I saw the dark waters rippling with the wrinkled movement of cruising alligators or water moccasins.

"Further in," he whispered.

Bugs flew up from everywhere, feasting on my bloody cuts. I shook with each sound, the eerie calls of the nightbirds and the bellowing of bull alligators.

"Just a little further, then we'll sink her. Come back for the booze in a week," Jon whispered again.

"You're thinking of saving booze. I'm going to save my neck."

"I gave you the show of a lifetime, didn't I, George?"

"Is it over?"

"Soon." He looked around to get his bearings. "Now rock her over. We'll capsize her."

Once we got the boat half out of the water, the weight of the booze sank her.

Searchlights flashed over our heads. Bugs trapped in vapor hung in the gray green beam of light. Jon and I ducked.

"Come out of there!" a man shouted.

"You see 'em?" another one asked.

Jon whispered, "We've got to get inland. Worst comes to worst, we spend the night in here and get out in the morning. Come on."

"We know you're in there!"

I followed Jon even though I heard the sloshing of those coastguardsmen behind me. Jon had swept me up completely in this dangerous game we were playing. I followed him blindly.

Up ahead was a clearing and a patch of dry land. We stopped for a moment and rested. A figure darted out of a maze of trees.

"What was that?"

We peered into the darkness. Someone sprang out. It was the Negro I'd let out of the sweatbox. At his side was the foreman's shotgun. I couldn't believe my eyes. At least here was something, someone familiar. I got to my feet and ran over to him.

"Do you have a hiding place? We're being followed."

"You brought police heeyah?" he slurred.

"They're following us."

All three of us froze as a coastguardsman's voice bellowed, "We're coming in after you. You can't hide in there all night."

"You brought dem heeyah?" he asked again.

He brought the shotgun up to his shoulder, and suddenly I was staring up the wrong end of it.

Jonny scrambled under me, knocking me to the ground; the Negro discharged one shot, and then another went sailing over my head.

Jon dragged me back into the thicket. We started running, but I looked back and saw the Negro jump into the water, firing at anything and everything—birds, trees, sand, even his own reflection in the water. The coastguardsmen began exchanging volleys with him. They couldn't see him. They didn't know he'd gone half mad. Finally their bullets cut him down. His shotgun flew out of his hands. His head toppled off his neck before he hit the water.

The sun was starting to come up by the time Jon and I made our way back to town. Once we got to the house, he piled blankets on top of me, but I lay shivering in my bed.

"It's all right," he kept saying. "We're home. It's all over."

"How can you say that?"

"It's gonna be okay."

"Those Indians will talk. They'll come for us."

"Not a chance. They been caught before. Sheriff just gets them drunk and sends them home. It's a game. Nothing ever happens. They know the booze is bought. We know they know. Devane has too much on everyone, anyway."

"It's more than a game. There's a dead man lying out there."

"That crazy nigger. We didn't do that."

"I can't believe I saw that. His head went flying off."

Jon covered his eyes with his hands. "God, I'm tired. Move over." He stretched out on the bed next to me. "This make you feel uncomfortable? I mean with all you know about me."

I was tense all right, but I said nothing.

"I do make you feel uncomfortable."

I shook my head. "Forget about it. You go out and find yourself a pretty young girl."

"I've already had pretty young girls."

"You try to sound as jaded as a Roman on his way out of an orgy, but you don't fool me. You're a damn innocent. Innocent of danger. Nothing scares you, does it?"

He rolled over away from me, cradling his head in his arms.

"I scare me, George."

We lay there silently for about half an hour, then he turned toward me again.

"You asleep?"

"No. I keep thinking about that Negro."

"You sprang him, George. You did your job. I guess he repaid you, poor bastard. They would have gotten him anyway, or he would have starved out there. Now they'll blame the rum run on him."

"I'm going to clear out of here."

He got up and moved over to his bed. "You don't have anything to worry about. They won't pin it on us, but you do what you have to."

His assurances did not comfort me that night. I had a feeling that Columbus, Ohio, was a far safer place for me.

The next morning I told the family I was going home for a while. Bea was upset. She said she had great plans for me, because I had such a good, clear head and that would be useful when the time came to invest her money. Sam thought I was out of my mind. I was confused. I left, but I knew I'd be back.

II

Shalimar

8

My fear of being apprehended by the Feds did not disappear with a departure from Miami. It lingered well into Georgia, and with each stop my pulse raced as I waited for cops to board the train and slap handcuffs on me. When we were well into the hinterlands of Indiana, then Ohio and finally Columbus, I was able to calm down. Being home, however, was a confusing experience. It gave me a chance to put what I'd been through in Miami into some perspective; I wound up feeling both appalled and exhilarated by my experiences down there. No one took much notice of my confusion. Everyone else was too confused.

It wasn't as if the rest of the country paled in comparison with Miami, it was just that in 1925 there wasn't that much left to compare it with. America was "in abandon," abandoning everything from corsets to common sense. No one was paying much attention to anything. President Coolidge wasn't making waves after his predecessor's exit in '23. It was reported that Coolidge spent two to four hours of each working day napping. While he slept, the rest of us played, and a good many played the stock market. At one point during the height of it, my family's housekeeper, Essie, had a larger stock portfolio than my father. She took to showing up for work in silk stockings, alighting from the running board of her midnight blue phaeton. Not bought and paid for exactly, but bought and being paid for. People watching time tick away in installment payments for new refrigerators, radios, and cars were pushing their way of life like a drug.

My father was disgusted with most of this nonsense. He was a real doom sayer. At the time many people scoffed at him, but he didn't believe in spending money he didn't have. For most of those early boom years, he sat back and waited for the end. "Squandering is what you're doing," he was fond of saying to me.

"I'm not squandering. I'm investigating possibilities."

"Which possibilities?"

"The land business, for one."

"You mean that nonsense in Florida?"

"It's making a lot of people rich."

"There is no shortcut to that, my boy."

I chose not to tell him that I'd already made a small pile of money that way. I don't know why. I suppose I would have angered him all the more.

"You should have taken your grandfather's money and used it for law school."

"I think granddad would have wanted me to have a little fun with it."

"That could be," he'd say, turning his attention back to his evening paper, "your grandfather didn't have a serious bone in his body."

Our relationship was as strained then as it had ever been.

A couple of months into my stay, my Aunt Clara came down with pneumonia. She died quickly, her second night in the hospital. The doctors said that her lungs and heart had just given out. My father made all the arrangements for her funeral. He asked me to help with some details; he wanted me to go down to the courthouse and file her death certificate. I looked at it before I reached the courthouse and was surprised to see that my aunt had only been fifty-two when she died. I couldn't believe it. She'd been so withered looking, so old. That night at dinner, my dad and I ate silently. I stared at him. He had that same dried-out look that she had. It scared me. After dinner I went up to my room and stared into the mirror, searching for traces of age. There weren't any as yet, but I was still scared. My dad and I never discussed my aunt's death. She faded from this earth as unobtrusively as she had lived on it.

Maybe it was her death or those long, silent meals with my father, but my drinking bouts became more frequent.

I spent the remainder of my time in Columbus sitting out evenings in speak-easies with the kids I'd gone to school with, who were now looking a bit desperate. Girls with hungry eyes, wearing undergarments for dresses. They reminded me of Diana Willig, the way they took lovers and took chances. Diana was best at that game because she played as if she were staking her life on it. I couldn't keep her out of my thoughts. All the girls who tried taking her place were pale imitations. They danced, camouflaging their boredom in idiotic songs.

They hid their timidity behind veils of provocative perfume. After a while, I saw through all of them.

No one saw an end to it, and it was all leaving me with nagging mornings after and short cash. Sam had persuaded me to leave half of what I'd made in the First National Bank in Miami. Two months after I got home, I'd gone through what I'd brought with me. I thought that the rum-running trouble had cooled down, and I itched to get back there, but there was always one more party to go to.

What finally did get me back on the southern train was a letter I received from Bea Willig:

George dear,

You have no idea how many times I've thought about you during the last couple of months. I hope your stay with your father has been enjoyable and that you are well.

We can hardly catch our breaths down here. The news of the day is that the tax people in Washington are sending down men to look into all of the money being made down here. Everyone is running for cover. The tax men want us to pay taxes on everything. The locals only want to be taxed on the cash they've made. You and I know that only amounts to about ten percent of what everyone is flashing around. People are money-mad. My money is sitting tight, probably right next to yours at that cavernous vault in the First National. Their man is very conservative. He is assuring me safe yields, little margin, etc. But listen to me go on—the money fever has spread to me as well.

The family has me troubled. I don't know what changes all this money will have on them. If what I am seeing is the first sign of it, well, I just don't know what to make of it. Jonny has been spending more time by himself. I want him to look at eastern schools, but you know how pigheaded he can be. Jack and Diana have moved into their own house. We had plenty of room here, but they obviously don't care how much money they spend. Sam dreams his pipe dreams, and they will keep him from working if he can manage it. He's down at the beach every day—scheming and dreaming. I could certainly use your levelheaded advice around here. Will you come down for a while and spend more time with us? Sam says you are our good luck charm. He misses you. We all do. So please wire us and tell us you'll come.

Hope to see you soon.

Fondly,
Bea Willig

P.S. If you decide to come, try to make it during the middle of next month. See you then.

My fellow travelers had changed considerably on this second trip down to Miami. Gone was the air of merrymaking that had me gambling and boozing all the way down a few months before. In its place was business. Money talk. Hard cold faces not in search of tans, but in search of deals. Business with a vengeance. If you possessed any inside information, and I did, they swarmed in. They took me off to their private cars and tried extracting it from me.

Roadways that ran alongside the tracks in the South were a testament to this change as well. They were jammed with cars heading for Florida. With them came people catering to Americans on the road. Selling them, putting them up for the night, feeding them. New towns sprang up and were thriving because they'd awakened one morning to find themselves at a crossroads of the Dixie Highway. With the sales job came a marvelous invention called the running billboard, which kept me chuckling as I gazed out my train window. Spaced every hundred feet or more was a message: EVERY SHAVER ... NOW CAN SNORE ... SIX MORE MINUTES ... THAN BEFORE ... BY USING ... BURMASHAVE!

After making sure there were no cops waiting for me at the Miami Station, I hoisted my bags down from the train.

"George! Over here. George!" Sam was screaming through the crowd the moment I stepped down from the train.

When I saw his round, grinning face, I realized how much I'd missed him. He may have missed me, too, and pined away, eating whatever he could jam into his mouth because, from the looks of him, I figured he'd put on about twenty pounds.

"Life seems to be treating you well," I said, patting his paunch. He gave me a bear hug.

"I'm feeling pretty flush."

As we made our way through the station, people came running up to him to introduce themselves to him.

"Sam, don't tell me you've gone and gotten famous."

He beamed. "Don't you know it. I'm the man who made a million on Flagler."

"A fifth of that might be closer to the truth."

He guffawed. "Now don't you go pokin' holes in my reputation. I'm glad to see you lookin' so well, but we've got to get you a tan. Then I got big plans for us."

"You still after my money?"

"No, it's your name I need now."

"My name?"

"Well, your Anglo-Saxon charm to be exact, but your name will do for starters."

He raced ahead with my bag, and I had to wait until we were settled in the car to be filled in on the details.

"What's all this nonsense?"

"Something real big, but I know you now, George Sloate. You got to be there with it staring you right in the face before you'll make a move. So if you can wait until I can show it to you, then I can wait for you to agree to go in on it with me."

"Sounds pretty mysterious."

"It's hot."

"Bea sure is worried about you."

"She should be—I don't need her any more. Oh, I could have used her help, but Jack and Diana got to her before I could."

"How so?"

"They needed money to buy that house of theirs."

"Bea said she wasn't too happy about their move."

"Don't you believe it. Mama couldn't wait for Diana to pack up and get out of there. I swear, those two women, they'd tear each other to shreds if it wasn't for Jack and me—and I thought he was my friend. He won't even cut me in on his new action."

"Hold on, Sam, you're talking too fast. What's Jack into?"

"He's working for Devane, but that didn't stop him from takin' mama's money when he needed it."

"If he's doing so well, what does he need her for?"

"Jack's just hedging his bets. Mama's a little more legal than Devane."

"Jonny working with him, too?"

"Sure enough." He slapped me on the shoulder. "It's good to see you, old man. I'm glad we're back together. So mama wrote to you, huh?"

"She wanted to see my shining face again."

"Oh, yeah? Well, I don't mean to insult you, George, because you know we all think the world of you, but don't ever take anything mama does at face value. She's got reasons for everything."

"I imagine she thinks I'm a good influence on Jonny."

"That's not it. Mama was pretty eager for a new house guest, so she could get rid of her present ones."

"Who're they?"

"Her sisters!"

By the time we pulled up in front of the house, I was filled in on them. "The beauties," is what Bea called them. They were younger twin sisters who were on a southern tour sans husbands and men friends. Cynthia liked to be called Sunny; Frieda was as grim a Teuton as there ever was. Sunny was a singer who had recently made her debut in a Sigmund Romberg operetta road company outside Pittsburgh. Sam told me she'd been fired because her temper outweighed her talent, and the William Morris Agency was having a tough time booking her. Frieda was taking a fling with the Workers' Party, having recently been seduced by a little toad of a man who was trying to get William Z. Forster elected president of the United States.

When I first saw them, Frieda had evidently put her politics away long enough to play a game that was the current rage of the bourgeoisie.

"Two crak."

"Pong!"

"Two bam."

"Red."

"Damn! Seven crak."

"Two dot."

"North."

"Damn!"

"Don't break the rhythm!"

"I can't help it."

The two sisters were sitting in the lotus position; Sunny was wearing an authentic hand-painted Chinese robe, Frieda a drab little gray dress. They didn't look up from the game when I walked into the living room. In front of them was a board stacked high with beautifully colored tiles, which they were picking up and discarding like two madwomen.

"Two crak."

"Flower."

"Two bam."

"One crak."

These, I gathered, were the names of the tiles, although they could have been throwing Chinese food at each other for all I knew.

It was Frieda who was breaking the rhythm by taking too long to study her hand. Sunny wanted none of that.

"Let's go!"

"Pong of nines," Frieda cried after she'd drawn.

Sunny stared incredulously. "How'd you pull that out?"

"You mean, how'd I do it after you'd done such a good job of dogging my hand all game?"

"Let's get on with it."

"Two crak."

"Three bam."

"Dragon."

"Nine dot."

Snap went the tiles as the sisters turned them up and then discarded them on the leather board.

I coughed. Sunny looked up without breaking her rhythm.

"Red dragon. Who do we have here?"

"I'm a friend of the family."

"Two crak."

"Chow south wind."

"We are the family," Frieda smirked. "Two crak!"

"Is Bea around?"

"Flower. She's out in the kitchen."

"You a friend of Bea's? Flower."

"Green dragon. He's too young," Sunny offered.

"Chow nines," Frieda beamed, then exposed four tiles in her hand.

"You are not going to beat me again. Three bam."

I walked into the kitchen on the next "two crak, three bam."

Bea was sitting on a stool, staring out the window with her back to the kitchen door, her hands covering her ears. The tiles snapped on in the living room. The sound would have driven me crazy, too.

I tapped her shoulder. She turned, heaving a sigh of relief as she hugged me. "George, thank God you're here!"

"I came as soon as I was summoned. Thanks for the invitation."

"Have you met them?" She pointed at the door. "The two Jewish Chinese women."

"We weren't formally introduced."

"You're lucky. I've got my hands full."

"So Sam said."

"Where is he?"

"He dropped me off and said he'd be back in a little while."

"That man."

"He looks as if he's doing well."

"You believe it?"

"No reason not to."

"He's doing well at the race track they opened down here."

"Everyone in town seems to know who he is."

"If he's such a big shot, how come he's living over my garage?"

I had no inclination to argue the point further.

"How's your grandchild?"

"He's the best of them, in spite of his parents. The one good thing about the business closing is that I don't have to see Tildy all that often. I tell you, I've had my hands full."

"If the house is too crowded, I can find myself another place to stay."

"Don't you dare! I want them out of here."

I believe it was Sunny who finally screamed, "Mah-jongg."

Bea shuddered, then ran to the door.

"Will you please not yell in this house! What will the neighbors think!"

"Bea, it's a game, you stuffy old thing," was Sunny's reply. "Let's meet your friend. We'll have a four-handed game."

"Over my dead body," Bea whispered to me. "Come on, George, you're in for a treat. The one in the robe is the artiste. The other one can't crack an egg any better than a smile."

When we walked in, Sunny was gathering up her tiles as Frieda puffed on a cigarette and leafed through a magazine.

"George Sloate, I'd like you to meet my sisters, Cynthia—"

"That's Sunny."

"Cynthia and Frieda."

"Call me, Sunny, okay? What kind of a name is Sloate?"

"I beg your pardon."
"Skip it," Sunny said. "Where you from?"
"Columbus, Ohio."
"I played Columbus once. Bea, you remember?"
Bea shrugged. Frieda puffed, and Bea coughed.
"If you don't like cigarette smoke, open the window," Frieda commanded.
"It's disgraceful," Bea replied. "Mom would have been outraged."
"Please leave her out of it."
"Let's see, in Columbus I played Roseanne in *Five Minutes Too Late.*"
"That's what the critics said," Frieda snickered.
Sunny ignored her. "My stage name is Sunny Shays."
"Call her Schwartz, and you'll hit a little closer to the mark," Frieda added.
A four-handed game of mah-jongg was sounding better to me all the time. Bea said something about iced tea and left me stranded with them.
Frieda grunted, tossing her magazine aside.
"Capitalist bunk." She sighed.
Bea's head popped out from the kitchen. "And I will have none of that talk in my house."
Frieda commenced to recite the "historical" implications of everything from the land boom to the Listerine advertisement in *Life* magazine.
"Politics," Sunny sighed. "I came down here to have fun. Let's go out to the beach."
"No," Frieda said.
"Oh, you. You're just gonna sit around here and lick your wounds. He wasn't worth it, honey pie. I'm sure you'll find another Bolshie cuter than him."
Sunny got to her feet and stretched, revealing an enticing slice of cleavage under her robe. "You look like you want some fun. Let's all go out to the beach."
Bea sailed into the room with a tray of iced tea.
"Nothing stronger?" Sunny asked, hugging Bea. "My older sister is such a prude. You a friend of the kids?"
"Yes."
"That Diana. What a treasure. I hope Jack knows what a treasure he's got in her. Isn't she something?"
"That's my daughter's best friend. Her aunt. Not her mother. Her aunt."

"Two peas in a pod," Frieda said as she and Bea exchanged the first smiles of the afternoon.

"I don't want you giving Diana any more talks like the one you gave her last night," Bea said.

"What did I do?"

"You're encouraging her. She's got a husband who's very good to her, and she shouldn't be told to go out and kick up her heels."

"You're being too hard on her."

"A lot you know about children."

Sunny smiled sadly at me. "Diana's always been my baby girl. Can't have any myself."

"She's not yours, and I'll have no more talk like that."

"Tell me, George." Frieda smiled. "Doesn't it sound as if we've overstayed our welcome?"

I sat there the rest of the afternoon watching, smiling at them, feigning interest at first, but then I actually did study their maneuvers. A definite pattern was developing. Bea versus Diana, versus Tildy, versus Sunny and Frieda. Jibes and subtle pain both their mean and their ends. What ends? These women raced around Bea's house like seven-year-olds who knew the right things to say for the worst effect. Sunny and Frieda whittled away at each other, weakening each other just enough to play into Bea's game of control and power. All were thriving on the attack, the resentment, the anger, the something titillating about provocation. If a tingling on my skin was beginning to register with each jab and parry, they must have been positively aglow.

At dinner I entertained the ladies with anecdotes from my college days. My presence seemed to have a soothing effect; battle was kept to a minimum.

"Did you drink a lot on your campus?" Sunny asked me.

"Two gallons a day."

"George!" Bea's eyebrows inched up disapprovingly.

"Mixed it myself, Bea."

"He's cute," Sunny said after realizing I had the leverage to play *Peck's Bad Boy* with Bea. "Real cute."

Frieda tugged up her skirt and took a flask out of her garter.

"Me, I'm having vodka," she said, pouring a double.

"Frieda!"

"Pick that up at Party meetings?" I ventured.

She scowled but offered me a shot.

"George!"

"Bea, the kid and I want a drink. It looks like water, anyway. Your neighbors will never know the difference."

Bea shrugged but said nothing. She shouldn't have backed down that easily.

"You have any radicals on your campus?" Frieda asked.

"I beg your pardon?"

"Any members of the Workers' Party?"

"None to speak of. Oh, there was an attempt sophomore year to get Tories resurrected, but it never came off."

"You get all lump-headed in those colleges."

"We've produced a very decent crop of boozers and murderers." The Leopold and Loeb extravaganza had ended its run in the tabloids last year.

Bea sighed. "And from Jewish homes, no less."

"That's a big one for Bea," Frieda jabbed. "Nothing about how their ruthlessness reflects the ruthlessness of their millionaire fathers. No, it's just two Jewish boys from good families—"

"And how do you think it looks? What do you suppose they're saying about us now?"

Frieda stifled a yawn. "My sisters are not at all politically aware."

"And where did you receive your education?" Bea countered.

Frieda downed another shot.

"What was his name again?" Sunny chimed in. "The little Bolshie?"

"Don't *you* start in on me," Frieda snapped. "Not when your husband is walking all over you."

"I'm not starting in on you."

"He's knocking off chippie after chippie while you're down here."

"Oh, this is starting to sound so serious. Let's play some music. What time is it?" The clock above her read 7:26. "And it's Thursday." She sprang away from the table. "Do you get 'Jack Frost's Melody Moments' down here?"

Bea looked disgusted. "I wouldn't know."

Sunny tried the radio anyway and came up with a find—Paul Whiteman. She began buzzing all over the room.

"You're making me nervous," Bea said, clearing away the dishes.

"Well, let's go to a movie."

As I watched Sunny squirm around the room, I had the unmistakable feeling that Frieda's eyes were trained on me. I turned ever so slightly, and there she was, cigarette smoke streaming out of her flared nostrils, her blue eyes locked into mine.

"How old are you?"

"Twenty-two."

"You ever been in love?"

"Oh, this is getting serious," Sunny chirped.

"You ever been hurt by someone you loved?"

"No."

Bea came back into the dining room carrying a tray.

"Bea's been hurt."

"What's that?"

"I said, you've been hurt by love."

The tension this provoked was as severe as any I'd ever seen.

"Don't you dare start in on that."

"Don't start in on what? I meant that you'd been hurt because of the death of your beloved spouse."

Frieda pushed on, turning to me again. "See, Abe left the family up in Columbus."

"He didn't leave us up in Columbus. He didn't want us to go with him. He was going to send for us once he got down here."

"And he fell to some illness on the highways."

The tray in Bea's hand crashed to the table. "Don't you dare talk so smugly about it in my house."

"I'm not being smug—you think you're the only one who's been hurt. That damned Socialist of mine put the knife to me. Don't you know that? He wrecked my life."

"Because you're a weakling."

"You're the one to talk."

"Ladies, ladies." Where the hell was Sam when I needed him?

"You paraded around Columbus like the best version of a jilted woman I ever saw. Came running down here looking for him. What did you find? How'd you feel?"

"I think we should go to the movies," I said.

"Yes, George, take them," Bea said, tears welling up in her eyes. "They have no respect for the dead."

Sunny blanched. "'They'? Bea, I didn't say a word. I thought it was just awful when old Abe died."

Frieda downed the remains of her glass. "Okay, enough is enough. Let's go see who Gloria Swanson seduces this week."

The beauties and I left shortly thereafter and got in to see a

1922 tear-jerker called *Her Gilded Cage.* Frieda drank her way through it. Sunny sobbed. Gloria perfected her wiles all in the unrequited service of her man. Yes, sir, there was definitely a pattern in all of it!

When we got home, Bea was in her room. The beauties began setting up the mah-jongg board for a quick go at each other before bed. I made my way upstairs to Jack and Diana's old room, where I was about to sleep off the jagged remains of the day, when Bea knocked on my door.

"Have you found everything you need? I left towels out for you."

"I found them. Thank you."

"Sorry about all this excitement at dinner." She walked in and closed the door behind her. "I'm terribly embarrassed by it."

"Bea, you don't have to apologize to me. They're your sisters."

"They've always been like that. Caused my mother more pain than you can imagine. What my mother put up with. . . ."

"They certainly have strong personalities."

"You think so? There's nothing strong about either of them. The singer has rattled her brain with her high notes, and that Frieda talks a good streak, but that's all it is. Don't you pay attention to what she says. She was left at the altar by some radical—that's what it boils down to."

"I didn't take them that seriously."

"Well, good. I don't know. I always had my mother to talk with, but now she's gone."

"She passed away?"

"Last year. I do miss that woman."

"Is your father alive?"

"They're just like him. He put my mother through plenty, too, believe me."

I had no intention of straying into that no-man's-land with her. She was exhausting me. I changed the subject.

"Where's Jonny?"

But she wouldn't budge.

"You think I want him around those two? He's off somewhere with his friends. You think I want my children seeing this kind of fighting? It's disgraceful."

"It happens in the best of families."

Her hands flitted nervously with the folds of her robe. "Why didn't Sam stop by tonight?"

"I don't know."

"He's not talking to me. Did he say anything to you about it?"

"No."

"He's feeling mighty cocky now, but when he needs something from me, he'll come around. Okay, okay, you're tired. I've talked too much. Thank you for coming down." She quickly walked to the bed, kissed me, and then left. I felt about age eight.

I heard the snap of the tiles and the Chinese litany pick up again in the living room.

"Are you going to play this damn game?" Frieda asked.

"Why was Bea so mad?"

"I burst her bubble."

"What do you mean?"

"I'll tell you what, Abe Willig had enough of her and the kids."

"You mean it's true."

"I wouldn't be surprised to see the man come strolling in that front door one fine day."

"He better get here before the money runs out."

They cackled.

"Two crak."

"Three bam."

"Dragon."

Needless to say, *they* were shown the front door by mid-afternoon the next day.

9

"Trust me," Sam was saying as he tied a handkerchief over my eyes.

"I trust you. I just don't know why I have to be blindfolded."

"The element of surprise."

"You dragged me all the way out to the beach in the midsummer sun, made me dress in a business suit, and now I suppose I'm to be bound and gagged."

"Just take my arm."

"Where are you taking me?"

"Down to the water. No wait—let me look at my map. No, we're too far south. We've got to drive a little further."

He pushed me back into the car.

"Can I take this thing off?"

"No, this will be better. Just leave it on. Just a little further."

I'll never know how the tires made it through the sand. When last I had been privileged to look, we had pulled off what passed as Miami Beach's main street onto a road consisting of two parallel ruts scooped out of the sand, filled with rotting oyster shells.

"Okay, just a little further. There!" He slammed on the brakes. My head hit the windscreen.

"Where?"

"Now, hold on. I've got you. Just walk with me."

"This better be worth it."

"You know this is the first secret I've ever been able to keep."

"Between yesterday and today—that's a start."

The sun was burning through the gentle sea breezes.

"Now, for the total effect, you've got to make believe: you've been swimming all morning; you're as rich as Croesus, and you've come down here to the beach to unwind from the rigors of counting your millions up in the city. So you swim a little, then you walk." He walked me through all this, lifting my legs, one at a time in rhythm with his words: "Slowly, out of the water, the sun hits you, warms you, and you look up."

Voilà!

The blindfold was ripped from my eyes, and I was staring at as beautiful an isolated and sun-drenched stretch of beach as I'd ever seen—sand like talc and in the distance, the green, feathery tops of the cypress trees.

"Well?"

"It's beautiful."

"What do you really think?"

"It's like a desert isle in a Fairbanks movie."

"Exactly. What else comes to your mind?"

"Beauty."

"What else?"

"Three colors. The sky. The trees. The sand. Blue, green, white."

"Touch of the poet. Oh, you're the man for me, George

Sloate. Can't you see it? Think of the most exotic place on earth."

"The desert sands. Valentino."

"Where have you always dreamed of going?"

"Tahiti."

"That's close. More exotic. What was Valentino sheik of?"

"Araby?"

He hugged me and danced around, laughing like a raving lunatic. "You've hit it on the nose. Araby! That's it. Rich as Croesus, unwinding in the ocean, and you step onto your own private Araby. That's what I'm gonna build for them."

"You own this?"

That tempered his enthusiasm somewhat. "Not yet. But to hell with that. It's for sale."

"Where are we, anyway?"

"North beach. This'll be the first development on the north beach. A whole new town."

"How much land is for sale?"

"Fifty acres." His hand arched out in the air. "As far as you can see. We'll build towers and mosques."

"Mosques?"

"Hotels that look like mosques and desert tents. I'm gonna bring camels in and stage races on the beach. And houses the likes of which you've never seen. I got it all in my head."

"Why can't you just build regular houses?"

"'Cause everybody's buildin' regular houses. You got to catch the imagination of the public. I can do that. But there's one hitch, and that's where you come in."

I didn't open my mouth. Neither did he. Instead, he kicked at the sand nervously. What exactly did he want from me this time?

"Okay, anytime you're ready, you can lower away on me."

"What are you makin' such a big deal out of?" he whined. "I don't want your money. In fact, you're gonna make money on it. Ten percent of everything we take in."

"I see from the start that I'm on the ten percent end of things this time."

"Okay, fifteen percent, but you're not gonna lay out a cent."

"What do you want from me?"

"See, there's this problem."

"Which is?"

"They won't sell this land to Jews."

"And?"

"That's it. The old dry-gums who owns this stretch of beach is a Jew-hater from way back."

"You want me to buy it for you?"

"You catch on quick."

"With what?"

"For what you mean. She wants three."

"Only in Miami and Wall Street can a single number be mentioned, and it rings millions."

"On the nose. Here, have a snort." He whipped a flask out of his pocket. "See, I want you to front the place for me. You go to old Haley Hunter—"

"The owner?"

"Old bag! You offer her the three million she wants, then I'll come in and start building it."

"Sam?"

"What?"

"With what are you going to buy it?"

"Not with what—with whom!"

He pointed toward our car; another one was pulling up beside it.

"There are some old friends of yours, George. Remember Meeker at the bank?" I nodded. "Old Henry Mason—the man you started your career off with? And there's good old Stanley Jawitz, the man you unloaded the Mason place on."

"What are they doing here?"

"They haven't come to get your money back, if that's what you're thinkin'. They're all rich now. Made it in the last six months. Matter of fact, Henry Mason might just unload a grand on you for sayin' hello to him. Now quick, before they get down here. Will you do it?"

"I still don't understand."

"You've got to agree to front for us. Meeker would, but he's such a cheapskate he doesn't want to lose his job at the bank. Old Henry can't because I don't trust him to stay off the bottle long enough. And Jawitz and I hail from the same tribe. We're gonna give the old Hunter shrew ten percent down. Then I'm gonna build me a land sales office and turn three hundred grand into a million overnight. Just like Miamiland. Know what I'm gonna call it? Shalimar, that's what. Shalimar."

The name was uttered reverently, urgently, breathlessly. A colossal scam if ever there had been one.

"I like it," I said before I had more time to think about it. "But how do I make money—fifteen percent of what and from whom?"

"From the public, dummy. You'll get fifteen percent of the take at the land sale office. One hundred fifty big ones!"

The three men were coming closer.

"Hello, boys, welcome to it. Welcome to Shalimar!" Sam called out, then whispered to me, "Now, you just follow my lead. I got these guys in my pocket. Will you do it?"

"Do I have a choice?"

General handshaking, remembering, and back-slapping reigned. Sam blindfolded the trio and sent them through the same routine; the build-up, the pitch, *et voilà,* you had to be blind not to see it.

Meeker's high forehead and pale skin had been bleached out in the sun. He squinted and nodded and burped regularly, asking a lot of dull questions to which Sam supplied flashy answers. Henry Mason was pie-eyed and up for anything. Stanley Jawitz, on the other hand, said nothing. He paced nervously, letting the sand flood over his white bucks and black socks.

"I think you got something here," he finally said. "I think you definitely got something."

"What does that mean, Stanley? You in or out?"

"The land booming and all. It's gonna die down soon. This may be just the shot it needs. You got me."

"You see, we've all got good sense."

Henry Mason lurched forward, pondering the situation. "I want in, too."

It was settled in less than an hour. My part in it was questioned by Meeker, but Mason and Jawitz wouldn't hear his objections. Wasn't I the reason they were rich men that very day? Of course. And they needed some Episcopalian to do the leg work. Fifteen percent was agreed on and settled with a handshake.

After the three of them left, I stood staring at the water. The tide was going out, leaving shallow pools on the shoreline.

"Are you getting your mother involved in this?"

"What for?"

"She'd like it, Sam. She'd be proud of you for thinking of it."

"Proud of me? She'd just come in and jerk me around like a fish on a line."

"Point her in the direction of the water when you take off her blindfold. The water is what will sell her."

Time slowed down with each breaking wave. An ocean as big as the Atlantic, and all I could think about was Bea and her garden hose.

"She wouldn't do it for me, George. She'll never give me that satisfaction in my lifetime."

I knew he meant it, and I half-suspected he was right.

"When I'm up there on top, she'll rally around me, but not now when I'm working my way up. So I don't even mention it to her."

But Sam was his own worst enemy when it came to keeping quiet about a deal he had in the works.

Two days later, he and I went over to Hialeah Racetrack. We weren't there more than half an hour before rumors started circulating about Sam's rich young friend, George Sloate, who'd come down from Columbus again with rolls of dough that he was itching to unload up on the north beach. "He's gonna build a town up there," people were chattering to my face. "Gonna put a place called Shalimar up there—like some desert oasis, camels and all."

It didn't take too much thinking to figure out who had salted and spread that manure.

Like everything else in Miami, Hialeah ran according to its own rules. It opened in January, 1925, and was doing record business. The only hitch making things sticky, but not terminal, was the fact that a bill legalizing racetrack gambling was lolling around on some docket up in Tallahassee. Not to be deterred, industrious gamblers got around the legalities with a few of their own. Before each race, small syndicates were set up like corporations, and investors interested in taking the plunge on "Little Johnny in the third" were assembled to buy shares in him. He paid a dividend when he won; or went into bankruptcy when he lost.

Sam used his "George Sloate, my young friend who's building a town" talk wisely enough to nose into the biggest betting syndicates, which included the disparate likes of Al Capone and a smattering of Vanderbilts and Whitneys. I was paid handsomely, a quick thousand, for the use of my name.

I busied myself canvassing the crowd in the grandstands

through Sam's field glasses, hoping to catch a glimpse of Diana. I had this image of her emblazoned in my mind. Beautiful, golden-haired, sapphire-eyed Diana. Pliant, supple Diana. Images were running rampant. My mouth seeking her mouth. My hands fumbling with pins and buttons. Silk chemise drifting to the floor . . .

"George, old man." Jack Chason was plowing through the crowd.

Jack Chason, of all people. I checked an impulse to beg his forgiveness for taking advantage of his wife, then studied him because he looked different. It wasn't those basset-hound eyes; they were as mournful as ever. But there was something about the way he was carrying himself, decked out in a new, affluent splendor; pale green linen suit, green-and-cinnamon-striped silk shirt. He'd acquired a practiced jauntiness, an eagerness to befriend, which he wore with as much discomfort as his new clothes.

"How long you been back?" He popped a cigarette into his mouth, his eyes darting off into the crowds.

"Just a day or two."

"Some place, isn't it?"

"I love it."

The sunshine gets in your blood, keeps calling you back. You stick around any longer, they'll be calling you a founding father."

"That I'll leave to you and the rest of the daring young men."

"We're just seizing the time, if you know what I mean," he said.

"You're looking like a man of leisure."

He made eye contact for a split second, then darted off again.

"Too busy to relax. I hear you've been keeping yourself busy as well."

"How so?"

"You've got a grand scheme going for a town up on the north beach. What are you calling it?"

"Sam told you, huh?"

"He's buzzing around like mad."

"Shalimar."

"That's it. Quite an idea. You looking for capital?"

"Sam's taking care of that."

"He is, is he? Where's he getting capital from?"

"I don't ask many questions."

"Well, you should. If it's seed money you need, you may want to talk with some of my associates."

"You like the Shalimar idea?"

"Hell, yes. What with Sam and all involved. Why not keep it in the family? You talked with Bea about it?"

It occurred to me that I was being pumped and that Jack was about to hit pay dirt.

"No, Bea's not involved yet. I don't think Sam wants her getting into it."

That seemed to relieve him. He took a deep breath, then tossed his cigarette aside. "Well, she's got plenty of money. I don't know what that woman wants to do with it."

"You looking into investiments for her?"

"Bea is too much for me to handle."

Which brought me to a question I'd been itching to ask him from the moment I saw him.

"Where is Diana?"

The color drained from his face. "She's around here somewhere. She was looking for you. You should come over and see our new house."

"I'll take you up on that."

"You do that," he said, then pushed his way back into the crowd.

I followed him with the field glasses as he walked down two or three rows, then sidled into a box seat. Sitting next to him was Diana.

From the back she looked very sophisticated, very French, wearing a mauve and lime green patterned silk dress, and a little mauve cloche hat with a green feather swooping up the side of it. She was sitting there wedged in between her husband and Devane. What games she was playing, sharing herself with husband and lover for a day at the races. Devane grinned like a covetous monkey, teeth flashing, diamond pinky ring shimmering in the sun. Jack leaned over and whispered something in her ear, then she looked up at the stands. My God, she was as beautiful as I imagined—shining like pure gold. I couldn't stop staring at her, and I was glad the field glasses were providing me with just the right measure of anonymity to fuel a new set of fantasies. Those deep-set eyes seemcd more remote than ever, but she laughed like a surprised child when she picked me out of the crowd and signaled to me to meet her downstairs.

I waited until the horses circled another turn before looking for her.

On the lawn under an umbrella, she sat sipping a glass of tonic, nervously tapping her fingers on her lime green purse. When I walked over to her, her hand floated up into mine.

"My darling," she said.

"Oh, Diana, please."

"Kiss my hand, George, just like old times."

As I kissed it, her fingers traced over my lips.

"Are we the vamp these days?"

"Yes, that's it."

"You look beautiful."

"Thank you, George. Sit with me for a moment."

"You've been keeping yourself busy. Husbands *and* lovers."

"Don't bait me, George."

"I'm sorry."

She played wounded southern belle, and then giggled like a schoolgirl.

"Did you have many torrid affairs with the neighbor girls at home?"

"Who's baiting whom?"

"My, my."

"How do you do it, Diana? How can you sit there with the two of them?"

"You take me too seriously."

"Perhaps."

She looked away, annoyed by my needling.

"I've upset you. I'm sorry." I stood.

"No, don't go. Please sit with me. I think about you all the time, and suddenly you're here again, and now you want to go running off."

"I've thought about you, too," I said finally.

"Have you? I'm flattered."

We sat staring at each other.

"You have the strangest effect on me, Diana."

"I like that—how so?"

"I keep thinking there is something more I should know about you."

"Every woman likes to think she's mystifying the men she meets."

"That isn't what you're really like."

"And what is the real me, George?"

"I have a hunch that you're just like your mother."

"Now that I will not tolerate."

"Hear me out."

"She's the most closed-minded individual I've ever met. I'm nothing like her."

"Talk about closed-minded. And all this flapper nonsense. Do you know what you should be doing?"

"What?" she snapped. "What should I be doing?"

"Oh, nothing. Forget it."

"No, I want to hear it."

"Nothing."

"I know what you're thinking. What I should be doing, according to you, is settling down and having children."

"Well?"

"Of course, George, you're so well bred. Sitting there totally confused, not knowing whether you want to seduce me or tell me to go home and have a baby."

"I keep saying all the wrong things. I'm sure when you invited me to join you, you were looking for much lighter conversation."

"I don't mind talking with you. It's so educational."

I sat there silently.

"I suppose my mother put you up to this little conversation."

"That's not true."

"And of course I don't know if I can believe you. I will not run the risk of spawning more Willig women. Have you met my aunts?"

"What do they have to do with it?"

"It's enough to frighten me out of my family for life. What is it about us that drives our men away?"

"Look at what you're doing to drive your husband off."

"Jack? He doesn't give a damn about me. I think I knew that the day I married him."

"Then why did you do it?"

"To be with someone who'd leave me alone. I don't believe in love and marriage, George. Jack protected me from my mother. Now he's gotten me out of her house. Better still, he's going to be rich—I'll be free and well dressed."

"Your cynicism is not half as becoming as your hat."

She threw her hands up in disgust. "My god!"

"We make each other uncomfortable."

"Which is so sad because we're both so pretty. I'm just waiting for you to tell me again how pretty I am, George."

"You are pretty."

"And evil and willful. Admit that it titillates you."

"That it does."

The race must have ended because the lawn was filling up with people. Sam was in the middle of them all, counting his bundle of cash.

"Money," Diana mused as she watched him scurry through the crowd. "Money is the thing. That's what I don't have, even with my rich husband and mother. No money of my own. Why don't I give birth to a dollar sign instead of a child?"

Her eyes flashed, locking with mine, as her hand slid across the table and began stroking the blonde hair on my wrist.

"You do want me, don't you?"

"You're embarrassing me, Diana."

"That isn't difficult. I think you're mad about me. And if I have anything to say about it, you'll have me. There, I've said it."

She grabbed her little green purse and took off into the crowd.

"What's she goin' off in such a huff about?" Sam asked, strolling over to me.

"Women," I muttered.

"Don't I know it."

"Where *is* Tildy these days?"

"We've had a falling out. Did you see me working this crowd this morning? I'm makin' contacts for us. I see Jack and Devane over there staring at us. Not a word about this to them."

"You've been the one blabbering all over this track about Shalimar. You'll have people swarming all over it, grabbing it up for themselves."

"No way, they think I own it already. I'm gettin' out of here. Don't want Jack nosing around me."

Devane and Jack walked over to me before I could leave.

"George Sloate, ain't that the name, boy?" Devane asked.

Jack looked surprised. "You two know each other?"

"Sure, we're old friends."

"That's overstating it a bit," I quipped.

"What's that?"

"Why, George is a good friend of the family. He's my mother-in-law's house guest."

Devane eyed me. "You make a killing up north or something?"

"Miami is my only killing to date."

"You sure ran out of here in a hurry. Place get too hot for you the last time?"

"A bit."

He laughed a little too loudly. "For me, too, but that doesn't stop me. I'm expanding my operations all the time. Jack here is my right-hand man now. Looks like I'm a friend of the family, too."

"Good business partner, too," Jack said meekly. "The best."

"Yup, right-hand man and water boy," Devane said, nudging me ever so slightly.

Jack blanched but said nothing.

"I need reliable people in my line of work."

"That he does, George, if you know any who are interested."

"Hold on there, Chason, I'll do the talking. People been telling me about a project you got going for yourself up on the north beach. Shalimar?"

"It's been discussed."

"Well, when you want to get some money up for it, I'll be all ears. It sounds like a good proposition to me."

"I'll keep that in mind."

"You do that. You know where to find me. I'm still out there on the water."

He took himself so seriously I almost laughed in his face. Then he spotted someone he knew and took off. Jack lingered a moment or two watching him.

"He's not bluffing, George. He's a good man to know."

"I don't doubt that."

"And he's got plenty of money to throw around. Be a much better source than Bea or someone like her."

"I hope he's paying you a lot."

"What?"

"I said, you seem to enjoy working with him."

I patted his shoulder, then left him to think over what I'd just been nasty enough to say. The fact is, I didn't like Jack, and I didn't trust him. Any man who'd defer so completely to another man who'd seduced his wife and owned him lock, stock, and barrel had no reason to be trusted.

10

I got the option on the Shalimar land sewed up, earning my keep, I might add, because I was able to get that old witch Haley Hunter to sell the fifty acres for a cool $2,750,000.

Meeker, Stanley Jawitz, and Henry Mason coughed up the option money plus enough to open a sales office, and, needless to say, Sam was higher than a kite.

Bea, however, was getting edgy because Sam had never gotten around to asking her for help.

"Why can't I see that land office?" she was saying to me one morning about a month later as I tried to finish dressing. "Why won't he let me?"

"You'll have to ask him that yourself, Bea. I'm not playing go-between." A foolish remark, why else was I her house guest?

"George, you're my only contact with the outside world. Why won't you tell me?"

"First off, you're overstating the point, and secondly, if Sam wanted to have you look at his land office, he'd ask you to come down and see it. If you really wanted to see it, you'd get into your car and drive down there yourself."

"You're no help at all. What's the big to-do? You rent office space, and you open an office. What's he waiting for?"

I made a final run for the front door but ran into Tildy and Albert, standing there looking lost and forlorn.

"George, would you watch Albert for a little while this morning? I wanna go see Sam's office."

Bea glared at her. "He's got anyone filing in and out of that place, but his own mother has to wait on line."

"Tildy, I'm not a baby sitter. I'm a partner in your husband's real estate venture."

"I'm no baby sitter, either," Bea chimed in.

"Then I'm never going to see that office." Tildy pouted.

Albert fidgeted at his mother's side, one of his tiny fingers inching tentatively up into one of his tiny nostrils.

"Hasn't that child eaten breakfast?" Bea snapped, pulling his hand away from his face.

Tildy ignored her question but remained glued to her position, blocking the door.

"Tildy, I'm late."

"George, I just don't understand it at all. What's Sam's big secret?"

"To tell you the truth, I'm not sure. I think Sam's got some genius for selling people—he's got the whole town asking the same question. He's working all of you as if he were a barker at a circus."

Tildy was heaving sighs by this time, her eyes wandering off, staring at the street.

"Is it genius, or is he just pulling the wool over everyone's eyes?" Bea asked.

"Trust him for once in his life. He's the ringmaster. I've seen what he's doing. It's stupendous. That's all I can say."

Suddenly Tildy gasped, "Oh, gawd! Here comes the animal act!"

We rushed outside.

Chugging up the street were two trucks hauling two of the biggest camels I'd ever seen. Hell, they were two of the only camels I'd ever seen. Behind them were Sam's car and two policemen on motorcycles. Sam was waving his hat, shouting hello to neighbors, who were beginning to pour out of their houses.

"Don't you bring them here," Bea shouted as the trucks pulled up to the house. "Don't you dare bring those ungodly animals into my house."

"What are you talkin' about, mama?" Sam called out. "I ain't bringin' them inside."

"Or outside, either," she said, lowering her voice as her eyes canvassed the growing crowd. "This is disgusting. Hello, Mrs. Eckstein!"

Mrs. Eckstein came padding across her lawn in a robe and hair pins. "Beatrice, Willig, what on earth!"

"Sam, you get them out of here."

"I just want to park them here for a couple of days."

"Couple of days? Are you crazy?"

"Wait, wait," Mrs. Eckstein chirped, flying back across her lawn into her house. "Wait 'til I get my camera!"

"Sam, you get those animals out of here, or I'll call the police."

"I brought them along, too."

After the mounted officers smiled a good morning, I stepped in to see what I could do to straighten this mess out. "What is going on, Sam?"

"George, this is the topper. Two genuine camels for opening day. Have 'em posted outside the office. I've talked with the mayor. He loves it. The cops do, too. And the newspaper boys should be here any minute. They'll have a field day."

"But you can't leave them here on the lawn."

"Not on the lawn, dummy, out back in the forest."

"Out back," Bea yelled. "Loose, running wild."

Sam must have been drunk. He slapped me on the back. "Can you see it in the papers? Jewish family trampled by wild camels. I love it!"

"Sam, I don't think you've thought this one out."

"Sure I have."

"Who's gonna take care of them?"

"Jonny back from Key West yet?"

"Jonny?" Bea's tone was reaching shrill heights. "You don't expect him to—"

"No, I got a trainer and everything for them, although I'll be damned if I know what they eat."

He stroked one of the animals as it batted its eyelashes and bared its teeth.

Bea was so disgusted that Sam had actually touched it that she turned on her heel and headed into the house. "You cannot keep them here, and that's that!"

"Now what am I gonna do?" he asked after she slammed the door.

"Be damned if I know. Did you buy them?"

"Sort of."

"Where on earth did you get them?"

"Simon Ruppert, the circus king. He's got his winter quarters over on the Gulf Coast. He sent 'em over." Sam reached down, grabbing Albert up in his arms to show him the animals.

"Don't you let him near those things," Tildy said. "What on earth has gotten into you?"

"Don't any of you got any imagination at all? You got to razzmatazz things to sell 'em."

"Sell 'em what? Some deserted stretch of beach." Tildy sneered.

"You could take them out there," I offered.

"To the beach?"

"Why not?"

"And just leave 'em there?"

"Sure. March them through the center of town straight out to Shalimar."

His eyes lit up. "Like a parade. A day-long parade."

Sam was not one to resist an impulse. He put Albert down, then hopped up on top of his car.

"Listen everyone. I want you all to follow me. We're headin' out to Shalimar. The camels will lead the way. Tildy, you and Albert get in the car with me. George, go get mama and drive her car out!"

It was the damnedest thing the town of Miami had seen since Fischer had squeezed his damn elephants into that damn bank.

We started out simply enough: two cars, two policemen on motorcycles, and two trucks carrying the two camels. By the time we reached the beach bridge, there were traffic jams in our wake: fifty cars or more, and hundreds of people on foot rushing toward the water like Baptists heading for a mass dunking. The town got so excited a holiday was declared and offices emptied.

"This is disgraceful," Bea kept saying all the way out.

"Hell, Bea, look behind us. It's a carnival. Don't spoil it for yourself. And Sam's getting just what he wanted. There's gonna be a riot when the land sale office finally opens."

"I'm going to die of embarrassment. What do you suppose those neighbors of mine are going to say about all of this? I'll be the laughingstock of the neighborhood.

"They loved it. Old Mrs. Eckstein wouldn't even let us leave until she got a picture. And anyway, now you're going to see it."

"What?"

"Shalimar!"

What happened when we finally got out there was as frenetic a scene of public madness as I ever witnessed. Children led the way with kites and balloons, dragging parents who toted picnic hampers across the sand. Music and booze flowed freely. People who'd been bottled up in offices all week loosened up, trying as best they could to mirror the expanse of beach, sky, and water surrounding them. You couldn't resist it or those people. To be away from the town all of them had fled to from up North. Away from what they thought would be a paradise, which was slowly becoming just another city. Out to the beach and the sun and the wild water. I felt its freedom ringing in my soul as if this were my last chance to grab it before people like me had a chance to organize it out of existence. But we weren't in tune with this nature. Maybe that's what all the booze and music was for—to dull all of us down to size or into some harmony with it. As the afternoon wore on, it became wilder. One of the camels broke free from its tether as soon as it was unloaded. It ran off, at first down to the water, then north, circling around the trainer and the men chasing it with ropes. Stopping, starting, jerking into dazed trots, it exhausted the men who did not want to work at anything that afternoon. It finally disappeared

I stayed on the hood of Bea's car waiting for the carnival to overtake me, but I was not able to escape from being the onlooker. I was unable to lose myself. I began to cry because I wasn't as free as I wanted to be. I was held in check by my guilt about doing anything out of the ordinary that would not be rewarded.

"George," Bea whispered.

I dried my eyes, then hopped down to see what she wanted. She had tears in her eyes as well.

"What's wrong?"

"This frightens me."

"It shouldn't do that. Everyone's just having a good time."

"Fights will break out."

"Look at it, Bea. Look where you are."

"This is Shalimar?'

"The water. Come down to the water with me."

I had to coax her down there, but it had the effect on her I knew it would. We walked away from the crowds, and she sat on the shore watching the enormous Atlantic pound on the sand.

"A man after my own heart, George. It takes my breath away. Always does. I don't know why I don't come out here more often."

"Now it's your son's dream come true."

"More like his grandmother's dream. Is all this ours?"

"For as little as ten percent down."

"His grandmother crossed this ocean. Now we own a part of it." Tears streamed down her cheeks. I put my arm around her shoulders, which shook stiffly as she cried. "They traveled here. All our parents and grandparents did. Didn't they? Did yours?"

"Sure."

"But your's came a long time ago. We just came here, George. I'm a fool for crying like this, but it's all is new to us. Do you know what I mean?"

"Sort of."

"My mother's tears helped fill this ocean on her way here. Now we own a part of it."

"To the high-water mark is how the deed reads."

"We're in America. If nothing else—even if he doesn't get his town built—Sam's had this part of it. Doesn't matter for how long a time. He's had this."

Although I knew she meant it, I also knew she'd never say that to him. I wished he was there. He'd won her over completely for that one moment in his life.

I saw Diana playing with Albert near the water's edge about fifty yards away from us. Jack was watching them. Diana waved, and she and Albert raced over to us as Jack lumbered slowly behind them.

"Isn't it wonderful," Diana said. She was out of breath, her cheeks were flushed pink, and her bobbed hair was sticking to her temples.

Bea leaned over and hugged her. It was the first time I'd seen her do that. Diana curled into her mother's arms and stayed like that for a long time. Jack merely shook his head back and forth.

"Isn't this the damnedest place you've ever seen."

Bea brushed Diana's hair back with her hand as the two women looked at each other, perhaps remembering earlier years.

"What Sam's done is wonderful," Bea said.

"Sam's a madman," Jack sighed.

"No. He most definitely is not," Bea said adamantly. "He's a dreamer."

Jack shrugged. It was obvious he didn't like this new, conciliatory air blowing in with the sea breeze.

11

By the time we got back to the house that night, Jonny had come home from his trip to Key West. He was loaded with stories—some true, some exaggerated—about his fishing trip and the characters he'd met: sailors and drifters, artists and drunkards. They were romantic pictures he painted of a place at the edge of the world inhabited by some of life's forgotten souls lolling in the sun, drinking rum, waiting for that one perfect day when the fog of booze or discontent would lift to enable all of them to begin the life they always talked about in their bars.

"I'm going back there in a couple of days," he said to me after dinner.

"You liked it that much?"

He stared at the kitchen door. We could hear Bea washing dishes. "Tell you the truth, I was working for Devane. Paid me good money, and he's got more work for me."

"Don't you ever get tired of putting your life on the line?"

"Pay's too good."

"Your mother won't be happy about your leaving."

"She won't have too much to say about it. I've made up my mind."

"But she wants you to start thinking about your future. She's got the money now to send you up North to school. Get a career for yourself."

"That's not in the cards for me."

"You must want more than just running errands for the likes of Devane."

"Oh, I do. I'm on my way to big things, but right now the money is important. If I stay around here with mother, she'll be jiggling all sorts of gifts under my nose. Go to school, play tennis, be polite. I want to be my own man."

"You won't be with Devane."

"He's teaching me all I need to know now."

"You weren't even frightened that night we almost got caught by the Feds, were you?"

He laughed. "Scared the hell out of you, though, didn't it?"

"Damn right."

"Well, I'm used to it now."

"This is all bragging foolishness if you ask me."

That angered him. "No one is asking you. What should I be doing? Joining my brother and you in the real estate game? We're playing in the same league, George, and I don't like you judging me."

He left the table, and that pretty much ended our conversation for the rest of his visit.

The next night he went to Bea and told her he was leaving. As expected, she threw a fit, called him a bum, and said she would have nothing to do with him if he didn't get himself off to a good school. But Jonny's mind was made up, and he was gone again by the third day.

During the next couple of weeks, land activity started picking up, and with it came the promise of a record tourist season, which meant rich visitors, hotels filled to brimming, and speculators watering at the mouth for land deals. Sam saw it all coming. Playing the game with a finesse that surprised me, he only leaked information about Shalimar whenever interest seemed to be waning.

The remaining camel was paraded out regularly, accompanied by showgirls dressed in harem outfits who blew kisses to the crowd as they walked through the automobile-clotted streets.

A week before the opening, Sam closed the sales office to everyone but his designers. Even I was not allowed inside. All I was told was that he was bringing the project in just slightly over budget and the results would knock my socks off.

When the fateful day arrived, crowds began gathering outside the office in the early morning. The camel, its trainer, and the harem girls were posted outside looking like pieces of papier-mâché sculpture atop a birthday cake. Above them, in pseudo-Arabic lettering, was a gigantic sign featuring a picture of an elaborately striped tent and, in gold the words: SHALIMAR . . . THE DREAM OF ARABY, followed by: Open for business today at 11:00.

I pushed my way through the crowd with Bea on my arm. Henry Mason was standing guard at the door with four uniformed policemen who looked the other way whenever Henry opened his flask for a morning bracer. When we squeezed inside the glass doors, Sam's creation took my breath away.

Ceilings and walls had been covered with heavy canvas tenting. Ostrich-plume fans whirled overhead. Underfoot were intricately patterned Bukhara rugs. Bea's eyes were tearing because the air was a little heavy on the acrid-smelling incense, but the total effect was mind-boggling.

"Mama, mama," Sam screamed out as he barreled through the room, "what do you think?"

"Who's going to pay for this?" She coughed. "My God, can't you open a window in this place?"

"Money to pay for this?" Sam laughed, perhaps a little nervously. "You're thinkin' way too small."

Meeker, Mason, and Jawitz joined us and added a chorus of equally nervous titters.

"So far we've laid out three hundred grand, and I'll be damned if I don't double it by noon." Sam clapped his hands. More harem girls and Negro boys filtered in, carrying champagne.

He grabbed a bottle, poured drinks, then lifted his glass in a toast. Padding over to a table that had a dropcloth thrown over it, he grandly swept the cloth away to reveal a model of the town of Shalimar. Housing plots were numbered and damned if he hadn't turned mosques into hotels and restaurants, post offices, courts, and libraries. There was even an oasis, complete with palm trees and a reflecting pool in the middle of it.

"Gentlemen—and mama—let's drink to millions and to Shalimar!"

"Sam, we'll get arrested for this," Bea complained.

"Drink, Bea. Drink!" I said, tossing the champagne down in one gulp.

"Now, just like rich men," Sam yelped. "To hell with the glasses."

He threw his at the tented wall opposite us. We followed suit, but the tenting was too thick, and our glasses rolled off onto the floor.

The sales force began showing up, and I recognized some as ex-binder boys who'd gone legit. Gone were the knickers. In their place were conservative suits, polished shoes, Vaselined hair, but the same flushed-faced, ah-sucker smiles. Sam snapped them into action, getting them as riled up as if he were Knute Rockne with his tackles at half time.

"This is razzmatazz, but it's business. We want as much cash as you can take in. We'll take checks and binders but no trades on other property. Cash, cash, and more cash. Jawitz, Meeker, and me will be in the back room. So you send the money over to us as soon as you get them signed up. Mason. Mason? Where are you?"

Henry was as good as gone on a bottle of champagne he was chugging in a corner while he groped one of the harem girls. "Henry! Shape up! Get your hands off her!"

The front door inched open as Tildy exploded into the room with a red-faced little man in tow.

"My goodness gracious. Never did I dream. Never." She ran up to Sam and kissed him.

"Tildy, there is a time and place, and this ain't it."

"But sugar, you cannot believe what I saw this morning."

Bea muttered, "Disgusting," under her breath.

"Later, Tildy."

"I want you to meet Mr. Fletcher here. Come over here, honey, join the party."

"Tildy—not now!" Sam tried prying his way out of her embrace.

"Mr. Fletcher here has heard all about how rich we're gonna be. Oh, Sam!" Her wide, sullen eyes registered dollar signs as she took the room in with one glance. "Never did I dream it. But Mr. Fletcher here knew it all along, didn't you? He's a real estate salesman."

"George, help me. Get Tildy and this character drinks."

I pulled them aside and plied her with champagne.

"Mr. Fletcher has been taking me around all morning," Tildy said, slurping down the bubbly. "He's been showing me houses. He says we got to diversify with all this money we're gonna have."

Fletcher smiled smugly.

"What money?" Bea asked flatly.

"Why, Bea, you can just smell it. He showed me this fabulous little mansion right on the water with a pool and everything."

Bea could stand no more of it. She inched her way over to Sam and gave him one last bit of encouragement before leaving. "Sam, you're gonna have your hands full."

But Sam was in no mood to pay any attention to her. He merely clapped his hands again. "Okay, children. Let's get this show on the road."

At 11:00 on the dot, the doors opened, the salesmen took their places, and the crowd started throwing money around as if there were no tomorrow.

Police had to be called in fifteen minutes later because buyers were not only content grabbing land, they wanted souvenirs.

Sam, Meeker, Jawitz, and I sat in the back room trying to count the cash as if we were a group of bona fide land barons. And wasn't that the truth? We were getting richer by the minute. Lots selling for five grand at 11:00 skyrocketed to twelve grand by 11:30. Mason, who was as stewed as a prune by this time, crawled into the back room with more champagne, which we all helped ourselves to as pandemonium reigned. Thousands more dollars were thrust at us. Women carrying babies clawed their way up to the sales desks only to be slammed back by grown men who were selling and reselling the same lots for quadruple their prices. One harem girl ran screaming through the piles of cash; her top had been ripped off by some over-amorous investor. No one could get to her to help her, so she stood whimpering, trying to cover her nipples.

"Keep up the money-counting, boys," Sam urged, but after a while it was no use. Meeker began shoveling all of it into paper bags.

I don't know on which exact champagne bottle I passed out or how I got out of there alive, but someone must have been watching over me. I remember seeing nothing but dollar bills; then being pulled through some woods and kissing that damn camel; then nothing, thank God, nothing but a drunken, spinning, blank abyss.

12

But what was a tin-sounding ukulele doing in the abyss with me? And a scratchy little voice that went with it?

" 'I'm the sheik of Araby, your love belongs to me!' "

Near me, somewhere over to the left of me. I didn't want to open my eyes.

" 'At night when you're asleep, into your tent I'll creep.' "

My left hand lurched out in the darkness, hitting a silk-clad ankle and an ankle strap.

"Naughty," she said, whoever she was.

"Don't stop talking. You sound familiar," I groaned.

"And don't open your eyes, darling. The coming dawn will knock you senseless."

All eight of me collided into an upright position as I opened my eyes.

"Diana." It was early morning of some day. My head almost rocked off my neck when the light hit my eyes.

"Now don't you go vomiting like a baby," she said, quietly strumming the uke, sitting on a log in someone's garden.

"Where are we?"

"Gertie Walsh's place."

"What the hell are you doing here?"

"Me? I think you'd be asking yourself that question."

"Gertie allows girls in? Oh, the light is too much to take. How'd it get to be morning?"

She laughed. "Is that my cue, for, 'Oh, Sweet Mystery of Life?' "

"Oooh, my head."

She fished around in her purse for something, then brought out a pair of bottle green sunglasses. "Here, this might ease the pain somewhat." She slipped them on over my eyes, then put a pair on herself. "There, that's better, isn't it?"

"I can't stop the spinning."

"The spins are the best part. You just lie back and enjoy it."

She bent over me, massaging my temples with her fingers.

"You feel so good."

"Just lie still, dreamer. . . . I followed you out here. Reno introduced me to Gertie a couple of months ago. She and I are pals. Even lets me entertain out here. See, I've arranged everything to get you, just like I said I would."

"Where is everyone else? What happened at Shalimar?"

"You are rich beyond dreams, dear boy. They're all upstairs with the loves of their lives. All but Meeker—boy, is he a creep. Went on with the money-counting all night. Jack's in there, too. So is Reno. We're all here, but they don't know I am. You think Jack feels he has to go blow-for-blow with prostitutes for Reno's sake? To prove something, I mean."

"I think you'd get your bottom bruised by both of them if they knew you were here."

"Nonsense. Can you get up? I'll get you something to take

away that hangover and give you an entirely *new* hangover."

She got to her feet, slowly tugging me up with her, walking both of us over to a sandy-colored stucco house.

"These must have been slave quarters once, but we all know Gertie doesn't keep slaves any more."

The door creaked open. I leaned on her shoulder, gently kissing her neck, which smelled of gardenias.

"You drive me wild, dreamy boy. Come. Inside."

There were no windows, only amber-colored lights flickering from candles in the corner opposite two beds, which had satin sheets on them. Above were tarnished mirrors, reflecting the murky light. I could make out the shape of a blonde head reclining on one of the beds. A tiny hand was holding a long silver pipe. A thin wisp of smoke wound out of the bowl at the end of it. Diana reached down for the pipe, prying it loose as the blonde head fell forward, slowly turning toward me. It was the young girl I'd made love with the last time I'd been here. Her arms reached out for me. Her eyes opened in an opaque gaze. I knelt by the side of her bed and kissed her.

"Why didn't you come back?" she whispered. "All the others are so old." She tried taking the glasses from my eyes, but Diana stopped her. I held the girl tentatively as if she were a dream of youth that would disappear. The smoke was heavy, making me so drowsy. Diana stretched out on the other bed, smoking the pipe, holding it limply, candlelight dancing in the green lenses covering her eyes.

The blonde girl watched her, then slipped from my arms and slowly made her way to the door. She walked as if she were in a trance. I wanted her again. She'd been so easy, so young, but she left.

"Make love to me," Diana whispered, taking the smoke into her mouth.

"What is that?"

"Opium. Come. Try some."

I hesitated, then she slid over onto the bed I was leaning against. Her fingers traced my lips. I sucked one of them into my mouth, and she pulled me closer to her. She wanted me, came after me, pulled insistently as she undid the buttons on her gauzy dress. Then she slipped the dress from her shoulders, took my hands, and offered me her breasts.

"Sip the pipe. Hold the smoke. Good. Again. Slowly. Good. Again. Now me. Me again."

Her hands were in my hair. My head was swimming out of focus. Who was she? These glasses.

"Don't take them off. No eyes."

We undressed each other. She cradled her head in my lap, then cupped my penis in her hands. She blew some smoke into the hair surrounding it, then stretched back, her foot inching up my chest, playing with my chin.

"What are you thinking?"

"Is this what you want?" I asked.

"What do you want? Name it, it's yours. Like that little girl said, they're all so old, George. I'm as young and blonde as she is. Aren't I? Tell me I am."

Was it her frailty I was after? It excited me more than her insistent finger tips. I traced my tongue over her body. Glasses eased away from our eyes, revealing tears. The movement of her hands was like wings beating over my back, tracing patterns down my arms. Our hands circled in and out of each other, playing games, trying to outfox each other with more and more intricate hand game patterns until her fingers floated down across my belly to my flaccid penis.

"You don't have to be inside me."

But frail young girls were to be overpowered.

"You don't have to," she kept saying, my penis resting limply against her thighs.

We rolled over the bed, the sheets sticking to our wet bodies, the smoke blurring everything out of reality. My penis did not respond at first, then it slowly crept up between our bellies. I held onto that image of it making its way to her.

"Please—you don't have to—just lie here with me, that's all I want."

Didn't she understand? Of course I had to. Reality came in now in short, sharp jabs behind my closed eyes. Seeing Devane on top of her. Seeing faceless others. Being on top of her. Overpowering her. She was gasping now, losing herself as I was filling her. Then my penis slipped out of her, spurting all over her belly, the only tangible evidence of having had her. And she looked so empty and angered.

I slipped into a drugged sleep beside her. Hours later, I heard her moving around the room. She hated me now. I could feel that in the air, but I remained feigning sleep so we would not have to confront each other. Did she get what she wanted? Did it matter? Did I? I will not face it now, I told myself. And again, a merciful sleep settled in between the sheets.

The door whipped open. Light flooded the room. I was alone in the bed.

"Aren't you the one," Sam was saying, throwing the satin sheets over me to cover me. "You had the little blonde one again, huh? You can have months on end with her now if you like." He was dumping money out of a sack all over the bed. "Months of it. Twenty-five thousand dollars of it, if you want."

"Not now, Sam," I said, burying my head in the pillow.

"Not now?" Sam was laughing like a devil. "You must be drunk again. Say, what's the funny smell? Aren't you ever coming out of here?"

"What day is it?"

"Great question! It's the afternoon after the day of the big killing. We made millions."

I ran my hands over the bills. "Is this all of it?"

"Your part. We split the rest this morning. Boys made their money back and then some. The rest of it went over to the construction people. Ten percent down like everything else. Those other boys sprinting out of this whorehouse like banshees this morning. Everyone grabbed a wad. So we made a little and then plowed the rest into Shalimar to build it. Made a little and now we're in hock up to our necks. How do you like that?"

"Come back later, Sam. I'm too far gone now. I can't follow you, and I don't want to listen to you explaining it any more. Are you happy with what happened?"

"Hell, yes, aren't you?"

"I don't know. I never made so much money for nothing before. Get out of here. Go get that big redhead of yours, then come back and we'll talk women. It's the only thing I can concentrate on now."

"I'm no one to talk women with. Like mama said, I got my hands full. Gonna have to go out and buy Tildy that house she wants. But I got the money to do it."

"Please, Sam, no more money talk, only women. Tell me, why do we go out and buy them their houses?"

"I don't think too much about that. Oh, sure, when I'm here I buy me that redhead, but I know the score on that one. Money paid down. I'm just a homely little fat boy sneakin' some icing off the cake."

"Is that how they make you feel?"

"Women always did. Thank the Lord for every one of 'em who laid down for me. The fat boys always feel indebted to them for doing that. That's why they get their houses. Tildy picked me to lay down for. She was my first. Never told that to another man, and I'm not proud of it, either, but it's the truth. Do you know what I'm talking about? How can you, huh? You're so tall and handsome, you never felt that way."

"Not in the same way. I'm not 'grateful,' but I'm still plagued by them. I think I love them, but when it comes down to it, it's me I can never lose sight of. I fantasize about them, but I don't care who they are, and I never satisfy them."

"Oh, my, we are up for confession today, aren't we. Well, if the truth be known, I stand before them with my little tadpole in hand, waiting to be invited in. I love them for taking me inside. I'd do anything for them just for that."

"That makes you the better man."

Sam smiled wryly as he patted my leg. "But you're the one they want," he sighed. "Enough of this. No more melancholy. I can't stand it."

"You feeling letdown by yesterday?"

"A little."

"That's what money does."

"That's what anything does if you let it. Come on, let's get out of this hole."

"Where's Diana?"

"Why are you thinking about her?"

"Where is she?"

"Damn girl was drinking up a storm with that Devane character out at the beach. Do you know why she hangs around with him so much?"

I shook my head no, but I knew. People like Diana were crazy. They never got what they wanted. They just went after more of what they didn't want.

13

No matter how he tried, Sam could not get me caught up in the continuing chaos of Shalimar. In the months that followed, while I was banking my money and sinking into a depression over Diana, Sam was losing no time swinging into action out at the site every day, managing builders, designers, spending money as if it were water. While Sam was away, Tildy hopped onto the money express, buying a beautiful old mansion on the bay, to which she laid claim with the most garish flags ever hoisted.

"The whole thing is gonna be a vision of the sea. Everything I can think of. Seashells for lamps, and mermaids and things. It's gonna take your breath away," she said every time I happened to be out there.

"That's nice, Tildy."

"What's with you? Can't you just imagine it? Come look at the bed I bought."

A hideous representative of what later came to be called kitsch: a headboard that curved over the mattress in white and gold swirls that made my stomach turn. Bought on time. Ten percent down without a thought about the bill that would arrive like clockwork at the end of every month.

I spent a good amount of time with Tildy because I didn't consider myself fit company for anyone else.

After Diana and I had our go-around, I pursued her as doggedly as she had pursued me, but she wouldn't see me. I felt as if I owed her something. As if I'd treated her cruelly and had to make up for it; and she did nothing to dispel my illusions. She took to her bed, playing the invalid, complaining of severe headaches, of migraines, vomiting, knee trouble, back trouble. Each week brought another symptom. With all the dope and booze she downed, she was probably suffering from little more than an extended hangover, but I'll be damned if I didn't think it was in my power to make it all better.

Bea swung into action at first, shuttling back and forth between Diana's house and her own with food and offering hand-holding sessions. But this show of maternal selflessness did not extend to being taken for granted.

"I just won't go there any more. I cook all morning for that girl, and when I drive over, she's lying in bed smoking cigarettes. Doesn't even ask how I feel. And I had that terrible cold the other day."

"Bea, please, I can't take any more fighting."

"Fighting? Why don't you just go out and have some fun, George?"

"Have you heard from Jonny?"

"Don't talk about that boy with me."

"Where is he?"

"Down in Key West. I got a card the other day. What did I do to deserve such disrespect from my children, George?"

I didn't know. I didn't care. I couldn't stop this nagging feeling that cropped up every morning after a fitful night's sleep. My eyes would spring open. My fists would be clenched. My mouth would shut tight against a howl building up from my gut. I'd lay there plotting, fantasizing: I'd run over to Diana's, tear her out of bed, challenge both Devane and her husband to a duel, and then snatch her away in the dead of night. The more tales I heard about Diana's pains and troubles, the more insistent my fantasies became. I said it was love, failing to realize that all I wanted to do with my love was to change her, make her into the girl who floated through my fantasies like some glorious sun-drenched phantom. Why do we spend our youth exhausting ourselves with people who really don't care about us or themselves?

Perhaps Diana was getting what she wanted—me, confused and running after her as if I were a repentant puppy who'd soiled her rug.

Finally I couldn't stand it. I drove over there one morning but had to wait in the bushes opposite her house until Devane's car pulled out of the driveway.

A Negro maid tried to keep me out of Diana's room.

"Miz Diana, I ast him to wait outside, but he rayn ride in," she said after I walked into Diana's room.

Diana peered over the novel she'd been reading. "It's all right. Mr. Sloate won't be staying very long."

"Why are you avoiding me?" I asked as soon as we were alone.

"Do I look as if I'm doing that?"

"Why are you mad at me?"

"George, I'm sick. What on earth are you doing here?"

"You're not talking to me. I didn't do anything wrong, did I?"

"Oh, really, George."

"You're doing this on purpose. Please stop it!"

"You're as mad as an old coot. You're all so old," she cooed, mocking the prostitute at Gertie's.

"What did I do? You wanted to have me, and you did—in the slave quarters, no less. That happened, didn't it? You had me, then you hated me for it."

"How you do go on."

"Stop playing games with me."

"What would you rather have me do?"

"Diana, we can take this very lightly. We can go out to the beach. Get you away from these people who make you so miserable. But you're locking yourself away, having everyone wait on you, and it's not making you any happier. I'm in love with you, and you're making that out to be a crime."

She sneered. "Get out of here! I didn't ask you to come here! I didn't ask you to fall in love with me!"

"You did. You played me along the first day we met—tossing your curls in my face."

"I've had it with all of you. I'll take my own sweet time drinking myself into oblivion if that's what I want to do."

"Please give me a chance. We can make love again. Anything you want this time. We'll just lie together somewhere."

"I don't want any of you. You're all driving me crazy. Men like piston engines, parading around like bantam roosters." She started crying. "I don't want any of you."

"Tell me what you do want."

"A way out of here."

"All right. If you want to go away, we'll go away. I want to try it with you."

"Do you? But it's always going to be this way for me. Run for your life, George. People like me can't be saved. Start hating me. You'll hate me soon enough."

"I don't understand. I came here to tell you that I love you."

"Don't do it. Go find your whore. She's uncomplicated. She'll tell you she loves you."

"Please—"

"I do this all the time. You don't know me at all. I spend half my life in these bedrooms drunk or smoking that silver pipe."

"But why?"

"I won't answer any more of your questions."

"Please, Diana."

"I can't stand this. Don't expect me to help you. Get out!"

She ran from the room, slamming the door behind her.

I drove around aimlessly all afternoon, then found myself at Gertie Walsh's in the arms of the blonde girl who stroked and soothed me, cradled and excited me. She sighed with delight as I pounded into her. I forgot for a moment that I paid her to sigh with delight. I was losing sight of who or where I was. My eyes were shut tightly. A memory from childhood came up out of nowhere. I was standing on a beach staring at a giant turtle that had washed up on shore. I made no move to help it as it flailed around on its back, trying to flip itself over to return to the water. My eyes opened. The girl writhed underneath me. Her face became Diana's dancing in the candlelight.

"Don't think about anyone but me," the blonde girl was whispering. "No one but me."

Each soft breath carried a moan. Faster and faster. Losing myself in anger, until my sperm spit into her like an injection of acid.

In the end she kissed me gently. We lay together exhausted, and there was nothing but the comforting warmth of her. I allowed myself the pleasure of clinging to only that.

Gertie let me stay around for a week or more. In the early mornings I worked in her gardens, which were in full bloom. The blonde girl knew the names of all the flowers: pink frangipani, flame rose oleander, pink and white periwinkles—all overshadowed by giant African tulip trees with pale leaves and bursts of orange blossoms; and bare jacarandas and drumstick trees that stood like skeletons waiting for spring.

In those late, fragrant afternoons, I lolled around in a hammock on the side lawn with my beautiful girl. I would have been content to stay there for the rest of my days, but I began thinking about the family, the tension of their lives providing me with a counterpoint to the unreal idyll I shared with the girl in the garden. What miracle of perversity had produced the Willigs? Bea always poised for combat, Jon and Diana on the edge of self-destruction, and Sam forever chasing his dreams.

14

When I finally got back to the house, Sam and Bea were in the middle of a row.

"Where the hell you been?" Sam said to me, looking as nervous as I'd ever seen him.

"I wanted to get away for a while."

"You should have left word or something, George," Bea said. "I've got one son running off to the ends of the earth. I don't want my house guest disappearing on me."

"I'm sorry. It was just a spur-of-the-moment trip. Is Diana feeling any better?"

Bea shrugged in disgust.

"We got a lot of trouble. I been looking all over for you," Sam said insistently.

"Don't you include George in this. It's your trouble."

"What happened?"

"Not enough money came in on the binders and down payments at Shalimar. The construction boys need more money. We got to keep them happy, or the whole thing goes under."

"Don't you listen to a word of it, George. It's his own fault. Went off and bought that mansion because of that wife of his. What did you do with all the money you had?"

"The money keeps gettin' eaten up faster than it comes in. Everything's workin' against me now. The ports are all jammed up. The rail lines may go on strike—that means no building supplies. I'm spendin' a fortune bribin' people to get materials to us. I don't know what to do."

"I told you he'd come around here when he needed some cash. Didn't I tell you that, George?"

"Please, mama, it's bad enough as it is."

"I can let you have ten thousand if you want it," I said.

"Don't be a fool, George. Hold onto your money. Keep it right in the bank. Listen, Sam, if you want some spare change, I'll give you some money to go down to Key West and bring back that brother of yours."

Sam shrugged disgustedly. Bea left us alone.

"This is real bad. Ten thousand is chicken feed compared to what I need."

"What about the others?"

"They're spreadin' themselves too thin. I thought we could rake in barrels of it, month after month, but money seems to be drying up. I'm in hock up to my teeth. And that damn house is eatin' up more and more. I knew I shouldn't have listened to Tildy. She told me to come over here with Albert.

She said Bea wouldn't turn me down if I brought him. But I couldn't do it, George."

"Just try to calm down, and we'll think this out."

"I'm not any good at that," was all he said. He threw up his hands and left the house.

The next day, rumors started spreading like wildfire through town that Shalimar was in serious money trouble. Most people didn't believe it simply because they could not afford to. After all, Shalimar was the most successful new development of a record tourist season. If it went under, where would everybody be? And anyhow, they said, receipts from land sales were still being totaled up from 1925, and rumor had it that the figure they'd reach would be over two billion dollars. It didn't seem to matter that eighty percent of that was paper and would remain paper. Sure, people asked themselves where all the money was, but no one stayed around too long to hear the answers. There simply wasn't enough time to do that. Too many diversions. Hotels were filling up. The Roney Plaza opened and was sold out, as were the Deauville, Floridian, and King Cole. Florenz Ziegfeld mounted a huge extravaganza at the Royal Palm, and if your tastes ran to something a bit snootier, Paderewski held court at the White Temple Auditorium.

The truth of the situation as Sam Willig knew it was a little less lightheaded and getting worse. The rail lines were a mess, with cars stalled on the tracks from Miami to Jacksonville. Finally, things got so bad a rail embargo was put into effect. Steamship lines followed suit, calling an embargo that cut off all water shipping. A search was on for any old schooner in mothballs to be pressed into service and loaded up with lumber.

In a month's time, thirty-two schooners put in at the Bayfront Park and as many as fifty more were waiting out in the channel. Aboard were forty-five million board feet of lumber from the woods of Georgia and the Northwest—all for the land boom in Miami. It was the greatest armada to pass the Florida coast since the Spanish sailed by two-hundred years earlier. But no one was working on this armada. Strikes started. First telegraphers, then railmen and dockworkers, all wanting a piece of the action: New York wages—sixty cents an hour. Shortages of milk and ice, poultry and meat cropped up.

No shortages of booze, however, and that kept a veneer of dim-witted joy spread over everyone. But on the night of January 10, 1926, a 240-foot barkentine named the *Prinz Valdemar* became the straw that broke the camel's back.

It had been bought from the Danish Navy by some savvy young promoter who wanted to turn it into a floating hotel. All well enough and good, but the young goon never did figure out how to get the damned thing in the channel. It stayed out in the ocean for a couple of days until some brave tugboat captain suggested floating it in at high tide. He volunteered his service, hitched it up to his tug and several others, and then proceeded to get roaring drunk while towing it in. When he cleared Government Cut, a rousing cheer went up on shore, but a wind blew up out of nowhere. The basin began churning like a boiling caldron, and then the wind caught the *Valdemar*'s giant masts, capsizing her and successfully blocking the channel for twenty days.

That was the first disaster. Another followed in its wake a week or two later: the *Lakevorte* ran aground in the middle of Government Cut and completed the mess by isolating everything, preventing all pleasure boats, steamships, and schooners from trafficking across the bay between the beaches and the mainland.

Those who weren't drunk were tearing out their hair. Needless to say, Sam was more sober than most. His debts were mounting, his cash dwindling. But Bea started to soften, which got another rather sober individual plotting and planning faster than ever. Jack Chason sprang into action with a grounded ship of his own, cutting Sam off from ever getting a hand on any of Bea's money.

It happened one balmy, moonless night in early February. I was sipping lemonade on the front porch when Jack pulled up to the house.

"Evening, George," he said nervously. "You still living here? I thought you were getting a place of your own."

"I've been thinking about it."

His eyes darted into the house. "Bea here?"

"She's around somewhere."

"I was wondering if you'd do me a favor."

"What's that?"

"Well, I've got to talk to Bea about some real important family business, and I was wondering if you'd make yourself scarce for a while."

I was about to get up and leave when Bea came walking around the house from the garden.

"Nonsense, Jack. Something wrong with Diana?"

"No, nothing like that," he said, rocking back and forth like a toy soldier. "Something else, Bea. I don't know if you want everybody hearing about it."

"I think you're being rude. George is a guest of mine. It's nothing to do with Jonny, is it?"

"Yes—it has something to do with him."

Her eyes narrowed. "What's wrong?"

"Come inside, Bea. I think we should talk this over alone."

They walked into the living room, and I decided to sit still and listen. I turned in my chair and watched Jack pacing up and down in front of her.

"What is it?"

"Bea, there's been some trouble."

"What trouble? Is he hurt?"

"No, he's all right but, oh, I don't know how to break this to you."

"Break what to me?"

"He's been arrested."

"What?"

"They got him yesterday. I just found out about it."

"That's not true."

"It is. I saw him before I came over here."

"Why's he been arrested? What's he done?"

"It was out of my hands. I didn't know he was doing it."

"What are you talking about?"

"He was running booze in. The Feds nabbed him, and that's all there is to it."

"What do you mean you didn't know? Running booze, my God!" He'd cranked up Bea's hysteria quotient a decibel or two.

"Now calm down. Everything's under control. There isn't a soul who knows about this but you and me, and as far as the cops go, I can take care of that."

"How? We need a lawyer."

"You don't need a lawyer down here. Just an ample spread of cash will do. Believe me, Bea, I know these people. That's how they make their living."

"I can't believe he's done something like this. I let him run loose, and now he does this to me!"

"He hasn't done anything so awful."

"Who got him into this? Did you?"

"No, I swear to you, I knew nothing about it."
"Who was he working for?"
"Reno Devane."
"That scum you hang around with? Don't tell me you had nothing to do with this."
"He's been doing it for a long time. I just found out about it, and as far as that Devane character is concerned, he's done me dirty, too."
"You?"
Jack turned his back to her, hunching his shoulders, letting loose with a sob or two.
"What's going on?" Bea demanded. "What's he done?"
"It's Diana."
"She's involved with this, too?"
"She's having an affair with him. I've tried reasoning with her, but she goes on with it. That Devane has gotten them both, and the only reason I've come to you is because I can't handle it alone any more."
He sank into a chair, covering his face, but I swear that big ape must have been grinning all the while.
"Stop it," Bea sighed. "Calm down. Don't cry. Men don't cry!" He timed his crying perfectly. Now he needed her to comfort him; what else does a mother do? "Isn't this something," she kept mumbling. "Isn't this a fine thing."
"I swear I want to beat Devane to a pulp."
"Calm down. Just stay calm. We have to think this out. What are we going to do?"
He took control now. "I can get Jonny out of this jam in a couple of hours. All I need is a couple of thousand dollars, and he'll be out. I've already talked with the police captain down there."
"Why has the likes of Reno Devane gotten hold of my family?"
"He's rich and powerful. He sits out there on his big boat and rakes in money. He suckers everyone into his little schemes. Diana's probably out there with him now. Right now, as I'm talking with you, that man is wining and dining her and doing God knows what else."
"Enough!" Bea ran her hands through her hair. "How much do you need to get Jonny out?"
"Two thousand will do it. But that won't be the end of it."
"Why?"

"We've got to do something about this Devane. He's got them hypnotized with all of his fast talk and easy money."

"No, let's not get involved with that now."

"We've got to. Listen, Bea, I'm going to be very honest with you. I'm probably the only man in this town who can get Jonny out of jail tonight, but I need your help with this other matter."

"What other matter? What are you pulling on me, Jack?"

"I want Devane out of the picture. Not just for my sake, but for Diana's and Jon's, and you've got to help me do that."

"How can I help you?"

"I need some money. Just to borrow some for a little while to get Devane out of the picture for good."

"Are you trying to blackmail me?"

He walked over to the windows, looking for me on the porch. I tiptoed off it and stood in the garden.

"This part of it is business, Bea. A business deal, pure and simple."

"You come in here running off at the mouth about my son in jail and my daughter doing whatever, and you want to talk business."

"It's all tied up together."

"What is it that you want?"

"I want you to just calm down."

"Don't patronize me. If you want to talk, talk!"

"I can set the family up for good, Bea. None of you will ever have to worry about a thing for the rest of your lives if you help me now. You stand to lose Jon and Diana if Devane's allowed to continue on the way he's been going."

"So I lose them. What's this have to do with me?"

"You talk tough, Bea, but I know you better. Let me talk tough with you. I want to take over Devane's operation."

"Get further into this bootlegging business?"

"Hear me out. I want that operation, and to get it I need some money from you. In exchange, I will get your son out of jail and your daughter back home under my roof. I'll also make you a very rich woman."

"I've got enough money."

"Where? In the bank? With Sam's land deal? Bea, I don't think you see what's coming. This land business is too crazy. The banks, the dealers are all tied up with each other, and they're going to go down the drain. The only operation in town that keeps getting bigger is Devane's. He's got the town in his hands. When the land boom winds down, prices will fall; then we can take the booze money and buy land dirt-cheap. We'll get out of bootlegging altogether and build hotels."

"You're crazy if you think I want to be associated with anything like that."

"You won't have to be. No one will ever know about your part in it. It will just be a deal between you and me. I can do it, Bea. Trust me. Devane will be out of our hair forever."

"This is some dirty business you're offering me."

"Do you think booze will be illegal forever?"

"I don't know. Where's George? I don't want him hearing this."

"He's taking a walk. Listen to me, Bea. This makes sense, and it's anything but dirty. Some of my best customers are the richest men in this country. I can swing this. But I need your help."

Bea was lost in thought. Jack knew better than to pressure her any further. He was tempting her with what she liked best: he was coming to her for help; it almost didn't matter for what.

"How much do you need?" she finally asked.

"One hundred thousand."

"You must be crazy."

"No, I'm just a good businessman. I never would have done this if Devane hadn't pushed us all into it."

She sank into her chair. "I need time to think this over."

"There isn't much time. Jonny is sitting in jail."

"Oh, there's time for that. You let him sit there another day or two until he learns his lesson."

"Then you'll do it."

She stared at him, a sly smile starting to light up her face. "You and I will draw up a contract tomorrow, Jack Chason. Everything will be in writing. I want a good return on my money for this—a nice piece of your pie."

"I knew you'd see a good business deal when it was laid out for you."

"You're very smart, aren't you." He blushed like a schoolboy. "The others are nothing compared with you. Jonny's just young. Diana's a fool—but you're the smart one, huh? Meet me at the bank tomorrow at eleven. Now get out of my house!"

Jonny was released from jail two nights later. All evidence connecting him with the booze-running episode was destroyed.

When she saw him that night, Bea was as cold as ice. "You dare do this to me," she said.

"I didn't do anything to you, mother. It happened to me, remember? *I* had to stay in that jail."

"And who do you think got you out of that jail? First thing in the morning, you report to Sam. You have him give you a construction job until the fall. Then I'm packing you off to school."

"You're very good at that, aren't you. Packed my father off, too."

Her hand sliced across his face. "Don't you ever say anything like that to me again. Next time I'll leave you in jail."

She stormed out of the living room. Jonny stood there defeated, turning to me for consolation.

"Devane says I was set up. He told me he thought Jack did it, but I didn't believe him. Jack wouldn't do that to me, would he?"

"I don't know." What right did I have to tell him how he'd been used.

"I know it's not true. Besides that, what would Jack have to gain from it?"

"Nothing, I guess."

"People just don't do that to each other."

So much for youth and innocence.

By the time March rolled around, people were doing worse than that to each other. Ripples of fear were turning the land boom into a bust. Suddenly people were packing up and leaving; construction all but stopped. Then the New York Stock Market quivered, dropping thirty points in two weeks. All that eastern money that had poured South started drying up, leaving people like Sam Willig more frantic than ever.

He'd borrowed money from everyone. Everyone had borrowed from someone else, and all the loans were being called in. I finally gave him the ten grand and then five more. He got up a second, then a third, mortgage on Tildy's dream house, which enabled him to limp on a while longer. Meeker, the creep, was the first of the partners to jump ship. Henry Mason's wife and son got a court order stating that good old

Henry was not capable of handling his own finances. (Henry was putting away about a case a week by that time.) They clamped down on him, getting him out of Shalimar as fast as they could. Stanley Jawitz declared bankruptcy and then disappeared in April. Some said he went down to Key West; others swore he'd taken off for the jungles of Cuba. Wherever, he was gone, leaving Sam with all of it. I've got to give Sam a lot of credit because he stayed with it, overseeing plans and construction.

He stayed on Bea's back, asking her to bail him out, but she wasn't able to do that. She'd signed over half of what she had to Jack, and she was not about to gamble with the rest of it.

I waited for Jack to make another move, but it seemed as if he were taking his sweet time. Booze flowing into town still sported Devane's mark) a twenty-five-cent piece pressed into wax on the cap of every bottle of Scotch, bourbon, or rye.

I was taking liberal slugs from one of them one spring morning as Jonny and I drove out to the beach.

"You know that load of hooch we sank the night we almost got caught," he was saying.

"What about it?"

"It's still there. We can make a pretty penny on it if we go out there one night and resurrect it."

"Nice talk for Easter."

"I'm serious, George. What's gotten into you? I've never seen you so down in the mouth."

"Unrequited love," I mumbled.

"Don't talk nonsense. All we have to do is get that boat up."

There was no stopping the kid; he'd get himself arrested again if it was the last thing he did.

There was an unusual amount of traffic on the beach road that day; packs of cars were parked on the shoulder as people watched a regatta of needle-nosed speedboats in the bay.

"What day is it?" Jon asked.

"Sunday."

"Stop the car!"

"What for?"

"I forgot all about it. Devane's in this race. That's what everyone's turning out for."

I parked under the shade of some palm trees; then we walked along the bayfront pilings, spotting Jack and Diana up ahead. Jack, as always, was pacing nervously as if he were a man with three bugs caught in his trousers. Diana sat staring down into the water, looking childlike and decidedly eccentric in a sort of gypsy outfit: a wide-brimmed straw hat with lavender feathers, a tiered gauzy skirt, and scarves on her shoulders, fluttering in the breeze like wings. My reaction to her was instantaneous and not altogether pleasant. What on earth would we say to each other? When Jack walked away from her, she caught my eye and came running over to kiss me as if nothing had ever passed between us.

"The dreamy boy—isn't this all too exciting," she said. There was a cast in her eyes that made me wonder if she knew who it was she was kissing. "Jonny, your friend Devane should put on quite a show. How have you been, George?"

I decided then and there that she was as mad as a hatter. "I'm all right. You feeling better?" I asked, keeping my distance.

"Infinitely better. Now why on earth was I cooping myself up in that house when all I really needed was a little fresh air and sunshine?"

"That son of a bitch," Jonny suddenly yelled. "That son of a bitch is crazy. That's him. I know it is!" He was pointing to a cream white boat off in the distance, overtaking the others. "That's Devane's boat—got a special hull outfitted to carry about fifty cases, but look at that son of a bitch go."

The boat flew across the water in pounding spurts, turning on its side, then straightening out, heading for a pack of about twenty others in front of it. There was no mistaking the driver, his red hair flying in the wind, his wide, toothy grin flashing to the crowd.

"He's making a run in broad daylight," Jon panted. "I can't believe he'd risk it."

The crowd knew exactly what he was doing, and they cheered him on all the more for it. After all, it was their booze he was risking his neck for.

"Is it Devane?" Jack asked, running up to us. "I knew he'd be fool enough."

"He's out of his mind!"

"Can't resist a good show," someone in the crowd shouted as all of us surged toward the water, running along the pilings.

The boat bobbed skillfully in and out of the pack. Firecrackers were set off; puffs of smoke appeared in the sky above him. Someone behind me screamed, but I didn't look back until a man called out, "Hit the ground! They're firing at him!"

Two police boats were barreling into the channel in pursuit of him.

"Let him go!" the crowd chanted. "Let him go!"

Spurts of gunfire erupted again from the bows of the police boats, hitting the water like sheets of rain on either side of his boat. Other drivers cut their engines or jumped for safety when Devane pulled his gun out and began firing back. More volleys sailed over his head. He ducked and fired again, but it was useless. You just had to feel sorry for him running out there alone, with no goons to protect him and these gargantuan police boats closing in on him for the kill. Suddenly he swung his boat around and headed straight for them. Two cops, Tommy guns knotted into their guts, crouched on the bows of their boats, showering waves of bullets over him, cutting his body to ribbons on the final pass. It was over before most people knew what had happened.

They laid his body out on the lawn of Carl Fischer's Flamingo Hotel. A Jesuit priest gave the last rites.

Jonny was shaken by what he'd seen. He and Jack and I stood apart from the crowd.

"Damn fool cops," was all Jonny said.

I couldn't take my eyes off Jack Chason because I knew he'd set Devane up and this was his shining moment, but the poor fool didn't know how to react.

Diana came walking out of the crowd. There was no mistaking the hatred in her eyes. Her right index finger had a spot of blood on it.

"You paid for this, you might as well wear it," she said, wiping some of the blood on Jack's lapel.

He grabbed her wrists roughly, looking as if he'd strangle her, but he merely led her away.

"What did she mean? What's Jack done?"

I don't know, maybe I was angry or disgusted with my own tacit complicity in all of it. I just couldn't let Jonny off unscathed.

"Your brother-in-law set you up, Jonny. Set Devane up, too. Got your mother to finance his takeover of the booze running operation; got Devane killed. He's in control now. Don't look so goddamned dumbstruck. You like playing with danger, don't you? Join the family. Jack was just biding his time, playing the long shot."

I tried convincing myself that this was what he needed, but I couldn't stop feeling ugly and old and jaded for having been the one to do it. He stared incredulously at Jack, looking frightened for the first time since I'd met him.

15

Slow, languid summer days followed. With tourists gone, the beaches were deserted. Senses dulled in the rippling heat, spreading a plague of indolence over everything. Trapped inside was the smell of sulfur, decaying fish on shore, brine and jasmine, mint and sweet odors from a hundred different blossoms.

In the Northeast and Midwest, it is usually autumn that brings such melancholy reflections, but it's not like that in the South. Summer broils, enfolds you in a dream of cooler days, of their industry and activity. If you're lucky, you find yourself a shaded spot under a pink shower tree or a crevice of damp earth in a grove of umbrella trees where, with loosened shirt and tie, you can fan yourself with a leaf and do nothing but sleep or remember.

What I remembered were feelings of having let down everyone around me. I know I kept letting the Willigs slip by me without exerting much effort to help them or be helped by them. When umbrella groves did not soothe me, I went off to forget with sloe-eyed girls from Gertie's stable. Thinking myself a libertine or a renegade, I spent my money and my time, but I was not finding that much consolation at Gertie's that summer. Even Sam's rosy dreams were no consolation, although I longed to get lost in them. The heat made his labors seem laughable, but to his credit, that didn't stop him. He stayed out at the beach even though construction was now limited to menial trim work. Money was drying up, but he wouldn't let go.

I happened to be out there one day toward the end of August while he was taking some town officials on a tour of Shalimar. Struts and grillwork lay baking in the noon sun. His mosques and plazas were frames and gashes in the sand at that time. He looked as if he knew they were going to stay that way for a while. When he saw me, his eyes lit up as if I were his only ally left on earth.

"Get them out of here for me, George," he said watching a group of officious-looking men pick their way through his site with their canes.

"What do they want?"

"Come here telling me what I should do. It's mine, George."

One of them, a Commander Moss, I believe, had an imperiously drawn face that alternately registered disdain and indifference.

"This won't do, Mr. Willig," he said.

"Won't do what, commander?"

"A group of us from town are forming a committee to look into the kind of construction work you people are putting up out here. Many of us were here before any of you knew this place existed. We know what storms can do."

"What's he talking about, Sam?" I asked.

"They think one of those hurricanes can come in here and destroy the town. These buildings will hold, and, anyway, there's never been a bad storm in these parts."

"That's just not true, Mr. Willig. We had a little taste of one in July, and none of you remember the one that hit back in 1906. If one like that came again, we'd all be wiped out. The town government has to protect its citizens."

"I know what your story is, Moss. All you care is that some little Jew named Willig managed to buy a stretch of land on your precious north beach. You don't care a damn about saving lives or writing building codes. It's the Jews you want to get rid of." Sam stormed off into the stucco house he'd been using as an office. The old commander stared after him.

"How did you get involved with *that* lot?" he asked me.

"What do you mean?"

"That Jewish cabal. You're a fine young man from a good family in Ohio, I hear. There are other opportunities for you in Miami."

"My 'good family' taught me all about people like them and people like you. You are a credit to no one's race, commander, and if I didn't think my good father would disapprove, I'd like nothing more than to wipe up the floor with you and your merry band. I suggest you get yourselves out of here."

"I'm sorry to hear you say that."

"I'll bet you are. So let me tell you another thing. I'd sooner stand with people like Sam Willig than you any day. At least he believes in something. You don't believe in anything except taking a leak on the guy two rungs below you."

Sam reemerged after they left, and both of us walked over the site. We didn't talk much until we climbed up on a low dune and surveyed the foundations.

"They won't take this away from me. I've staked my claim here with you, George. I've never had anything like it before."

"Maybe you should let go. You've got the deck stacked against you. Wait until next winter for the tourists to come back."

"All the money's gone."

"I've got about ten grand left if you need it."

"No, hang onto it. You'll need it. You've been a good friend to me, George. Just the fact that you're still here with me is enough. Anyway, I'm sure that when it comes down to it, my mother will help me out."

"Don't depend on that, Sam. I hate to see you get hurt."

"You sound like you know something."

"Just past history."

"I know something is going on. Something to do with Jack and all the money he's starting to pull in with Devane's operation. He got to my mother before me, didn't he?"

Sam didn't need to hear it from me. "I don't know about that. I just think you should let go."

"She'll help me. I'm her son. Jack doesn't have that over me."

Fate has a way of making mincemeat of dreams no matter how well-intentioned they may be; Sam's were washed away with a rain that started early in the day on September 17, 1926.

I'd set myself up in the back room of the land office in town, trying to figure out the mess Sam had made of the Shalimar books when the phone rang. It was Bea.

"George, you've got to get out to the beach and get Sam. Jonny just came back from there, and he says there's a storm brewing. The paper is going to post a hurricane watch, and that madman will stay out there. I know him."

"I'll see what I can do."

I went back to work, then lost all sense of time. When I looked up again, it was dark outside and the rain had picked up somewhat. Staring out at Flagler, I could make out the shapes of two people huddled in doorways, swapping drinks from a flask and laughing. I poured myself a stiff drink, then straightened up my worktable and headed out the back door.

While I was trying to start the car, a wind blew up. It was like nothing I'd ever heard before. Rumbling like a freight train, it barreled overhead, shaking windows and walls, stripping the leaves off trees. I held my breath as my car shook violently, but the motor turned over, and I pulled away from the curb, only to be blown onto the sidewalk. Then a torrent of water surged up from the bay on the heels of another gust. People in the darkened passages screamed as windows gave way and electric lines crackled, sputtering blue white light into the street.

"Over here," I yelled to the young couple seeking shelter, but they couldn't hear me above the rumbling. They lost their footing, and the woman fell into the stream rushing up Flagler. Her husband ran after her and then fell himself. As another galė wind screamed by, the woman was blown into a plate glass window. Her body was lost in a jumble of mannequins': arms, legs, and heads swirling away into the street. I ran to help but lost sight of them.

The land office door nearly blew out of my hand when I went to open it. Signs crashed down around me as awnings over the sidewalk gave way, their canvas ends slicing the wind like the snap of a hundred bullwhips. Inside, the room was filling up with water, carrying a Bukhara rug around as if it were a magic carpet that couldn't quite get off the ground. Hopping onto one of the desks, I closed my eyes and prayed. Another crackle. Bolts of energy penetrated the air, illuminating everything with a surreal blue light. The wind pounded my eardrums. Glass exploded everywhere. I thought I heard a voice calling to me, but there was no one in the office and no one in the street, only the gale wind driving a drenching rain, buffeting the office with a force that shook the doors for hours.

It kept up like that all night until the first gray light of morning laid bare the damage that had already taken place.

Wind had peeled plaster from the walls. Steel girders on the hotel they'd been building on the Willig store site were twisted into pretzel shapes. All the wheeling and dealing—lost in a couple of hours with a wind that came from nowhere to devour everything.

At dawn the wind subsided. Patches of blue appeared behind the gray stretch of sky. I made my way up Flagler, walking like a war casualty. All around me lay fenders and signs, bricks and dead tree limbs.

"Get back inside," a man called to me. "It's just the calm. We're getting more of it. Get off the street!"

Only later did I find out that these storms were circular things with dead centers, and what I'd passed through that night was only the head of it—another even more powerful blast was about to be delivered.

I paid no attention to the man. Instead, I found my car sheltered in a doorway. By some miracle, it started. Floods in the street created huge pools, and only five feet of dry pavement were passable. I made my way to the bay front, where the damage had been more devastating; boats had been thrown up on shore from their moorings as if they'd been toys tossed from a bath by a naughty child. All the royal palms lay twisted on the roads, palm fronds trailing behind the trunks like manes of hair covering sleeping bodies on the beach.

After I crossed the causeway, the storm returned, stopping all traffic on the roads and water. It now blew in frenzied repetitions like the blasts of a cannon firing over the ocean. Translucent sheets of water slanted across the waves, tossing the small craft along the shore and causing their moorings to pitch heavily. All were smothered in the mist. The gale blew the top of my car off, then it blew the rain away. But when the wind subsided, the rain was unleashed, pounding harder than before. I prayed it would stop, but there was no letup. What was I doing out in it? I forgot about my mission to retrieve Sam. Forgot about everything and everyone but the fierceness of the wind, the enraged determination with which it battered me.

I abandoned my car and tried making it on foot to Shalimar, feeling totally lost and alone amid the sky and sand and wind gone mad, whirling around me, pulling me with its will. I couldn't fight it any more. I gave myself up to it, allowed it to cut me down to size, and then I began to cry, but even then I felt that my tears were not my own—it was the rain and nothing more. I tried holding myself together, but I was whipping myself as the wind whipped me. How I had used this place and the Willigs, felt so little for them except for the trickling of events that crossed my mind now like splay-legged girls wide open without comment, without love. I was lost again, bound up only with the green limbs of trees, detached flying through the air the way the Negro's head had severed that night in the swamps. I cried for all of it. Cried because I had allowed myself to be cut off from everything: from Bea and her insane sisters; from Jon; and from Diana's perverse love. I felt nothing but the words to describe how they looked when they talked or made love. I could not tell you what mysteries of feeling there were inside them. I asked the storm to take me away. I am tired of mysteries, I told myself. I want new mysteries, mysteries of feeling. I wanted to escape from my body, to seek out some inner world of love and caring. Force me out of me. To be a human being blown free of time and place, not frozen in torrents of wind and water. Not walking though this raging convulsion of earth, sea, and sky where I was merely a body in a body, holding onto a body.

I struggled in the wind for what seemed like hours, hearing voices off in the distance, seeing corpses scattered in the sand. One man who'd climbed a tree to what he must have thought was safety, now lay dead, cradled in its bare branches; both body and tree were so disfigured that their twisted shapes seemed joined in some outlandish sacrifice to vengeful gods.

Ahead lay the road to Shalimar, and finally I remembered my mission. Now I wanted nothing more than to see Sam again, to embrace him, shake him alive with my friendship and love of him.

The wind cut back as I climbed up the low dunes and stood staring at the dream town, the beach, and ocean. Very little was left of Shalimar, and what was left looked like a sunken galleon that had been dredged up from the sea after a long sleep. Gone were the pink and white hotel, the liver red tiles, and the plantings. Sam couldn't have survived this.

The ocean had receded, extending the beach fifty feet or more. All the secrets of the bottom sand now lay covering his hopes and dreams. Everywhere I looked I saw more of them twisted out of all recognition: a piano, floating in the oasis pool; little blackamoor statues looking now like charred babies buried in the sand; beds and couches with fan backs ripped apart and scattered—everything gone for all time.

I cried again, this time feeling my own tears streak across my cheeks as I picked my way through the rubble, searching for him. Out of the corner of my eye, I spotted a figure dressed in white, walking by the shore off in the distance. I fought against despair to believe that it could be Sam, but whoever it was was walking with an incredible pace and shoulders swaying just like his. I ran down to the water, flailing my arms, screaming. It was him. He was alive, and we were running toward each other until I could see his eyes, saddened but alive, his skin ashen but alive. He ran with a pace that matched mine as we swung into each other's arms, dancing like children, jumping up and down, mimicking the waves, faster than them, clutching on to each other with affection that came from our friendship and the fact that we both had survived.

"Alive, alive, alive!" The sound tore from my throat. "We're alive!"

Crying now, we sank to the sand, still huddled in each other's arms, roughly feeling for each other's muscles and bones just to confirm what we saw with our eyes.

"I tried to get out here all night," I panted.

Beaming, he took my head in his hands and cradled me against his chest. "Damn fool, George. Damn fool." Tears streaming down his cheeks, he pushed me away playfully. "Jonny make it home all right?"

I nodded.

"Thank God for that. The family okay?"

"I don't know. I've been out on the road all right."

"I'm sure they are. Mama's got an instinct for survival, don't she? That damned Jew-baiter Moss was right. Shalimar floated out to sea on the first wave. I barricaded myself behind the dunes all night, praying to God I wouldn't die, but as I watched it all going before my eyes, I stopped caring and wanted it to take me out, too. All gone in an hour. Everything's over for me."

"You'll get it back."

"No. I had my shot. People like me only get one."

We sat there in silence for the longest time. He wept, and there was no comforting him. And no reason to sit out there any more to remind him of what he'd lost.

As the sun broke through, a rainbow arced across the sky, beaming through the scattered gray clouds that were making their way out to sea. Sam and I walked into town, holding onto each other as if we were two dazed schoolboys returning home from a shattering adventure.

16

Somehow, the destruction we passed on our way back to town did not seem real. We had to wait until the next day when the *Miami Herald* published statistics to fully understand what we had passed through. First estimates said that seventy-five were dead and hundreds injured. At the height of the storm, winds had reached a velocity of 128 miles per hour. The Miami River had risen eleven feet above the mean tide mark. As the days went on, the figures got worse. New estimates: three hundred dead, twenty-eight thousand injured, over one hundred million dollars in damages. A state of emergency was declared, then, unbelievably, rescinded.

The mayor and town officials, all of whom had made big money in the boom, could not see their way clear to admitting the extent of the damage. This was paradise! It had an image to maintain.

"The plight of the destitute and homeless cannot be exaggerated," the mayor said, but he was quick to add that "Miami's famous tourist facilities have come through with little damage."

People now living in the streets wanted to string him up, and although his cheery statements hindered fund-raising for a few days, Red Cross dollars and food finally began pouring into Miami.

Bea, Jon, Jack, and Diana came through the storm with little or no damage to their houses. It was Sam who suffered the worst of it. His house on the bay was all but demolished. That bastion of Tildy's garish empire with its seascape rooms of green and gold was dragged out to rest on the ocean floor. Fate wound around Sam like a vice, showing him how dependent he was once again on his mother. In the end, it was that dependence that became too painful for him to bear.

We had all been invited to Diana's for dinner one night. I'm sure Jack prompted that because he so enjoyed his new status as family provider and host. He served booze and food as if there were no shortages at all in the streets of Miami. Jonny was there in body but not in spirit. He stayed in a corner all evening, studying us as if we were a man who was about to make a decision. Of course, the main topic of conversation was the storm and the destruction it had caused.

"I don't want to hear any more of it," Bea was saying.

"Just like you, mama," Sam replied. "She thinks if she doesn't hear it, it will go away."

"Is that so? I've been down at the hospital all morning helping out. I just don't want to discuss it during dinner."

"There are certain things we have to deal with."

"Like what?"

"Me. Me and Tildy and Albert. Everything is gone."

"You can get settled into my house for a while, then we'll make plans for you."

"We can't stay there," Tildy chimed in. "We need some help to rebuild our house."

"I can't move back into your house, mama. I need a loan to get me back on my feet."

"Will you listen to this madman! He's saved from death by some miracle, and now all he wants to talk about is money. I don't understand my children. I swear I don't."

Jack stood now, taking a commanding position in the middle of the room. "Listen, Sam, you can't rebuild that house."

"It's not just the house. It's Shalimar. We've got a good couple of months before another tourist season. I can scrape that place together by then."

"It's not feasible," Jack added.

Sam's anger was growing now as he stood to confront Jack. "I'm not talking with you, anyway. This is between my mother and me."

"What do you want from me?" Bea wailed. "I offer you my house. What more do you want? I spoiled you children, and now you think you can go on the rest of your lives getting anything you want from me."

"Don't aggravate yourself, Bea," Jack said. "I'll handle this."

Sam was dazed by the fact that his mother was allowing Jack some measure of control.

"What will you handle?" Sam asked.

"Stop this yelling. Both of you. I will not have any more aggravation."

"It's all right, Bea. I'll handle it. You go inside and help Diana."

"Mama, please," Sam pleaded. "I need your help now. You can't leave it to Jack."

"Sit down, Sam," Jack was saying. "If you don't want to live at your mother's, then Diana and I will put you up for a while."

"It's not a matter of that. I need the money to rebuild what I've lost."

"Rebuild what?" Jack snapped. "A town that's growing barnacles at the bottom of the sea? We can't throw away money on that."

"Who's the 'we' he's talkin' about, mama?"

"You listen to him, Sam," she said, her words ringing like a death knell.

His eyes flashed around the room, seeking support from Tildy, and when she looked away from him, he turned to Jonny and then me, but I remained silent.

"You're all glad to have me done in like this, aren't you? I made all that money for you, and now you desert me."

"That's not true," Jack condescended. "It's just that we can't throw away money on harebrained schemes."

Sam pointed his finger at his mother and raged on. "You've destroyed me on purpose. You couldn't stand it that it was me and not you who made a big success down here. You waited for me to land belly up on the bench to show your hand."

They were mute, locked in their own private selves, surrounded by fear and resentment. Why is it that no one moved when all that they wanted was a small sign of affection? They sat there denying themselves the pleasure. Finally I could stand no more of it.

"She loved what you did out there. She told me. Tell him, Bea. He needs to hear it from you."

She said nothing.

"You should have heard her, Sam. That day the crowd of people came out to Shalimar—she had tears in her eyes. I wish I could remember her exact words. Help me, Bea—something about how you finally owned a piece of this country. How you'd build this dream for yourself. She's proud of you for that."

Bea's nervous eyes signaled me to stop.

"It's the money she cares about," Sam sobbed. "Don't let her fool you."

"That's right, bit shot, go on talking. You'll talk your way out of my house in a minute. It's only money is it? Why is it that when you need it, you think of me."

"Calm down, Bea," Jack said.

"Stop talking to her that way," Sam screamed.

"Hold on, boy, you're a guest in my home."

"This is all your doing, isn't it?"

"Sam, don't," Tildy said.

"Don't you understand that I'd rather starve than be a guest in anyone's house?"

"Now you're talking," Jonny said; his first words of the evening.

Sam raced for the front door, railing at Jack as he crossed the living room. "You brought this on me, and you'll pay for it. I swear you will. I don't care how long it takes. You will pay." He slammed the door behind him.

Tildy stood in the hall, her hands fidgeting at her sides. "He'll be back as soon as he blows off some steam."

"Don't bet on it," Jon said.

"Sure he will," Jack said, consoling Bea who'd been shocked speechless by Sam's one and only blast of anger. "We're just convenient targets. The storm took everything, but he's got us to blame."

"You're wrong about that." Jonny heaved a heavy sigh. "He's finally seeing the way things work. We all see it, Jack. You're calling the shots, aren't you?"

"Don't start in on me, Jonny. We don't need any more of that tonight. You just behave yourself."

"What are your plans for *me?*" Jonny asked.

"You're going up to school in a month, just like your mother wants."

Jon glared at her. "Is that what you want? Letting him take over?"

Again she said nothing.

"You're going to lose all of us," he said, then quietly retreated to his corner of the room.

Later that night as I was tossing and turning in my bed, I heard Jonny rummaging around in his room. I walked downstairs and found him packing.

"Where are you going?"

He spoke as if he'd been in the middle of a conversation with himself. "None of you really knows anything about me. I thought maybe *you* did, but we just met a year ago—how much could you know?"

"We've been through a lot together."

"Not so much. Not in the whole scheme of things. I have got big plans for myself, George. That's one thing I thought I made clear to you. I can't stay here or go to school or go anywhere they want me to go. My mother will never let me have half of what I want for myself."

"What is that, do you know?"

"Right now, it's just the running away I want. I have those same dreams Sam's got chasing around in his head. But I won't get them here. Let the rest of them battle it out. I want to hit the road. You didn't know anything about us, George. We were just Jews in the Midwest, playing life undercover, you know what I mean? Everything is too safe. My mother keeps it that way. Now she's got Jack to front for her. Everybody fronts for her sooner or later."

I followed him into the kitchen.

"You tell my mother I'll be all right. I know how to take care of myself."

"Your leaving will destroy her."

"That's where you're wrong." He took canned goods out of the pantry. "You want to come along with me?"

The temptation was great, but I didn't share that restless need to prove myself. I shook my head no.

"A Bexley boy is what you'll always be. I like you very much, George. We'll run into each other again. We'll laugh about all of this."

He stowed the food into his duffle bag, then swung it up on his shoulder, and walked out onto the front porch. We stood there staring at the night sky; at a sliver of moon cloaked behind spangled clouds flying like sails across vast, black space. His leaving and the cool breeze blowing pierced me through and through with waves of sadness and excitement.

"Wish me luck, George."

"You know I do, although I always felt you were the only one of all of us who didn't need it. You seem blessed with it."

He smiled a sly, boyish grin. "I feel it, too. Great things in store for me." He stared up at the house. "You leave here, too, George. This is no place for you—never was."

"What do you mean?"

"You want something from my family you thought you didn't have inside you. Our drive, was it? You don't need anything from us. I'm afraid we don't have all that much to give."

We hugged each other; then he left, slipping through the shadows, leaving me behind this time.

Next morning I told Bea that he'd gone.

"Please, George, I can't stand any more. I'll call Jack. He'll get him back."

"I don't think so."

"But where did he go? What's he going to live on?"

"I don't think that kid ever had to worry about that."

"What did I do to them?"

"It has nothing to do with you, Bea. Jonny just wants a chance to find something on his own."

"What nonsense. First Sam, now Jonny."

"Just let go of them. They won't die out there."

"You don't understand it, either, George. They want something I can't give them. My hands are tied."

"It isn't a matter of hands with Sam—it's a matter of heart."

Again, I thought about the woman standing at her window watching the water pulse from a garden hose. "Sail away," she'd said to herself. "Leave me alone," was what she really meant. "I cannot do anything for anyone. Don't pressure me. Just leave me alone."

As I packed to leave her house later that week, I thought perhaps she'd feel I was deserting her, too, but I know now that she must have been relieved.

"You, too," she said, standing in the doorway of the upstairs bedroom, looking like a child who was about to get her own room back.

"Me, too." I laughed.

"What will you do?"

"Take my money and run."

"Very funny."

"I'll go to school and settle down. I think that's what I'm best at."

"What will I do with this empty house?"

"Invite your sisters down."

She grimaced.

"Oh, don't look so glum, Bea. It's not the end of the world."

"George, I just saw something in you that frightened me. Cynicism. Don't ever give in to that. You're too fine a person." She embraced me warmly. "You'll come back again. You love the meshugas."

"What's that?"

"Yiddish—the craziness. It's what keeps me going."

"Say goodbye to Diana and Jack for me."

"I will." She sailed out of the room, heading down the stairs, laughing to herself. "Come back for the palm trees and the meshugas—remember!"

The train station was teeming with people. I wondered how many of them had come to town with nothing in their pockets and were now leaving with nothing. I was glad it was over, but there was something unfinished that kept nagging at me.

As I waited with my ticket, the porters loaded bags and people streamed past me looking dazed and unfinished themselves. Diana came walking out of the crowd.

"I knew you'd leave. Couldn't take it any more, could you?" she asked, stroking my cheek with her hand.

"There's not much for me to do here."

"There never was, George. You could have been my lover. If you'd only let me be myself."

"But you don't know what you want."

"I want acceptance."

"I think it would be better if we try to let go of each other."

"But we're just starting out," she smiled. "We'll see each other again. Just don't feel obligated to make things easier for me. Let me alone, and we'll be lovers again. Wouldn't you like that?"

"I don't know."

"Don't beg the question. I'll always come back to haunt you. That's what I wish for. It's easy enough, isn't it?"

I smiled. "Nothing is easy with you."

Whistles blew, and people surged onto the platform as porters started their final calls.

"Will you stay married to him?"

"He and I understand each other, I suppose."

"Okay, Diana, kiss me goodbye."

"Oh, yes, one kiss to remember me by." She laughed, then parted her lips and pressed them onto mine. I felt the warmth of her but knew she was laughing at me when she kissed me.

Even so, I never did get her out of my mind. She haunted me all right.

I sat in the club car. The land, flat as a table top, passed by like pictures on a screen. My life was irrevocably changed. I was up for some milder form of adventure. I wanted something to soothe me. We rode north through Georgia, through Indiana. I was on a route I had already taken, but now it offered me the prospect of more comfortable mysteries.

III

Separate Lives

17

I must escape into the present for a moment to get my bearings. All morning I've been wandering around my little library, denying myself the glories of a perfectly beautiful spring day, sure that the dam will break any minute now, setting loose a torrent of recollections, sending me off on the wild-goose chase of finding out exactly who Jon Willig really was and what motivated him. Tabloids and news magazines that tried doing just that are scattered over my desk, but I never have been wholly satisfied with their attempts.

There was not a month that passed in two decades in which I did not see his face staring out at me from the covers and stories in *Life, Vanity Fair,* and *Time* as he departed or arrived, danced and drank in dozens of countries and cities all over the world. They called him the Master Showman, but what they revealed about him was only a surface reflection: the willing smile, the secretive eyes shining out from the newsstands as if he were looking at you and you alone. "Boyish, dashing, romantic"—those were the words they used to describe him, but few people knew how carefully he orchestrated his public persona. In many ways Jon was taunting all of us: take one step closer, and you'll destroy my illusion and yours.

If you had penetrated that veneer of his as I had, maybe you would have felt as betrayed as I did to find out that he was just like the rest of us, succumbing to life with as much grief and heartbreak. Perhaps I do that image of his a disservice, but it is important to demystify such people, if not for their sakes, then for our own.

Jon and I corresponded regularly from 1926 until the middle thirties. During that period, I enrolled in law school and eventually went into practice with a large downtown New York firm. Settling into a rather mundane career, I found myself waiting for Jon's letters each week to fuel my imagination. I will use those letters now to fill in the pieces of his life that I did not witness firsthand.

By his own account, it was simply the running away from things he was after when he left Miami, but I think there was more to it than that. That night in 1926 Jon Willig went off in search of himself wrapped in something I'll choose to call his destiny.

Fall was settling into the steamy Florida nights. Cool breezes were blowing, and birds were flying in aimless circles, coasting under long, thin clouds that were weaving around the moon like strands of loosely curled hair around a pearl comb. Jon walked through the back streets of the hurricane-ravaged city counting his blessings and his money. He could make do with what he had for a month before having to put on an all-out search for work. His plan involved some risk and great adventure; he'd salvage the haul of booze he and I had sunk in the channel that night the Feds chased us, then he'd take off to sell it on the Gulf Coast.

Homer, the Seminole who had been in Devane's employ, agreed to help Jon. He found a small motor sailer in good repair, and together they hid the booze beneath its deck boards.

Jon spent days alone lazing up the Miami River through the inland routes. The midday sun baked all trace of fall away. Crickets in the high grass played their scratchy tunes as herons circled and water fowl thrashed in the low grass, fleeing from the boat coursing through the thickets.

Jon crossed vast Lake Okeechobee, then reentered the streams and rivers passing the tiny towns of Goodno, La Belle, Denaud, Olga, and Tice where the waterways opened up once again to the broad Caloosa past Fort Myers to the Gulf of Mexico, where water, beach, and sky were layered in the softest tones of silver blue, white, and gray.

The towns that dotted that coast of Florida were also hit by the land boom of the 1920s. Many suffered through those scenes of public madness we saw in Miami, but the west coast of the state always had a sleepier quality, and giddy speculation there was on a more reasonable scale.

What it lacked in boom time action, however, it made up for in the amount of wealthy eccentrics it attracted, who had no inclination to engage in the rigid social whirls spinning to the east of them in Palm Beach and Miami.

One such eccentric was a man named Simon Ruppert, who played an important role in Jon Willig's life. He had carved a kingdom out of the pines and acacias of Pine Key, a fishing village twenty miles north of Fort Myers.

There were a number of reasons why Ruppert chose Pine Key, not the least of which had to do with his desire to one-up his greatest living rival, John Ringling. Beginning in about 1890 and continuing on for most of this century, Ringling's Greatest Show on Earth and Simon Ruppert's Show Of The Century battled to control what was the circus empire of America. Although the two men never met, their lives followed similar patterns as each spring their shows began crisscrossing the country, fighting to capture the imaginations of what Ringling used to call, "America's children of all ages."

When word went out that Ringling was about to build a winter quarters for his circus in Sarasota, Simon Ruppert followed suit, losing no time buying all the land he could find some fifty miles south of there. Construction began, and in the early twenties Ruppert took up permanent residence on an estate he called Georgia Hall (named in honor of his wife, Georgia Barstock Ruppert, whose ten-thousand-dollar dowry had gotten the Show Of The Century off to a flying start in the early 1880s).

Ruppert transformed about two hundred acres of a deserted tropical island into a fifty-two-room palace, complete with private circus grounds, marble swimming pools, an air strip, countless rose gardens and terraces draped with bougainvillea, a yacht basin, and the beginnings of one of the greatest private art collections in the world. Quite an accomplishment for a man who had started out carting a medicine wagon, two donkeys, a parakeet, and a balding parrot around the Midwest, charging people two bits to hear wild stories about his adventures stalking baboons in the Amazon.

Ruppert's greatest asset was his charm and vigor, which had managed through the years to ride herd over the disparate needs of unruly investors, elephants, and highly strung lion tamers. But by the middle twenties, at about the time he was creating his Pine Key empire, his energies waned. The Show Of The Century was now big business, run and operated in a no-nonsense corporate way by dull men who were more adept at figuring balance sheets than creating spectacles. Ruppert began devoting more and more time to amassing his art collection and catering to the needs of his wife, who was a strange, frail woman with a penchant for art, astrology, and anything at all that defied science and common sense. Together, they ruled the Pine Key estate with quixotic and whimsical hands.

Jon Willig wound up in the bay between the mainland and Pine Key, which happened to be the front doorstep of the Ruppert domain. He had decided to head north once he reached the Gulf at Fort Myers, but at this point the hand of fate dealt it's most fortuitous blow; his little boat ran aground at low tide one moonless night. After much useless cursing, pulling, and tugging, he dropped anchor and wrapped himself in a blanket, deciding to sleep off his minor misfortune until high tide came rolling in again from the Gulf.

Before closing his eyes that night, he thought he saw the twinkling of lights and the outlines of a towered fortress in the distant pine trees, but he merely shrugged it off, considering that two weeks on the water were playing strange tricks with his eyes. It wasn't until mid-morning of the following day that he realized these weren't hallucinations at all.

"I say there, wake up!" an Englishman's bass voice rumbled somewhere above him.

When he heard the voice, felt the nudge of someone's hand on his shoulder, Jon lifted his head. He was staring into the watery blue eyes of a man dressed in black and white livery who was leaning over the motor sailer. He was trying to steady himself in a small dinghy pitching in the choppy water.

"I'm afraid we cannot have you anchored off here. You have to move."

"Where did you come from?" Jon asked, squinting into the sunlight.

"You've got to be on your way. We have people coming in here today."

"I ran aground last night."

"You are no longer aground. I must ask you to leave."

"What seems to be the trouble, Raymond?" a voice boomed across the water from shore.

Jon twisted around to get a better look, but his mind could hardly comprehend what he saw. Off to the west, rising out of the water was an island with a pink-and-cream-colored palace on it. The morning sun angled on rows of amethyst-and-aquamarine-colored glass windows fronting two hundred feet of marble dock. A tall, lean, gray-haired man wearing a striped blazer and white flannel trousers stood on the dock holding a megaphone over his mouth.

"I'll have him out of here in a moment, sir," the Englishman called out.

"Where am I?" Jon asked.

"What's he doing out there, Raymond?" the megaphoned voice boomed back.

"He ran aground last night, sir."

Jon's eyes darted incredulously between the Englishman's fleshy, red-veined face and the island. "Does he own this place?"

"He does, and he does not like people trespassing on it."

"Will he need help?" the man on the dock called out.

"The tide has freed him now, sir."

"Well, then, get him on his way!" the man said, turning to walk back to his house.

Jon leaped to his feet, flailing his arms toward shore. "No, wait!" Then to the Englishman, "Tell him to wait. I have something he might be interested in."

"What the devil is going on out there?" the man on shore demanded.

"Is the house stocked with booze for the winter?" Jon asked. The butler looked properly ruffled, but, oddly enough, the smell of his breath and the glow of his cheeks made Jon suspect he was already half-bagged. "I've got fifty cases of it. Scotch and Tanqueray Gin. I'll give you a commission on all of it."

The Englishman stole a furtive glance toward shore, then sighed. "I dare say you are barking up the wrong tree."

Jon was not about to be put off by that. He'd never seen such a tangible display of wealth in all his life. Running to the bow of the boat, he cupped his hands over his mouth. "I've got something to sell here you might be interested in."

"What is he going on about, Raymond?"

"Fifty cases of Scotch and gin," Jon answered. "I don't know who supplies you now, but I know I can cut their price in half." He dropped to his knees, pulling up the deck boards to show the Englishman his entire cache. "Tell him it's all here, fifty dollars a case. Two thousand for the whole load. Not a bottle has been cut with anything," he said, offering the Englishman one of the bottles, which the latter inspected and then held over his head so that the man on the dock could see it as well.

"Does it look real, Raymond?"

"Real enough to me, sir."

"What about taste?"

"It is rather early in the day for me, sir."

The man on shore threw his hands up in disguest as Jon quickly rummaged through his duffle bag for a cup. He cracked open the wax label of a gin bottle, pouring the butler a stiff shot.

"Do you think I dare, sir?"

"Business is business, Raymond. I don't care what time of day it is."

Raymond sniffed above the cup, then raised it in a toast to the man. "To your health, sir." Eyes, then head rolled back as he took down the shot. He smiled. "I'll have another short one if you don't mind," he said quickly, licking his lips.

"Well? What do you make of it, Raymond?"

"Reminds me of home."

"You, there," the man on shore shouted. "What's your name?"

"Jon Willig."

"Bring your boat in, and we'll have a good look at what you've got. Raymond, let the young man tow you in. We know what two shots of gin do to you. I'll go get the glasses." He headed up the lawn, then stopped. "Where are the glasses?"

"Behind the bar, sir," Raymond said.

"Who is he?" Jon asked.

"Simon Ruppert."

"The circus magnate?"

Raymond hiccuped.

"You just sit tight, Raymond," Jon said, securing the lines that held the anchor. Raymond sat, nursing another drink, thoroughly baffled, and not all too happy about being out on the rough water.

The tiny power motor sputtered on as the boat bobbed up and down, cutting toward the dock. The house looked like an elegantly dripped sand castle with terra-cotta tiles laid atop two towers that arched above a rambling loggia. The jeweled colored windows alternately sent off jets of blue, green, yellow, and purple lights that danced on the water. The tall, elderly man ambled out of one of the glass doors carrying a serving tray with three crystal glasses on it. His face was large and bony but ended in loose folds of flesh below his jaw line; he had a pleasant assortment of features dominated by large, deceptively sleepy-looking eyes.

"My name is Simon Ruppert," he said. "I'm always in the market for a good buy. You cannot imagine the prices I've had to pay lately. You are a bit young to be plying the sea with this trade, aren't you? I wouldn't want to be accused of corrupting the morals of minors."

"No need to worry about that. I'm almost twenty."

"Yes," Ruppert said suspiciously, although he certainly admired the young man's style. Of all things, he thought, this extraordinary young man winding up in the bay to sell booze. Ruppert inspected the color and odor of the gin. "Well, nothing ventured, nothing gained. Raymond, pour yourself another."

Ruppert's eyes closed as he downed the shot; then he nearly fell over, coughing and hacking, stamping his large feet. "By God! That's good! That really is." His voice was rasping as he tried catching his breath. "Let's have a look at it."

Jon fetched another unopened bottle as Ruppert and Raymond helped each other down the marble steps above the boat. Raymond was wobbling by this time, so Ruppert grabbed the bottle and poured three more drinks himself.

"Damn good! What did you say? Two thousand for the entire lot?"

"It's pretty evenly mixed. Gin and Scotch."

"How did you happen upon this?"

"I'm not at liberty to say."

Ruppert let out with a childish wheeze of laughter. "That's a good one. Didn't sail it here from England, did you?" he said, looking over at Raymond to share his joke, but Raymond was pretty well gone by that time. "Well, this is quite a young man. Let's drink up!"

While master and servant polished off their third and sixth of the day, Jon deferred to his better judgment and poured his over the side. He refilled their glasses to the three-quarter mark. The drinks were polished off with considerable aplomb—and imprudence, considering the strength of the sun beating down on their heads. Jon took a minute or two to stare up at the windows, to follow the serpentine designs set in marble casings surrounding them. A sparrowlike woman with sharp features and gray hair cut in a short Chinese bob appeared in one window upstairs, waving at him as if she knew him.

How strange! He knew where he was—he'd died and gone to heaven which, oddly enough, looked very much like earth, but with a bit more polish. Sitting there, swapping rib pokes with the old man who owned the circus. Strange was hardly the word.

Ruppert was in his mid-sixties and on his way to a noontime nap if he didn't watch out. Jon, sorry now that he'd mentioned the price as early as he had, put on his best poker face; he still had a business deal to get through.

"What are you looking at?" Ruppert asked.

"The color of the glass. The designs. It's fantastic."

More trickles of laughter poured out of Ruppert, accompanied by hand wavings requesting more drinks encompassing the land and the house in one sweep.

"Yes, wonderful, wonderful. Such great fun," he drawled. His accent shifted ever so slightly, heavy traces of Midwest appearing through the faintly British. "We traveled all over the world. Took us a decade to cart all of it in. Then by ferry boat out here. Every piece of it."

Raymond, silent and sturdy though he was, gently slid back and snoozed.

"I thought perhaps you'd seen someone up there in the windows. My wife disapproves of morning nips, says the psychic powers diminish, or something of that sort," Ruppert said offhandedly and then poured himself another drink with all the caution of a schoolboy playing hookey. "Are you a believer in the great planetary scheme of things?"

"I beg your pardon."

"And well you should. I'm a double Taurus. Georgia says everyone has to know where they fit in, cosmically speaking."

"I suppose it helps to believe in something."

"Oh, yes. It helps. Always a comfort to know that when you wind up on your ass, the stars said you would."

The downstairs doors were flung open as the woman Jon had seen in the window came rushing across the lawn toward them. She was tiny, not more than five feet tall, and wore blue silk Poiret lounging pajamas. As she ran, the breeze picked up, and her coat flew open. Her face was brightened by the reflection of the coat's orchid-colored lining.

"Is this a visitor?" she chirped in an excited but refined voice. "This is too good to believe. Did he just drop in from the blue? Madame Treach said someone was coming."

Ruppert dropped his glass in the water, then jumped up to help her down the steps.

"Quite extraordinary," he said. "This young man's boat ran

aground out there in the bay last night. He had it loaded with wonderful liquor."

The woman's luminous dark eyes opened and closed as if she were trying to regain some trance state; then she rushed down the steps to shake Jon's hand. "Madame Treach said nothing about liquor, but this is fortuitous, anyway. What is your name?"

"Jon Willig."

"And I am Georgia Ruppert," she said in a more lilting tone. Her face was finely chiseled, with almost transparent skin held tautly over her bones, which arched her cheeks and jaw in clean, delicate lines. "Madame Treach also said nothing about your coming by water, but I like the symbolism of that even more." She turned to her husband. "This is very important to us, Simon. Madame said it would be."

Ruppert stared down at his wife, one eyebrow raised superciliously. Jon was totally confused. Was he being offered an invitation? He thought he was, but he tempered his emotions cautiously so as not to appear too eager, which his mother had always told him was impolite.

Georgia fished through the pockets of her jacket. "You must choose a card. Right now, so we can catch you almost at the moment of your arrival. It will be very telling."

A deck of oversized playing cards was brought forth and thrust at him. He looked at Ruppert for guidance.

"Don't ask me." Ruppert sighed. "It's all in the stars." He laughed.

"Oh, you hush. Now, dear boy, you must pick one very quickly. No thinking at all, just pick."

Jon did as he was told, extracting one from the center of the deck. On it was a picture of a man hanging upside down. His right foot was tied with a thick rope to a brace made of tree branches.

"The Hanging Man," Georgia mused. "Very interesting," she said intently.

"What is this all about?" Jon pleaded.

"The Tarot," Ruppert whispered in a mock reverential tone.

"Fortune teller's cards?"

"More serious than that, I can assure you. Give me a minute or two to digest this, then I'll tell you all about it." She closed her eyes as Ruppert and Jon shrugged. Raymond's snoring suddenly broke the silence. Her eyes flashed open.

"It's Raymond there. He's disturbing my concentration. Awaken him, Simon. Take him away."

"Whatever you say, my love." Ruppert bent over and kissed his wife's head, then helped Raymond up to the house.

When she and Jon were alone, Georgia began to study his face again. "The Hanging Man is very important. He is literally hung in his karma—do you know that word?"

"No."

"Sanskrit, from the root *kr*. Simply put—the consequences of our actions. The Hanging Man is hung in his, but it isn't his fault. You see, as long as you are identified with your mortal body, you are bound to the task of paying off old debts—unraveling the web of your fate."

"I just came here to sell your husband some Scotch."

"No, do not stay with that thought. Do you follow the Karma Yoga? No, of course you don't, but you should. You may be able to untangle the knot of fate. Become more of what your immortal higher self is, do you see? You can redeem yourself. Christ was also in your position."

"Oh, my."

"Listen to me. Christ was hung on the cross, but he was called the Redeemer. Trust me with this. This is very important."

Jon was enchanted. Who would not have been, confronted by this ethereal woman ranting and raving about the stars and Christ and the cosmos in this most earthly of paradises. He wanted to stay with them for a while, but more than that, he wanted what they had to be his own.

"Yes, yes," Georgia was saying, "I know what you are thinking. Why shouldn't you have anything you want, but you will have to pay a price for it—that is the karma of the Hanging Man."

Jon was stunned into paying strict attention to her.

"Now that you've chosen the Hanging Man, I must put that together with what Madame Treach said. She said you were coming. And something about usurpation. That was the key word. Usurpation. Don't look so skeptical. Madame Treach knows these things. You'll meet her. You must. And when you do, you must listen to her. She knows. She predicted my death coming soon. A very pleasant death, she said. Before my time, if you ask me, but see there, that is the price I must pay. Now, you must stay here for a moment while I go talk with Simon and arrange everything. Just sit on the dock and enjoy the day."

Off she went, flitting across the lawn, leaving Jon to contemplate his cosmic destiny, which suddenly seemed fraught with commercial possibilities.

In a few minutes Ruppert reappeared, casually strolling across the lawn toward him. "You've made quite a first impression."

"And vice versa, if you don't mind my saying, sir."

"I don't mind at all. You are quite an extraordinary young man, keeping your wits about you while Georgia gave you the cosmic once-over. Tell me, do you think it is madness setting in?"

"Who is to say?"

"That is what I keep saying. After all, this planetary nonsense got me where I am today. Now, about more earthly matters—what did you say, fifteen hundred for the entire load of liquor?"

"Two thousand, and I'll wager your business ability had a lot to do with what got you where you are today," Jon said lightly.

Ruppert chuckled. "Just testing. It is good to know what caliber of man is about to become my house guest. You have clothes with you, I presume."

"I do."

"Well, get them then. I'll have Raymond—no, Raymond won't do—I'll get you settled myself," he said, turning to leave. "That is, if you don't have any other engagements?"

"No, no."

"Good. We'll see how you take to this continuing lunacy."

18

Not only was Jon welcomed as a house guest, but Georgia Ruppert would not permit him to leave until the mysterious Madame Olga Treach arrived to divine what was in store for all of them. Jon was more than happy to oblige.

Both Simon and Georgia were late sleepers. Jon awakened at seven every morning to explore the house undisturbed. He sat in the heavily carved cinquecento chairs and perused the paintings in the gallery. Alone, he felt perfectly comfortable with his imaginary role as lord and master. When the Rupperts were with him, however, he became timorous in conversation and awkward at meals, waiting for them to begin eating to see which fork or knife they used for the different courses.

Charmed though he was by Georgia, he still had a nagging feeling that she was out of her mind. He walked with her every afternoon in her rose garden where she discussed alchemy, astrology, and life after death. When not talking about these subjects, she sat in the main hall working on her needlepoint.

The room was of immense proportions, with high, cambered ceilings. In the late afternoon the sun slanted through jewel-colored windows bathing the marble floors in an unearthly light.

Simon Ruppert worked in a small office on the bay side of the gallery, and the halls echoed with what Jon came to think of as Ruppert's telephone voice—a bit rougher than the one he reserved for polite conversation. In the morning he'd be shouting orders to the circus managers who were winding up summer and fall seasons in the Midwest. On the wall above his desk was a huge multicolored map, which he used to plot the circus's moves. He prided himself on knowing the timetables of every rail crossing in the country and kept all of that information in his head. For the most part, whether he was reading in the main hall, walking around the grounds, or inspecting his paintings, he kept a watchful eye on Jon.

One day while they were walking through the ballroom, studying the collection of paintings there, Ruppert stopped in front of a large canvas, the *Bacchanal* by Titian, in which a glorious nude lay with her head thrown back as revelers circled near her.

"She's marvelous, isn't she? She is the first one I bought."

Jon nodded but said nothing.

"What a revelation she was when I first came upon her. Some New York dealer had her tucked away in the back of his shop. He said she was a Guercino, but I knew she was a Titian. Paid him next to nothing for her, then I brought her down here and my experts confirmed my suspicions. I wish I could see her with your eyes."

"I don't think I'm old enough to fully appreciate her. That comes later, doesn't it—when there's enough time."

Ruppert smiled sadly. "I suppose so."

"Do you ever leave this place?"

"Not so much any more. When I was your age, I spent all my time on the road, never seemed to tire of it, but when we came down here, it stopped—I stopped."

They walked through the ballroom, then into the main hall past the Tintorettos and Breughels, Bassanos and Rembrandts.

"This is a place for an old man, isn't it," he mused. "I often think about the future. After my death perhaps someone will keep this place going. Georgia and I are all alone—no family—never wanted children. But I know someone will keep this place going. People will come and wonder who we were. They'll call us madmen, no doubt."

"Or dreamers."

"How very perceptive of you. I dreamed this place into existence, and the value of all we've managed to collect here is not worth a fraction of those dreams."

"When they came true—" Jon began.

"Go on."

"No, I don't want to pry. I'd be impolite."

"You couldn't be that, dear boy."

"Well, it seems to me that when your dreams came true, they never measured up. When I hear you on the telephone in the morning, you run your empire like a hell on wheels, but when we walk around here, you seem trapped. Do you feel that?"

"Very perceptive, indeed. You must be a dreamer as well."

Jon looked around at the paintings. "I know what I want."

"And you'll stop at nothing to get it?" Ruppert smiled gently.

"Exactly."

"That's a start, dear boy."

A glass door opened. Georgia ran across the main hall to greet them; her face was flushed with excitement.

"Madame Treach has just called. She will be down this evening. Oh, Jon, you'll love her. I told her about the Hanging Man, and she said that it all fits. We must prepare you, she said."

"For what?"

"She didn't say. Oh, she's so mysterious, but you must trust her." She looked at Ruppert. "All of us must trust her."

That was all but impossible for Jon Willig when Madame Olga Treach arrived later that afternoon. Only two words came to his mind concerning her: bamboozler and charlatan. She was an effusive, bawdy woman in her early forties. Dyed raven black hair framed her sensual face; dark, piercing eyes were set deeply above an aquiline nose.

"My darlings, my darlings!" she cried, her heaving bosom buried beneath layers of scarves and chains on which amulets dangled. She held Georgia close. "The place looks marvelous. I've just been out in California. Nothing out there rivals it."

She was a bit more cautious with Simon, keeping her distance, shaking his hand as if it were a water pump.

"Simon, you look wonderfully well. And this must be the young man."

She saved her most seductive expression for Jon.

"Those wonderful eyes," she whispered breathlessly. "And the golden hair. Just as I thought. And he is a Jew, isn't he?"

All three of them stared as Jon nodded affirmatively.

Georgia squealed with delight. "Oh, I told you she knows. She knows everything."

"I see the ages behind those eyes." As she studied him, her tongue darted over her full lips. "When do we eat? I'm famished."

Dinner was served in the state dining room. Madame Treach filled her mouth with heaps of pâté and caviar, stopping every now and then to stare at the paintings, Flemish still lifes of slaughtered stags and rabbits.

"I don't know what prompted you to hang those dreadful beasts in here—it all but takes my appetite away."

There was no need to worry about that. Course after course was devoured with enough alacrity to cause Jon to wonder whether or not California had been good enough to feed her. She eyed him suspiciously, then tenderly, devoting most of her attention to Georgia, who was chastised for not keeping up with her yoga, Blavatsky, and Gurdjieff.

"You must devote at least an hour a day to it. You too, Simon. The yoga will keep you limber, Blavatsky will soothe the soul—" Her sentence cut off when she began choking on the bones of a Cornish hen. Raymond appeared behind her, pounding on her back as she gulped down wine.

"No need to worry—no fuss at all. It will take more than a little bird to do me in. What's for dessert?"

"Bombé surprise," Georgia said.

"Oh, surprise me, Georgia—I love surprises."

Jon doubted that.

"Georgia says you predicted the arrival of our young friend here," Simon piped in.

Madame Treach's eyes crossed, then focused. "We shall see if he is the one," she whispered cryptically.

"We must have a reading after dinner."

"If all augurs well." She burped.

They took brandy and coffee in one of the tower rooms. Two enormous Mexican wedding hammocks were strung in it, and tacked to the ceiling was a circus tent that flapped lazily in the breeze coming up from the water. Madame Treach stood, leaning over the rail, staring out to sea, a coolly calculated mystical expression floating across her eyes.

"Yes. I believe we are in alignment. We may commence." She turned suddenly, stretching her arms out again, the breeze billowing out the draped sleeves of the loose tunic she was wearing. "Take lotus positions on the floor, and we'll cleanse ourselves."

"Oh, must we again," Simon protested.

"Don't you dare go and ruin this for us, Simon," Georgia scolded.

Ruppert and Jon exchanged knowing glances but sat cross-legged beneath one of the hammocks as Madame Treach began chanting:

"Close your eyes and fix your mind's eye on that place six inches above the center of your head where all your energies reside. Showering light on your body in that upper temple of your body. The upper room of your soul." She stopped here to swig down some brandy.

"My upper room is vacant," said Jon.

"Funny, mine has a To Let sign as well," Ruppert added.

"Please be quiet and concentrate—bathe yourselves in the light of your own energies, your own immortal souls."

She went on like that for an hour, her voice becoming husky and mellow, intoning, beckoning the light in their souls until they sat there dazed, either by the light of their souls or dog-tiredness—none could say which. It was then that Madame Treach got all the information she needed to know about Jon. His birth date and approximate time of birth. He, too, was a double Taurus and that augured well (whatever that meant).

Then she dealt the Tarot. Hers was a more elaborate deck which looked soiled from wear. First, she read for Simon and Georgia. Theirs were surprisingly similar; they were coming to the end of life cycles. Jon was next. She placed five cards down, each representing some aspect of what had passed and what was to come to him. Oddly enough, the Hanging Man reappeared in the "passing" position. Georgia and Treach exchanged knowing smiles. The key card, the integrating factor of his life, was turned over as breaths were held. The Magician was revealed.

"Very telling," Treach announced. "The shape shifter. Prime moving force of the cosmos."

"But what about usurpation—you mentioned that when you predicted his arrival?" Georgia asked.

"It is all here. The Hanging Man, the Magician and the High Priestess. I see things very clearly. He cannot allow himself to get too close to anyone. He has fearful secrets"—her eyes were closed; she appeared to be in a deep, trancelike state—"things he cannot tell anyone. That is where the usurpation comes into play. He must do away with those who try to help him. He cannot define himself."

Jon wanted her to stop. He didn't like this at all. It sounded too filled with the foreboding despair that he had suspected was there lurking inside himself.

"Boundless energy," she was saying. "And you must give him room to grow. He will be a provider. You must not stand in his way."

"I think that is enough for now," Ruppert said when he saw the look of alarm in Jon's eyes. "Jon and I will take our brandy downstairs. You've provided us with more than enough food for thought, Madame Treach. I thank you."

He rose and walked into the house.

Jon was left staring at Treach. "How do you see these things?"

"It is a dubious gift, my friend," was all she said.

Jon joined Ruppert in the main hall. A roaring fire was lit, and Ruppert sat staring sadly at it.

After pouring himself a brandy, Jon sat next to the hearth. "What do you make of all this?"

Ruppert shrugged.

"You don't actually believe it, do you?" Jon asked. "You can't. You're a man of the world. My God, this is senseless and useless."

"And what I've chosen to occupy my time with, it seems."

"But you certainly are not powerless to change that if you want to. I think it's too depressing for you here. This whole place is getting to you. Maybe she's right—you do need to end a cycle. Do you mind my being this honest with you?"

"Not at all."

"Art collecting is fine, but not as a full-time occupation. You can't turn your back on the way you spent your whole life. Why I imagine you've traveled all over the world, and surely the circus must be the most exciting life anyone could want."

Jon realized he was talking for himself as well. He was tired of dawdling around in this rambling house. He was eager to persuade Ruppert to leave it, to take him out on the road.

"Perhaps you are right," Ruppert said, his face suddenly infused with life as Jon urged him on.

"I'd like to run off with the circus—with you, if I could. I think I'd like nothing more than that."

"You'd love the life out there on the road. Each day a new city or town. The tents billowing above like a ship's sails. It is fantastic." Ruppert rose and paced excitedly in front of the fireplace. "When I was a boy, there was very little joy in our house. My parents were dirt-poor, dissatisfied people who never left their farm, never saw anything of life. And I ran away from that and built a dream the likes of which you've never seen. The color of it alone. Mind-boggling. Clowns and animals—you are right, you must see it!"

He crossed the great hall, ran up the staircase to the upper gallery. "Dear boy, you are saving my life. I'll order the train. We'll travel in my car and meet up with the rest in Minnesota—they'll be there in two weeks." He stopped when he reached the railing in front of his office. "You gave me the talking-to I needed, and I promise I'll repay you for it."

"Will you teach me about the circus?"

"Anything you want to know. You'll see, I'll come alive again," he shouted, disappearing into the office. In a few minutes the house was buzzing with the sound of his telephone voice.

As Jon sat listening to it, he wondered whether or not he was being completely self-serving or whether or not that mattered at all. Perhaps that mystical harpy was correct. This was merely the manifestation of what was already written in the stars.

That night his head was too filled with plans to sleep. He tossed and turned and then heard a rapping at the door. Before he had a chance to pull on his pants, Olga Treach sauntered in wearing a white robe. She sat on the edge of his bed as he covered himself with his sheet.

"You are a beautiful one," she whispered, then looked at the stately Empire furniture in the bedroom. "You've done all right for yourself. I guess we both have," she cooed. "Don't worry about me. We come from the same place, my beautiful darling. I'm just a smart little Jewish girl from Brooklyn. And you?"

"Jewish boy from Miami."

"Don't go thinking harsh thoughts about me. I can read the future. Yours looks very rosy if you play your cards right."

"From the Tarot deck."

"Don't laugh. They need us. They're too rich."

"Simon and Georgia?"

"All of them. You should see them. The movie stars are the best. They get all that money, and they don't know why. Of course, Simon worked his ass off for his, but he's as guilt-ridden as the rest. They don't wear it very easily, especially the American ones. They overspend to soothe themselves. Then I come along offering them something they can't see to believe in." Her hand circled his leg. "You seem to have offered them youth and beauty." She massaged his groin. "Simon's second chance, the way I figure it." Her long nails trailed up his chest, leaving faint red lines on his pale skin. "I believe in anything that feels good. I'm not being too cynical for you, am I?" She laughed. "Is that possible?"

Jon shifted his position on the bed, trying to ease away from her, but she was very persistent.

"Do I scare you?" she asked, cupping his hand, placing it on one of her pendulous breasts.

"No."

"Too much of a woman for you?"

"I like going after what I want."

"That's an easy answer. Don't you want me?"

She kissed him before he could speak, her tongue snaking between his lips, her teeth nibbling at them—softly at first and then urgently, until he wanted to cry out in pain. But his hands burrowed in her thick hair, tugging her closer to him. She pulled away suddenly, throwing off her robe, proud of her round body, sitting there open-legged, casually dangling her foot from the bed.

"Roughhouse is what you really like," she whispered, encircling his erect penis with her hand, creasing the broad vein at its base with her nails. "Just a little pain helps. So I don't have to be too beautiful, do I?"

"No," he said, lunging at her; but her hand tightened around him, forcing him back.

"Works wonders." She laughed.

Her head dropped into his lap, licking the wiry hair on his scrotum. Tightening the grasp of her hand again, she began nibbling, grazing the sensitive, puckered skin of his glans with her teeth.

"You can be as rough as you like with me," she panted, again tightening her fingers around him. "In fact, I'd like that now. Get on the floor in front of me!"

He didn't say a word as she held him and directed him to the floor, her fingers parting the crepelike skin of her thighs, twining the black mat of hair. "In there," she commanded. "Lick into me. Hard as you like. Bite me. Again. Pull at me."

Her thighs held his head, blocking out the sight of her. As his mouth worked over her, he heard her laughter chiding him, coaxing him.

"Pain is the best part," she was saying. "Always the best."

He once talked about this encounter with me.

"She did read my future, George," he said one drunken night many years later. "Sealed my fate, in fact. Because for years I never found any comfort with a man or a woman. The power struggle was too exciting. To have them or be had by them. She was like that nude in the Titian *Bacchanal*—something to conquer. Have you ever tried it, George?"

"No."

"My city of darkness. My religion, you could say. A deadly serious business. There was no joy with any of them. That is something I regret, but that doesn't stop me from paying good cash to get it. Not like that first night with that fat sow; that was for free."

"The Freudians would call you a classic case study of denial."

"What do they know? Denial of what?"

"Romance. Love. Any number of comforting things. What about all those women you spent so much time with?"

"Just so much newsprint."

"And what about our friendship?"

"You've been a good friend, but I thought we were talking about love."

"What about your father, or Ruppert?"

"One I never knew. And the other. . . . I didn't have the time to be comforted by Ruppert. All I wanted was what he had—the business, the house, and all that money."

19

Fueled by Jon's youthful energy and his own desire to recapture the magic of his youth, Simon Ruppert once again went out on the road with his circus. The years they spent traveling were a revelation to Jon, which were best expressed in the letters he wrote me. I have edited them down somewhat and present them to you now.

December 18, 1926

Dear George:

Your decision to enter law school is a commendable one, I suppose. Perhaps you are better suited to that monkish existence, but I can't help thinking that you robbed yourself of some golden opportunities by not shipping out with me. I'll pull you along with me one way or another one of these days. Ruppert says that lawyers come in handy.

Where to begin? The train, of course. Ruppert has his own string of cars, which he calls the SIGIA—short for Simon and Georgia. (Dotty old Georgia looked more than reconciled when we left Pine Key. She and Treach stood there in the drive, looking as if they were going to throw the bones or cast the dice to read what the road had in store for us.)

We made our way to Duluth, Minnesota, via New York City of all places. Ruppert couldn't do enough for me there. He bought me an entire wardrobe, and I must admit I'm becoming something of a fop. Please don't look as smug as I imagine you are looking at this moment.

The circus pulled into Duluth just six hours before we did, and I can't tell you how excited I was to see it being set up for the first time. During the train trip out, Ruppert kept filling my head with the intricacies of booking and scheduling, making me memorize those route cards he memorized years ago. But to actually see it! Men swarming over the lot as if they were an army of ants. Mostly Negroes, hundreds of them, working their tails off, lugging poles and tenting.

At first they work with the center poles; they're as tall as masts from a clipper ship, and each weighs about a ton. They're hitched to wagons and pulled by elephants. Meanwhile, the Gilly wagons trail after them, dropping stakes for the guy ropes. Behind them come the Negroes swinging sledgehammers. What a sight—when it goes up, the tent is about five hundred feet in length and about two hundred feet in width. I persuaded Ruppert to let me work with the men that first week. It was long and back-breaking, and something I'm not too eager to repeat.

The circus performers don't know what to make of me. Tell you the truth, I don't know, either. Ruppert doesn't want me getting too friendly with them. I watch him in awe as he calms tempers and pampers his stars. One in particular is a woman who used to be the main equestrienne act. Her name is Belle, and I believe that she and Ruppert once had something going. Now she must be in her sixties, and Ruppert still pampers her. He's created an act for her in which all she does is make an entrance in a golden chariot.

The other performers are as moody an aristocracy as I've ever met. Most of them are from Europe and had families in the circus for generations. Only the top acts make big money, and even then the pay is not extraordinary. For most, it is the only life they know. I understand what they see in it and want to stay with it as well. Ruppert says he is prepping me to do just that.

* * *

May 12, 1927

Dear George:

Pulling into New York again for the spring show, which seems to be traveling under a cloud of doom this season.

Just two days ago, a little child who'd come to see the circus for the first time got too close to one of our elephants. The elephant grabbed her with his trunk, then knelt on her, killing her instantly. The poor baby was gone before we could help her. The elephant's trainer went wild, thrashing the great beast with a prod until we had to drag him away. We took the animal out to the meadowlands in New Jersey to destroy him. Yesterday at dawn, Ruppert and I stood there with the circus vet and this dumb beast who I'm sure knew what fate had in store. The Doc loaded a syringe as big as a jackhammer with strychnine and eased it into a vein in one of the elephant's flapping ears. He stood there calmly and proudly for a moment, then came tumbling down like the wall of a monstrously large building. I was crying when it ended. For the child and the animal, too, who had no idea what crime he had committed.

* * *

February 16, 1928

Dear George:

Will be leaving for Europe soon to scout new acts for the fall show. Ruppert will go along with me, and I'm looking forward to that.

I've just heard from my mother who was asking about you and wondering when I was coming home to Miami to see her. I keep meaning to, but something stops me. She says Sam has cut himself off from everyone. Jack is getting into the hotel business, and he and mother are making a lot of money. Diana, of course, is off on a rampage, traveling all over the place. As usual, my mother is disgusted with her. I don't want to face all of them.

* * *

March 7, 1929

Dear George:

You must be proud of yourself—not even graduated and you've wrangled a position with a firm. I'm impressed. We'll celebrate the next time I'm in New York. Some bad news on this end—Georgia Ruppert has taken ill. The doctors are not optimistic, and Simon is returning to Pine Key, leaving me here to run the show for him. Of course, I'm eager to try my wings, but I'm sorry it had to happen under these conditions.

What on earth is going on with the stock market? You must keep an eye on it for me—I'm a man of means now.

* * *

September 30, 1929

Dear George:

Georgia Ruppert died in her sleep this morning at about five. I was there with Simon when it happened. Such an eerie night. I'd gone to bed after seeing her. She could hardly talk by then, but she was muttering something about accepting the end—she knew it was coming.

Simon's crying awakened me before dawn. I looked all over the house for him, but couldn't find him. I dressed and searched the grounds and finally found him in the rose garden. He was lying there, crying like a child. "I am all alone in this world," he kept saying. There was no comforting him, but I was able to coax him back into the house. He's aged in just hours. He sits in the main hall as if he were a captive. He doesn't want to go out on the road again. He wants me to run it for him.

* * *

December 4, 1929

Dear George:

I suppose all of us will always remember Black Tuesday. I was in Chicago on the telephone with Ruppert, trying to convince him that all was not lost. He's like a frightened spinster. The investments he made were wiped out. All the money from the circus was put into the house and mining stocks—railroads and land. He was telling me he was ruined, but I had a show to put on that night. It was doing average business—average, yes, but still money coming in to keep the show afloat and keep him well stocked at Pine Key. His art alone would net him a fortune, but he says he will not sell any of it. His blessed Georgia Hall! That's no way to do business. I do think that Ruppert and I are heading for our first major confrontation.

Last week, on a whim, he fired half of our acts. Economy measures, he called it, notifying me just hours before he let them go. What I think he fails to see is that in the bleak times coming, people will still need to amuse themselves, and the circus will thrive. But he's frightened, and nothing I say convinces him. It is time for me to do some serious thinking about my future, and I wish you were here to help me plot my strategy.

* * *

March 15, 1929

George Esq.:

I'm sorry about the mix-up. Ruppert and I were supposed to be in New York in February to negotiate the new contract with Madison Square Garden, and I thought you and I would get together then, but you have no idea how unpredictable the old man has been and how much money that is now costing us. He seems bent on a very destructive course. He simply refused to show up for his meeting with the Garden management, railing all the while that if the Garden wanted to negotiate with him, they could damn well come down to Pine Key to do it. He says he's made enough money for them all these years. But these management men he's dealing with are as stiff as hell, and with the Crash and all, they're as nervous as everyone. They were enraged when he didn't show up. He says they were looking for an excuse to put the squeeze on him, but I don't know.

The next thing we heard from them was that they would still negotiate with us, but they'd be cutting us out of Friday night showings so they could bring the fights in. I imagine that is rather lucrative business these days.

Ruppert's reaction to all of this was to tell them to shove it. Now we're locked out of the Garden. Can you imagine a spring without the circus there? There's no reasoning with him.

At any rate, I will be up there in about a month trying to straighten this mess out. Will call you then.

* * *

He did call when he arrived in New York that spring, and I was taken aback by his tone of voice. Gone was the reckless young man who'd taken me on rum runs; he'd become a businessman.

"We've got a crisis here, so I can't meet you downtown. Come up to the Plaza," he said.

"What's going on?"

"I can't talk now. It's this Madison Square Garden deal. I'm trying to hold everything together."

"Sounds interesting."

"That's a word for it. What are you doing?"

"They've put me into Estates and Trusts. The partner who supervises me plays taskmaster to my galley slave."

"Good God, George, I expected better things for you. But you always needed a cattle prod to get you going. Come up to the Plaza. Ruppert's suite. About two. We'll talk."

When I arrived there later that afternoon, there was an argument in progress in one of the bedrooms. Raymond, who through Jon's letters was now as familiar to me as any old friend, asked me to wait, but no sooner had I taken a seat to do just that when one of the rear doors slammed open and Simon Ruppert came in. Big, bluff, and energetic, his vitality shattered any notions I had of his being a doddering old man mourning the death of his beloved wife or frittering away what remained of his empire. He brought his argument in with him like a March wind blustering in a cold front; his eyes glowered, and I guessed that the target of all this rage was Jon.

"They do this to me, and you want me to appease them? Never!" he was saying, canvassing the room with one ferocious glare. When he spotted me in a corner, he snapped, "Who are you—one of their henchmen?"

"I beg your pardon."

Jon's appearance on the scene was all that saved me from a fusillade of abuse. I rose as he bounded across the room, shook my hand, and then explained to Ruppert who I was and why I was there.

Jon had gone through a major transformation in these past three years. Now he was well turned out in that leisured, European way as if he'd been born to it. He was wearing buff-colored gabardine trousers, a camel's-hair jacket and a green silk tie and shirt. His hair was longer than was the style then, neatly parted and falling over the collar of his shirt.

"So good to see you, George. I'm sorry about all this."

"You needn't make excuses for me," Ruppert bellowed.

"We are under a great deal of pressure today," Jon added.

"Would you like me to come back later?" I offered.

"My question," Ruppert continued, "is why you are here in the first place. Why on earth do we need young lawyers hanging around us?"

Jon planted his fists squarely on his hips as he turned to confront Ruppert. "This is a friend of mine, and you are being incredibly rude. I don't want you talking this way to him. Do you understand?"

Suddenly Ruppert's vitality diminished. He looked around the room as if he were a lap dog who'd just been spanked. "Don't you start in on me, Jonny. We have to stay together on this." He stared benignly at me for the first time. "He's something—this friend of ours. Puts me in my place when I need it. I'm terribly sorry if I offended you."

"I'm not offended."

"That's good. I'm not much on amenities these days. Where are my working papers?"

"In your bedroom."

Ruppert didn't want to offend me further, but it was obvious that he had more pressing problems on his mind.

"If you two don't mind, I'll go back there and work this out. There are a few phone calls I have to make. You see that your friend is well taken care of," he said as he left the room.

"What on earth is going on here?"

Jon stared at the empty hallway. "Bad situation and it's all his fault. They've completely locked him out of showing at the Garden this spring. Their management wanted to spite him, so they signed with some dinky circus, the Palladino Brothers, for the entire season. It's the first time they've ever done that. Now Ruppert wants to buy the Palladino—lock, stock, and barrel. He's got those Wall Street boys convincing him to put what remains of his holdings in hock to do it, too."

"Will he?"

"You're damned right he will. It's nonsense, but they've lured him into this spite war, and he won't quit."

"Sounds like you've been having a difficult time of it."

"I'm just biding my time. Experience like this doesn't come along all that often. But enough about me," he said politely. "What have you been doing, tell me everything."

He didn't look as if he wanted to hear it, but I told him, anyway, that I was rather disenchanted with law after all, or at least the part of it that had been consuming my time lately. I noticed that he kept his eyes trained on the vacant hallway as if he were straining to hear the telephone conversation going on in the bedroom, and so I was brief. I turned the conversation back to him.

"What do you mean when you say you're biding your time? Have you any other offers?"

"No, not really. I've been thinking lately that his going into hock to buy this other circus might be very useful for me in the long run."

"How so?"

"All the holdings will be in a very vulnerable position on the open market locked up in a note."

"How much capital will be involved?"

"About a million and a half. I tell you, he cannot afford to keep up the payments on a note of that size. We are in a depression, I don't care what Hoover and those other idiots say."

"How does that help you?"

"After a while, I think anyone with funds could step in and buy up the note and control the whole show."

"And you'd do that to him?"

He looked at me with a startled expression that implied a measure of disdain for my having asked such a childish question.

"It's not as if I'm doing him in, George. The circus was his life's work, and the time has come for him to pass it on. I even think that in his heart of hearts he knows that."

"You can't be serious. He took you in."

"You surprise me, George. Yes, it's all true—he was my benefactor and mentor, taught me a great deal, but he knows I want out from under his wing. He's expecting it. I don't think he'd respect me if I didn't make a try for it. The reason I was taken in with him is very simple. We're both alike, and he knows that. Sure, I showed up at his place without a nickel in my pocket while he was playing lord and master, but under the skin we're just two boys with our noses pressed up against the candy-store window. I tell you, he never wanted it to get this big. He's old, and now he's scared."

I was taken aback by his display of ingratitude, but Jon wanted me to believe it was all perfectly moral: the old giving way to the young; the law of the jungle; and a hundred other perfectly sound reasons. I felt a need to temper his enthusiasm.

"And where will you get a million and a half?"

"I'm not saying I'd do it now. I can afford to be patient. Let him strap himself, and then I'll find sources."

"Anyone I know?"

He smiled. "There is a lot of Willig money in Miami these days."

"Your mother."

"I imagine she'll be eager to have me back in the fold again, and I'm not above going to her when the time is ripe."

"She might have the only money left in Miami by then."

"I've heard from friends that Jack is making it hand over fist," he whispered. "And if I know my mother, she is taking a very nice cut of it. Simon doesn't know about any of this, so please keep it under your hat."

"How is your family? Are you in touch with them?"

"Occasionally. Letters. Telephone calls. Mother asks about you all the time and wonders if you are as disenchanted with law as you say you are. I think it would be worth your while to go down there and talk with her. She needs advice."

"I've thought about it. How is Sam?"

"It's too sad. He's cut himself off completely. Living in an old run-down place with Tildy and the boy."

"And Diana?"

His eyes lit up. "You know, George, I've always had a sneaking suspicion that you were in love with her."

I couldn't control my blush.

"I thought so. But she's trouble. Or have you already found that out?"

Ruppert's voice boomed out from the bedroom. "Jon, let's get back to work!"

"I have to run," he said, standing and adjusting his tie and sports coat. "But we'll stay in touch. I want us to work together again."

I looked around at the ornate gold and white suite.

"It will be a far cry from rum-running when and if."

"Safer, too."

"You're doing very well for yourself."

"Everyone keeps saying that to me as if they didn't expect that I would. Don't ever underestimate me, George. I have always gotten what I wanted. I expect I always will."

20

Our correspondence was spotty during the next three years. I did learn, however, that Simon Ruppert had put all of his holdings up as collateral for a million-and-a-half-dollar note to buy the Palladino Circus, which he promptly absorbed into the Show Of The Century. He played the Garden that spring after all.

Jon said they were heading for lean years, but he was content to wait it out, to make cautious moves that would solidify his own position before grabbing Ruppert's.

I, in the meantime, was inching my way up the ladder at Barnes, Thatcher and Stokes, having been made a junior partner in my third year and having learned how to deal with the heap of abuse leveled at me by the old curmudgeon in charge of Estates and Trusts, who simply refused to retire or die.

In 1933 I celebrated my thirty-first birthday, a milestone that I thought would be fairly innocuous until I lapsed into a short but wrenching depression. It was becoming painfully clear to me that the adventures of my youth were truly behind me and I was speeding toward middle age. It was simply a matter of adjusting to a new set of expectations. After all, the notion of making a small fortune in dubious land deals had, by that time, been thoroughly supplanted by my slow creep up to full partnership.

I was living in a small, one bedroom apartment in a brownstone in the Turtle Bay section of New York. I entertained an assortment of rather staid friends from the office and a collection of women who were either the friends of friends or divorcées. There was not one special girl, and that got me down, but I only had to look around at the sad shape the world was in to realize that I could not complain. I had a job and friends, and Mr. Roosevelt had just been elected on a smidgen of hope.

A week after my birthday, I received a phone call from my father's secretary. She didn't want to alarm me, she said, but she thought it would be best if I returned home for a short visit. My father had suffered a heart attack and wanted to see me. I boarded a train that night, but in the time it took me to get to Columbus, my father died.

I don't remember being aware of other people at my father's funeral. I remember standing there, surprised at how unchanged everything seemed to be. My loneliness was more acute. I felt a lack of resolution, but I had always felt that with him. I wanted to have one more talk with him. I wanted to show him some humor and emotion. I wanted to look for it in him just one more time.

I returned to New York, got back to work, and realized what I was going through was not the only tragedy in life. Routines helped for a while, then they began wearing me down again.

Perhaps that is why I was very excited to hear from an old friend in the early days of 1933. My secretary told me a Mrs. Willig was on the line.

"Bea Willig?"

"She didn't say. I'll find out."

"No, don't bother. There is no other."

It had been seven years since the last time I'd talked with her.

"Bea Willig, my favorite older woman!" I began.

"What? Hello? George, what damn fool nonsense is that?"
"That you're old or my favorite?"
"Both." She chuckled. "Please, dear, your secretary is probably listening in."
This was Bea all right, as suspicious and easily embarrassed as ever.
"To what do I owe the pleasure of this phone call?"
"You sound older," she chided. "But that must go with your law degree and Barnes, Whatever, and Whatever."
"What is going on down there?"
"I'm building a new house. Jack talked me into it, and I must admit I'm having the time of my life."
"A big place?"
"I suppose you could say that."
"How is the family?"
There was a long pause.
"George, I want you to come down here."
"What's wrong?"
"Any number of things, but that's not why I want to see you. Jonny tells me you work with estates. I want you to draw up a will for me."
"Surely there are attorneys down there you can use."
"No one I trust. My estate is growing, and we're getting into a great many new enterprises. Jack has proved to be quite a businessman. I need some advice from you."
"Business advice or just a will?"
"Both. I need someone to look out for my interests. It's all getting rather complex."
"Has Sam gotten involved in it with you?"
"That's another problem altogether. He's not in very good shape. Tildy ran off with some low life, which is what I expected from the likes of her, and Sam's living in a horrible place. My sister Frieda is taking care of him. He won't talk with me, but Albert is living with me now. I just couldn't leave him there with the two of them. I know Sam will snap out of it if he sees you again. Won't you come?"
"Well, I do have a week's vacation coming to me."
"Are you happy with your work?"
"Not ecstatically happy."
"You're too young to file yourself away in some office. Why don't you come back down and look around? Opportunity is in the air again. I know we can work out a suitable arrangement for you."
"Hold your horses, Bea. I might be able to get vacation

time to come down to draw up a will, but I won't promise you anything else."

"That's good enough. When can you be here?"

"In a month."

"I suppose I'll have to wait."

"What is Sam's address? I'd like to write to him before I show up."

"That's a good idea. Tell me, have you seen Jonny?"

"Not in a couple of years. Haven't you?"

"I get a letter every now and then. He's out on the road for that Ruppert character. You'd think he'd spare me a day or two, but no. It's been years."

I cut her off in the middle of what seemed to be a budding tirade.

"And how is Diana?"

"George, you seem to be asking all the wrong questions. No one knows where she is. She travels with a strange pack of people. Out in California, then back here. I never know when she's going to show up. But you will come, won't you?"

"Have I ever disappointed you?"

"Not that I recall, and that's why I called today."

"I'll wire you when I leave New York."

Before she got off the phone, she gave me Sam's address, and later that afternoon I sent him a lengthy, cheerful letter to which he did not reply.

Because I did not have very much time, I decided to take my first airplane trip down to Miami. Eastern Airlines had a scheduled flight that made an interminable number of stops, and the only thing I remember about it was that I was given an air sickness bag, which I used as soon as we were airborne.

After sixteen vibrating, ear-shattering hours, we landed at the Pan American field at Northwest Thirty-sixth Street. Although I was in need of a good sleep, I decided to go directly over to Sam's apartment. I caught a cab and sat back, staring out at the place that now seemed like a second home to me. Of course, many things had changed in the intervening years. Gone were the street corner realtors; most of them were driving trucks or operating drug stores. Bungalows that had rented for 3,000 bucks a season back in the twenties were now going for $20 a month, but there was still the brilliant blue sky above, the cushion of soft, wet heat, and glimpses of splendid Miami-styled haciendas with their red-tiled roofs, moss-covered walls, and lush gardens.

They were quite a contrast to Sam's place, which was a flophouse somewhere on Sixth Street. I asked the cabbie to check the street address, but he said this was the place I wanted. Sure enough, I found Sam's name on one of the mailboxes; then I climbed the rickety stairs to an apartment on the third floor. The door was ajar. I peeked in and saw Frieda looking as grim as ever, sitting in a chair, puffing on a cigarette, reading. I knocked on the door.

"You back already?" she called out without looking up. "He's out with the kid."

I stuck my head in as she stared at me.

"Oh, it's you. I thought it was Bea's chauffeur coming to get Albert."

"How are you, Frieda?"

She studied my face for a moment, trying to place me, then snapped her fingers to get her memory going.

"The young one," she finally said. "The house guest. Don't tell me. George something or other."

"George Sloate."

"Right—come in, come in."

Sam had certainly chosen a squalid retreat for exile; there were stray bits of rattan furniture scattered about, and I noticed one of Tildy's seashell lamps on an end table, its shade tilted and burned.

"What are you doing down here?"

"Just came to see Sam."

She looked around the room. "How the mighty have fallen, huh?"

"And you, what have you been doing?"

"I came down here to help Sam out when Tildy ran off. I guess you heard about that."

I nodded.

"Yeah, she left a couple of months ago. So I came down here to help him out with the kid, but Bea swooped down and carted the poor little bugger off with her. Bea was always good at managing everyone's life, you know." She paused for a moment to pour herself a drink. "You want anything?"

"No."

"Become a teetotaler in your old age?"

"No."

"Well, you're looking pretty well fed, aren't you? What have you gotten yourself into?"

"I'm a lawyer."

"Grifter, huh? Going to Washington to work for the new administration?"

Leave it to Frieda to edge into politics the first chance she had.

"No, I don't think so," I said.

"We'll see what that blue-blooded son of a bitch Roosevelt does. Did you vote for him?"

"Where is Sam, anyway?"

"I asked you a question."

"Yes, I voted for him."

"Fat cats—he'll skin all of you alive." She was looking for a fight, but I didn't have the energy.

"You say Sam is out with Albert?"

"Back in the alley. Stick around, he'll be up in a minute."

"I think I'll go looking for him."

"Yeah, you do that," she said, turning her attention back to a newspaper lying near her chair.

Behind the rooming house was a narrow alley littered with garbage and laundry carts. At the far end of it sat Sam and Albert.

Even before I walked up to him, I could see the change in him; he weighed well over two hundred pounds, and his shoulders were stooped protectively around his chest. His trousers and shirt looked worn and unlaundered.

"Sam Willig," I called out as I walked toward him.

His head turned heavily toward me; those jovial eyes of his, once so filled with life, had all but gone dead.

"Is it you?" he said, huffing and puffing, trying to rise.

"It's me all right."

He stood there staring at my new suit and polished shoes, measuring his own defeat against my outward display of success.

"Well, look at you. City slicker *beaucoup*."

I put my arms around him and hugged him to me. He reeked of liquor and sweat.

"Don't get too close, now, you'll spoil yourself. Remember Albert?"

I looked down at the boy, who had Tildy's heavy-lidded eyes and dark complexion. When he shook my hand, he avoided looking at me.

"He's grown some, hasn't he?"

"I'll say. How old are you, Albert?"
"Twelve."
"Mama wants to pack him off to some military school or something, but we won't hear about it, will we?"
The boy shrugged, embarrassed.
"Well, George, what do you think of this?" Sam asked, waving his hand around at the lines of laundry overhead. "Couldn't call this Shalimar," he added bitterly.
"Far from it."
"The last souls on earth come to live here. How do you like that for your old man, Albert?" The boy stood there, his moody eyes darting between Sam and me. "His mother ran off."
"I heard about that."
"Who told you?"
"Bea called me."
"You up in New York now?"
"Yes. I'm with a law firm."
"My, my. Took the money you made off me and invested it in yourself. That's good," he said absent-mindedly. "Bea called you, huh? Well, she was glad to see Tildy run off. She and Jack must have had a good chuckle over that one. Just another nail in my coffin."
"You think we should talk about that in front of—"
"Don't worry about Albert here. He knows the score. Knows all about Jack—how that dirty son of a bitch did me in."
I was uncomfortable talking about it in front of Albert, so I tried changing the subject. "You're looking well, Sam."
"Don't bullshit me. I know what I look like. How come you're down here?"
"Bea asked me to draw up a will for her."
"That's a good one. Well, she's a rich woman by now. Sold me down the river, but she made a killing. Do you know how that bastard brother-in-law of mine made off with all her money?"
"Why go into that?"
"Why not? Don't you like talkin' about the good old days? Sure, you all made money off me and then left me to rot. Tildy runs off with some cardsharp from New York. Some gangster. Don't even know what his name is. Leaves the kid here. And that bastard Jack keeps movin' up. Bigger houses. You should see that damned place he's in now. I stand

outside his gates some mornings just waiting for him to come out. Just stand there—let him see what he's done to me. Start his morning off real good that way." He chuckled, but it didn't cover the self-pity he'd been wallowing in. "We'll fix him, won't we?" he said to Albert. The boy's eyes narrowed, and I couldn't tell what he was thinking. "Albert's living with Bea—did I tell you that?"

"No, she did when she called."

"What didn't she tell you, huh? How I'd come to ruin. She got you down here to save my soul, I suppose, but it's no dice, George. I ain't up for salvation. All I got is revenge on my mind. Went to the Feds about Jack, but he'd been there before me. Paid them all off. Now he thinks Repeal is just about the corner; then he'll have himself a bonafide distributorship and start buying land. Bea tell you that they're gettin' into that?"

"She mentioned something about expansion."

"Sure, that's a good word for it. She'll get you into it, too. Gets everyone in but me. . . . Do you know what came of Shalimar? Wasted, my friend. Left it to rot. Some banker has it now. Pretty soon, Jack'll buy it, throw that up in my face. That's like him." He was lost in thought, staring at Albert, regret and humiliation written all over his face. "Let's you and me get drunk, George. Albert'll wait back at the house with his aunt."

"Can't I stay here with you?" the boy asked.

"No, you go back there and wait until your grandmother's chauffeur comes. Imagine that, George, she's got herself a goddamn chauffeur."

Albert ran out of the alley.

"She's not goin' to poison my kid against me, that much I do know. I've told him everything. How all of 'em did me in," he said, pulling a flask of rotgut out of his back pocket. He offered me a drink, but I passed. "I told him how Jack got Devane killed and got my money."

"Jesus, Sam, it was all so long ago. Seven years have come and gone."

"Easy for you to say. You pulled out of here with a nice little bundle."

"I'm sorry you feel that way about me, too. Really I am." I reached out and stroked his shoulders. He started crying like a baby.

"That damn woman of mine runs off. I told you once, George, the fat boys don't get a second chance. I didn't give a damn that she was foolin' around on me. I just didn't want her to leave. I loved her."

"But you're still young, Sam. Still got those dreams of yours."

"Killed off. No second chances for me."

He looked so smug, standing there in his pain and frustration. Strange how people who've failed get so self-righteous, turning up their noses at any hint of life or vitality. I wanted to console him, but he was beginning to anger me.

"I thought you and I could talk about old times, thought maybe talking would help you, but you don't seem to want to do anything to help yourself."

"Maybe you should go wait upstairs for the chauffeur, too, then. Come back some day when you can stand the sight of me."

"Now, wait a minute. I didn't mean that."

He started lumbering away. "Sure you didn't. Just come back some other time. Don't waste yourself on me, George."

I ran over to him, draping my arm around his shoulder. "Don't turn on me, Sam, I never have harmed you and never will. You were a good friend to me. I'm just trying to help."

He looked at me with that old jaunty glint in his eyes. "Remember those binder boys all over me, everywhere I went? 'Want a fast land deal, Mr. Willig? Got a piece to trade me, Mr. Willig?' Man, I was so hot then, George. Fastest talker around. Almost talked you out of your two thousand dollars that first day you hit town, but you had to go blow it on the Mason place."

"I'll do it again, Sam. I swear I will."

"We got people coming back in here now for the winter. Depression is on, but you wouldn't know it. Just like the last time." Then his mind wandered off into a consideration of some indignity he'd suffered, some debt he had to settle. "I don't feel young any more. I've been eaten up alive. That bastard, Jack, is little more than a criminal. That's what he's done to my family. Turned them all into lowlife. I got a plan for him."

"What's that?"

"Gonna kill that bastard. Been planning it for years."

"Come off it, will you, Sam," I said nervously.

"I ain't jokin' around about it. Even Frieda says I should. Says it would serve that capitalist bastard right. So I even got history on my side. Go on up there and talk with her. She makes a lot of sense." He pushed me away from him. "Go on. Get outta here. I got too much on my mind to talk with you now."

He walked away slowly, and this time I didn't follow him.

My better judgment prevailed, and I did not go back upstairs to discuss the plight of the world with Frieda. Instead, I grabbed my bag and waited in front of the house for Bea's car. About a half hour later, a maroon Packard limousine pulled up to the curb, and a Negro driver went upstairs to fetch Albert.

He and I rode over to Bea's in silence. He was the most contained child. He had a world of ideas floating around behind those moody eyes.

"Do you like living with your grandmother?"

"It's okay."

"And you come to see your father often?"

He turned to me and came straight to the point. "Were you really in cahoots with the rest of them?"

"What do you mean?"

"What my father was talking about. How my grandmother and uncle did him in. He never said you were part of it before. I thought you were his friend."

"Your father seems to be going through a difficult time."

"You don't have to talk down to me. I'm not that much of a child. I just want to know whose side you're on."

"I didn't know war had been declared. And I wasn't talking down to you. If you want my honest opinion, I don't think your father has any right involving you in this. One thing you may learn as you get older is that sometimes it is best to just let things lie and go on from there. Sure, your father has suffered a setback, but that's no reason for him to wallow in it."

"He'll get back at them."

"There's no point to that—that's what I'm trying to tell you."

"You're wrong. If he doesn't get them, then I will."

21

Bea's new house was on the main highway in Coconut Grove. Set on about five acres and fronting the bay, it was a long, low Mediterranean structure with heavy Moorish overtones, a style that has always been very popular with the rich of southern Florida.

When we arrived, Albert disappeared. Bea was busy with a contractor in the back, and a maid in a starched black and white uniform suggested I sit in the living room to wait for her.

On the bay windows were beautiful grates that had been handcrafted in bronze, creating an underwater feeling of starfish, sea horses, plants, and tube weeds bending with the currents. All in all, a very pleasant room with its terrazzo floors and light blue and green chintz-covered chairs and sofas. Bea was certainly enjoying her new riches, but she was not overstating the point.

She joined me after a little while, and I was astounded to see how wonderfully well she looked. Wearing a pale rose Shantung dress and delicate emerald hair clips, she had the chic style of a woman half her age.

"Don't you look lovely!"

"Please," she blushed. "Don't embarrass me. What do you think?" she asked, turning around to appraise the room herself.

"Perfect."

"Not too much?"

"No, it's wonderful."

"I simply wanted it to be comfortable. Would you like a drink?"

"Bea, don't tell me you've gone over the edge of Prohibition?"

"Nonsense. Repeal will be here any day now. You know he's in town."

"Who?"

"President-elect Roosevelt. He'll be speaking at the Bayfront Park in two days."

Money or age or something had worked miracles with her. She wasn't even taking the trouble to hide her girlishness anymore.

"Now, let me look at you. Tall, blonde, and gorgeous. No wife in the wings?"

"None that I know of."

She called for the maid and ordered two daiquiris, which we took outside.

The blue green bay water lapped at the edge of her property, which had been sumptuously planted; it had a small Japanese garden near the house, majestic royal palms, a rose garden, and a gazebo near the water.

"Now you've got the water all to yourself."

She was lost in thought as she sipped her drink. "I suppose you've seen him."

"Sam?"

"He won't talk to me, you know. Why has all this happened? None of my children comes to see me. What did I do to them? I tried giving them anything they wanted. Maybe that's where I went wrong."

"Well, you have Albert with you."

"He worries me. Don't you think he's a very serious child for his age? I don't know, when I was that age I didn't have a care in the world."

I found that hard to believe—one doesn't become as cautious or methodical as Bea overnight.

"I think their lives are in their own hands now."

"We'll see." She sighed. "Whenever I see Sam I ask myself where all his suffering comes from. Was it because his father died? He's so bitter. It scares me. Is that in me as well?"

"That's hard to say."

"Of course, that wife of his is more to blame than anyone else. I told you about her the first time I met you. I know my customers, don't I?"

"I don't suppose that makes Sam feel any better. He seems to have focused all his anger on Jack."

"Jealousy—pure and simple jealousy. I'd like you to talk with Jack again. I know there is something going on between the two of you, but that should be in the past now, and I think you two would make good friends."

"He's done well for you."

She dismissed that with a flick of her hand. "We can talk about money after dinner. I know Sam is trying to turn everyone against Jack, but you shouldn't listen to him. You know we're getting into the hotel business. Jack can explain it all to you. He's been a very good son to me. Made me a very rich woman."

I reached out and took her hand. "Bea, have you tried helping Sam? An offer of money, anything?"

She bristled, retracting her hand as old defenses sprang into action. "It is not a mother's job to go begging for attention from her children. If he wants me, he knows where to find me. If he'd rather hang around with that crazy sister of mine, that's his affair. I'm not going out looking for trouble with him. You couldn't get through to him, could you?"

"No."

"Then what do you expect me to do? He's a sick man. I have no choice but to wash my hands of him. Oh, don't go thinking I'm cruel. There is nothing I can do—believe me, I tried."

And that put an end to that.

Dinner was elegant: poached red snapper in a wine broth. Albert ate with us, behaving even more cautiously when his grandmother was around. His manners were letter perfect, but he still had trouble looking me in the eye, and after dessert was cleared, he quietly left the table and did not reappear that night.

"It's time you and I got to work on my will."

"If you say so."

"I've got everything ready for you. You know I was Mr. Willig's first bookkeeper," she said, leaving the table, "so I have quite a good business sense. You wait for me in the living room, and I'll bring everything in there."

She came back lugging a bunch of ledgers, saying that I was the only one who would be privileged enough to know all there was to know about her finances. There was only one thing she wanted to make clear to me at the outset: everything she possessed was to be shared equally by her three children in the event of her death. She wanted no squabbling then. I suppose it didn't matter that they were waging war while she lived. As she offered me these keys to the kingdom, I had the distinct impression that I was being pressured into accepting something more than a will-drafting job from her. After I'd gone over her ledgers, which were indexed and cross-indexed in a manner worthy of the Library of Congress, she settled back and gloated.

"Now, what do you figure my net worth to be?" she asked.

She had been understanding the point when she said Jack had been very good to her; from what I saw, she was now worth in excess of three million dollars.

"A couple of million," I said lightly.

She sat upright and grabbed a ledger out of my hand. "Is that all? You're not very good at math. I bring it closer to three and a half."

"Was there really that much money in running booze?"

She blanched but pretended to ignore the jibe. "Now I suppose taxes will start eating away at everything."

"You've diversified."

"Of course. I'm rather shrewd when it comes down to it. I own apartments and hotels. But it's all there in front of you, George. I picked up blue chips for nothing. Got out of that dirty business before Jack did, I'll tell you that much. And another thing—I was always the one in control. Jack signed his life away to me years ago to get my money. The damned fool. I'm still in control."

"Why are you telling me all this?"

"Because I want you to help me manage it."

"I've got a job, Bea."

"At what sort of salary?"

"Seventy-five hundred a year, but I'm just starting out."

"I'll double that."

"I don't know what you want from me."

"All right, I'll pay you $17,500. Do you know how much money that is?"

"But what would I do for you?"

"You're a lawyer, aren't you? I want you to look out for my interests. Be a liaison between Jack and me. Get me into this and out of that. Simple enough."

"I don't know."

"Don't be a fool, George." She snapped the ledger shut. "Opportunities like this don't come along every day."

"There's something I want to know. Sam says Jack is little more than a criminal. I can't be involved in anything like that."

"Do you think I would? We can keep Jack in line. Devane was nothing more than a two-bit gangster, but Jack kept his nose clean. There is a lot of criminal money showing up down here, but that is not the route we're going to take. I want you to go out to the beach tomorrow and have a look at the hotel Jack bought for us. You look it over and ask Jack to show you the books. I'll arrange it. You tell me what's going on."

"I have to think about your offer."

"Of course you do, but that's exactly why I want you. You're cautious. I like that in a man. You take all the time you want. I'm patient."

She rose. Business was obviously over, so we said good night.

The next morning she was nowhere to be seen, but the limousine was waiting to take me out to the beach.

Miami certainly was prospering again. The skyline I'd left in '26 had been a deserted wreck of twisted girders, but now all those buildings on Flagler had been completed. Out at the beach were the first signs of what was to become "hotel row" north of the Roney Plaza.

The driver pulled up to a hotel called the Aztec; an art deco palace with prismatic sunset reliefs on pale white stucco. Thunderbird designs were painted on the exterior walls and inset above the doorways. Standing next to the gates at the base of the driveway was Sam, looking shabby and unshaven. I told the driver to stop.

"Sam—what are you doing?"

He squinted up at me. "Going to do business with him?" He wore a wrinkled suit that might have fit a man fifty pounds thinner. He was bleary-eyed, I thought I saw a flask in his jacket pocket.

"Got yourself the limousine now, too. Go on, go see him. You're no better than the rest!"

I got out of the car, tried reasoning with him, but he ran away from me. "Don't tell me any of your stories, George. I've heard them all. Go on. Go do your business. Just remember that I'm out here watching."

I stood there staring incredulously as he walked away.

Jack spotted me as soon as I entered the lobby.

"What's happened to you?" he asked.

"It's Sam."

"Is he out there again? He won't leave me alone."

When we walked outside, Sam was still standing at the base of the drive shaking his fist and mumbling to himself.

"I'm sorry about this," Jack said. "I know you don't think too much of me, but I didn't do anything to Sam. I swear I didn't."

"I think that's beside the point. He's in trouble."

"Sam!" he called out.

Sam's head reared up like a wounded animal's. "Don't you summon me, you son of a bitch. I don't work for you."

Several hotel guests stared in shock, then hurried along the paths leading to the beach.

"There is no reasoning with him. Come inside. I've got a business to run. If we stay out here, he'll never let up."

As we walked through the lobby, guests greeted him. Jack appeared to be very pleased with himself.

"This is a lot less risky than other ventures I've been in. Bea and I are starting out very slowly with this hotel so that I can get the lay of the land. She says you want to look over the books."

I couldn't talk business with Sam standing out there like that. "What are we going to do with him, just leave him out there all day?"

"Forget about it. Say, George, we could use a sharp young lawyer." He stopped near the entrance to his office. "You don't like me very much, do you?"

I was suddenly at a loss for words.

"You think I'm the worst one in the bunch, but you're wrong about me. Regardless of what you've heard or who you've heard it from, I didn't set up Devane!"

I knew he was lying, but I didn't care. Perhaps the years were mellowing me, or Jack seemed to be supremely rational in contrast with Sam's ranting and raving. Suddenly I didn't give a good goddamn who'd set Devane up; the world was just a little bit better off lacking him in it.

"You're not talking very much today, George."

I nodded.

"Getting pretty bored up there in New York?"

"You people always had a talent for action. It's tantalizing."

He stood there, puffing on a cigarette, surveying his little kingdom. "I like this business. Selling people a fantasy for a couple of weeks. Although I confess I don't know where these stiffs get their money these days."

Parading by just then were two swarthy hoods with goons in tow.

"Oh, we get them in here," Jack mused. "Old friends of mine, but they're more like decoration than anything else. The swells love rubbing elbows with a little danger."

"You've got a taste for that as well."

"You've got me pegged all wrong. What I was running was a clean operation. Sure I made a bundle on booze, but I never got involved with any of those hoods. Hell, Sam was into them more than I was."

"Sam?"

"Sure, you remember a character named Stanley Jawitz?"

Remember him? There wasn't a night when I didn't thank my lucky stars for him; he'd helped me make the bundle that had paid my way through law school.

"What about him?"

"Stanley is a front for the big league hoods. How do you think he made all that money he was always waving around? Fronting for them. In Shalimar, in any number of operations. Still works for them down in Havana, running their gambling joints. I expect good old Stanley will show up here again one fine day now that the hotel business is picking up."

We strolled out onto the beach. Tourists were sunning themselves, running in and out of the water, jabbering like crows. I looked behind my shoulder and saw Sam following us at a safe distance.

"Sam's still there."

Jack didn't even flinch. "Forget about him," he said, walking down to the water.

"Where is Diana?"

He stared out, a grim expression registering in those tired-looking eyes. "God knows. That's how I pay, George. She's a penance I'm serving."

"She'll come around to her senses."

"You think so? I gave up waiting."

I turned and stared up the beach at Sam, who was fumbling through his jacket pockets, looking for his flask, I thought. But the maniac pulled out a revolver and aimed it in our direction.

"He's coming after us!" Jack turned and saw it, too.

"Sam, don't be crazy!"

"Don't tell me what to do. You ruined my whole life, and you'll pay for it!"

That crazy bastard clutched the gun with both hands, closed his eyes, and pulled the trigger. A shot whizzed past my shoulder, pumping the shallow water behind me. I looked for cover, but we were out in the middle of the beach with nowhere to hide.

"Put that thing away, you lunatic!" Jack yelled.

He charged us, cursing, eyes crazed as he crouched and

sent off another shot. Jack and I hit the sand and began crawling toward the cabanas. Guests were screaming by this time, pouring out of the hotel to see what was happening.

"He's gonna kill us," I whispered.

"Hell, that dumb bastard couldn't hit the side of a barn. Just keep down. I'll get him."

Another shot landed with a thud in the sand beside me as Jack got to his feet and tried to rush him.

Several busboys had circled behind Sam who looked panic-stricken as he tried to steady the gun. He fired one more shot, which caught Jack in the shoulder. Jack stumbled to the sand, groaning, holding his hand over the wound.

Sam suddenly threw his gun away and then bolted up the beach. Blind fear or rage, I couldn't tell which, seized me as I got to my feet and sprinted after him. All that weight he'd put on slowed him down considerably, and I gained on him in no time, lunging at his feet, grabbing his ankles, bringing him down on top of me as we struggled in the surf, turning over and over until I pinned him and held him.

"Let me go!" he wailed.

"Now you've gone and done it."

"Did I kill him?"

"You're goddamn crazy."

"Did I kill him?"

"No, you didn't kill him," I screamed, my face just inches above his. "Now they'll lock you up for good."

"I wanted him dead."

"You hit him all right, but he's alive. Damned lucky for you."

"I want him dead."

I shook his head until I thought it would roll off.

"All these years it's been your problem, Sam, not his. They didn't set out to destroy you. It was business. That's all it was. Take your goddamned life into your own goddamned hands." I went on like that for what seemed like an eternity until help finally arrived and men pulled me off him. But he hadn't heard a word I said. When they got him to his feet, he spit in my face.

"I would have killed you, too."

Once again I became an indispensable member of the Willig family, trying to calm nerves, keep the story out of the papers, and sort through this mess. Jack was out of the hospital that night. I tried contacting Diana, but no one knew where she was, and I doubted that she'd care enough to come home to take care of him. That wasn't the biggest problem. Sam was the problem. What to do with him? Where to put him?

Bea did not want this ending up in a courtroom, so I played go-between, arguing with Jack, who finally agreed not to press charges, and cajoling the cops, who were once again more than eager to be plied with Bea's money. My biggest problem was with the press boys, who were always on the lookout for a juicy scandal, but a better story cropped up that saved the family from notoriety.

President-elect Roosevelt had been on a fishing trip aboard Vincent Astor's yacht, the *Nourmahal.* On February 15 the town was buzzing with excitement because Roosevelt was scheduled to make an appearance at the Bayfront Park. Crowds of people had been gathering there all day waiting for him. In the crowd was a thin, angry-looking Italian named Zangara who was concealing a hammerless .32-caliber, five-shot revolver and a wealth of anger and resentment for the rich and powerful Roosevelt.

The president-elect made a short speech about his fishing trip and then began handshaking with politicians who happened to be in the area. One was Anton Cermak, mayor of Chicago, who had just reached the car to pose for pictures when suddenly two shots rang out in the crowd. Zangara was running through it firing wildly. Three more shots were fired as Secret Service men threw themselves over the president. The crowd went after the Italian, almost killing him.

Needless to say, this kept the news machine blazing for days. The president-elect was unharmed, but Cermak, who had been hit, died several weeks later.

While all this was going on, Sam remained in the county jail.

Jack and Bea and I finally decided on a course of action; Sam was to be released in Bea's custody, and she arranged to have him put away in a psychiatric facility with an alarmingly reassuring name, La Hacienda. All of this was accomplished swiftly before anyone but the family knew what had happened.

The day he was taken away, Bea sat in her living room questioning herself about what had gone wrong and why this had happened to her. There was nothing I could say to comfort her.

"He's being taken care of now. You've done the right thing."

"Where are Jon and Diana when I need them? The whole lot of them—useless."

Albert, who had been sitting quietly in a corner, finally said, "Why can't I see him?"

"George, take him outside. You talk with him."

Albert glared defiantly at me. "Don't you touch me. You tell me where my father is."

Bea lost control. "This is your home now. There will be no talking about what has happened and no mention of your father. He's disgraced this family."

The rage in Albert's eyes was all too familiar. It frightened me. In the end, Sam would win—he'd passed on all his resentment, and Albert kept it quietly buried inside under layers of acquiescence, moodiness, and manners that I never trusted.

I walked out of the house in search of comic relief, which was conveniently supplied to me by Frieda, who was at that very moment skulking around the garden chugging vodka. I padded across the lawn to the gazebo where she was sitting. When she saw me, she winked drunkenly.

"Some place," she said.

"This is a very sad day."

"Oh, don't be so frigging grim, George. It's just more of the same. Have a drink."

I took the bottle.

"More of the same shit—it all boils down to shit, don't you know that by now?"

"Not in those terms exactly."

She laughed. "It's the winding-down process. Bea is at the tail end of civilization, that's her problem. Accumulation of fortunes, perversity, the beginnings of empires." She squinted up at the sun. "It's too hot for an empire."

"Marx in Miami."

"Fortunes made and lost. What do you think that produces after a while? Little more than crime in the streets for the lower classes and limp dandyism for the upper. So Bea comes from heartier stock, and hers produces insanity in the second generation. What can I tell you? Jews are ahead of their time."

"I'm trying to follow you—"

"Come on, George, say it—shit. You can smell it in the air."

"That's oleander, I believe."

"Smart talking white man," she groaned, retrieving the bottle. "Bea wants to overachieve—let her have what comes with it. Don't feel sorry for her. Feel sorry for yourself. You're so young, and here you are hopping on a doomed train."

"Is the train called the *Civilization Express* by any chance?" I asked smiling broadly.

She gave a wink of recognition. Had she met her match? I don't know. She took another drink and trundled off. "Banter, banter, banter. So smart, George. So frigging smart."

Malcontented, irritable old cretin. Hopping trains, indeed (I was feeling arch by that time). Watching her walk off, slugging down vodka, spewing *Das Kapital* in the Japanese garden.

I left the next day without having decided what to do about Bea's generous offer to board the train on its downward spiral.

22

I eased back into the humdrum life at the office, routines I walked through with zombielike proficiency. When fall arrived, I decided I'd had enough of it, and it gave me great pleasure to tell my superiors I was leaving. The next day I called Bea.

"I've decided to take you up on your offer."

"Good. I have something very important for you to do," she said as if she knew all along that I'd be going to work for her. "Are you ready for a vacation?"

"Is this going to be business or pleasure?"

"Both, if you play your cards right. Jon will be down in Havana scouting acts for his damned circus. I want you to go down there and bring him back to Miami."

"Have you been in touch with him?"

"Yes, but he won't give me a definite answer."

Not bad for a first assignment, I thought. I agreed to fly down to Miami and from there hop a boat to Havana as soon as I tied up loose ends in New York.

Havana was called the Pearl of the Antilles in those days. It was a bit too pristine a nickname for my first impressions. The city was more like a glorious old harlot squatting over the sea. When I first saw it, I was standing at the deck rail of the tourist boat I'd boarded in Miami. A bunch of farm equipment salesmen from Duluth, dressed in Sears Roebuck sharkskin, were on deck as well. Each had his pink tourist card waving in the balmy breeze. They rib-poked and joshed me all the way into the harbor.

"They got sex shows," the red-faced one nearest me said. "Live ones and movies!" he added for emphasis.

"You down here on business?" I inquired.

"I plan to be on the buyin' end this time," he said, exchanging benignly lecherous snickers with his friends. "Live sex shows, imagine that. Those mulatto broads spreadin' the wide and pearlies for a buck with a tool the size of Lake Erie."

"Won't put you to shame, Henry," Henry's companion offered.

"Where you stayin'?" Henry asked.

"The Nacional."

"First class. I like a man who travels first class. We're bunkin' in at some el cheapo. Thank god the missus ain't with me, or she'd have me spendin' like a sailor on the goddamn room. No dice, I told her. Not with her this time. Gonna drink rum and sneak a peek at the Chinese Quarter. You heard about it?"

"Can't say as I have."

"My buddy from back home says they got two theaters there"—he searched through his pockets for a piece of paper, which he read—"called the Shanghai and the Venus. Show blue movies."

"Interesting."

"I'll say. But first I'm hoppin' over to Sloppy Joe's and get tanked on some Bacardi. Why don't you come along with us?"

"I'm afraid I can't. I've got business to attend to. But thanks for the offer."

"Well, we'll probably see you around. Gonna gamble?"

"Maybe."

"Well, don't be a stiff. All work and no play, you know."

I assured them I would do my bit of debauchery to uphold the role of the American male in Latin America. They sauntered off, laughing like delinquent schoolboys. I wondered how many of them would return home with a dose of the clap, and what they would say to the missus when she got it.

The Nacional was the grand hotel of Havana, attracting the rich of Miami who had a penchant for gambling and the murkier side of life. It was a wide, low hacienda structure with lush gardens filled with flame red poinsettias and the heavy scent of Chinese lily trees. As I stood at the registration desk, I heard someone calling my name.

"George. George Sloate is that you?"

Thin, nervous, shifty-eyed Stanley Jawitz, like Lazarus, was back from the dead, running through the lobby toward me.

"What on earth are you doing down here?" he called out.

"Down on business," I said as he shook my hand. "Long time no see, Stanley. I heard you wound up here after the Shalimar fiasco."

"Fiasco? Why say that? You didn't lose any money on it, did you?"

"Not really, but I heard you were wiped out."

He jumped around like a puppet on a string. "Not me, old man. I land on my feet."

"I wish I could say the same for Sam."

"Yeah, I heard. Good news travels fast. You seen him yet?"

"He's locked away—no one sees him."

"The kid told me all about it. He's down here, you know."

"Who's that?"

"Jon Willig—the youngest one. What a hustler he turned into. Breezes in here looking like a million, gives press conferences. Wines 'em and dines 'em. I'm impressed. You staying here?"

"I'm trying to register."

He stepped up to the desk and exchanged some garbled Spanish with the man on duty. The clerk rang a bell, and a bellboy carried my bags over to one of the elevators.

"Got friends all over this town," Jawitz said expansively. "You have any trouble here, you just mention my name. Come on, I'll buy you a drink."

"I need my key."

"Don't sweat it—it's all taken care of."

We walked through a long corridor with thick glass windows that had tiny perforations in them.

"Bullet holes, in case you're wondering," Stanley said out of the corner of his mouth. "When Batista came in last September, he lined up his enemies on the back lawn and did away with his opposition overnight. He's playing ball, though. Smart man, Batista."

We sat in a room filled with ferns and white rattan furniture. Stanley ordered something called a *mojita criolla* for us.

"What's that?"

"Rum, vermouth, sugar, lemon, and *yerba buena. Muy buena.* Hell, after the third one you won't give a damn what's in it."

When it arrived, I concurred; it was sweet and lethal.

"What are you up to these days?" I asked.

His eyes darted around the room. "Right now, I guess you could call me a sales agent for an American company."

"Which one?"

"Molister."

"Never heard of it."

"You clean-cut types slay me," Jawitz said, his fingers tapping nervously on the table. "Prohibition company from New Jersey. We're down here buying molasses for booze. We'll be as legal as General Motors when Repeal comes in. Cuba's got a lot of molasses. We're getting real friendly with Batista. Keep the supply coming—you know what I mean?"

"You have a piece of the company?"

"I'm strictly an employee. You may have heard of my boss, Mort Lister."

Who hadn't. He was as shadowy a figure as there had ever been on the American crime scene. Mr. Lister had recently made the newspapers in connection with some bloody business involving a buddy of his, Lucky Luciano.

"Nice company you keep, Stanley."

"He's one of Batista's closest friends."

"You fronted for him in Miami, didn't you?"

"Who told you that?"

"Just local gossip."

"Yeah, I did some work for him. Made you a nice bundle with it, didn't I?"

It seemed to me that no matter how hard I tried, I was

bound to get my skirts dirty. I wondered what Barnes, Thatcher and Stokes would say if they knew I'd bankrolled my law career with Mort Lister's front money.

"We're getting into a lot down here. Brought in gambling at the Nacional."

"None of this newspaper talk about Lister and Luciano and Bugsy Siegal bothers you?"

"Don't get so uppity, George. It's business. What kind of business are you doing down here?"

"I'm working for Bea Willig."

"I hear she and Jack made some killing on the booze from Bimini," he said emphatically to show me how clean my money smelled to him. "Into the hotel business now?"

"Something like that."

"So you're looking into Havana for her."

"No."

"I'll give Jack Chason a lot of credit. He kept himself pretty clean after he got rid of Devane. What are you doing for them?"

"Looking for Jon Willig at the moment. I'm supposed to meet him."

"Funny he didn't mention it to me."

"You've met with him?"

"Sure, he's down here to talk with me. We got a lot of money to spread around, and Jon seems to be in the market."

"I thought he was down here on circus business."

"I guess you could call it that."

"Is Ruppert with him?"

"Jon calls him the recluse. The old man never leaves that house of his. No, Jonny's trying to raise some capital for a project of his own. We're pretty interested in it."

My pulse raced. If Jon had thrown in with that lot, he'd be a goner, and Bea would wind up blaming me for losing him.

"Lister, too?"

"I can't really talk about it, George. But you can find Jon around. He's got himself a suite on the top floor."

Business conversation stopped, so we bantered on about the good old days in Miami. Then Stanley made my pulse race for the second time.

"You know the sister is down here, too?"

"Diana?"

"That her name? Strange broad. Jon and I ran into her the other night. Seems like they hadn't seen each other in years."

After Jawitz and I finished our second round, I staggered upstairs and promptly fell asleep.

The telephone next to my bed was doing an unmerciful thing—it was ringing. I propped myself up and stared at it as if I'd never seen one before. I prayed it would stop. My mouth felt like cotton, and I cleared my throat before answering.

"Hello."

"George, you old swine." It was Jon sounding a bit too energetic for my frame of mind. "Stanley Jawitz told me you were here."

"I'm not too sure I am."

"He get you loaded on Bacardis?"

"Something like that."

"Get some clothes on and come upstairs. I had people up here, but I'm clearing the place out for you."

"Give me about a year to pull myself together."

"I'll give you fifteen minutes."

The last remnants of Jon's party were straggling out of his suite into the hallway when I got up there. A decidedly curious collection of beautiful Cuban demimonde—two men and a woman with pale honey skin. It looked as though Jon was paying dearly for his pleasures these days. He was rather embarrassed when he saw me with them in the hall.

"Right this way, George," he said, tucking his shirttail into his pants as he ushered me into the living room.

"Quite a crew," I muttered.

He was not interested in my observations.

"Can I get you a drink?"

"Never again."

"Fight fire with fire. Let me look at you. You look wonderful," he said, mixing up some rum concoction at the bar.

"And you do look like a million."

He smiled that effortless grin, still looking boyish, his skin burnished like copper.

He handed me a drink, and we settled into about ten minutes of small talk.

Like most men, Jon had concocted a good story for himself. It kept him going through good and bad times, and it had all to do with his being a raconteur and sophisticate, a driven businessman and ardent lover. But I knew him better, and there was no mistaking his edginess that night. I finally grew tired of our badinage and launched a frontal assault.

"What's all this nonsense about you hooking up with Mort Lister and Jawitz?"

"Stanley does shoot his mouth off, doesn't he?" he said without blinking an eye. "You getting prissy on me, George?"

"I'm on no crusade. We're friends, and I don't want to see you doing something stupid like that."

"It's a long story."

"I've got all night. The last time we saw each other you told me you were biding your time. Has your time come?"

"Something like that. It's Ruppert."

"What happened to him?"

"He's a lunatic. He was in hock for a million and a half because of that Palladino deal, but that wasn't enough for him. He went off to Sotheby's the next year and bought the place out. He's got nothing left. Now he's sick. Doctors say it's his heart. He's overextended and about to default on the note. My time *is* ripe, George."

"What's your plan?"

"I'm down here trying to line up financing to buy the note from the people who are holding it so that when he defaults, the show will wind up in my lap. You should see what I've done with the circus, George. Revamped it, added acts. Fantastic profit potential, but the old coot is sucking it dry. We had to close down in September because of him. He's got to step down."

"Do you honestly think you'll be a free agent if you get involved with a killer like Lister?"

"Lister doesn't bother me. Where else am I supposed to go to raise money like that?"

"Have you tried New York?"

"I don't trust them."

"But you'll trust a bunch of hoods."

"They've got the money, George. Not too much of that around these days. Those prohibition boys are the only ones who are looking to bankroll operations like mine."

"Is it already yours?"

"Just inches away. I've got all the information I need, detailed lists of Ruppert's holdings—the works. If I can pull this off, the whole thing falls in my lap."

"He won't go down without a fight."

"He has no other option. Anyway, I won't be doing it. My corporation will. Circus Investments. You like that?"

I shook my head.

"You can help me, George. I need a lawyer like you now."

"Oh, I can help you, all right, but not on those terms. Not with the likes of Lister and his cronies. I've got other plans for you."

"What's that?"

"Have you forgotten your first plan—the one you made years ago up at the Plaza?"

"You mean my mother? I haven't forgotten. I've reconsidered. She doesn't have that kind of money. And as far as my mother is concerned, I've run off with the circus, and I'll be home for dinner any minute now."

"You're wrong. She wants to see you, and she thinks more of you than that. She's a rich woman now, Jon."

He smiled, his eyes trying to reveal little, but he seemed nervous. "Is that why you're down here?"

"I'm working for her now as a liaison between family members. I might be able to put a deal together for you, but you've got to promise me that you'll stall Jawitz and Lister. Give me time to talk with her. Then you and I will go up to Miami and present a business opportunity to her. But I'm warning you, it better be good. She's a tough negotiator."

"Then she'll have me back under her thumb again."

"Don't be a fool. You should know that she can't do that to you."

"Couldn't do it to Sam, either, that poor bastard."

"It was his fault. Don't forget that. He let her do it, and don't forget something else. He's out of his mind."

"Lovely bunch of people." He sat there nursing his drink. "Jawitz keeps pressuring me to make up my mind. I don't know. I don't want Jack involved in this."

"Don't worry about that. Bea says she can handle Jack, and I believe her."

"Jawitz wants us to go out partying with him tonight. I said we would. Give me tonight to think this over." He got up and stretched. "Enough business talk. Get your dancing shoes on. I'll give you a taste of those ardent Cuban nights. Got a surprise for you, too."

"Is her name Diana?"

"Stanley ruined it. Still carrying the torch?"
"That's your married sister we're talking about."
"I'm a very open-minded person, George."

Stanley Jawitz met us downstairs and drove us to the outskirts of town to a district known as *La Frita,* which was the Cuban equivalent of Coney Island. We bar-hopped for a while and then settled into some serious drinking at a dance hall called *Los Tres Hermanos* where, Stanley assured us, we'd see the best rumba dancers in Havana.

He was not exaggerating; we saw the best dancers and the most beautiful prostitutes. Sloe-eyed boys offered the trade as girls with pale copper skin and kohl-darkened eyelids sauntered past us. When the rumba band picked up the tempo, the floor was cleared. A lithe golden women and a coal black Negro began dancing. Their movements were slow and steamily erotic. He swayed with her, held her hands behind her back. She laughed softly as he dipped her, grazing her neck with his teeth.

Through all of this, the Cuban men sat watching, nursing their drinks. They were self-contained and expressionless, with casual lips and graceful, cruel hands.

As more dancers filled the floor, Jon's eyes were trained on the original two, his face flushed with excitement.

"Which of those two dancers would you pay for the pleasure?" I asked.

"Don't you know me well enough by now, George? I'll take both."

A group of rich American tourists walked in, laughing, carrying champagne glasses, passing around a bottle of Moët. Diana was with them on the arm of a large, raven-haired woman."

"Here's your surprise," Jon said and then drew in his breath excitedly. "My God, she's with Treach!"

"Your Treach?"

"That woman shows up in the most unexpected places."

Diana was laughing. Her hair was longer, falling to her shoulders in loose golden waves. Her dress was pearl white satin, cut low in front and in back and held up by tiny straps.

"Olga. Diana. Over here," Jon called, standing and waving to them.

When she saw me, Diana stopped halfway between the

dance floor and our table. She laughed again, pointed at me, but remained where she was. I was obviously a pleasure she hadn't counted on that night.

"*La Belle* Jon," Olga Treach bellowed as she hugged Jon to her. "Of all people. What on earth are you doing here?"

"I could ask the same of you and more. You're with my sister."

Treach was momentarily stunned and stared back at Diana standing alone on the dance floor.

"Of course," Olga said. "The eyes. I should have known it immediately. My darling, tell me all. Introduce me. Diana, come join us."

She wouldn't move. I excused myself and walked up to her. "Diana, you look beautiful."

For that, she offered me the rest of her champagne.

"One thing about me, dreamy boy, I survive."

I toasted her. "To survival."

Her hand brushed through my hair as her face softened into the loveliest, bemused expression. Perhaps she was thinking about a night so many years ago when she'd touched my hair like that and made me fall in love with her.

"You never change," she whispered. "So innocent and fine looking. Has my prediction come true? Have I come back to haunt you?"

"Always."

"Oh, that's good to hear. I need to hear that."

We stood there for a moment staring at each other.

"You've been traveling."

"The wandering Jewess. So many stories, George. So many things come back to haunt me."

"But tonight we're having a party, and there's no need to talk about it."

She stared over my shoulder at her brother and the Treach woman, who were now chattering away with each other like two sparrows.

"They know each other?"

I nodded.

She squinched up her nose. "You're right as always, George. No need to go into my craziness now. But there is a long, sad story I have to tell you. I think you'll appreciate it. Perhaps later."

We started inching our way through the crowded dance floor toward the table.

"How did you wind up with Olga Treach?"

"She leeched onto some friends of mine. Been traveling with us for a month now." She stopped suddenly, twisting her head around to stare at me. A stray lock of hair fell across her forehead.

"You know all about my craziness, don't you, George? You know too much."

"You never change, either, Diana," I said lightly, losing myself in her eyes.

"I always think it's wonderful when people do not let on how crazy they really are."

"But surely they do in private. You never know what's going on inside."

"I know that, but hopefully they don't expose it to us—that's what I mean. So if we don't see it, it doesn't affect us. I'm always glad when people keep it to themselves and present a decent front."

She headed off toward the table again, the sweet scent of gardenias trailing after her.

"This is hardly a joyous reunion," Treach cooed after Jon and Diana stiffly kissed each other's cheeks.

"We had a nice long talk the other night," Diana said.

"And who are *you?*" Treach asked me.

"I'm the friend."

"That's oblique enough." She sat back staring at Diana and Jon.

"Will you just look at the two of them. Enough beauty to blind the eye. You two should go around together—you'd get the most amusing offers."

"I prefer to travel alone always," Jon said.

"But we've all gone South, haven't we, dear?" Treach smiled covetously, stroking Diana's arm.

"Have you been a naughty girl, Diana?" Jon teased.

"I always get in with the worst sort of people," she said, staring Treach down.

"Well, perhaps you should take a rest. I can recommend an excellent masseuse."

"That's a very generous suggestion, Jon," Diana shot back.

A deadly silence fell over the table. Treach felt compelled to remove it, and she began talking nervously. Her words curled up in the air, as insubstantial as cigarette smoke. All of us were waiting for her to say something of value, but all she said were things like, "I've read so much that I don't have to read for the next ten years." Or: "You know what Machiavelli said, 'I am as I appear.'" Or: "You know what Oscar

Wilde said about youth. . . ." But she didn't follow up on youth or Wilde or anything at all. Just talk and more talk.

"Will you look at those gorgeous Cubans. How much do you think they cost?"

That did it. It was a bit too jaded for my blood. I excused myself to join Stanley Jawitz, who was standing at the bar by himself.

"Still drinking rum?" he asked.

"I'll drink anything."

"The addled rich getting on your nerves?"

"How very philosophical of you, Stanley. Yeah, I'll drink anything with rum in it."

"What have you been sayin' to the kid?"

"To Jon?"

"Yeah, I think you came down here to queer this deal for me. I don't like it, George. He's not half as interested in my money since you arrived."

"Don't blame that on me. I don't mean to insult you, but I'm taking my drink outside."

Off I went in a huff, planting myself under the first palm tree I could find, where I stared up at that ardent Cuban sky.

In a little while Jon and Treach came piling out of the dance hall with some of the other Americans in tow. Diana was not with them, and Jon was a little tight. He was being lead by the Treach harpy, who spotted me and came running over to my palm tree.

"Up for some fun?" she asked.

"No."

"We're going to prowl the streets."

"What a lovely turn of phrase," I spat out at her.

"How bizarre! You sitting out here looking gloomy and romantic. And Diana sitting inside looking gloomy and rheumatic. You are quite a pair."

"What in God's name do you know about romance?"

"A drunken non sequitur if I ever heard one."

"Get out of here."

"You're unfriendly and oblique."

"Away." I closed my eyes, hoping she'd vanish.

"I will, but not before I lay one pearl of wisdom at your feet, my dear. It has to do with men and women."

"Which is?"

"If we women hadn't been built to be screwed by you,

you'd probably be out in the forests hunting us. Good night."

I struggled to my feet. "Jon! Ditch this group of vile climbers!" I screamed.

He smiled drunkenly as he was pulled into a convertible.

"You take it too seriously," he said and then sped off.

Diana stood in the doorway, framed by the light of the honky-tonk.

"Left us to fend for ourselves," she said softly. "Let's walk on the beach. Isn't there one around here?"

I grabbed her hand, and we went off in search of it.

We walked along some deserted stretch of sand near the water's edge. She ran ahead of me, and when I caught up to her, I encircled her with my arms, pinning hers to her sides. My tongue grazed over her neck as she quivered, and I longed to dive into the heart of her again, to get lost in the smell of her perfume.

"I really did sting you, didn't I, George?"

"I want you now more than ever."

"I took you for granted," she whispered. "I'm sorry I did that."

One of my arms released her. I slipped a satin strap from her shoulder. My fingers traced lines from her collarbone across her chest. I bent my head forward, licking her nipple until it puckered up in my mouth.

"Took you for granted. How I paid for that."

Gently pushing herself free, she stood staring up at me. "You make me feel so lovely. I thank you for that." She walked away from me. "I want to tell you a story. . . . I fell in love last year for the first time."

"What do you mean?"

"I met him in California. A poet."

"How perfect for you," I said lightly, but my stomach knotted.

"Yes. Romantic. Will you listen to my story?"

I nodded.

"We traveled together. He had the most soulful face. Fine bones, just the hint of a cleft in his chin, and this wild mane of hair. Golden brown with streaks of gray in it. His face was so innocent-looking, although he tried covering that up with these impenetrable stares. He didn't fool me. I know all about impenetrable stares. I saw right through him. He was the most sensitive lover I've ever known. He loved me, George," she said again as if I wouldn't believe that were possible. "He wrote me the most fabulous letters all about how we'd run away together and lock out the rest of the world.

"He was the son of a rich Jew. His father wanted him to be a banker or something, but this boy only wanted to write. The father paid him off, and so he traveled. Did I tell you he took me to France last summer? We had a yellow touring car down in Provence where we leased a house for a month in a town called L'Isle sur la Sorgues. In the afternoons I'd sit on a stone bench brushing my hair, and he'd be circling around me, snapping pictures with this funny little box camera he'd bought. . . ."

She looked so sad I wanted to stop her.

"I couldn't accept it. I began smoking opium all day. I tested him constantly. I lied. I told him I tried killing myself, told him I was sick. Then the headaches began again. After a while he said he couldn't watch me destroy myself. . . . I lost him. . . . He tried comforting me for a while, but I accused him of hating me. I told him he was glad to see me like that. I convinced him that he hated me. And now I want to die."

"Don't talk nonsense," I said, taking her in my arms again.

"I just want to die thinking about him."

"Why don't you go after him?"

She smiled ruefully. "The sad thing is that he'd want me again."

I kissed her gently.

"Why have I done this to myself?"

I had no answer.

"Will you make love to me?" she asked.

I eased the straps of her dress from her shoulders. It slithered off and lay like a shimmering boa on the sand. My hands stroked her. She closed her eyes and kissed me.

"Let me lie under you. I will only think about him for a little while. Then I'll get lost in you, George. I swear I will."

We made love at the beach, and then I brought her back to my room where we slept, wrapped around each other in careless harmony, like two satisfied children.

When I awakened in the morning, she was gone.

23

By mid-morning I gave up any thought of going after her or trying to locate her. Instead, I placed a call to Bea in Miami and sat waiting patiently for it to get through. The connection was made by noon.

"Have you found him?" she asked.

"We talked yesterday."

"And?"

"He's down here on circus business all right; he wants to buy it."

"Ruppert's?"

"It seems the old man is in hock to a New York group. He's about to default on a note, and Jon wants to buy the note and take over when Ruppert goes under."

"What do you think about it?"

"It's hard to say. Jon says there is a lot of money to be made. He's revamped the show, but I don't like where he's going to get his capital."

"What do you mean?"

"Does the name Mort Lister ring a bell?"

"My God! He's not in with that bunch?"

"Pretty close to signing a deal with them."

"You get him back here."

"Bea, I told him you might put up the money."

"Why did you do that?"

"The Show of The Century made Simon Ruppert a very rich man. He may be in bad shape now, but I think Jon can turn a profit on it."

"You just bring him back here, then we'll talk."

"He wants some kind of a commitment."

"Listen, George, you just tell him to come home and talk with his family before making any rash moves."

"Can I pin you down to a definite answer?"

"No. I'll see you in a couple of days."

I met Jon for lunch and told him to hold off on any agreements with Jawitz until he talked with his mother. I suppose my little speech about Lister had gotten to him, for he was amenable to my idea. We arranged to leave Havana the next day.

That night I went out looking for Diana. Jon said she was staying aboard some friend's yacht, but when I checked the dock listings, I discovered that the yacht had left for Barbados that afternoon.

The next morning I packed and went to pay my bill.

"Señor Jawitz has already taken care of that for you," the bellman said.

"Jawitz? I won't hear of it." I took out my billfold and placed my cash on the counter. I did not want to be even remotely indebted to him any more. "Do you have a piece of paper and an envelope?"

He slid them across the desk, and I wrote Jawitz the following note:

Stanley:

Thank you so much for the thought, but I have already paid for my room. Please check your statement when you leave. I'd hate to think you were double-billed.

Cordially,
George Sloate

Bea's driver met us at the dock and drove us directly over to her house. Jack was standing in the driveway when we pulled up.

"Well, will you look at the prodigal son," he said nervously, appraising Jon.

"How are you, Jack?"

"Can't complain. Oh, we had some trouble a while back with Sam, but I'm all right now."

Jon sailed passed him, looking for his mother. I saw her peering through the grates on her living room windows.

"I saw Diana in Cuba," Jon said lightly. Jack lit a cigarette.

"Where is mother?"

"Inside, waiting for you."

Bea was in the living room. A queen receiving an errant subject was what I thought she'd be playing, but when Jon walked up to her, she melted and hugged him warmly.

"How could you have stayed away so long?" She held him

at arms' length. "Just like your father. Do you know that? Just like him." She stared at his face as if it were a landscape she were about to paint; then she turned to Jack and me. "You two make yourselves busy somewhere. I want to talk with my son."

Jack and I sat by the bay drinking, talking. Occasionally we'd look up and see Bea and Jon walking near us but taking no notice of us. My bitter feelings for Jack had continued to mellow. I found myself feeling sorry for him. He was an anxious man, obviously controlled by Bea, trying as best he could to run his growing empire and not rock the boat. He told me he wanted to have children, but that was impossible with Diana. I asked him why he hadn't divorced her, and he shrugged, saying he loved her and that when she was finished with her travels and love affairs she always came back to him to be comforted by him. I could easily empathize with him. Both of us were involved with the impossible idea of possessing her. I suppose it was enough for him to have some sort of legal claim to her, but for me it was an endless series of frustrations—to have her and then lose her again so quickly. Perhaps it kept me safe, kept me from entering the world or risking my emotions. I wanted to stop questioning it.

Jon and Bea spent the next couple of days together. It wasn't until the third night of my stay that I learned from Jon that she was willing to provide him with the funds to go up to New York to buy the note and take over the circus.

"But how did you manage it?" I asked as he sat on my bed recounting his talks with her.

"She says I'm most like her. She doesn't want to stand in my way."

"Tell me everything."

"She keeps scrapbooks about me—newspaper clippings from all over. As soon as we were alone, I told her what my plans were, but she kept fencing with me, changing the subject, steering away from business. She wanted to tell me things about herself. . . ."

* * *

"You look like your father," she said. "He was a very temperate man, your father. But I pushed him. Always wanted to push ahead. I think you've got that in you."

"That's what Ruppert said. I told him about you."

She scowled at that—doesn't like anyone knowing anything about her. "What sort of a man is he?"

"A dreamer like us." She loved that. "But he's old now, and he's squandering all of his money."

"That happens to them. They live on make-believe, then they need to surround themselves with young blood at the end. That's where you came in. You mustn't give him any more ideas, he's just using you."

"That's not completely true. He's paid me for my ideas, treated me more like a son than an employee. He's taken me all over the world."

"Sure. You were his life line. He's washed up, and he knows it. He's not a father to you—in the end, he'll just take what he can from you."

"That's not true."

"You're being too soft. I tell you I know these men. They get what they can from you."

"I don't like you talking about him that way."

"I've seen those pictures of his house in the papers. That's what really got you hooked up to him, isn't it?"

"It's more of a palace than a house."

"I know all about it, but where has it gotten him? He's in hock up to his ears. Don't be fooled by the things people own.

"I understand what you saw in him. I did the same thing myself. You know when I was born, my folks had just come over on the boat. We had very little money. Lived in a ghetto filled with refugees like us. Filled with the sons and daughters of the anti-Semites we'd left in Europe. Hell is what it was. After a couple of years, my father made some money in the construction business, and I wanted us to move into some nice middle-class neighborhood, but my father wouldn't do it. He had no vision. But I did—even at that age.

"There was this pretty little gentile girl in my class at school I was friendly with. I used to love visiting with her at her house. Her mother was always busy in the kitchen or entertaining her bridge club ladies, and I'd sit there watching it all, studying them until my eyes hurt. When I left their place, I'd trudge over to the library and take out all the books they read and study them. That's when I went to my father and told him I wanted to move, but my father, with his miserable temper, hit me and sent me off to my room. That's when I made up my mind to go out and get what I wanted for myself. Even at that age—I was no more than fourteen or fifteen—I moved out of that ghetto and went to live in my gentile friend's house. They took me in. I was so well-mannered. I helped around the house. After a while my father came around. Bought us a beautiful little house right near where I was staying. We finally had a back porch and a parlor where I could entertain my friends. So you see, I know all about what you want."

"It is a little more complex than that. I'm talking high finance—I want to seize control."

"Hold your horses! There's plenty of time for you to do that."

"Now is the time—don't you understand? I know this business. I can't afford to let this slip by me."

"You can't go running off like a wild man. Everything takes time. You want to talk business, but I want to take my time. You're the only one left I can talk to. You're going to have to sit and listen to it. I want to get these things off my chest—understand?"

"I enjoy listening to your stories."

"Good, that's a start. Sometimes, when you want something from me, you've got to let me take my time to give it to you. . . . Now I've lost my train of thought. All right, so we're talking business—you want to seize control."

"Yes."

"And you'll need some money from me to do that."

"Yes."

"Of course you do. Do you think I'm a fool? I know what you want. I won't stand in your way."

"But there is something I want to get straight with you. I see what Sam and Jack have gone through to get your support. I don't think I can put up with that."

"What are you talking about? Sam and Jack. Flies, my boy, flies on the wall. That's all they are. I've got bigger plans for you. I'll give you the money you need, and I'll leave you alone to make your own mistakes. But don't fool yourself about me, Jonny, you won't find better counsel than mine."

"Then you'll do it?"

"I'll do it, but you'll have to pay me back. We'll see how responsible you are. . . ."

* * *

"Then you got it just like that?" I asked him. He seemed wholly unsatisfied with his accomplishment.

"Just like that."

"And it came so easily."

He got up and walked over to the window, staring out at the bay. "Oh, there will be a price to pay. She always demands a price."

"I think she's being very honest with you. After all, she can't gobble you up. She said it herself, you'll be a free agent."

"I don't know."

"Hell, man, don't back down now. What's the next move?"

"She's reading over the financial statements. When she sees that everything is in order, she wants you to go up to New York with me to negotiate with the note holders. Then comes the hardest part."

"What's that?"

He turned back to the window again. "Let's call it what it is—I'm burying a knife in Simon Ruppert's back."

24

Jon and I left the next day for New York where we met with the United States Mortgage Company. After two days of negotiations, the note was signed over to Jon's Circus Investment Corporation.

He stayed in touch with Ruppert while we were in New York. He said that the old man had no idea what was in store for him. Everything was going according to plan. Ruppert would default on the note, and Jon would step in, but Jon was living under a cloud of guilt.

"I've spoken with his doctors," he told me one day over drinks in his suite. "They say he's in very bad shape. I don't know. I feel as if I'm stealing something away from a dead man."

"Better to do it now, than after his death," I replied, using my best legal sense. "It might be a hell of a lot better than dealing with his estate."

"I suppose," he said quickly and then turned his attention back to the deal. "What we'll do is this. We have the Show Of The Century obligation in my corporation, so we are the new creditor group. We'll take twenty percent of the company up front as a bonus for assuming the debt. Then we'll have Ruppert pledge all of his holdings as collateral until the note is payed off. He'll have to come up with fifty-five thousand in the first quarter, and that will break him. During this time, we'll be easing more and more voting shares away from him. He'll have to make those concessions; then, after a while, we'll vote him out of the picture."

"An elegant procedure if I've ever heard one."

"As elegant as a noose."

Ruppert's private car was waiting for us at Pennsylvania Station. We were alone in it for the entire trip. I spent most of my time reading, not seeing Jon all that much. He locked himself up in his compartment—drinking, I suppose. When we reached the Pine Key Station, he reemerged, looking as ill at ease as a sixteen-year-old. He couldn't look me straight in the face. I assumed that I had been relegated to the position of collaborator in the dirty deed. I don't know whether he thought he was out to get what was rightfully his or if he saw himself as being little more than a thief, riding off with a fortune in the dark of night.

We got off the train and saw Raymond waiting on the platform.

"Thank goodness you're here, sir."

"What's wrong?"

"It's bad, sir, very bad."

"His heart?"

"Another heart attack. Then a stroke two days ago."

Jon stared at me, a mixture of pain and alarm in his eyes.

"Shouldn't he be in a hospital?"

"He won't go. We've tried to reason with him, but he won't leave that house. He wants to see you, sir."

Jon's early descriptions of the Pine Key place could not match my first impressions. It was simply colossal, a spun-sugar fantasy studded with fiery jewels. A ferry brought us across the bay to the Key. As soon as it docked, Jon ran up the drive to the house. Raymond and I were close behind him.

When we reached the house, I could tell by the stains on the walls that all the paintings had been taken down in the galleries.

"What's happened to them?" Jon asked.

"He wants them up in his room," Raymond said as Jon bounded up the marble stairs. But a man in a pin-striped suit stopped him when he reached the upper gallery.

"I'm Jon Willig."

"He's sleeping now. I'm Dr. Peterson."

"He wants to see me."

"Yes, I know all about it, but you cannot disturb him now."

"How bad is it?"

"Very bad, I'm afraid. There isn't much more I can do for him. Why don't you wait until he gets up? I'll call you."

Ruppert slept for most of the afternoon as Jon and I sat in the main hall drinking whiskey and sodas. It was a chilly November day, and although the sun flooded through the windows, Jon had Raymond light a fire in the huge hearth.

"What do we do now?" Jon asked, staring into the flames.

"We wait."

"I can't do it now—you understand, don't you?"

"Of course I do. We'll have to wait for another time."

"He'll know something is up. I was supposed to be in Europe looking for new acts. And your being here. He'll know what I've come to do."

"Don't do this to yourself, Jonny. Weren't you the one who sat in a hotel suite in New York telling me that this was the way it had to be, that nothing would stand in your way?"

Dr. Peterson leaned over the upper gallery railing.

"Mr. Willig, Simon will see you now."

Jon grabbed my arm. "Come up there with me."

"I'm right behind you—don't worry."

Ruppert's bedroom looked like an auction gallery: paintings were scattered on chairs, priceless treasures all over the floor. With one sweep, my eyes passed over Tintorettos, Guercinos and Bassanos. The drapes had been drawn. The air, musky and fetid, hung in the room. Death was so close you could almost taste it.

Simon Ruppert had aged decades since last I'd seen him. His skin was the color of a pale rose. His eyes had a rheumy cast, seeming lifeless and lost until they focused on Jon leaning over the bed.

"My young friend. I waited for you."

Jon sat on the bed, stroking Ruppert's frail hand. "I'm sorry I didn't come sooner."

"I can hardly see your face. Are the pictures in here with me?"

"Yes."

"Good. After this damned thing is over, you put them back where they belong. Can you remember where each was hung?"

"I've walked through those halls so many times with you—I'll remember."

"You memorized all of them." Ruppert smiled. "Are we alone?"

Jon looked around at me, motioning to me to remain silent in the corner.

"We're alone."

"We must talk," Ruppert whispered. "How many years have we known one another?"

"Eight, almost eight years."

"That long. We've had a wonderful time in those eight years, haven't we?"

"Yes."

"I want you to know how much they meant to me. Through you I was able to live part of my life over again. Showing you all those places I saw when I was your age. After Georgia died, it meant everything to me. You helped me get over her death. You know that, don't you?"

Jon pressed the old man's hand to his lips and cried.

"Don't waste your tears now, Jon. We must talk. It's me who should be crying. I don't like this dying business. It's too painful. I would like to remember the expression on your face the first time I showed you the main tent going up. It was just like mine. And the first time you saw this house. You were so young and eager to have it all, weren't you? I knew that. So young and eager. Although you bullied me, I was thankful for you. I'm frightened now. It's nothing you can help me with—you don't know how to do it."

"Just lie there. I'm here with you."

"There is so much for me to do. I wanted everything to be perfect for you, but I've run up debts."

"Forget about that now."

"No, I can't. I've left everything to you. The circus, the house, all the paintings. Everything will be yours."

Jon buried his head in his hands and wept. "What have I done?" he whispered to me in the darkness.

"There is not enough time for you to cry. We must talk. Georgia wanted me to leave it all to you that first night we met you. She said, 'He's perfect, what a lark. Let him have it,' she said. 'Let's see if he'll be blessed or damned by it. Let him play.' We had no one. We were waiting for you. What a crazy thought, wasn't it? But no crazier than my dreams—not half as crazy as my winding up in this place dying." Ruppert laughed. "Do you think I'll see Georgia again?"

"Yes."

"You'll bury me in the rose garden where she is?"

"I'll take care of everything."

"And Raymond—I've left him something, but he'll stay on with you. And I've arranged to wipe out all the debts. You must sell some of the paintings to do that. All of it is spelled out in my will. You'll sell as many as you need, then the rest of them will remain here. After your death, I want the house given to the State. I want it to be filled with people again. I told you that once. They will come in here and wonder who we were to have surrounded ourselves with so much beauty. I want them to remember us. That's what I am most frightened of now. I don't want to be forgotten. . . . Do you know any prayers for the dead?"

"No."

"Aren't there any Jewish ones?"

"I suppose so, but I don't know them."

"I don't know any of mine, either. Will you stay with me?"

"As long as you like."

"Stay with me until it's over. Talk to me—maybe you can talk me over to wherever it is I'm going. Then Georgia will be there. I know she will be there for me." His face was suddenly lit with excitement. "Where is the Titian? My first one."

"Right here near the bed."

"Tell me what she looks like—the nude in the *Bacchanal*. Start with her. Describe all of them to me, but start with her. Is she glorious?"

"Yes."

"Is she resting?"

"Yes. Her head is thrown back. She doesn't seem to notice anyone, but the others are drinking and letching after each other under the tree."

"And she is so self-contained, isn't she?"

"Yes."

"And the sky is that glorious color."

"Yes."

"All this life floating around her, and she is in love with her beauty and her youth."

"Yes . . ."

We stayed with him for hours. Jon sat there describing the pictures as if he were reciting stories or myths from some other time, and it seemed to me that those treasures were there for him to show him how miraculous life had been at its best. It was with all that beauty emblazoned in his mind that Ruppert finally eased into death in the early morning.

25

The funeral was an outlandish spectacle. Ruppert had spelled out all the details for it in his will, which was read the night after his death.

All performances of the road shows of the Show Of The Century were canceled for two weeks. Performers were asked to join Jon and the servants at the Pine Key estate, and there stage one final show.

The funeral was conducted under the big top, which had been set up next to the house. After a short memorial service, Jon and I sat in the bleachers with about two hundred press people gawking at this spectacle of spectacles. Most of the performers had been with Ruppert's show for at least ten years, and there wasn't a dry eye in the house when Belle made her entrance dressed in a flame red costume, pulled around the arena in a golden coach drawn by two white horses. The spots were trained on her, and even though she must have been near seventy, her beauty was dazzling. As she came alongside our box, I saw tears flooding down her cheeks. Jon leaped from his seat and embraced her, then the entire company gathered in the center ring and sang "Auld Lang Syne."

A week later the tent was pulled down, and the companies were off again on the road. Newspapers were filled with accounts of the elaborate ceremony and stories about Jon, whom they were calling, "the heir apparent." His biography appeared in dozens of editions, and marriage proposals—proposals of all sorts—began flooding in. After a week of it, Jon had no choice but to kick the remaining newsmen off the island so that he could get down to the business of managing his new empire.

Phone lines to and from the island were jammed during this time, but Bea Willig managed to get through on a number of occasions, offering her condolences and counsel to Jon. When she could not get through to him, she pumped me for information.

"What is going on over there?"

"It's pretty hectic. Is it all right if I stay and help him settle in?"

"Of course. It's family business now. That falls within your job."

"Well, that is something I've been meaning to talk with you about."

"I knew something was up. Jon has been so cryptic. Is it true he's inheriting the whole thing?"

"Yes."

"Where does that leave me? Where is my money?"

"That is the point. He's going to be paying you back."

"Paying me back? I don't want that now. It was our understanding that the money would come from me. It would be a family operation. George, I thought you were keeping your eye on things for me."

"Well, I was when it involved you, but it looks as if Ruppert came up with a way for Jon to pay off the note and keep control without the use of your money."

"Well, I won't sell the note, that's all."

"You don't own it, Bea."

"Who does?"

"Jon's corporation."

"George, who are you working for—Jon or me?"

"I'm paid by you, Bea. My loyalties are with you, and I don't see any conflict."

"Yes, yes," she said quickly, wanting to dismiss me. "This is not what I wanted. I wanted Jon brought back into the family."

"You haven't lost a son, Bea."

"I know my children, George. I'll never see him again."

"Don't be foolish."

"Don't you be foolish, George. I know them. Oh, there's my doorbell. I've got to get off."

There was no one at her door. She simply could not take this failure. She'd lost control over Jon for good now, and she knew it.

Men from Sotheby's and Christie's began to sniff around the art collection during the next couple of weeks. Ruppert had stipulated which paintings were to be sold first to pay off the 1.5 million-dollar note, and ten of them were carted off to New York and London for that purpose.

In less than a month, eight were sold at auction, netting $1.6 million. Commissions were paid, and then a check was made out to Bea. Jon's obligations to his family and other creditors were over. He was starting life anew at the top of the heap.

This, oddly enough, did not seem to console him. I stayed with him for the next month, living a fairly Spartan existence in the midst of all that splendor, and that rankled me. Jon was not up for parties or other people. Night after night I was forced to sit in the vacant main hall drinking, listening to his maudlin stories about Ruppert. I did not wish to be cold-hearted, but in my opinion, the mourning period was just about over, and Jon was refusing to face up to living again.

"You said it once yourself, George—everything comes too easily for me."

"I hope you're drunk," I said sharply.

"What does that have to do with anything?"

"Because if you are not drunk, then I'm packing my bags and getting out of here. I'll give you just one more night of this damned soul-searching." I stood and screamed out at the top of my lungs. Butlers and maids came rushing in as the sound of my voice echoed through the rooms. "Look at what you've got, you idiot! Look at all of it!"

He started laughing, leaping across the room, trying to cover my mouth with his hand.

"Look at it! Jesus H. Christ. Rembrandts!" I pulled a soaking bottle of champagne out of the bucket near the hearth and then began stripping off my clothes. "Come on, Jonny, let's run bare-assed through this place. Come on! Let's open the doors!"

"It's nothing," he said to the servants lining the gallery. "We're all right. You can go back to your rooms. George, not your pants!"

"To hell with it all, Jonny. I want one night of undisturbed debauchery in this mausoleum. Just one night!"

Lunging at him, I began pulling his shirt out of his pants, forcing champagne down his throat. "Live a little, Jon. Ruppert died and left you everything. Come on. We'll play football in the gallery. Anything!" The servants wouldn't budge and stood gawking at me. "Join us!" I yelled up at them. "Or don't. I don't care. The young master here has to let go a little. Raymond, two more magnums. Three more."

As the last of my clothes went sailing over my head, I groped for the door handles out to the piazza and wound up slipping on the cool marble, barely saving the bottle in my hand. Jon followed me, but I ran from the dock through the gardens, laughing like a loon.

"George, you're a lawyer. I've never seen you like this."

"This whole island is yours—all yours. If you aren't going to enjoy it, then I will all by myself."

I wound up sleeping in the gazebo in the rose garden where all the dearly departed were now at rest.

The next morning I awoke with a cramp in my neck and one hell of a head cold, which I took up to my bedroom with my incredible hangover.

Jon resisted every move this side of sullen and depressed until the last morning of my stay. We were having breakfast in the garden room. We talked about business, and then the mail was brought in. He began sorting through it.

When he read one piece postmarked Duluth, Minnesota, his eyes bugged open, and he began roaring with laughter.

"What is it?"

"Wait—let me finish. Oh, no. Too perfect! Too much to believe! Here—look at it. Read it. My poor mother."

He shoved two pages across the table. The letter was written in a backhand sort of scrawl.

My dear son,

There is no easy way for me to begin this letter, but I'm hoping the shock of receiving it will break the ice sufficiently. I expect that you must hate me and wonder why I left you and your mother and sister and brother as I did, but you will have to trust me when I tell you that what I did, I did because I thought it was best. Perhaps you will understand it, if we ever meet face to face and are able to talk man to man. I see your picture in the newspapers, and I want you to know how proud I am of you. You've done very well for yourself.

I'd like to ask you to keep this letter secret between the two of us. It would only upset your mother, and I don't think your brother or sister are as strong as you are, and they, too, would be upset. I have a feeling that you are the only one who can accept me as I am. So it will be our little secret, okay?

My name is no longer Abraham Willig—I changed it years ago, so I don't think you will be able to find me if you try. You will have to give me a little more time until I am ready to see you. For the time being, I want you to know that you are in my thoughts and that I watch your life unfold with a great deal of pride.

Your loving father,
Abe Willig

"My God," I whispered as Jon lapsed into another laughing fit.

"Did you finish it?" He panted. "The best part—the end—how did he sign it?"

"Your loving father."

"Yes, Abe Willig. Your loving father—don't you just love that?"

"What are you going to do?"

"What do you mean, what am I going to do? . . . Raymond? Raymond, where are you?"

He began running around the garden room, cackling like a lunatic.

"Raymond, bring out some champagne. Now this is something to celebrate, George. This is the event."

"But what about your mother? What about Diana and Sam?"

"Poor George, you wanted to celebrate and only wound up drunk, with a hangover. Not me. The old man dies, leaves me the world, then old Abe is back from the dead. This is the limit."

"Will you calm down."

He jumped up on the table and squatted there like a seven-year-old.

"Will I calm down? Not on your life. This is true southern gothic! Don't you see anything?"

"Maybe I should wax philosophical here—put things in some sort of perspective for you."

China and flower arrangements went flying as he scrambled down the table at me.

"Oh, yes, let's do that. What do you suppose the old guy saw in those newspaper pictures that made him want to get in touch with me?"

"I don't know."

"Think he wants to hit me up for a loan?"

A champagne cork exploded from a bottle in Raymond's hand. "Will you need glasses, sir?"

"Just hand it over." Jon knelt on the table guzzling a fourth of the magnum in a minute. "He's probably down on his luck, poor bugger."

"I don't like the way you are handling this, Jon."

"Listen to you. Two nights ago you went screaming like a naked banshee, trying to get me out of the doldrums. And now listen to you—you didn't even hear yourself talking the other night."

I scratched my head in wonder.

"This is what is left to celebrate, George. Life and its infinite possibilities. Oh sure, we suffer forever, but then these fabulous spurts come along, and it's this lunacy that makes it all worth the wait."

He could tell that I was not getting the message.

"Okay, good lawyer George, who only goes on one-night benders. You finish your packing and head out for Miami. But you must keep daddy's secret." Another chorus of excruciating laughter followed that. "I'll be just fine here. No more guilt. I swear it!"

He picked up the letter and stuffed it into his pants pocket.

"Daddy's secret!" he bellowed, hopping off the table. He threw open the glass doors of the garden room and screamed out to the sky:

"Thank you, daddy, wherever you are. Whoever you are—thank you!"

He was still sailing as high as a kite when I left later that afternoon. After seeing me off, he returned to the house and ordered the staff to move all of his belongings into Ruppert's bedroom. After all, the lord and master was not going to bunk down in a guest room any more. He ordered no dinner than night. Instead, he asked the servants to leave the house and come back in the morning. He wanted to be alone.

After they left he wandered the halls, inspecting the paintings, the statues, the wall moldings—anything and everything. The enormity of it humbled and bewildered him. Who was he, anyway? How had it happened? He felt like an interloper or a proud deception artist. For years this had been his fantasy, and now it was in his hands. He was awed by the accomplishment and somewhat frightened as well.

He walked up the grand staircase to the master bedroom. Everything there was in its proper place. Evening clothes were lying on the bed.

"Protestant America dresses for dinner," he mused to himself as he walked into the master bath.

The tub was set into the bronze marble floor. There was the sweet scent of Chinese sandalwood soap. A bureau stood opposite the washstand. On top of it were silver and tortoiseshell brushes and combs, all with Ruppert's initials on them. He had never seen so many brushes. Then that old persistent thought cropped up in his mind. How had he wound up there? He'd lived in that house for eight years and was now in the master suite, but none of this was familiar. Even the face in the mirror above the bureau looked as though it were a stranger's.

IV

Revenge

26

Abe Willig did not break his silence during the following ten years, and I don't think Jon had much time to concern himself about it. He took masterful control of the circus and gave it the injection of vitality it sorely needed. The generation that had danced and dreamed through the twenties had now been supplanted by a world-wearied generation clamoring for escape from the oppressive contagion of the Depression. Jon's answer to the problem was sophistication and greater spectacle.

During the latter part of the thirties, the Show Of The Century was completely revamped. Broadway lighting designers, costumers, and musicians were brought in to weave the spell. Theme shows with names like "Jewels for the Eye," "Ice Extravaganza," and "Wild in Africa" became the bill of fare. In just one season the big top itself was transformed—dyed midnight blue so that the lighting effects could work their wonder without daylight interfering. Once inside the tent, it seemed as if the world as we knew it ceased to exist. In its place was a dazzling display of ferocious animals, exotic acts, beautiful women, and muscled men performing in a world of perfect make-believe, as if they were dolls in a store window. Klieg lights swam around the arena, illuminating the golden sashes looped around the center ring. Torches blazed. Finales built to dizzying crescendos as the arena became a sea of undulating color, with animals dyed red, gold, or green depending upon the theme of the season. Sometimes, if the mood moved him, Jon would dress in white tie, tails, and top hat to announce the acts from the center ring. Of course, the newspapers ate that up, and Jon fed their voracious appetites with dazzling pranks.

In early 1940 he was hot on the trail of a German acrobat he wanted to bring back to the United States. This particular acrobat did a swan dive from a height of eighty feet onto a slide that catapulted him at more than a mile a minute up a ramp off into a net. (Everyone has to make a living, I suppose.) At any rate, traveling to and from Germany at that time was becoming perilous because Hitler and his gang of henchmen had just rolled over Poland. Anti-Semitism was screaming in the wind and from every crevice of the German psyche, but that was not going to deter Jon. He formed an entourage of press agents and journalists and set off to capture the acrobat.

Here is a sampling of the letters I received from him during that trip.

Dear George,

We found our acrobat in Magdeburg—an industrial town lacking anything close to the charm of the good German life these Germans keep talking about. He works in a private circus that was expropriated from a Jewish banker named Steinmetz. Mr. Steinmetz was forced to sell out his holdings about five years ago, and he has since disappeared. Our acrobat was eager to come to the United States—no loyal German, he—especially after we offered him an exclusive contract and he got a whiff of our money. But the goverment would not release him to us. I had to go up to Berlin to negotiate with the immigration authorities and was put through the third degree by the bureaucrats. When they saw the name Willig, they asked if I was German. I said no, then they wondered if I was Jewish, and I wondered if I was going to make it out of there at all. One of the journalists with our group told me to keep my mouth shut. There are horrible rumors one hears everywhere about detention camps for Jews—how some of the wealthiest, like our Mr. Steinmetz, have been forced to sell their holdings for a fraction of their worth. It scared me, but I was determined to leave with our acrobat in tow. We had to pack him in a trunk to get him over the border on a night train. We ran into trouble in the Netherlands when we showed up with an extra, somewhat crumpled, man in our party. That's where we are now—waiting, the interminable waiting, for papers, for visas. The rails are clogged, and we hear that boat passage is getting hard to come by.

* * *

May 20, 1940

Dear George,

Sometimes I think that Hitler is hot on my trail. I'm taking it all very personally. We were forced to put our acrobat back in his trunk as the German armies swept over the Netherlands. I do not want to get caught here. It is terrible. At the rail stations they line everyone up and take away passports at the drop of a hat—no matter if you are American or French; it's the Jews they're looking for, and the Germans who are running for their lives. En route to Paris where we can arrange passage back to the States. I will kiss the ground if I see it again.

* * *

George,

Ran into a friend of yours who happens to be a sister of mine. Diana sends you her love. She was on the Riviera, traveling with a glorious-looking, albeit androgynous, American heiress named Suzanne Osbert. What has Diana fallen prey to? All of us are in Paris now, trying to get off of this smoldering continent. War is everywhere, permeating the air, the food, the wine. Parisians anticipate a German invasion at any moment. Some are reduced to tears, others are ready to unfurl their swastikas. They are so ripe for invasion. Isn't that in their history? Always raped. The Franks (Germans, too) gave them their name, didn't they? And the French have that German spirit in them, but it's a bastardized version. All the rigidly intricate ceremony. In Germany it is in the war machine. In Paris it is in the way a waiter pours sauce over duck l'orange. The world seems to be falling down around all of us. I am taking Diana home with me. Our acrobat will once again nest in his trunk. Diana's friend, Suzanne, will be off to England tomorrow. I don't envy her.

* * *

That was the last letter I received.

France fell a few weeks later, and Bea, Jack, and I waited nervously for some word.

It finally came in July: a wire from Diana saying that she and Jon had arrived safely in New York. Jon was going off again to the Midwest on business, but Diana now wanted to come home.

Jack and Bea were as nervous as children before she arrived. She'd been away from the family for so long, neither of them knew what to make of her or why she was now interested in making an appearance.

In the intervening years, I'd developed a very agreeable working relationship with Bea and, through her, with Jack. I handled all their legal matters, which were involved with the management of the hotels Jack had bought and the liquor distributorship he'd set up after Repeal. Oddly enough, the Depression had not played havoc with the tourist economy. If anything, promoters were beginning to smell another boom coming. Hotels at the beach were jammed every winter season, and Jack was eager to try his wings with an extravagant venture—the building of an enormous luxury resort on the north beach, which would cater to the wealthy northern Jews who flocked to Miami. But Bea held the line.

"There is war coming," she would say whenever he brought up the subject.

"That's in Europe. It won't touch us."

"You're wrong about that. Roosevelt will get us into it. You think we're going to sit by and watch England go under? You listen to me. We're not investing another nickel down here for the next couple of years. We're doing just fine as it is—don't be so greedy. I'll tell you when the time is right."

As always, she was proved right. In August the Germans began launching air attacks on England. Lend-Lease came into existence, and war was in the air, even though people still went out to the beach for carefree Sunday picnics; or stood in line to see *Gone with the Wind,* or plunked nickels into jukeboxes to hear Wee Bonnie Barker warble, "Oh, Johnny, Oh." They ran like children, trying to forget a bad dream called Nazism and Axis power that was devouring Europe, raping China. Two oceans away from us, everyone said reassuringly, but it was getting closer all the time.

I was out at Bea's house the afternoon Diana arrived. We were going over financial statements when a taxi pulled up. Diana got out as the cabbie unloaded her luggage. I was surprised that she hadn't stopped off at her house first. Something was up. I knew it, and Bea's nervousness confirmed my suspicions.

"She looks beautiful," Bea whispered, peering through the living room windows as Diana paid the cabbie. "Why do you suppose she's coming over here first?"

"Probably wants to see you."

"She's never done that before. I wonder what she wants."

"Bea, she's your daughter. You take my advice and play it very slowly with her."

"I know my children, George—she wants something."

"Bea, please."

"She just can't walk in and out of our lives every time she damn well chooses."

"I'm sure you can do without my help," I said, shuffling my papers together, closing my briefcase. "I'm not up to watching family scenes this afternoon."

Her eyes were filled with panic. "No, stay. You're like a part of the family."

I began walking out of the living room.

"George, please."

"Oh, no, Bea. This is none of my business. I'll say hello to Diana, and then we'll meet again tomorrow."

It was a muggy, overcast day—a gray sky promised no rain, just more of the same. Diana stood in the courtyard in front of the house wearing gray crepe man-tailored slacks and a lavender linen blouse. She looked fresh and lovely, although her eyes were distant and worried-looking.

"Coming home to mama?" I asked after I kissed her.

She studied the house.

"Oh, she's in there all right," I added.

"That's comforting. I'm sorry about the last time in Cuba." She concentrated on my face, then kissed me again quickly. "Is it my imagination, or am I always saying I'm sorry to you?"

"Must be imagination—there's nothing to feel sorry about. I love the time we spend together. I don't expect any more than that."

"You're living here now?"

"Got myself a small house out at the beach."

"Can I visit you there?"

"I don't see why not."

"No lovers in your life?"

"That's become a rather expensive habit."

"Oh, George, getting so cynical."

"I'm true to you in my fashion."

"But always so gallant—doesn't anything ever change?"

I stroked her honey-colored hair. "Not with you."

"I've got to see her."

"Well, take it easy and don't lose your temper. If you need me, I'm around."

I left, although I felt as if I were letting both of those women down—they needed some arbitration to get them together. Afterward, Diana told me all about what had gone on when I left.

She walked into the room and embraced her mother, who remained cold and mistrustful in spite of herself.

"A kiss on the cheek does not undo what has already been done," Bea said cryptically. Then she studied her daughter's clothes. "So chic—must have spent a fortune on yourself over there."

Diana remained silent—probably scared out of her wits.

"Oh, well," Bea continued. "Thank God you and Jon got out of Europe when you did. Where is he, anyway?"

"He's in Chicago on business. He sends you his love."

"I'm sure of that. He's really quite something, isn't he?"

"I'm proud of him."

"Oh, yes, that, too. Lots of money, I suspect. But I was talking about the fact that he never comes to see me. Why do you suppose he's never here?"

"We didn't talk about it," Diana said quickly.

They stood, passing an awkward moment. There was so much catching up to do, but neither could make the first move.

"Would you like something to eat?" Bea asked politely.

"No."

"Something to drink?"

"No."

Bea sat and stared out the windows, then her eyes focused on Diana's.

"Well then, why have you come back?"

"This is my home."

"Your home is with your husband. Have you seen him?"

"No."

"That's where you should be."

"I wanted to see you first—we haven't talked in a long time."

"Yes, I remember we often talked when you were about ten."

"You're going to make this impossible for me, aren't you?"

"Whatever do you mean?"

"You're going to leave that wall up between us, mother. Isn't it ever going to come down?"

"This sudden interest. It's overwhelming. I don't know what to say, Diana. Don't know what you're talking about, either."

Diana knelt in front of her.

"Get off your knees, you'll ruin your pants."

"Just listen to us, mother, listen to it. I'm not ten any more. I'm almost thirty-five. A grown woman. Can't we talk like two grown women? Just let your guard down for once?"

"I can't afford to do that. My whole life I've had to live with the likes of you—those two sisters. I know how to protect myself."

"From what? I'm not going to hurt you. I don't even know what you mean."

"Of course you don't, because you've never taken the time. Too busy with this one and that one—think more of your aunts than you do of me."

"That's not true."

"Do you know what I've put up with? But I see the way those two turned out. Frieda, so bitter and Sunny—what a damned fool. We'll see how you turn out."

"Please, mother, give me a chance."

"Give you a chance. What have you done with your life but chased men on every continent and drunk yourself senseless? Why should I give you a chance?"

"I want to try and make a go of it with you."

"What for? What are you after?"

Diana's head dropped as she muttered, "Oh, hell—this *is* impossible." She stood and looked around the room for the first time. "Okay, so we won't make a go of it. Okay, what am I after. . . . For one, I want what's mine, just like the boys. I want something to do and some money to do it with. Is that clear enough for you?"

"Europe is closed because of war, isn't that it? All your rich friends have closed their houses, and you've no place to go."

Diana shook her head mechanically, without feeling or thought.

"I want to go into business," she said. "I want you to teach me about money. You've never done that, and I'm begging you now."

"You've got to be kidding."

"I'm deadly serious. I want to save my life. I want something of my own now."

"You haven't a serious bone in your body—you've broken my heart with your stupid, unfeeling ways. And now you come back here asking for money. Go ask your husband," she screamed. "You're his problem, not mine."

"You own him. Please mother. I can't beg any more. Please—can't there be a truce?"

"Go talk with your husband," Bea said. Then she left her alone.

It was early evening by the time Diana got home. Jack was in his den, sitting in the dark, a bottle of bourbon propped up on the couch next to him. He looked mean and bitter. She had never seen him looking like that.

"You know how I found out you were home?" he whispered in a raspy voice. "Your mother's chauffeur told me. There is no end to the crap I take from you, is there?"

She stared coolly at him, then shrugged. "Jack, please, this has been one hell of a day."

"Close the door. I want to talk with you."

She reached behind her, shoving the door shut before she walked over to the bar and poured herself a drink.

"What went wrong?" he taunted. "Who did you in this time? How many men has it been this time, Diana?"

She smirked. "You surprise me, Jack. You're always so happy to have me home. Isn't that enough this time?"

He threw the bottle to the floor. "No."

"I don't want another scene today, Jack. I've already had one with my mother, and I don't want any trouble from you."

She walked to the door, but he blocked her way.

"I want to take a bath."

"You're not going anywhere!"

The oafish fool was playing strong man, she thought. She was about to laugh in his face, but the rage in his eyes startled her.

"I want to know why you've come back again. What do you want this time?"

"I wanted something from my mother that she's not capable of giving me. I want something of my own. Some money—anything."

"What did she say?"

"She told me to talk to you about it."

"That's a laugh—I won't give you another penny."

Without thinking, her hand slashed across his face. "Get away from me—get your hands off of me."

His hands encircled her neck and held her pinned to the door. "I might consider coughing up something for services rendered," he slurred.

"Leave me alone."

He tightened his grip. "You've made a fool of me, and now you come skulking home asking for things from your mother. She's laughing at me. Don't you see what you've done? She thinks I'm a fool."

"You are her fool—she paid for you."

Diana wriggled free, and then he lunged for her, ripping her blouse.

"Get away from me, you disgust me. All you care about is that witch and what she thinks. You've never cared a damn about me."

He struck her across her face, and she fell to the floor like a broken doll. He stared at his hand; he never realized he had that power over her. He lifted her head and struck her again. It was so easy—she fell so quickly and lightly.

"Tell me about all the men. Tell me more about it," he screamed at her.

"Please stop, Jack—please." This is how it happens she thought, I push too far and it becomes as prosaic as a headline: "Husband Kills Wife."

"Say it sweetly—say everything sweetly from now on." Again, his hand came down on her. "Let me give you the new house rules. You want to hear them?"

Her head shook convulsively.

"Say please."

"Please—oh God, Jack, please let me out of here."

"Say please again."

"Please."

"All right—you will live here in one wing of the house, and I'll live in another. If I want to bring women in here, you won't say a word about it. I don't care what you do outside this house, but not here, you understand? No more money for you—nothing. You will put in your time here and not say a word about it. You understand?"

She nodded like a mute, then he released her. When she got to the door, she stared back at him, crouching on the floor like a sullen animal.

"If you ever touch me again, Jack, I'll kill you!"

She slammed the door, then ran into her bedroom, and locked herself in for the night.

At about two in the morning, she heard him rumbling in the hallway outside the room. She approached the door carefully and heard him weeping. Then he began knocking.

"Diana. Please, Diana, forgive me. I'm sorry. Diana? Are you there?" He was sobbing now, spasms echoing through the halls. "Please Diana. Please forgive me. I was drunk. Never again. I swear. Just stay with me, please. I won't come near you."

She let him wail on in the hall as she walked over to her dressing table and stared at the bruises on her throat, at her casual expression—so evil, she thought. She stood listening to his pain. Finally she opened the door. He was huddled on the floor like a child. She bent down and put her arms around him.

"It's all right," she said, staring off into space. "It's all right. I brought it on myself. It's me, Jack. Not you. It's all me."

The next morning her maid found her unconscious in bed. A bottle of Seconals lay next to her.

Jack rushed back to the house with a doctor, and they pumped it out of her; afterward, she lay in bed staring up at him like a child.

"It was an accident," she said. "It won't happen again. I just wanted to take a rest from all of this. You won't put me away, will you?"

"No," he said sadly. "It will go on the same way."

"And you won't tell my mother?"

"No."

"Don't tell her, Jack. I'll be all right now. I just wanted to take a rest."

She told me about this two weeks after it happened. She came to see me one night, and without saying a word, she undressed, led me to the bed, and slipped down beside me. I was beyond asking questions of her, beyond explaining the beauty of her, always fragrant and exciting in spite of the booze and drugs and excesses. I would stare at her in the candlelight for hours. She was one of those wondrous women who continue to exude an almost adolescent freshness and who, perhaps, suddenly become lamentably old one day without transition.

"Why did you tell Jack it was an accident?"

"That is what he wanted to hear."

"But why suicide?"

"Don't you ever think about it?"

"No."

"I can understand that, George. You probably think to yourself, why kill myself when dying seems so orderly a thing to do even without planning it. Why waste the time, right?" She laughed.

"I suppose so."

She continued laughing. I think she knew her laughter disturbed me, but she could not hold it in. It flowed up from her throat and spilled over her mouth and eyes. The heaving of her breasts and the deep sound of her laughter made her even more desirable. I covered her mouth with mine, and we made love again.

Afterward, she propped her head up in her hand and stared at me.

"George, do you still love me?"

"I don't know."

"That's good—maybe it will stay this good for a while."

"Why do you say such things?"

"I don't want to hurt you, that's all."

I reached out and stroked her hair. "Who do you love?" I asked.

"I still love my poet, I suppose. And you, George, I love being here with you. I'm going to blow out these damned candles. Do you mind?"

She stretched, then hopped out of bed, went to the window, and blew out the candle on the ledge. She stood there for a moment with her back to me, staring out at the sand.

"George, there's something I've been wanting to talk with you about."

"Sounds serious."

"There was this woman in Europe—"

I remembered Jon's letter—the androgynous heiress.

"She and I—well, it scared me half to death at first—"

"Come back to bed."

She turned with a child's expression on her face, expecting a reprimand, but not getting it.

"We don't have to talk about it," I said.

"Why are you always here for me?"

I kissed her. "Beautiful eyes. And your hair. And your soft skin."

"The woman in Europe—her name was Suzanne. We were lovers."

"You sound as if you're taunting me."

"No, I just want you to know everything. Tell me again, George. Why are you always here for me?"

I listed all the reasons again, knowing that they wouldn't satisfy her.

"Am I the only one in your life?" she asked.

"Yes."

"How I envy you. I'm still waiting to find myself, and you're so settled. Will you wait with me? Tell me you will even though you don't mean it. Lie to me. That's all I want. Tell me you don't love me. That I'm beautiful, that you'll wait for me."

"Yes."

"That's it. Again."

"I don't love you. You're beautiful. I'll wait for you."

"Good. Now I'll stay with you for the rest of the night."

It didn't matter any more—she was miraculous. She was sweet confusion, hours and days of sweet confusion.

27

For one of the few times in my life, I was feeling very comfortable. I'd bought a small house on the beach—an old cypress wood shack, which I fixed up by myself. Although my place often looked uncared for, it suited me. I always left the windows open, and after a while the salt spray coated the glass with a fine opaque mist. The sea smells invaded all the rooms, and my furniture was often damp with that too-sweet fragrance of mildew. There was always gritty sand underfoot, but the place reflected what was simple and uncomplicated about my life.

We were pretty safe out on that northern stretch of beach back then. No reason to lock doors or windows when I slept. Often a wind would blow across the sand, and I'd awaken in the middle of the night, listening to it rustle the wind chimes on the porch. Those bells made sad sounds, as though they were little souls strung apart, which touched every now and then with a melancholy sweetness. One night in fall, however, the wind awakened me. Gusts of it, shuddered the storm sashes against the house and slammed the chimes in a raucous chorus. It sounded as if the wind of '26 were back at my door. I went downstairs to investigate. My front door was wide open. I could almost see the sea mist rolling into the living room. When I went to close the door, someone called my name.

"Georgie, boy."

No one I knew had ever called me that.

"Who is it?"

"It's me, the lunatic."

It was hard to tell where it was coming from—outside or in. I made one complete turn around the darkened room and called out:

"Who is it? Where are you?"

"Wanna play games?"

"No, I do not want to play games."

"I'm harmless—I'll tell you that much."

Whoever it was, was in my living room. I slammed the door shut.

"Sam?" I ventured. "Is that you?"

"I'm harmless, Georgie, I swear it."

"Where are you? And stop calling me Georgie."

"Find me," he said.

"Sam, that is you. Stop this nonsense. How did you get out?"

"Mama sends me money every month to soothe her conscience. I suppose I really don't have much to spend it on. So I pay off my attendant, who likes to go out for a night on the town every now and then. He takes me along, then picks me up later when he's finished. This isn't the first time I've been out—don't be insulted that I didn't come to see you sooner. I had a lot of serious thinkin' to do about you until I decided you were all right. You aren't insulted, are you?"

"Of course not. Where are you hiding? Aren't you going to come out?"

"I'd rather not."

"Why not?"

"I'm a bonafide lunatic, George, I don't have to give explanations, do I?"

"If you are hiding in my living room, you do."

"Well, as I recall, the last time we met face to face, we weren't on the best of terms."

"That's an understatement—you wanted to kill me."

"See—that's what I've been thinkin' about. I'm feelin' a lot better now."

"Have you escaped?"

"No, I like it in there. Have you seen it? Beautiful little house. Plenty of food. Lots of time to think and write. That's what I'm doing these days— writin'."

"I see. Sam, I'm going to turn on some lights."

"No, please, just leave it like this for a while, okay?"

"But why?"

"I'm not ready for lights yet. Give me some time. Maybe next time. I have trouble talkin' directly to people."

"Do you mind if I sit while we're doing this?"

"Not at all. Fast moves aren't what bother me."

I took a seat on a straw couch near the fireplace.

"Do you mind telling me where you are? I won't look."

"Right under the couch."

"Jesus!" I jumped off it and pulled up a rattan chair. I could see his hulking body on the floor. A hand waved at me, but I couldn't see his face.

"Hiya, George. Just stay there, and I'll tell you why I've come to see you."

"I'm spellbound."

"Well, you see it's like this. I like it in there all right, but there are a few things I can't do, and I was wonderin' if you would take care of them for me."

"Like what?"

"Well, my kid is one thing. That's the big one."

"What about him?"

"You aren't mad at me, are you?"

"Sam, I think you're mad enough for both of us."

He cackled. "Good goin', George. I like it when the rest of you are honest with me. I can stand it. Anyway, about Albert—what do you know about him?"

"He's in school."

"I know that. Bea bribed enough people to get him into the Kentucky Military Institute when he was fifteen. The kid didn't like it there—took a lot of abuse from everyone because he was the only Jew."

"I didn't know about that part of it."

"Albert keeps things to himself. He spent two years there, and then she packed him off to the University of Pennsylvania. Now he's comin' back."

"I've heard about that. He says he doesn't want to finish his last year."

"You know how kids are. He's got a girlfriend. Old Commander Moss's granddaughter. Albert gets around. Bea wants him to go back up there, but he doesn't want to."

"What do you want me to do?"

"Keep an eye on him for me."

"Bea does that."

"That's just the point. I don't want him taken in by her."

"I see things haven't changed all that much," I said.

"Yes, they have. I don't care if she gives him money or supports him. I just think he needs a man to look up to—to pal around with."

"I'm hardly pal age any more, Sam."

"But you're a good man. That's all I ask. He's a very impressionable kid. Hot tempered, too. I want you to take him in hand. Maybe bring him out where they keep me every once in a while."

"So that's it, then. He comes to see you."

"Not since he started college. I may be an embarrassment he doesn't want to deal with."

"He's always been very loyal to you, Sam."

"You can never tell with kids," he muttered.

"No kid of yours, that's certain. Will you please come out from under my couch?"

He giggled again but stayed put. "I got a letter from Tildy last year."

"Oh? What did she have to say?"

"Who remembers? Women! I shouldn't have wasted my time on her. She was nothin' but trouble. But that's enough of that. I'm goin' to leave now."

"Are you planning to crawl out?"

"No. You go on back to sleep, and I'll leave. I'm going to leave you one of my poems. It will be on the mantel. Read it after I've left, okay? Go on up to bed now."

"For goodness sake, Sam, come out of there and let me see you."

"Don't get me angry. You know how crazy people are. I'm liable to go into some foamin' at the mouth and attack you. You just do what I say."

I walked to the staircase and looked back at him huddled on the floor.

"Anything you say, Sam. Just slam the door when you leave. And Sam—"

"Yes."

"Come back whenever you want to."

"I'll do that. I liked this a whole lot."

I went upstairs and waited for the door to close. When it did, I rushed down and stood on my porch. I could just barely make out the shape of his back scurrying along the beach.

I went back inside and found the following poem:

> We are sailing homeward bound
> From Eastern countries old
> And on our journey home we carry
> Silk and Gold and Spice and Violins . . .

Dear George,

You like it so far? I haven't been able to end it, but I thought maybe you could—you've got such a good grasp on the english language.
Remember—keep an eye on the kid.

Sam.

28

". . . keep an eye on the kid." The kid.

Somehow, I was never able to think about Albert in those terms. He never was a kid. At fifteen, when they shipped him off to military school, he was shaving a tougher beard than mine. He was tall and swarthy and massive, looking nothing at all like the Williges. Perhaps that is why he was shipped off;

he was too much a reminder of Tildy's side of the family. Not that Bea didn't love "the kid"—she did, all right—that is, if anyone could love Albert. The more I thought about my ad hoc custodianship of him, the less I seemed to be suited for the role. I don't know. Maybe it was that sullen expression of his. The know-it-all air. The size of him. Something always got in the way of my developing an actual liking for him. And I did try.

I knew in my heart of hearts that when Sam wasn't wanting to kill me, he had been a very good and understanding friend. It was the least I could do for him. So I racked my brain to find some redeeming side of Albert, and when I was about to draw zilch, I decided that it all had to do with the loyalty he'd shown for his father in those bad years, after Sam had hit the skids and gone batty. That was it. Albert was a loyal son—you could almost say a devoted son. I recalled his earliest years as an errant nose picker and Pablum slinger. Poor kid (see, I was getting into the swing of it). He was a victim, spinning like a dervish between his grandmother's covetous arms and his mother's petulant displays of affection. No wonder he'd turned into such a cautious little brat. And when the money started rolling in at Bea's place and Tildy ran off and Sam went off, Albert merely grabbed what he could.

I remembered dinners at Bea's house when he was home from school for Christmas. He'd sit there, not taking part in the conversation unless he was commanding center stage; and when he wasn't, he'd taunt me with his dark, brooding eyes, waiting for me to pause in mid-sentence so that he could seize control and ramble on about something or other.

Bea's attitude was benign, to say the least. She treated him as if he were a guest in her house. Whenever he was particularly difficult, she'd tell me that it was just a stage he was going through, as if he would one day hop that stage and haul himself out of there. A child of adversity is what she called him. I think she liked playing lady bountiful with him, lavishing gifts instead of affection on him, hoping that he wouldn't be as much of a disappointment to her as Sam had been. But Albert had integrity when it came to any disparaging remarks concerning his father's bad luck. He'd rail at Bea, telling her she was responsible for it.

She took it in stride. After all, it wasn't Albert talking, it was this stage he was in.

My, how we all underestimated "the kid." Victimization took its toll, and everyone wound up paying for it.

Much of what I know about Albert came to me second and third hand. I believe that most of these stories are true. Others I had to use my imagination to recreate. I want to be fair with Albert, and I think I'm objective enough to try.

He finally showed up in the early summer of '41 in the throes of a new stage—love. Outright, dogged, unrequited love for old Commander Moss's granddaughter, Faith.

Bea was none too pleased with it. For once, I didn't blame her. Faith was one of those girls who never once felt a twinge of guilt or remorse in her life. Too rich. Too pampered. Batting green eyes in that helpless southern girlish way. But behind the eyes lurked a steel-trap mind ready to spring into action.

"My, what a lovely place," she said to Bea on her first visit to the Coconut Grove mansion. "And it's so nice you were able to use all that heavy furniture you carted down from up North."

"I bought most of my furniture down here," Bea replied.

"And I love the fact that you stuck to a style you were so obviously used to," Faith cooed.

Little things like that. Like the time she kept us spellbound at dinner, telling us all about Rollins, the school she attended, where in late spring they celebrated Old South Day.

"All the boys dressed up like l'il pickaninnies and cavalry officers, and the girls wore hoop skirts. My mother let me wear one of her mother's dresses. Simply lovely. Yards of taffeta and ruffles. But grandmummy must have had a twelve-inch waist. I looked high and low for a dressmaker who'd let it out for me. Finally found one who wanted to charge me an arm and a leg for it. But I Jewed her down."

"What a lovely turn of phrase," I said.

Bea shushed me. "And I'm sure you looked lovely. But you poor wilted thing, having to wear taffeta on a sweltering June day," Bea purred.

As I recall, Faith's l'il ole mouth froze as Albert shifted in his chair uncomfortably.

I suppose there is no accounting for the places love takes you. I'll admit she had a certain loveliness. Masses of sable curls, a firmly set jaw, and a smile she reserved just for Albert, an absolutely cow-eyed grin that made her appear almost vulnerable. But she had this nasty habit of always boasting about her ancestors, as dull people do who are aware that they have done nothing themselves to boast about. She boasted about Commander Moss in particular, who as we all know, was as pedantic a prig as there ever was.

"My granddaddy, the commander, says the strangest things about you, Mr. Sloate. You two once have a go-around?"

"I wouldn't call it that—just ethical differences."

"Sounds pretty high-minded to me," she chirped. "But granddaddy is always on such a high level."

"A real second-story man," I quipped.

"Come again?"

"Forget it."

After a number of these visits, Bea finally put her foot down.

"Albert, I do not want that girl in my house any more."

"Don't talk to me like that."

"I'll talk to you any damned way I want. This is my house, and I will not tolerate any more abuse from a little snot nose who eats my food, swims from my dock, sits on my chairs, and then rips the whole place apart with one sweet phrase. You may be taken in by her, but I am not. She's just like your mother. Get rid of her."

"Don't talk to me that way, damn it. I happen to be in love with that girl—and you leave my mother out of it."

"Your love life is of no interest to me, young man. And if I had my way, I would have liked your mother 'out of it,' years before she took off. But how you can pal around with a bunch of people who talk down to you to your face is beyond me."

"You don't even know the Moss family."

"That damned commander and his crew. Foul Anti-Semites, the whole lot. I will not have that girl talking about our people that way."

"Since when did you get religion?"

"Since the day I was born. And you, too, Albert. You are a Jew, and I don't want you hanging around with trash like that."

"Some trash—you've never been to their house. Gentlemen—all of them."

"Oh, the hell with it," Bea groaned. "Drink your own poison. You'll learn fast enough. Just don't bring her here again, because I will not spend another pleasant minute sitting around here being goyish with her."

Faith's hook in Albert was clear—the boy was getting his taste of life, lily-Wasp style. He sat there with all the white gentlemen to get his fair share of abuse, and he didn't see them for what they were. Gertie Walsh used to have a word for that lot: "Piss-elegant."

That took care of Albert. But what was l'il ole Faith's stake in all of this? The same difference, the way I figured it. Albert was different, and like many girls of her class and disposition, Faith was cool and placid on the outside for all the world to see, but inside she was a bit racy. "Charged" might be more accurate. Underneath all those yards of taffeta and ruffles, Faith was simply a good old girl who liked to tumble in the hay, and not with those pale, hairless boys at the country club, either. She socialized with them, but she "sexualized" with Albert.

"Look at those arms," she'd murmur, snaking her fingers through the coarse black hair covering his forearms. "I'm damp in the seat touchin' those arms. Get undressed in front of me again, Albert."

"Not here."

They'd be out at the beach or in a park, some semiprivate place. Not only was he illicit because he was Jewish; not only was he built like some great dark stallion set out in a field to stud; not only did he handle her as though she were made of porcelain, but he was hers anywhere she wanted to have him—in the sand, on the grass, in a car, in a theater. Any time she wanted to, she could reach out and fumble with his fly, insert her hands, and twine her fingers in all that dark, coarse hair. He was completely hers, and beyond all that there was the added excitement that she might get caught in the act of having him all to herself.

"Don't be such an old silly. No one's around for miles. You old fuddy. I'll do it first. You think I'm scared?"

He'd stare at her in wonder, never having known a more capricious girl. She'd pull her dress over her head and stand there—her arms and shoulders tawny gold from the sun.

"Now you."

He was powerless to refuse. He'd undo his shirt and pants, and she'd inspect every inch of him.

"How thick the hair is here on your chest and here on your belly and down here—the very root of it. So thick." She'd press her nose to his chest and breathe in. "So thick and musky." She'd pinch his nipples until he thought he'd scream. Standing there defenseless, staring at their two bodies like the dark and light sides of the moon, she was so willing to tease and stroke him. His penis filled with blood, standing out from him. "So large. I can't get my hands around him. So thick. He won't fit inside me—he'll never fit."

And Albert, now erect, now feeling powerful and filled with his sense of brutish masculinity, would chide her, "He's fit in there before—just lay down for me."

Down she'd go, legs wide open, slick folds oozing like honey in the sunlight, as he stooped above her, working the glans of his penis on her thighs, in the dark tangle of her hair.

"Let me hold him," she'd pant, grasping him with both hands, pushing him inside herself, filling herself, her breasts heaving, her breath coming in short, fierce beats. Her hands raked across his back and chest, tugging on the hair, pulling him closer and closer, until she brought him to the brink of it.

"Not inside me—on my stomach. You can't do it inside me."

And that was all she would allow. She could have him, but he couldn't have her—not in that way—not in a hundred other ways, either. They could go at each other for hours, but in the end he wound up feeling like nothing more than the two or three viscous blobs of fluid that landed on her stomach. She was saving herself for the pale, hairless ones at the country club or the ones in their starched navy uniforms who started to flood into town that summer before war was declared.

"Don't all of them look marvelous—just like my daddy," she'd say as they walked on the beach, after she'd been saluted or waved to by the men in her father's command at the naval base. "Don't they look swell."

How he started hating the sound of that word. Everyone was "swell," all her set was "swell." Uniforms were "swell." Moonlight dances at the country club to which he was not invited were "swell." She reeked of "swell," pelted him with it—made him play the clown for it. And yet he was determined not to lose her.

"I'm going to get into it as soon as I finish school," he'd say.

"The war might be over by then."

"Hasn't even started yet."

"Old you! A lot you know. The Germans have taken everything. Daddy says the Japs are coming next. Coming soon," she'd say, as if it all were a damned coming attraction at the movie house.

"My grandmother wants me to finish school first."

"A lot she knows—that old witch. I don't know how you stand it in that gilded cage of hers."

"She treats me okay."

"She hates me, I know that. But I'll tell you something. I'm not all that wild about her. Hello, Ensign Burtrom." She waved at a passing sailor. "That man positively rolls with the sea when he walks, doesn't he?"

"I didn't notice."

"Just like you. All those beautiful young men going off to a glorious war. Don't you feel it in the air?"

"It's hard to avoid."

"You sound like an old crab. Look at those beautiful young men."

"Will you stop looking at them!"

"Old jealous you. Don't you want to go marching off into it? I can see you in uniform. All tan and muscled like some god, going off somewhere to fight—not navy, though, I don't think they'd let you be navy."

"What are you talking about?"

"Family ties and all—I don't think they'd want you in there with them. But the army or the cavalry or something. Like Mars, armored for combat. You'll leave, and I'll rush to the train. I'll be late, of course, you know me—I'll have spent the afternoon in a tub soaking, primping for your farewell. I'll run down the platform searching the cars for you with tears in my eyes because I think I've missed you. And then there you are, your head stuck out a window searching for me. Our eyes meet, and you reach down, pull me up in those arms of yours, and we kiss once—just once—then it's over, and I'm standing here, tears streaming down my cheeks."

He was beaming by that time—seeing the train pulling away, seeing her tears, waving goodbye, blowing kisses; kisses getting lost in the steam and the clank of the wheels.

"My, how I go on—got me damp in the seat again. Let's find your car and go off somewhere."

How many young men went marching off to "glorious war" with the strains of that tune ringing in their ears? Did it matter that the war was glorious? What could compare with those glorious goodbyes?

I was having late breakfast on my porch one morning in midsummer, when Albert pulled up in his car, a determined look in his eyes.

"I want you to come out to see my father with me this afternoon," he was saying.

"What for?"

"He trusts you, and I want your help."

It was the first time he'd ever approached me, so I was more than willing to listen.

"I'm going to enlist."

"In the army?"

"I've been down to the recruiting post. I'm legal age, and no one can stop me. I just want to get my father's blessings."

"What do you need me for?"

"In case he makes a fuss. I want you to tell him you think it's the right thing for me to do."

"That's all—just like that?"

"Listen, George, I'm not going to be able to finish college, anyway. War's coming on fast now. There's no stopping it. I want to get in early."

"What about your grandmother?"

"What about her?"

"She wants you to go back to school."

"A lot she knows. I'm sick of living in that gilded cage of hers. I want to get in there and get my licks."

"As you said, Albert, your time will come anyway. Why not wait it out—get more schooling under your belt?"

"I don't need to listen to you, you understand? I simply thought you'd want to make it easier for my father. So either go along with me or I'll go off myself—I won't even stop to see him. Take your pick."

As I suspected, he could not suppress the bully in him.

"Don't do that to him."

"I leave it in your hands."

In the car on the way out there, I ventured a guess as to what had gotten Albert so fired up for war.

"Does that girl have anything to do with this?"

"You and my grandmother don't like her, do you?"

"She's all right."

"You surprise me, George. A fine, upstanding Gentile like you. I'd think you'd see Faith for the girl she is."

"If that surprises you, Albert, you don't know me well enough."

Sam was waiting for us in one of the day rooms. Something had changed. He could face me without hiding under one of the sofas, but he appeared to be depressed.

"Albert has something to tell you, Sam."

"What's that?"

"I'm enlisting."

Sam's eyes clouded over. He sat rocking back and forth for a moment and neither Albert nor I could tell how he was taking it. Finally he sighed. "I wish I could do it with you."

Albert wrapped one of his massive arms around Sam's shoulders. "I knew you'd go for it. Goddamn it, can you imagine what it will be like? Fighting those bastards. I want it so badly I can taste it."

"Me, too," Sam said, slurring his words ever so slightly. I wondered if he was on medication. "I'd love to get outta this place and kick some ass over there. I'm young enough, aren't I, George?"

"Not quite—not yet at any rate."

"What about you, George?" Sam asked.

"I'm a mess. Bad feet and bad back. Not a chance."

"Too bad, huh?" Sam lapsed into silence.

"Dad, you'll come down to the station to see me off."

"Will I? I don't know. Tell me something—does mama know anything about this?"

"I haven't told her yet."

"Or Jack?"

"No."

"They won't let you do it."

"Can't stop me. I'm above age. All I have to do is sign on the dotted line. Don't worry about those two, pop, I'll take care of them."

"Break it to her easy. Don't get her going wild, because I want you to ask her something for me."

"What's that?"

Sam looked around and studied the vacant hall leading out of the day room before he spoke.

"George, you listen to this, too," he whispered. "I want you to ask her to let me out of this place. I don't like it here any more." He started crying. "I don't want to stay here. They do these things to me, and I don't like it any more."

All the ebullience of Albert's war talk drained down to nothing. The three of us sat there like mourners crouched over a bier. Finally, I cleared my throat and spoke.

"What is it, Sam? What are they doing to you?"

"They don't leave me alone. And they drug me up. I'm so tired all of the time. I don't like it. You said it yourself once,

George, I'm a young man. I could make a fresh start somewhere. I don't want to stay here."

"I'll try, pop."

"But don't talk about it when that bastard Jack is around. He doesn't want me out of here. He wants me where he can see me. He's scared."

"I'll take care of him for you, pop."

"Yeah," Sam said absent-mindedly, "I know you will. That's all I can say for the time being—I don't trust the walls in this place."

Albert and I nodded as Sam got up to leave.

"You try springing me before you go marching off into it."

We watched as he lumbered down the hall. His slippers were scraping like sandpaper over the terrazzo floors. It was the only sound I could hear, grating and measured, the loneliest sound I ever heard.

"Who put him up to this?" Bea stalked around her living room listening to Albert. "That is what I want to know. Who put these damned fool thoughts in this boy's head?" Her eyes locked with mine. Jack was standing behind her, shaking his head mournfully.

"Don't look at me, Bea," I said. "The boy has made a man's decision."

"Don't talk nonsense."

"It has nothing to do with George. It's my decision. I'm going, grandmother. There is nothing more to it than that."

Bea just went to pieces. "Don't any of you understand what I'm trying to do? I've been trying to keep a family together, but you block me at every turn. I can't take much more of it. Don't you know what this means to me? My daughter will not talk with me. My youngest son hasn't seen me in years, and the other is out of his mind. I can't let you go off like this. One of you has to stay here with me."

"There is no way you can stop me."

Bea's eyes shot over to me. "Is that true, George? I mean legally—can't I stop him?"

"He's of age."

She started crying again. Albert dropped to his knees in front of her and held her hand for a moment until she pulled it away.

"Isn't there one of you left for me? I know you'll have to

go sooner or later, but couldn't you wait? I want one of you."

"I've got to, grandmother."

It suddenly occurred to me that Albert had not really been taking this seriously. Now, seeing his grandmother in tears, he was shocked into reality. This was war, and while there might be lovely southern belles blowing kisses into the steam pouring from the train, there was also this—a woman in tears because she knew what war meant: fighting, the possibility of being blown away forever.

"Wasn't I good for you, Albert? I tried taking care of you. But I didn't do it right, did I? You just want to go off like the rest of them."

The tenderness of the moment was just as suddenly broken as Albert got to his feet and looked around at us. No, he thought, nothing had been good enough for him in that house, and so why was she crying now?

"There is something else—I want you to get my father out of that place. I saw him today. They're drugging him. I don't like the way he looks. I want him to come back and live here."

"I'm afraid that's impossible," Jack said.

"I'm not talking with you."

I was reminded of a scene like this so many years ago. Bea and Sam were trying to find some common ground as Jack stood there blocking them, and their fears stared them straight in the face.

"Let Jack talk," Bea said again as she had on that night so many years ago.

"But it has nothing to do with him."

"I've got a scar on my shoulder to argue that fact with you."

"I don't care about that. That was years ago. You should see him now. You ever go out there?" This was aimed directly at Bea. She bristled with anger.

"He doesn't want to see me. I've tried. Why should I be the only one to take all the abuse?"

"You should see what's become of him. Wandering around that place like a sleepwalker. You've got to get him out of there. He's paid for his crime."

"I don't trust him," Jack said quickly.

Albert looked ready to haul off and belt him, but I stepped between them.

"You don't trust him," Albert said. "What's he doing in there in the first place? Who's not to trust around here?"

"Stop it this instant," Bea said, rising to her feet. "I will not have any more of this, do you understand?"

"I would like you to do this for me before I leave," Albert pleaded.

"No one is going to do anything. He's in my custody. I won't do it. He's a sick man. I can't trust him. He will stay where he is."

Albert sneered. "So it's on your head, grandmother. I guess he was right about the two of you all along."

He stormed out of the room, and again it ended the way it had the first time.

Faith never did make it to the train station for her farewell performance, but Albert figured it didn't matter. They had played the scene that day on the beach once, anyway.

"I suppose it is better this way," he said, ticket in hand, standing with countless others just like himself who were there waiting for the war to overtake them. "Thanks for seeing me off, George. Give my father a hug. Tell him I'll be all right."

He was gone in a flash, and as I walked out of the station, I saw Bea running toward me, looking over my shoulder at the train chugging off into the distance. "I missed him," she said sadly. "I didn't want to. It keeps happening to us. We keep missing each other by seconds."

I held on to her as I walked her back to the limousine.

"He'll come back, won't he?"

"I hope so."

"But it won't be the same. I missed my chance with him." We stood there in silence for a moment, then she got into the car. "My God, George, I'm starting to feel so old."

29

Albert went off to boot camp in South Texas and was eventually assigned to the Eighth Army Division.

I don't remember hearing all that much about his war experiences, but there was one story Sam used to tell me every time I went out there to see him.

The Eighth Army was shipped out to New Guinea, where an invasion group was assembled and eventually fought in the battle for Mindanao.

One night Albert and a buddy of his named Stan were camped on a ridge overlooking a coastal town. Air fire started coming in from some Japanese planes. Albert and Stan had been sleeping, and it caught them by surprise. Albert was hit, but he was able to scramble into a hut. Stan hadn't been as lucky. When Albert looked out, he saw his buddy's body lying out there in open ground. He crawled out of the hut and saw that the kid had been cut almost in two by the bullets and debris. One leg had been ripped off, and yet he was still alive.

Albert leaned over and listened to Stan's breathing before calling in the medics. Stan whispered, "Just shoot me, Al. Get it over with. I don't want to go home this way. . . ."

Albert scrambled to his feet, searching the hillside for help, but the attack had caught everyone off guard; a dozen men lay dead or dying near him. He rushed back to Stan and told him to hang on.

"No, please—just kill me. I'm going, anyway. Just kill me."

Albert reached for a gun and a sleeping roll to muffle the shot, but before he pulled the trigger, Stan died.

Back home, we saw no war like that. No battles. No bloodied bodies; only caskets, mercifully closed. Sometimes it came close to us; during the height of it, the Germans torpedoed tankers off the Miami coast. I remember seeing pillars of black smoke one day out in the Atlantic, but the army brass hushed up any speculation about it. For weeks afterward, however, charred bodies washed up on shore, and the coast guard came in and carted them away.

Bea had been right back in 1940—Miami closed down tighter than a drum as far as tourists were concerned. The town became one huge navy, army, air force, and coast guard base. Now, when I ate breakfast on my porch, I saw entire divisions doing calisthenics or parade drills up the beach.

With that many servicemen around, the town became a very pious place. Each week brought crackdowns on brothels and gambling joints. As soon as they were raided, others opened, and any serviceman who had the money could wile away the hours at the Colonial Club, or the Lime Tree out at the beach. At that time this was all local action catering to the boys, but toward the end of the war that changed. I started hearing about Chicago groups coming in and bringing a black market in with them. A thing called the S and G Syndicate came on the scene, with it came bookie joints, and suddenly Stanley Jawitz was back in town again, managing a gambling joint called the Palm Club, out on the south beach.

The only business Jack and Bea's hotels did was connected with the military. The pleasure palaces were more or less requisitioned as barracks and officers' clubs. I was the legal liaison between the hotel owners and the military brass. Sometimes I shuttled back and forth between the beach and Washington two and three times a month to make sure everything ran smoothly.

I saw Jon several times while I was up in Washington. He'd turned several units of the Show Of The Century into a USO operation that traveled Europe and the Pacific. He often accompanied them, dressing in white tie and tails to announce the acts from center ring. Whenever our paths crossed, we'd sit for hours and talk over old times. He'd send his love to his mother, but there never did seem to be enough time for him to get down to Miami to see her. He seemed to be thriving: a bit grim, but as driven as ever.

After France was liberated, he took a unit over there and was on his way back to the States from England when he ran into Suzanne Osbert, that friend of Diana's, who wanted to come home with him. He got the necessary clearances for her and brought her back. She was from New England, and from what I learned, she spent only a month up there before coming down to see Diana.

After she appeared on the scene, Diana stopped coming by my house. I expected as much to happen, but I was upset—I missed her. About six months went by, and I neither ran into her nor heard from her. Jack told me she had moved out of their house and was now living up in Lauderdale. He rarely saw her.

One night, however, quite unexpectedly, she showed up at my place alone.

"My goodness, you look smashing."

She was walking around the living room in her bare feet,

fingering the driftwood and sea glass I collected. She looked like a little girl who had a secret she was dying to have me pry out of her.

"All right, I give up. What's going on?"

"I'm growing up, George."

"Well, to quote an old aquaintance of ours named Treach, that's 'oblique' enough. Do you want a drink?"

She settled into the couch. "Yes, I'd love one. I'm feeling wonderful. Can you really tell that I am?"

"Of course. The way you move—so serene and relaxed."

"It's Suzanne's doing. Do you want me to tell you about her?"

"If you'd like to," I said halfheartedly. I was feeling rather displaced by this Suzanne person.

"I want the two of you to meet. She's changed my life, George."

"How so?"

"She's taking care of me."

"And you're in love with her."

"Oh, but it's more than that. I'm transforming myself."

I handed her a whiskey and soda. "I don't know much about this transformation stuff," I quipped. "Never trusted it."

"But that's just the way you are. I'm off pills completely now. Have been for more than six months."

"I didn't know you were on them."

"Yes, all the time. Seconals and opium when I could get it, and more booze than you can imagine. Still have that to fall back on, but I'm getting there."

I lifted my glass to her. "To transformation."

We drank. Then she studied my face. "You're not in love with me any more, are you?"

"I don't know about that." I shifted nervously in my chair. Suddenly this conversation was becoming a little more than I could take.

"I'm making you feel uncomfortable. I don't want to do that." She got up and came to me, then sat on my lap. "Not for a minute. I love you dearly for all the time you've given me."

I don't know, perhaps I'd been out there on the beach alone for too long, or hadn't had her in my arms for so many months. I don't know. It was something overwhelming. I began to cry. Why now, I kept wondering—why cry after all these years?

"I keep thinking that it doesn't matter. I think when you aren't here, well, that's just the way it has to be, but then you come again, and now I've lost you, haven't I?"

"No, never, George, I'm here now. No one is going anywhere."

"Will we make love again?"

"Yes. Now? Would you like to now?"

When we did, she took care of me, undressed me, led me down to the bed. It was all for me, she kept whispering. Anything I wanted from her was mine.

"Will you come back again?" I asked.

"Yes."

"Come to me at night. I like that. Just the two of us tucked away in this bed waiting for the night to end. We once did that, didn't we?"

"Of course I remember."

The pain was welling up inside me again. "It's always going to be this lonely. So many years chasing after what . . . who are you Diana?"

"No more phantoms, George. It's me. I'm feeling whole."

"It's too painful for me. Why is that?"

"Suzanne—"

"I don't want to hear what Suzanne says."

"Please listen. She said something to me one night about letting go. We're just a bag of suffering bones tucked away here at night. I like the way you say that—waiting for the night to end, locked away in our little cages in the moonlight. We stick our hands outside the bars to console one another, but it still comes from our own suffering. We've got to overcome that to really help each other—to reach each other. Do you see that? We've got to get beyond all that suffering. Try letting go of that, not me."

"You loved me once, didn't you, Diana?"

"I do love you. I can take care of you now. I've learned that from her. She's taught me how to do it by taking care of me. Do you see? I want you to meet her."

"No."

"It will be fine, George. She's lovely, really lovely. Please say you will. I'll always be here for you."

"It's too painful."

"And not as glib as you once imagined, but it will be all right."

But it seemed to be ending—our old game of passion and desertion, ownership and refusal, taunting and entangling ourselves in the web of our own devices. I tried, but I could not shake my loneliness.

A week later she telephoned to ask if she could bring Suzanne over for lunch. I agreed halfheartedly. Diana was feeling whole, and there I was feeling like a gaping wound with my emotions completely beyond my control.

I was not surprised or any happier to see how lovely Suzanne was. She had pearl white skin, pitch black hair piled loosely on her head, a swan's neck, and a sweetly cryptic smile. She was not of this time or place, and yet she studied me intently. She talked about Africa and India, places in which she'd lived.

"The color of those people," she said, "made me wish I wasn't white. All our cherished whiteness—we're simply blank pages next to those people."

Diana said she wanted to visit all those places when the war was over. Suzanne smiled at her so calmly. Diana cleared the dinner dishes and went off into the kitchen.

"You've had a wonderful effect on Diana. I've never seen her looking this well."

"It just takes time. She's got everything to work with in herself. She is just closer to it now. Perhaps if you had met her when I did, you could have done the same thing for her. But she didn't trust anyone for so many years."

Was she actually trying to reassure me?

"The time was right for her. She loves you, George. She says you are the only man who's ever accepted her."

"I wanted to possess her—that sound old-fashioned?"

"No, I think you have. I think she is deep within you now. You'll never lose her. She won't let you."

"And you will stay with her."

"Yes."

Diana came back into the room and began talking about the future. I started feeling uncomfortable again.

"Jonny is being so generous with me. Did I tell you that, George?"

"No."

"He's been wonderful. He's going to let us have one of the guest cottages on Pine Key. He says we can stay there for as long as we like—until the war ends. Then I'd like to travel again.

"You'll come over all the time, George. Jon will want to

see you, and I'll want you, too. You will do that, won't you? It will be so much better this way. I don't want to hang around Miami. It will get too complicated here with my mother and Jack and all. You will come, won't you?"

"Yes."

I struggled through the rest of the afternoon wishing her gone so that I could settle into the fact of her leaving.

When they did leave, Suzanne walked out to the car, and Diana stayed on the porch with me for a moment.

"You liked each other."

"You were right, she is lovely. You'll take good care of each other."

"Don't sound as though this were goodbye. You'll be at Pine Key as soon as we've settled in."

She kissed me and left.

I spent the rest of the afternoon nursing one bourbon after the other, trying to rid myself of the thought of her. That didn't work. All I could think of was how much I loved her. How much she'd changed me. I was able to love her without having her. I'd opened myself up, and I hadn't quite caved in for having done it.

It was late afternoon when I finished my boozy ruminations. I studied the sky. The light was fading from it, but it seemed so comforting. The richest light of day. There is no subtlety like it in daylight; purples and grays beginning their slow stretch across the sky, infusing everything with nuance. She is like that, I thought, always beyond my touch but leaving that pervasive sense of herself. I liked staying with those thoughts of her, just the way I liked sitting in those evening shadows.

30

Of course word about Diana's latest escapade spread like wildfire in Miami—how she'd run off with a woman and was living on her brother's estate.

Bea was horrified. Jack took the brunt of most of it. Bea accused him of being a weakling. She told him to go out after

Diana and bring her back, but Jack was in no position to do that. He was also in no position to talk back to Bea. She was still calling the shots.

Throughout the war years, Miamians learned another lesson in belt-tightening. The military, who now controlled the town, were a far cry from the free-spending tourists. That, however, didn't seem to have much of an effect on Jack's wallet. He was still spending money like a drunken sailor, and I'd often see him with showgirls drinking champagne and gambling the night away at the local hangouts.

One night, I saw him in Stanley Jawitz's Palm Club talking with an unsavory group of hoods who were starting to make big reputations for themselves. They were part of the S and G Syndicate, which had consolidated all the local gambling action. They were running bookie joints out of every hotel and barbershop in the county. As far as I knew, they had never managed to get their hands on Bea's hotels, but seeing Jack with them made me wonder about that.

He didn't see me walk in. He was sitting at a back table in the shadows, near a door that led to a small casino. I took a seat at the bar and watched him for a while. He appeared to be on pretty friendly terms with them, and that got me nervous.

After a while, Stanley Jawitz came out of the back room and waved to me. It was the first time I had seen him since those days in Havana. He was looking as flush as a gambler on a roll, but no matter how much money he had, he couldn't shake those nervous tics.

"Long time no see," he said, sidling up next to me. "I've never seen you in here before."

"Stayed away, thought it wasn't patriotic."

He laughed and ordered drinks for us. "Patriotic, I like that. . . . Heard that Sam's son got wounded? Any word about him?"

"They've got him in a hospital in Guam—should be home soon."

"That's good. How is the old bird, anyway—still loony?"

I pointed to Jack instead of answering. "He hang out here all the time?"

"Good old Jack has dropped a bundle with me. I like customers like him, although I'm not wild about the company he's keeping."

"What's he doing with them?"

"Brother, you *do* have your head in the sand."

"What are you talking about?"

"The S and G boys—Jack's involved with them."

"Betting with them?"

"Not the way I hear it. They're operating out of the Aztec."

"Jack's not doing that. Bea Willig would have his head."

"The old lady better sharpen up her ax. I know for a fact he's getting a cut of their action."

"How come you know so much?"

"I got my sources, sweetie. Listen, you can tell Chason that he's gonna be in over his head if he doesn't watch out."

"You're losing me, Stanley."

"Well, it's a long story."

I knew if given the opportunity, Stanley would unload it on me.

"What do you suppose I'm doing back here in Miami?"

"You're working for Lister, aren't you?"

"Sure I am. Havana operation runs without me, but the war scared a lot of people down there. The boys are coming into Miami in full force Lister himself is gonna be moving in here. You better warn Jack that his days with the S and G are numbered. We're gonna be taking over, and I'd hate to see him wind up on the wrong side when it happens."

I hated seeing him involved with any side. The more pearls of wisdom Stanley dropped on the bar, the more I started sweating. After all, whatever Jack was into, I was into, and my blood was starting to boil.

"You don't read much about Lister any more," I said.

"He likes it that way. You know he was working with the military a couple of years ago?"

"I doubt that."

"You'd be surprised. The dockworkers in New York were giving the military brass a lot of trouble. That's Luciano and his boys. The dumb S.O.B.s in New York State went and deported Luciano, so Washington went to Lister, asked him to come in and straighten everything out."

Just then a blonde floozy walked out of the casino and stood behind Jack. He smiled up at her, then finished his conversation, and started walking out with her. I turned back to the bar and followed him in the mirror—he still hadn't seen me. After he left I thanked Jawitz for the drinks and information and went looking for Jack.

I found him in the back parking lot, talking with the floozy.

"Ditch her, Jack," I said. "I want to talk with you."

He smiled nervously. "Why, George, where have you been?"

"I said, ditch her—we've got some business to discuss."

He laughed nervously and told the blonde to go powder her nose.

"Let's you and I take a walk on the beach," I said, grabbing his arm.

"What's this about?"

I waited until we had crossed into a darkened alley, then spun him around, slammed my hand up into his throat, and held him against a wall.

"Who are your friends, Jack?"

"Get your hands off me."

"I'll break your goddamned neck—start talking."

"I don't know what you're talking about."

"Your friends, Jack, the S and G boys. What in hell are you doing with them?"

"Just like you say, George, they're friends of mine—that's all. Get off of me."

"Not until you tell me the truth."

"What truth?"

"What are you doing with those syndicate creeps?"

"I bet with 'em every once in a while," he said.

I released him, turning away from him; but then, when he wasn't ready for it, I turned again, and my fist connected with his gut. He doubled over, falling to the ground, gasping for air. I dragged him up to his feet and held him.

"Don't you know who you're playing with, Jack? This is me—mild-mannered me. You aren't going to lie to me, do you understand? I want the truth. What do you have going with those creeps?"

"It's nothing, George, I swear it. They run book out of the newsstands—at the hotels."

I rammed his head into the wall.

"Stop it, George, goddamn it—it's nothing."

"I'm going to tell Bea everything I know unless you come clean. You want me to do that?"

"No."

"I've read all the agreements you have with her. She can cut your balls off at a moment's notice."

"You think I don't know that?"

"Then talk."

"They make book, that's all. They came to me a couple of months ago looking for a lease. They call it a lease or a key concession—just a stand where the soldiers place their bets. They wanted one out at the Aztec—offered to give me a little split of the action for it. It wasn't hurting anyone. Soldiers have to spend their money. So I did it."

"Very nice."

"It's not hurting anyone. The S and G pays off. No one got burned."

"I'm burned, and Bea would be plenty burned if she knew. How do you think it looks, you dumb bastard? What happens when they raid the goddamned place?"

"No one is gonna be doing that."

"You taking out an insurance policy on that one?"

"I don't have to. The S and G took care of it."

"What does that mean?"

"They own a lot of people, George. They even own Jimmy Sullivan."

"What?"

"They own him!"

Jimmy Sullivan had been something of a fixture on the streets of Miami. They used to call him the "smiling cop" when he was stationed at the intersection of Southeast Second Avenue and Second Street. He had a reputation for walking old ladies across the street. Everyone in town referred to his beat as "Jimmy's Corner." He'd recently run for sheriff and won by an overwhelming margin.

"I don't care who they own. They won't own you or me or anything Bea has a hand in. You better get that through your head, Jack. I won't stand for it."

"George, listen to me. These guys aren't what you think they are. They're businessmen."

"I know who they are—they're gangsters, and I don't care what they look like this season."

"You've been listening to Stanley Jawitz."

"That's right, I have. Jawitz may run off at the mouth, but I saw the way he operated in Havana, and I see what he's into now—he still fronts for Mort Lister. Those boys play for keeps, and they're not about to let some nickel dime book-making operation flourish while they're busy taking over everything that moves in this town. I'll tell you another thing, too—you get those S and G people out of the Aztec by next week, or I'll go to Bea."

"Sure, George."

"You better say that as if you mean it because I'm serious. By next week." I started walking away.

"I'll do it, George. Just don't tell the old lady. I'll take care of everything."

When next week rolled around, I drove over to the Aztec and went to the newsstand to place a bet on a horse running in the fifth at Hialeah. A Negro was there minding the store.

"I want to put something on Jock in the fifth."

He looked around nervously. "Can't do that here no more."

"What do you mean? A friend of mine told me to come to the Aztec and lay my money down."

"No more—boss says we can't do that no more."

"Thanks."

That took care of that, but I knew I'd have to keep my eye on Jack from now on.

31

Albert was someone else I should have kept my eye on. But I didn't, and I suppose I'm partly responsible for all the trouble he caused.

He came home near the war's end, decorated to the gills for what he had suffered through in the Pacific. He wasn't softened by his war experience the way some men were. He was angry and more cynical, more the bully than ever.

He flew into a rage when he discovered that Bea had kept his father under lock and key out at La Hacienda during the war. He stormed out of her house, vowing never to return.

He and I went out to see Sam, who was now more of a sleepwalker than ever. Albert's bitterness was refueled when Sam went into one of his tirades against Bea and Jack. He called them his jailors, thieves who had stolen everything from him. Twenty years had not dulled his pain. You had to see him as I did to understand Bea's position; he was deranged, there was no getting away from that. At a moment's notice, he'd be out of control, and I believe that without all the medication they kept him on, he would have been waving a gun again at me or Jack or himself.

That fact did not assuage Albert. He left La Hacienda more bitter than ever. What was more frightening was that he seemed to be adrift—not knowing who his friends were or when his own family would strike out against him. There was only one person left for him, and he was naive enough to believe that someone of Faith Moss's sensibility would be able to comfort him.

A week after his return, after he'd taken a dumpy little apartment and gone on a drunken binge, he shaved and showered, put on his starched uniform with all its medals, and went to see her.

The butler held him at bay in the vestibule.

"Who shall I say is calling?"

"Sergeant Albert Willig."

"Yes." The butler sniffed disdainfully. Very few men lower in rank than captain came around. "I'm afraid Miss Moss it not at home."

"When do you expect her?"

"Soon."

Albert pushed past the butler. "Then I'll wait for her."

"I'm afraid you can't do that."

"Don't bother me, pal. You just tell her I'm downstairs waiting."

Albert went into the library where he found the old commander, now a senile drunkard, dozing in his wing chair near the fireplace. When Albert took a seat opposite him, the old man opened his rheumy gray eyes.

"Who's that?"

"It's Albert Willig, sir. How are you?"

"Willig? Don't know any Willig. What do you want?"

"I'm here to see Faith."

"What's the name again?"

"Willig, sir."

"Those beach people?"

"I'm their grandson."

"Didn't know they had any."

"I'm Sam Willig's son."

"Who invited you into my library?"

"I'm waiting for your granddaughter."

"The hell you are." The commander reached over and pressed his service bell.

"Please, sir, I've just gotten home, and I want to see Faith."

"You are not welcome in my house."

The butler appeared in the doorway.

"Laughton, get this young man out of here." Albert rose. "Who invited him in here in the first place."

"I invited myself in," Albert said, his rage building. "And I'm going to stay here until I see her."

"Call the police," the old man ordered.

The butler stood there dumbfounded as Albert sauntered over to the commander's bar and poured himself one Scotch and then another.

"The effrontery," the commander said. "Get out of here. Don't you know when you are not welcome?"

Albert pointed to the medals on his chest. "You see these? They make me welcome wherever I go."

"I'm afraid you must leave," Laughton snipped.

Albert charged the butler pushing him out of the room. He slammed the door.

"I didn't risk my ass to get pushed out of anyone's house, you understand?"

"You people are all alike," the commander said, looking away in disgust.

Albert's face was inches away from the old man's. He began picking the medals off his uniform. "Fought your frigging war for you. I guess these are yours as well." One by one, he tossed the medals into the commander's lap.

The old man was struggling to rise. His hands flew up against Albert's chest, but Albert merely swatted him away as if he were a tiresome fly. He walked over to the bar and poured himself another series of shots. "You want a drink?"

"Laughton will call the police, then we'll get you out of here. Serve you right to spend time in a cell, you—"

"Don't finish that sentence. Let me finish it for you. You Jew—that's it, isn't it? That's the worst thing you can think of to say, isn't it?"

The commander screwed his face up and spit, hitting Albert's uniform on the shoulder. Albert brushed it away, threw his highball glass across the room, and left.

As he was walking away from the house, he saw Faith drive up in a green Cadillac convertible. A blond navy officer was with her.

"Well, look who's here."

"I want to talk with you."

"Have you met Lieutenant Greenway?" Faith went on as if Albert were an annoying pet. The navy officer got out of the car and extended his hand. "Larry Greenway, Albert Willig," Faith said.

"I don't want to meet anyone. I want to talk with you."

Faith blushed. "Why, Albert, how impolite." She studied his uniform. "Let's see. Army was it? And a sergeant to boot." She and Greenway giggled. "Can we talk some other time, Albert?"

Albert opened the car door on the driver's side. "Move over—we're gonna talk now." He was inside before she could answer. She leaned out the window and gave Greenway's hand a squeeze.

"Larry, would you be a darling and drop by tomorrow? This won't take long. I don't want to keep you waiting."

Albert rammed the car into drive, pushing the accelerator to the floor.

"My goodness, Albert. What do you think you're doing?"

"Getting away from that house of yours. I want to talk with you."

"Well, if it's sweet talking you want to do, you had better think of another approach. This won't do at all."

He stared at her. He knew she was not worth the love he felt for her, and yet he wanted another measure of abuse. His foot was riveted to the pedal, pressed to the floor, speeding toward some conclusion.

"You never wrote to me," he finally said angrily.

She turned to him now, playing the coquette, stroking his face. "It would have been too painful for me. I heard you were wounded. I was too worried."

"And how did you spend the war?"

"Don't make fun of me."

"Country club dances and all those navy men?"

"I volunteered at the Red Cross."

"Sounds 'swell.' "

"Making fun of me. If that's all you want to do, you can turn around now and take me home."

Finally, he pulled off the road on a deserted stretch of beach and grabbed her hands and kissed them. She stared down at him, a glint of mockery playing across her eyes. He was, after all, still her pet soldier, and she offered her hand like a queen, there for fealty and forgiveness.

"I missed you," he whispered. "You don't know what the nights were like out there. All the time I was thinking of you." His hands inched up her.

"I remember you now." She sighed, her eyes closed. Her thoughts riveted on the past, urging her memory with the feel of him—his roughness, which she could tame on a whim; his gentleness, which she could whip up to a frenzy with just one carelessly uttered word.

"I want you again," he said, tearing her clothes, discarding his own.

"Not now. Not like this."

"I want you. I won't let go of you. I won't let you play with me like before. This time you're going to be there for me anytime I want you."

But that had nothing to do with the fantasy spinning around her head. She pushed him away, gently at first.

"I've waited too long for you. Don't play with me. This time we're gonna play my way, with my rules—you can forget about those clean navy boys."

No, it was nothing even remotely like the past—this urgency was not hers, it was his. He pressed in on her roughly, unmanageably.

"Albert, don't—you're hurting me."

He reached under her skirt, pulling her panties down her legs.

"Don't you dare do that! Albert, stop!" Her hand fumbled for the door handle, found it, released it, and the door swung open. She tumbled out onto the sand.

"What do you think you're doing to me?"

He was bewildered.

"Don't you dare manhandle me that way!"

He was suddenly back in his place with her, shaking his head sorrowfully like a recalcitrant puppy. He scrambled out of the car to help her up.

"I'm sorry."

"I have a good mind to get into that car and leave you here. Would you like that?"

"No."

"No, I bet you wouldn't. You can't treat me like some common tramp, which is what I'm sure you're used to."

"No, I didn't mean it—I—"

"Oh, stop fumbling and help me. Look what you've done. You've ruined my top, you bumbling goon."

"Don't talk to me that way, please. I said I was sorry."

"Sorry? Look what you've done. You've ripped my beautiful top. What am I going to say to Larry?"

"Please," he snuggled close to her.

"Get away from me."

"Please don't see him again. I want it to be just the two of us."

"Don't make me laugh."

"I want to marry you."

She was stunned for a moment. This dull, brooding beast could not have been serious. For an instant the wedding ceremony flashed through her mind. His dark body stuffed into a morning coat. His crazy family talking loudly, braying like donkeys in a field. His wicked sister and her female lover—it was all too funny for words. She laughed at him, right in his face, positively roared with disgust.

"Don't laugh at me."

"But it's too funny. You thinking I'd marry you. Oh, Albert, you can't be serious."

"Stop laughing."

"But, baby, you're such a serious brute—can't you see how funny it would be?"

One of his hands came down across her face, and the laughter choked in her throat.

"You goon," she screamed, "you God-awful goon!"

He started shoving her, making quick lightning jabs at her slight shoulders, pushing her down the beach, toward the water.

"Stop it! I'll scream. Just stop it!"

His hand sizzled in the air, held aloft as if it were a hammer that would demolish her face with one blow. Down it came again, and this time she fell.

"You've hurt me."

He raised his foot to her shoulder, forcing her down on her back, then he stood above her, one foot planted at the nape of her neck.

"What are you going to do?"

He tore the shirt off his back.

"I want you to see the soldier you forgot to kiss goodbye at the train station." He bent over her, one knee pinning her down. For the first time, in the dim light, she saw his chest and back, which had been scarred, cut to ribbons— "Lick me," he commanded. "Touch them! Go on. Touch them!"

She covered her mouth with her hands, but he pried them away and ran them roughly over his body. Then he pinned her and mounted her.

"Please don't do this to me," she pleaded, but he pushed in on her, pumped her with all the strength he had, until he thought he'd split her in two. All the while he was thinking about the countless times she'd made him stop and pull out of her, and now he was taking his time, seeing the end coming, then switching it off in his mind to prolong her agony. He'd make her pay for all the laughter and lies, for all the indignities he suffered. Then she began to move with him. In her anger, he was driving her on, and she was flailing up at him. It was as though she were falling from a great height. He worked her as if she were a car, fueling her, pedal pushed to the floor, then easing up, then flooding her again. He did not want to see her enjoy herself. He stopped abruptly as she began crawling up on him, but he pushed her down. Her hands reached out blindly for his penis, pulling him back into her, but he pushed her away again. His semen shot out of him, landing on his hands, which he wiped over her face.

"You can't have me," he said. He walked away, leaving her crying near the water's edge.

"You bastard!" she shrieked. "You can't do this to me and get away with it. Don't you dare leave me here! Albert! Come back here! Albert!"

Two nights later he wound up at Stanley Jawitz's Palm Club. A card game was just breaking up in the back room. Larry Greenway and two of his buddies walked away from the table and spotted him at the bar. They ordered drinks and began talking in voices loud enough for him to hear.

"Impudent kikes," Greenway said. "One of them had the nerve to propose marriage to Faith the other night. She laughed at him."

Albert turned quickly.

"You want to make something of what I've just said?" Greenway taunted.

He shrugged at first, looking as if he knew he was outnumbered and wanted no part of their action, but just as quickly, he turned, slamming his shoulder into Greenway's gut, sending the lieutenant sprawling across the floor. The crowd at the bar began screaming as Albert went after the other two, who now held stools above their heads. One came crashing down across Albert's back. Then Jawitz ran out of the back room.

"What's going on here? Cut it out. Get off that guy!"

Jawitz's goons swung into action, carting Greenway and the two navy men out the door. Albert lay unconscious on the bar floor. Jawitz bent over him, studying his face.

"Hey, army!" He slapped him. "You all right?" Jawitz looked up at the bartender. "Get me some water. You two bring him back to my office."

The goons picked him up and dragged him through a door concealed behind the bottles.

He finally came around after Jawitz forced a little brandy down his throat.

"What happened to you?"

Albert's eyes blinked open slowly. He tried getting up but fell back and stared at Jawitz.

"Why'd you stop me?"

"Stop you? Those goddamned monsters were about to beat the life out of you."

"I could have taken them."

"Big talker—here, have some more brandy."

Albert took two more sips, then sat up and shook his head. "Son of a bitch. It's always a woman, isn't it?"

Jawitz smiled. "They're never around when the fists are flying, but they're the cause."

"You and that navy guy have the same girl?"

"Past tense, pal."

"From the looks of you, I'd say you could have taken that scrawny lieutenant one on one."

"Yeah, sure." Albert tried getting to his feet.

"You should take it easy. What's your name?"

"Albert Willig."

"Sam's kid?"

"You know my old man?"

"Sure, I was in business with him out at Shalimar—Stanley Jawitz."

"Yeah, he's mentioned you. I thought you were down in Havana or something."

"I was—I'm here now."

Albert smiled, then got to his feet. "Well, thanks for the brandy. Sorry about the trouble at the bar."

"Hold on, you're in no shape to go anywhere—relax."

Albert walked over to a mirror to study his face.

"So you're the grandson. How is your father? I know I should get out there more often, but I've been too busy. I heard you were a war hero."

"Some war hero."

"You're out early."

"I got enough wounds. They shipped me back. You got anything else to drink around here?"

"Sure, you sit down, take it easy. I'll get you a Scotch—you drink Scotch?"

"Sure."

"I'll just be a minute."

Albert stared at the office mirrored walls. Glass chandeliers. Jawitz certainly seemed to be doing well for himself. It seemed as if everyone who'd been connected with Sam had done well. He wondered how a two-bit sharpie like Jawitz had managed to put together a nice little bundle.

Jawitz came sailing back into the office, all smiles, carrying a fifth of Scotch and two glasses.

"Here you go. To better days—drink up."

Albert tossed one down, then poured himself another.

"Sam's kid, huh?"

Albert nodded.

"So tell me, Sergeant Willig, what are your prospects for the future?"

"Don't have any."

"What about your grandmother and uncle—they seem to be doing pretty well."

"That so?"

"To hear Jack tell it, he's got big plans. New hotels in the works."

"He won't do anything without my grandmother's approval."

"Yeah," Jawitz sighed, "she's got everything sewed up. Got Jack's balls in a vice, doesn't she?"

Albert merely shrugged and tossed down another drink. Jawitz kept rambling on in a friendly enough manner, but he appeared to be circling around, getting as much information as he could.

"You don't want to throw in with your grandmother, do you? I mean not after she cut your father out of the picture."

"What are you getting at?"

"Take it easy, pal. I'm just talking—just doing a little thinking of my own."

"How'd you wind up with a place like this?"

"I had connections. You could capitalize on yours if you wanted to."

"What do you mean?"

Jawitz stood and began pacing nervously. "What I mean to say is that you got a good name down here. Everyone knows the Willigs—maybe not Albert Willig, not yet, but the name sure stands for a lot of money and clout. You could use that to your advantage if you wanted to."

"You mean get into a business down here?"

"Why not? That's what I did. There are a lot of people around who got a lot of money they want to invest down here, but they're too busy to run things themselves. They're always looking for some young guy with a good name to run things for them. As a matter of fact, I could use some help with my importing company."

"Importing company? Jesus Christ, Jawitz, where did you get all your money?"

"I got an idea. You go into the bathroom and straighten yourself up. I want to take you somewhere, show you what's goin' on down here. You game?"

"Why not?"

"That's right." Jawitz smiled. "Why not."

Jawitz and Albert drove over to the dock area near the bay front. Patches of fog were rolling across the bay, blanketing the merchant ships that had put in that morning. Even though it was almost midnight, there were dockworkers unloading freight from one of them. When Jawitz and Albert walked by, the workers stopped what they were doing and waved at Jawitz. Everyone seemed to know him.

"These your ships?" Albert asked.

"Not mine exactly—they're leased to a company I work for. Molister, my boss, owns them."

"Who's he?"

"Ever hear of Mort Lister?"

"The hood from New York."

"Mind your mouth around here. He's paying these guys very nice money. Lister's a businessman."

"What's the cargo?"

"Well, you see, the war may be over for you, but I think you forgot to tell the rest of the world. We still got rationing. Molister is just making a little scratch from it, that's all—not hurting anyone."

"You mean black market."

"Ugly word, never liked it. We're bringing in meat, milk, and booze—things like that. I coordinate the Miami operation."

"Why'd you bring me down here?"

"Like I said before, I'm always looking for ambitious guys with good family names—guys who've never gotten their noses dirty. Black market runs like everything else—like my clubs, for instance. Ain't no one gonna bother us. I been running this operation since Pearl Harbor."

"I don't know."

"What's not to know? You getting a lot of scratch from your grandmother?"

"No."

"You on the outs with her?"

"She'd give me anything I wanted, but I don't want it."

"Takes a lot of money to live down here. I could make you some money. See my suit." Jawitz held his lapel out as if it were a medal. "Pure silk, from Tripler's up in New York. Now that's money. Have a feel. I can get you one like it. That's if you're smart."

"What would you have me doing?"

"Just make some connections for me. Sell the stuff to restaurants and hotels—easy stuff—nothing too glamorous to begin with, but Lister's organization has got a real future down here. We'll be out of the black market soon. Then the future looks pretty rosy from where I'm sitting."

"I got to think about it."

"Okay, suit yourself, but don't take too long. Opportunities like this don't come along every day."

They walked back to the car in silence. Then Jawitz moved in for his final pitch.

"I'm right about you, Albert. You're hungry, and you're smart. I know Lister would like having you in on it, the name and all—it'd be good for business. Let me tell you another thing, too. No scrawny navy man would ever dare take another punch at you again. We got ways of dealing with that."

"What kind of money you talking about?" Albert asked as they got into the car.

"Nothing too big to start off with, but when the war ends, there'll be more. There will be lots of everything with Mort Lister's name on it. I can start you off at a hundred and a quarter—that sound good?"

It sounded a lot better than the five bucks and change Albert had jingling around in his pockets.

"When do I meet this guy Lister?"

Jawitz laughed. "Hold your horses, pal. You report to me. I report to Lister. He'll hear about you in time. Do we have a deal?"

"Do I sign in blood?" Albert asked.

"Cute, kid, real cute!"

32

By the time the war ended, Albert was thriving. As Jawitz had predicted, the black market operation was eased out of existence, but the gambling joints were doing bigger business than ever. Albert took over management of the Palm Club while Jawitz went on to open a newer, gaudier place up in Broward County. The ubiquitous Mort Lister had moved down to Miami but was rarely seen. You played blackjack at his tables, placed bets with his bookies, drank his booze, and if you had those predilections, you paid his prostitutes. But for the most part he was invisible, living in a middle-class sparkle-stucco house somewhere on the outskirts of town.

The S and G was also thriving, but street talk about them was not good. It seemed that Lister was about to launch an assault, and although the S and G was a powerful group, they would eventually fall to Lister's rather primitive but effective business methods. If he could topple the S and G, Lister would be the most powerful racketeer in town. People were scared, but that didn't keep them away from his tables.

Of course, word spread quickly that Albert had thrown in with northern gangsters. Bea discounted that as pure rumor at first, but she could not avoid the truth. She merely crossed Albert off her growing list of friends and relatives who could not be trusted or saved, who could not even be thought of.

Bea, Jack, and I had regularly scheduled meetings the first Tuesday of every month. At that time we'd go over the books, look into real estate deals that had come up on the market, and talk about the future.

When I showed up at Bea's the first Tuesday in September, I thought it would be business as usual, but something was in the air. Jack was talking more nervously than ever.

"All the servicemen are leaving. This place is gonna dry up."

"Not on your life," Bea said. "All the boys we trained down here got a taste of paradise. Now that the war is over, they'll be back. This time they'll bring their wives with them. They never had it so good."

A line like that always made Jack change gears. Off he'd go soaring into the land of profits.

"If that's the way you feel, Bea, we've got to capitalize on it. Build something fantastic for them."

"Just calm down. What we should do is refurbish the dining room at the Aztec—put some more tables in there, maybe a new wing. What are construction costs like?"

"Pretty high. We'd be paying top dollar for building supplies for at least another six months until the war industries have time to convert."

"Well, we've got time. We should have a very nice season this winter, the way I figure it."

That didn't seem to satisfy Jack. "I heard some very interesting news today." He milked a long pause.

"Well, go on, you've got a captive audience."

"Some property that was once in the family is coming up for sale again."

"Shalimar?"

"Or what's left of it. About ten acres up on what's now Sixty-fifth Street."

Bea got up and stared out the bay windows at the beach. "I always liked that place."

"Sam's prediction comes true," I said lightly, but both Jack and Bea looked very serious.

"What's that, George?"

"He always said you two would wind up owning it."

"That's nonsense," Bea said, tossing my remark aside.

"Sam just couldn't hold onto it—that's all," Jack said nervously. "Anyway, when he had it, there was nothing up there. Now it's at the end of hotel row—prime location. We could make a go of it."

"It's a pretty stretch of land, I'll say that for it, but Sam would never forgive you," I said.

"Why would he have to know?" Bea responded. "George, you put some feelers out—see how much they want."

"They're asking about a million," Jack put in quickly.
"Who owns it?"
"The First National."
"They're fools to let it go at that price. You put out feelers—we'll see what we can afford."
"Then you'll do it." Jack was excited. "I've got great plans for a huge resort on a location like that."
"Oh, no, my good man, not yet. We've got time for that. I'd just like to hold onto it for a while. Then we'll see about developing it."
The telephone rang. One of the maids came into the room to answer it.
"It's for you, Miz Willig."
"Who is it?"
"Jon Willig."
An alarmed expression flashed over Bea's face. She waved at the phone as if she could make it disappear.
"George, you answer it."
"But he isn't calling me—he's calling you."
"What on earth could he want? No, I can't talk with him. You do it."
"Bea, please," I pleaded.
"No, I insist. Tell him I'm busy—see what he wants."
I had no choice. I took the receiver. "Jon, it's George Sloate—how are you?"
"Where's the old lady?" he asked.
"She is in the middle of something."
"In the middle of nothing, you mean. What's wrong? Is she mad at me?"
Bea was hanging on every word, waving to me to continue the conversation.
"No—nothing like that," I said. "How is everything going? Haven't seen you in a long time."
"Sorry about that—been a hectic time for me. We're gearing up for a new season, going to put on a show that will knock your socks off. But the costs, George, you can't imagine what the costs are like."
"Everyone's complaining about that."
"About what?" Bea said impatiently.
I held the phone to my chest for a moment. "If you want to talk with him, be my guest."
"No, go on—ask how Diana is. Does he see her?"
"Is Diana down there with you?"
"Not now—she and Suzanne left for Europe last week, but

I expect them back in a month. She's well. The two of them are happy. Diana misses you, George. She wonders why you never accept her invitations to come over here."

"I'll bet."

"She says she does."

"Well, anyway, what's going on? Why the sudden phone call?"

"I wanted to speak with mother. Can't you pry her away from whatever it is she's doing?"

"Let me try."

I dropped the receiver on the table and walked away from it. "He wants to talk with you, not me."

She was as flustered as a schoolgirl.

"Jonny? Is that you? How are you?"

"What's he want?" Jack asked me.

"I don't know."

"That's just like him, huh, calling out of the blue like that. Must be in trouble."

Bea was nodding and smiling, exchanging pleasantries, then scolding him for not having called sooner. After a little while she said goodbye and then hung up.

"Well, what's he want?"

"He wanted to tell me that he's opening the new show in Miami. He wants me to see it. I think it's strange he's not taking it up to New York."

"Maybe this is just for you, Bea," I said. "Perhaps he finally wants to show you what a success he's made of himself."

"That's what I was thinking. That's good. That's the way it should be, isn't it?"

The Miami show, Jon said later, was to have been the biggest one ever staged. All the units would be under one big top for the first time in five years. There would be new costumes, more acts, more news coverage.

"More schmaltz," Jon said. "They eat it up with spoons."

Teams of people were called in on the planning. It was going to be kicked off at the Pine Key place. Newsmen from all over the world would be assembled for the starting day, and then Jon was going to move the entire show across the state on foot. "The Circus Caravan," he called it. He rented planes and helicopters for photographers who were going to document every stop the Show Of The Century made. It would finally live up to its name, he said. There would never again be anything like it.

And so in October it began by flooding the airwaves, and rolling off the presses. Finally, the great golden chariots and calliope wagons, elephants and lions, clowns and acrobats began their trek. Champagne flowed, cameras clicked. An army of people intent on nothing short of the adventure of a lifetime tramped across inland Florida. It took two weeks.

Jon's private plane landed at the Miami airport and a cortège of cars drove out to the western part of the county. When the first elephants were spotted, cannons were set off, and huge balloons were sent aloft. Thousands of people jammed the roadways, screaming, laughing, drinking; it was boom-time reborn—all those mad parties and land sales rolled into one spectacular event. Jon, dressed in his white suit, marched into the center of town atop an enormous bull elephant. He was still the golden boy, still looking so young and dashing. The little girls swooned, and boys ran after him, reaching out to touch the mammoth beast he rode. He paraded everyone around as though they were his subjects, out to the beach for no reason at all but to be seen there. Then back into town and out again to the western county, down North Kendall Road, where the big top was being set up.

Through all the commotion and partying, the workers slaved with the big top, a brand new one, still dyed midnight blue but made of a benzene-treated canvas to keep it watertight. With all the excitement building up on the site, it was only natural that there were some slip-ups. A standing rule was overlooked; during all performances tractors with the circus's fire-fighting equipment were set up outside the tent, but that day there were too many people milling about, and the fire boss did not order the trucks into position. Fire extinguishers, which were normally placed under the seats, were forgotten.

Bea and I drove through the crush of people in her limousine. It took hours, but finally we saw the massive outline of the big top baking in the noon sun out in a field. The land around it sizzled in the heat, but the tent seemed cool and impervious, with flags flapping in the wind. The animals were parading around it as clowns and aerialists put on small shows for the children. When we reached the site, Jon was there smiling like the happiest man on earth, and Bea positively melted when he helped her from the car and showed her around.

"This is amazing," she said.

A crush of newsmen followed us wherever we went.

"Are you Mr. Willig?" they'd ask. Jon smiled at everyone. He waved at photographers, and signed autograph books, and all the while he was taking everyone away with him in some fantasy. When I got up close to him, however, I noticed that he looked tired and drained by his performance.

Bea was taken to center ring. It overwhelmed her. "I can't believe you put all of this together."

"Did you doubt that I would, mother?"

"Never doubted you for a moment. I expect the best from all of my children. But this—it's amazing."

"I thank you for that," he said, lifting her hand to his lips.

When he got us seated in the center box, he took off again, disappearing into the crowds of tourists and photographers. Bea leaned over to me and whispered, "He's changed, hasn't he?"

"What do you mean?"

"He's like two people now. To tell you the truth, when I see him here, running this show, I can't remember what he was like when he was a boy."

"But he still has that in him. Only a boy could run a show like this."

"It's as if he doesn't belong to me any more."

We stared down at the floor. The band was playing a Sousa march as the first performers—the beautiful girls on the web—swung effortlessly. The clowns rode in crazy cars belching purple smoke and horns blasting—all accompanied by the delightful trills of the children in the audience.

Workers brought out the steel mesh runways that were used to bring the large cats into the rings, and the crowd went wild. The first fifteen minutes of the show gave everyone a taste of what was to come. There were aerialists swinging above and horses prancing below; everywhere you looked your eyes were filled with something else—men being shot out of cannons, golden girls dangling from trapezes. It kept building until I thought my mind would explode. Then Jon grabbed a microphone. The band was silent. Performers waved farewell, and he began to announce the first acts of the day: The St. Lucia Stallions . . . a juggling act . . .

"And far above this world of make-believe, the Flying Sultans dangle on a thin wire! How do they do it? Six of them at once! Marvel at them! The wondrous Flying Sultans!"

Out they came as spots danced over them and the band

played "Pomp and Circumstance." Up they went on a towering platform—fifty, sixty, seventy feet in the air, dancing over the taut wire strung between the two main poles, dancing as though they were held in the palm of the gods. The crowd was cheering, the vendors were hawking their wares, and suddenly I heard Bea gasp.

"My God!"

She was pointing up at them. At first I thought she'd been excited by something they were doing, but she stood and screamed out:

"George, on top, up there—can you see it?"

I got to my feet and stood next to her. "What?"

"Up there!"

I saw a circle of flames glowing like the end of a cigarette in the darkness.

"It's an effect he's using, only lights," I said.

"No, look!"

The crowd near us heard her, and they stared up and froze. Eyes darted in unison as the roof of the big top suddenly erupted in flames. It was like a terrible flash of lightning fire, like guns exploding overhead.

Bea grabbed my hand, and we began running ahead of the crowd, who were now on their feet, pointing up at what we'd seen.

The band burst into "Stars and Stripes Forever," the traditional circus disaster song, and that was the last moment of calm. With the sun-baked benzene canvas roaring above, the crowd went wild, storming the front entrance, where they piled up against one another.

"Not that way," I screamed out to Bea who was now running ahead of me. She could not hear me, and so I lurched forward, grabbing her shoulders and forcing her to the ground. She groaned as she fell. I began dragging her under the bleachers until she got to her feet.

"Jonny!" she screamed, her eyes searching the crowd for him. "Jonny!"

"I'll come back for him, but we have to get out."

We scrambled like animals under the seats. A little girl fell from above and lay sobbing on the ground.

"Do you have anything sharp, anything to cut with?" I screamed out to Bea, who was now crouched over the little girl, cradling her in her arms and crying herself. She couldn't comprehend what I was saying. I pointed to the tent flap behind the seats.

"We'll cut through," I said, grabbing her arm and then reaching out for the little girl, who cried as I held her to me. The bones of her right arm had broken through the skin. Flames were flashing above our heads as we reached the flap. I pawed at it with my nails, trying to bore a hole under it.

"Look in your purse, a knife, a pen—anything." Bea was frozen with fear.

I grabbed her purse, emptied all its contents, and found a nail file. I cupped my hand around it and stabbed at the canvas again and again. I looked back for a moment and saw people dropping from the stands. Near the front entrance was a ghastly heap of humanity piled four and five deep: children screaming; the living writhing under the dead; the dank, awful smell of burning flesh.

Bea rushed to my side and began stabbing at the canvas with me, until we managed to pierce it. Then I clawed at the small hole, working it back and forth until my fingers were bleeding. We were finally able to break through. I got to my feet and rammed the hole with my shoulder until I fell through to safety outside. I reached in and pulled out the little girl. Then Bea scrambled out, and we started running toward a field. In the distance I heard the clang of the circus fire wagons.

"You stay here. I'll go back and look for Jon."

Bea was rocking the little girl back and forth in her lap. "You'll die in there!" she cried, but I ran back toward the blazing tent, working my way around to the animal cages, which were engulfed in flames that soared a hundred feet into the air. The animals were burning. Men ran through the smoke trying to save them. Other uniformed guards raced about with revolvers, shooting the poor creatures who were too far gone.

On the other side, near the front entrance, thousands of people stood watching helplessly. One man whose hair was on fire dragged four children out; then he howled in agony as he thrashed on the ground.

After five minutes the huge center poles began wavering. People moaned in anguish as they watched them totter and fall. Water was pumped from the fire trucks, but it was all over so quickly. So many lives lost in that furnace. Where the big top had stood, there was now a circle of charred earth. The steel skeletons of the stands rose like twisted fingers above it.

Searching for Jon, I raced amid the cries and shrieks,

clanging bells, and charred bodies. I finally saw him crawling through the rubble, dragging two children by their arms. He was howling like the dying animals in their cages. His face had been blackened by smoke.

"Help me with them," he cried out when he saw me. I ran to him and realized that the children were dead. He got them to safety, then clutched them to his chest and sobbed.

"They're gone, Jon," I said, trying to pry them from his arms. "They're dead!"

"My God, they can't be. They can't be dead! Please help me with them. Please save them. Oh, my God, they can't be dead," he sobbed. Then he got to his feet and began running like a man seized with madness, calling out incoherently, "I've killed them! I've killed them!"

Embers burned through the night. The bodies were put into trucks and taken into town for identification. The wounded were taken to hospitals. Bea stood watch over Jon. She forced him to eat, and when he regained some of his strength, he surveyed the damage and tried comforting his people. But there was no comforting him. I stayed with him.

When we finished touring the grounds, there were men from the sheriff's office waiting for him near his office.

"Mr. Willig?"

"I'm Jon Willig."

Bea stepped between them. I guess she knew what was coming. "Can't this wait until morning?"

"I'm sorry, ma'am. We've got orders."

"For what?" I piped in.

"We've got orders to arrest Mr. Jon Willig."

Jon nodded. I think he was relieved to have someone level the blame at him. He walked away with them without any protest, without even asking why they were taking him in.

33

"But it's a mistake," Bea kept saying in the hours that followed. She turned the Coconut Grove mansion over to the circus management men who flew into town that night. "They can't blame him personally. It's a corporation, isn't it?" One of their lawyers was on the phone with the sheriff's department, trying to get answers to those very questions. "I'm worried about him, George. If these men can't do something, then we'll do it ourselves. You go down there and offer them anything to get him out of jail. He can't stay in there all night—not after what he's been through."

The lawyer got off the phone. "These yokels don't know what to do. They've never had anything like this before, that's why they arrested him."

"But he's not personally responsible. They've got to understand that," Bea pleaded.

"They'll bring charges," one of the management men said.

"You're covered, aren't you?" I asked.

"We've got insurance coverage up to half a million."

"You'll need more than that."

Bea flew into a rage. "I cannot believe that you're all sitting here doing nothing to get him out. George, you get your coat on and get down to that jail and tell them they can have anything they want, but they must release him tonight."

"Simmer down, I'll call a judge I know over there and straighten this out."

About a half hour later, it was settled. The Judge agreed with me; there was no earthly reason why Jon had to be held personally responsible.

It was dawn by the time I got down there. They were still holding him, but another phone call to the judge fixed that. They showed me to his cell and left me alone with him.

The gray shadows of morning were creeping over the city. Everything was very still, the way it often is in a dream. He was sitting by a window, framed in the gray light, smoking a cigarette. He looked up at me blankly, then stared out the window again.

"She sent you this time," he said. What appeared to me to be a non sequitur apparently had great meaning for him.

"I don't follow you. I've arranged to get you out of here."

"Sit down for a minute. I've got time," he said. "I was thinking about the last time. I couldn't remember who came to get me out of here the last time. Do you remember?"

"Why don't we talk about that over breakfast?"

"It wasn't you the last time. I think she sent Jack over then. Wasn't it, Jack?"

"I guess so. I wasn't around. I don't remember."

"Yeah, it was Jack. Tell me, why doesn't she like to do this kind of work herself?"

His calm was irritating me. "Is it your mother you're talking about?" I snapped.

"She doesn't want to see us like this, does she? So she sends either you or Jack to fetch me. She can't bear to look at us when we really need her. This afternoon when I was up there on that damned elephant, she was more than happy to celebrate with me, but not now—not when I need her."

"What on earth are you blaming your mother for? She was willing to pay any amount to get you out of here."

"Oh, money. Yes, sure, I know about that." This *was* a dream we were walking through, but I didn't know if it was my dream or his. "You know, she's a born innocent, that woman. She has no idea how life works. You have to pay for success. She wants no part of that. That's why she sends you. Why she locks Sam up, sends Diana off in a rage. She can't bear looking at what it is we all do to pay for what we want. We're left to do that by ourselves." He smiled as if he were acknowledging another private joke. "I never heard from my father again. What do you suppose went wrong there? I'm not so sure any more, but she is: he's dead and gone and the case closed. Failure is staring her right in the face, so it's pushed away somewhere. Get money. Get power to cover it up. Leaves us alone to work it out. Doesn't even help us. It's as if she's saying, don't look at it—it doesn't exist. It will go away if you don't look at it. And poor you, George. You do her bidding. You're finally lost in it, too."

I rose slowly and walked across the room to place my hand on his shoulder, to confirm for him and myself that there was still human contact to comfort one another. He patted my hand quickly, affectionately, as if I were a born innocent as well.

"That's nice, George. Your hand feels real good."

"Please, let's get out of here."

"Sure, I'm ready. Tell me, are the corporation boys in town?"

"Over at your mother's place."

"Let them handle it. What's going to happen, do they know?"

"There will probably be a trial."

"No reason to go to trial. I'll cover it personally. You tell them that for me. Whatever the insurance company doesn't cover comes out of my pocket."

"Aren't you going to stick around?"

"No."

"Your mother is expecting us."

"She doesn't want to see me. I'm going home. Will you do me a favor?"

"Sure."

"Call the airport and see if my plane is ready. I want to fly out of here now."

"But your mother does want to see you. She told me she wants to help."

"Waste of time, George, too embarrassing, too uncomfortable for her," he said and left the cell.

He flew out of Miami without seeing anyone, and he remained holed up in Pine Key for a long time. When the judgment of the court was handed down, he saw to it that four million dollars of his own money was paid out to the families of the dead and injured. The circus continued playing the season, but the stigma of the great Miami fire was not erased for years.

Several weeks later, I received a telephone call from Diana, who had come back to the States after hearing the news.

"Where is he?"

"At Pine Key. He won't see anyone, Diana. Won't talk with me."

"I'm up in New York, but I'm going down there to take care of him."

"It won't do much good."

"I can try. Suzanne can help him if I can't."

"Good luck with it—and, Diana, stay in touch with me. I'm concerned about him. I'd like to do something, anything—you tell him that for me."

"I'll write to you."

I don't know what Diana expected to find when she went down there. I suppose she thought Jon would be in mourning, but he wasn't—he was in hell.

Olga Treach and a group of her better dressed friends had

moved into the main house, Diana told me later. Treach kept a constant stream of people running through the house, while Jon remained aloof, drinking himself into a stupor most days, footing the bill and not caring when the party would end.

Suzanne hated Treach on sight and would leave the room whenever the woman appeared, retreating to the guest house she and Diana shared.

"Why's your friend so fidgety?" Treach chided Diana.

"Too much excitement for her."

"She's a mousey little thing, isn't she? I expected better things for you, my dear."

Treach plied her mouth with figs and créme fraiche. They were walking through the lower galleries searching for Jon.

"Do you know where he is?"

"I don't think he wants to see you again today, my pet. You have been running off at the mouth with him, you know, and all this Eastern transformation stuff has got him quite nervous."

"And what have you done with *your* 'Eastern stuff,' Olga? Conveniently packed it away?"

"That's not what he needs," Treach said emphatically, more figs disappearing into her cavernous mouth. "He needs life around him, not asceticism. You really have taken the most dreadful turn, Diana. And you're not looking as well as you used to. Traipsing around serene in several little outfits with your hair pulled back—so dour, you look like a dyke librarian."

"I'm going to get you out of here if it's the last thing I do."

"Do you think you scare me? I've been living like this forever. Bags are packed at a moment's notice. Not that I'd like leaving here. It's the most glorious house in the States, but if I'm forced to, I'll leave—gracefully, I might add."

"I don't know how he can stand to have you around."

"My dear, you surprise me, or is it that you don't know your brother at all? He likes to feed the hand that bites him." She chuckled. "I can tell you the most amusing stories. La Belle Masochist, our boy Jonny, but doesn't that run in the family?" She laughed again, reaching out to stroke Diana's head, but Diana turned violently. The bowl of figs and cream went crashing to the floor.

"What a thing to do to figs." Treach smiled as Diana ran out of the house in tears.

Treach looked up at the vacant gallery, trying to pierce the walls of Jon's room.

"You see what a naughty boy you are," she yelled up at him, knowing that he was hiding up there, hearing everything. "Look what you've done to your pretty little sister.

"What shall it be tonight, my pet? Which one would you like? The burly man? Or the nervous little girl? I've got them both for you. I love playing Pandarus. I'll give you anything your little heart desires." She waited for his response, but none came. "Not talking? That's all right. I'm starved." And off she flew into the kitchen.

It was a warm winter that year. At about three or four in the afternoon, the sun was like golden honey pouring over the Gulf through giant clouds, which looked like birds with their wings extended over the pines and acacias.

Jon stayed up on the solarium he had built off his bedroom, staring down at people swimming in the pool, which sparkled like an aquamarine on the lawn. There were mattresses on the marble walks surrounding it; and on two of those, Diana and Suzanne were lying. Their heads were protected from the sun by the narrow shadows of the tower over the bathing pavilion.

Jon studied Diana's face through a pair of binoculars. She was troubled. Restlessly, she turned her head on the cushions this way and that, as though she were seeking, in vain, some relief from the heat or whatever it was that bothered her. In contrast, Suzanne was placid and as still as the air; as unmindful of the urgent heat of the day as she was of the faint breezes that cooled it.

When the last of the guests went inside to change for dinner, the two women were still there. Jon decided that the time had come to talk with Diana—to reassure her that everything was either all right or beyond her comprehension. She'd come to comfort him, but he didn't need it and did not want her to suffer with it any more.

He padded across the lawn in his white linen pants and shirt and took a seat by the pool near them. Suzanne smiled as if he were a book she were reading and she'd just gotten to a part she liked.

"You've been playing recluse," she said softly.

Diana awakened, startled, and turned around to look at him as well. "Where have you been?"

"Upstairs. I'm playing spy, not recluse."

"Either would become you," Suzanne said lightly.

"I'm worried." Diana rose and walked over to him. "What is going on inside that mind of yours?"

"Nothing fruitful."

"I am worried. These people you've got here—" She shuddered.

"Filling the time," he said.

"What happened wasn't your fault, don't you know that?"

"I think I'll leave the two of you alone," Suzanne said, collecting her towel and hat and walking away like some cool, elegant water bird.

"You've made a wise choice for a companion," Jon said, watching her leave.

Diana stroked his sullen face. "Jonny, what's going on? I know it was dreadful back there, but it is not the end of the world."

"Did Suzanne teach you how to take care of people?"

"Yes."

"How did you ever learn to make such good choices? I don't understand it."

"Just talk with me, Jon."

"I've been taking quite a philosophical turn."

"That's a nice place to start. Tell me more."

"I feel like an acrobat we have in the circus. He dances on a wire with a little ragged umbrella, dressed in clown make-up, always on the verge of tripping off the wire, crashing down on the arena floor. Diana, tell me, is it trite for me to say that all of us live at the edge of a void like that?"

"Trite or not doesn't make it less true. We do."

"It's as if we dance on the edge of it all the time. We jump at the bait it offers—should we laugh at it or put up our fists against it?"

"I don't think it matters."

"You're right. I'm foolish." He turned in his chair. "What a joke. Isn't that why we're so unmercifully outraged when accidents occur, when we're staring that void right in the face? It is the only thing about life that I know in my gut."

Diana shuddered again as a breeze blew across the lawn and rippled the water in the pool. "People like you and I weren't taught how to think about things like that," she said softly.

"Run away at all costs—that's what we've been doing all our lives. I want to run away from it and forget about it for as long as I can. Mother taught us to do that."

"That's true. Funny, isn't it, she stays put? One by one she's lost us, but she doesn't seem to notice. What do you suppose went on with her in that family—her mother and father and the sisters?"

"What went on with us, I suppose. They were frightened. They ran, too. Mother ran to the security of a marriage that never was and to the sanctity of money."

"That's all she believes in," Diana said.

"Oh, don't be so harsh with her. She loves us. She doesn't know how to show it, that's all. Money equals love to her. So she taught me to run after it, thinking that if I acquired enough of it, I'd feel loved. I've amassed a fortune in money." He turned again, looking more relaxed. "I'm realistic enough about myself to know that I'll probably go on needing it."

"But you must try to find someone, too. I know you. You're so cautious."

"Watch me," he cried out, childlike. He jumped off the chair and stood by the pool staring down at his reflection. "Narcissus won't risk it." He turned back to her, leaned over, and kissed her forehead. He had a fleeting urge to tell her about the letter he had received from Abe, but he didn't see much point in it. "I'm so glad we got to know one another." He chuckled. "I've got some money and love for you."

She smiled at him, seeing herself in his face; the affinity she'd always felt for him surged to the surface. It was in their eyes, dancing there like twin images, strobing back and forth between them.

"I've wired your bank in New York, deposited two hundred thousand dollars. Spend it or invest it. It's yours. Take my advice and spend it." He laughed.

"But you don't have to. Suzanne and I have enough."

"Please let me give it to you—and no 'thank you.' I want you to have it. And I want you to know that I love you deeply."

"Then let me take care of you a little while longer."

"No."

"At least allow me the pleasure of getting rid of that Treach woman."

"I'll do that when I'm ready. Trust me. I can take care of myself."

After Diana and Suzanne left, Treach stayed on to supply Jon with his entertainment—a variety of young prostitutes.

There was one in particular who intrigued him, a nervous snip of a girl with peroxide blonde hair and a cherubic face. She had a quality of innocence that suggested that she'd be appalled if Jon were direct enough to tell her to get down on her knees and start her work.

One night, however, he felt the need for some variation in their ritual.

"You always seem to be nervous," he said.

"I ain't good at talkin'."

"But I want to get to know you."

"Ain't much to know."

"What's your name?"

"Patsy."

"You shouldn't call yourself that—call yourself Pat."

"What for?"

"You aren't a child any more."

"I like it."

"It does nothing for me."

"You pay me enough, I'll call myself Pat."

He threw back his head and laughed. "That's priceless. That's true."

"You sure are actin' weird tonight."

"Why'd you bleach your hair like that?"

"I was blonde when I was a kid."

"It looks awful."

She seemed properly miffed at that. "You payin' me to talk? I thought you wanted me to beat you or somethin'."

"I'm payin' *you* to do anything I want."

"Pay me, I'll do it." She clacked a wad of gum in her mouth.

"That's not enough."

"Then I'll leave."

He grabbed her arm roughly.

"You're scarin' me, mister."

"I'll only pay you if it's the real thing this time—hit me like you really mean it." He reached over and handed her a wooden rod.

"But I don't hate you." She fondled the rod as if it were something she used every day, like a hairbrush or comb. "You pay me the money, and I'll do it."

"I want more than that."

"Then pay more."

He laughed at her again. She shook herself free and stood over him angrily.

"If you're makin' fun of me, you ain't gonna get shit from me."

"That's it."

"Shit is all you'll ever be to me, mister—"

"Indignation—that's a good place to start. Of course, indifference would be a whole lot better."

"I come in the front gate of your big house—"

"You want the house?"

"Huh?"

"I'll give you the house."

"First thing I'd do is kick your ass the hell out of here."

"Have your boyfriend move in with you, right? What's he like? Big guy, I'll bet."

"Yeah—Ralph's big."

"Treat you rough?"

"When I ain't good."

"How's he hurt you?"

"Punches me around. Whadaya gettin' at?"

"Where is he now, this Neanderthal Ralph character?"

"He's out in his boat waitin' for me."

"Now? He's out there now?"

"He's waitin' for me to finish up in here."

Jon raced to the front windows and stared out at the boat pitching in the water beside the dock. "Go out and bring him in."

"What for?"

"Tell him I'll pay him five hundred bucks to do to me what he does to you."

"Ralph's not that way."

"No, not sex. Tell him to punch me around like he does you."

"He won't do it."

"I'll make it a thousand."

"That's what you want?"

"A thousand bucks' worth."

Her high heels clip-clopped along the marble floor as she went out.

Jon was shaking nervously, hoping the whore and the boyfriend wouldn't disappoint him. He was about to call out that he'd double his offer when he saw the two of them coming back up the path together.

"Go along with him, Ralph, he's crazy. He just wants to be roughed up a little."

"I dunno," the big lug said in a thick redneck drawl. The

two of them were standing in the entrance of the main hall. "Whoooeeeeee," Ralph whistled as he looked around.

He's perfect, Jon thought—massive arms, a low, broad forehead, and a nose flattened in one too many bar brawls.

"You must be Ralph," Jon said, failing to rise. "Come in, make yourselves comfortable. That is, if you're capable of doing that."

"See Ralph, he's been goin' on like this all night."

"You don't have to explain anything to Ralph here, he wouldn't understand it, anyway, would you Ralph?"

"I dunno."

"Sure you don't, you were just going to sit out there all night while I tumbled in the hay with your girlfriend. You don't know anything, do you, Ralph?"

"How much money you talkin'?" he grunted.

"Money, yes, I forgot about that. Wait a minute."

Jon sailed up the main stairway into his office, where he got a thousand dollars from the safe.

When he got back to the main hall, he placed it in Ralph's hand. "A thousand—you've probably never seen a thousand in cash before, have you?"

Ralph grabbed the money and began counting it.

"Don't insult me, you idiot—it's all there." Jon ran his hand over Ralph's chest. "May I?"

"Get yo' friggin' hands off me, fairy."

Ralph turned to Patsy. "What's he want me to do?"

"Don't ask her. I'll tell you—just a little roughhouse, you know?"

"What's he, bonkers?"

"That's it, bonkers," Jon offered. "I'd like it now, please, with your shirt off if you don't mind."

His hands went up to Ralph's chest to undo the buttons. Ralph merely stood there staring down at his sprawling belly.

"Come on, Ralph. Now."

Ralph's lip curled, the fingers of both his hands meshed together.

This was what Jon wanted. When would it come? How much would it hurt? The fists sprang apart and then smashed into Jon's gut. He doubled over and fell, gasping for air, pawing the cool floor as Ralph cocked his leg and sent his boot into Jon's gut again and again. Jon crawled away, but Ralph came after him, lifting him off the floor, then swatting him with his open hand. Jon's head struck the couch, and he blacked out for a moment. When he came to, both of them were leaving. Jon lurched forward but fell on the rug in front of the hearth.

"Not yet." He groaned. "You haven't earned your keep."

"Pay me two grand more, and I'll kill you," Ralph spat out at him.

"Some people," Jon screamed, "will do anything for a buck, huh?"

They slammed the glass doors as he rolled over on the marble floor laughing. Then he winced in pain and lay on his back, staring up at the heavily carved ceiling.

"This is real, isn't it," he said to no one in particular. "Punishment for crimes, but I forgot to ask—which crimes? Does anyone remember?"

34

Jon told Raymond to kick Treach and her friends off the island.

In the end, she did not leave as gracefully as she said she would. She stood shouting in the hallway as Raymond ferried her bags out the door to a boat waiting to take her to the mainland.

"Don't drop me, Jon. I don't like it."

He did not answer.

"I can be vengeful."

Again, no answer.

"Is this final and irrevocable? Oh, hell, just don't drop me completely."

Jon had gone up to his room with bowls of fruit and hampers of caviar, cheese, and champagne. He ran back and forth in the passageway concealed behind the walls, which connected the master bedroom with Georgia's suite of rooms. The passage was lit with amber lights, the walls painted with nymphs being chased through forests by satyrs.

In the years since her death, nothing had been disturbed in Georgia's rooms. The closets were filled with her clothes, her shoes, her lingerie, and behind all of it, Jon discovered a hidden closet containing stacks of books dealing with alchemy, astrology, yoga, the I Ching and Tarot. Jon read them carefully now, pouring through them night after night. When all else fails there is always mysticism, he thought.

Every once in a while he came across a reference to the Hanging Man (his card from the Tarot deck), which he thought held a clue to the peace he sought. In the back of the closet, he found an unused deck, and in this new Tarot, the Hanging Man was standing with his feet on two separate buildings, a man and woman hanging from his wrists, the woman upside down. Tears were streaming down the man's cheeks. A reference book that came with the new deck said that when the Hanging Man unified the male and female aspects of his own nature, he would be redeemed. Jon took the deck and the book back to his room to think about the meaning of this new interpretation.

He'd never taken the time to explore either part of his nature. He'd been hung in his own calculations: to seize control of the business, to possess all the beauty Ruppert had collected. Wasn't that what he wanted?

After a while, he fell asleep and dreamed. He was thirteen years old again. Simon Ruppert was taking him to a hospital to visit Georgia who, he said, was dying of cancer. She was standing in an antiseptic hallway wearing an eggshell-colored burlap robe. Before he approached her, Ruppert whispered that the disease had eaten away at her face, only her forehead and eyes were left. In some places there were shreds of skin still attached to the muscle and bone. But he would be spared from seeing it—the dream was conveniently benign in that way. She was wearing a mask made of light plaster and gold leaf, which looked as if it would crack if she smiled. Jon saw his hands reach out to her, but he was frightened by the sight of her. Ruppert was calling to him:

"Mr. Willig! Mr. Willig, sir, Mr. Willig!" The voice pierced the still night like a siren.

Jon, startled, awoke, but he could still hear the voice:

"Mr. Willig! Mr. Willig!"

He huddled against the bed's headboard, covering his ears with a pillow, and still the voice called:

"Mr. Willig, sir. Are you in there? Are you all right?"

Jon shook the dream from his mind. It was Raymond at the door. Raymond.

"Mr. Willig!"

"Yes, what is it, Raymond?"

"Are you all right?"
"I was sleeping."
"I must talk with you, sir. There is someone here for you."
Jon stared out the windows at the dark sky.
"What time is it?"
"It is late, sir. A boat from the mainland arrived with a guest who wants to see you. Will you let me in? This guest, it's very odd, sir."
Jon pulled on his robe and opened the door. Raymond apologized and then walked in.
"It's your father, sir," he said as soon as the door closed.
"My father?"
"He's here, sir."
Jon ran out to the upper gallery railing and stared down.
"You can't see him from here. He was hungry, so I had Cook put some soup on for him. He's in the dining room eating. I didn't know what to do."
"Another visitor from the sea."
"What?"
"Are you sure it's him?"
"How am I to know? You'd better come down, sir. He said he cannot stay long, but he wants to talk with you."
Jon stared out the window, tapping his finger on the colored glass pane. "At least he shows up when I need him," he said quickly. "Draw a bath for me, then tell him I'll be down in a little while."
Raymond nodded, then left.
Jon spread his legs out like the man in the Tarot deck. His arms were extended, and he saw the man and woman dangling from them. "Redemption," he whispered.
Twenty minutes later, he emerged from his room, slowly making his way down the staircase. He stood in the doorway of the state dining room and stared at the gray head barely visible above the back of one of the carved chairs. The head dipped, then reappeared. Jon was unable to talk or to take another step. He stood listening to the slurp of the soup. Finally the man turned.
The eyes, Jon thought. My eyes.
"My, my," Abe Willig cried out, rising to his feet, and walking toward Jon. "Jonny, I can't believe it." He held Jon at arms' length appraising him. "So handsome and well turned out!"
"Is it you?" Jon asked tentatively.

"None other. You'll catch flies with your mouth hung open like that."

"I don't know what to say—will you give me a minute or two?"

"Sure, take your time. Helluva place you've got here—helluva place."

The old man stared around at the paintings as Jon inspected his face, remembering the clear blue eyes, the high forehead. He had a quiet sort of masculinity, strength, not a swagger, and a calm that came from somewhere deep inside him. He was wearing a dark blue suit, blue tie, and white shirt. On his pinky finger he wore a ring Jon remembered from his childhood—a small canary diamond set in platinum.

"You remember the ring, don't you? Your mother gave it to me." Abe's eyebrows inched up suspiciously. "You haven't told your mother about me, have you?"

"No, she doesn't know anything."

"That's good." His face relaxed again. There were deep creases on his forehead and around his eyes and mouth.

"Have you had enough to eat?" Jon asked nervously.

"Oh, yes."

"I'm sorry I couldn't join you."

"That's all right. Hey, stop looking so nervous. I haven't come here to fleece you."

"Don't be silly. I never gave that a thought."

"Sure, sure. It's a helluva thing, me showing up here like this."

The two of them stared silently at each other, trying to comprehend the situation, then Abe smiled benignly.

"You want to talk in here?"

"No, no—let's go into the main hall."

As they walked Abe gawked at the paintings and tapestries. "We got a place in Duluth like this. That's where I'm from now. Did I tell you?"

Jonny nodded.

"Yeah, we got an old courthouse that looks a lot like this. Wouldn't want to live in it, myself."

"Would you excuse me for a minute?" Jon asked quickly.

"Sure, sure, take your time."

Jon fled into a bar behind the gallery and paced for a moment; then he took a shot of bourbon and stared down at the bottle. "What the hell." He shrugged. There was no reason why they shouldn't polish it off together. He tucked the bottle under his arm and came back into the hall carrying two glasses.

"This calls for a drink," he said, pouring two more shots.

"Good idea."

"Tell you the truth, I'm flabbergasted. You must be as well."

"Oh, no getting away from that," Abe said, tossing one down and then pouring himself another.

The two of them sat there drinking, warming themselves near the fire, trying to play at this reunion as if they were old war buddies who hadn't seen each other since the last big campaign. But it wasn't working. Jon was tingling with questions, with remorse, with anger, with any number of emotions he couldn't even identify.

"Why now? You've got to tell me. Why on earth are you here now after all this time?"

Abe sank back into his chair, staring over the rim of his glass. "Had business down here and then there was that fire in Miami. I had a feeling you needed to see me after that."

"It was bad."

"And you're moping around this place, aren't you? I thought that's what you'd be doing."

Jon said nothing.

"I don't have that much time to spend with you but what time I've got I want to use to help you. Will you let me do that?"

Jon took another drink, feeling a bit lightheaded now, more willing to be honest with this stranger sitting opposite him.

"If this isn't the damnedest thing. I still can't get this straight. What do you want from me?"

Abe finished his drink and then sat up, cupping his hands in his lap. "That's your mother talking now. There always has to be a motive for everything with her. You've got to believe that I don't want anything from you. I want to know what *I* can do for *you*."

"But I've got everything," Jon said cynically.

"That's not enough. What do you want to do with it?"

"I want to get rid of it."

"Then do it."

"But I've got responsibilities."

"You say that to me as if I don't understand, but here I am, thirty years after the fact, staring one of my responsibilities in the face. I ran away, Jonny, and I say do it."

"That's the point, isn't it?" Jon added snidely. "You did run, and you think I'm better off because you did."

"Did any of you turn out so badly?"

Jon wondered whose responsibility it was that Sam had wound up so badly. How could Abe Willig be made to pay for that?

"Things haven't turned out so well. Do you know where Sam is?"

"No."

"He's in a psychiatric asylum—he went mad, tried to kill Diana's husband."

Abe sat back, staring reflectively for a moment. "Poor Sam, how'd he wind up like that?"

"There's too much to fill you in on, but there was this scramble for money and Sam was cut out."

"I'll bet that was your mother's doing."

Jon stood angrily. "How dare you say that! All hell breaks loose, you're nowhere to be found, and when you hear about it, it's her fault. How very convenient."

"I don't blame you for being angry, but you haven't heard my side of it. I'm just asking you questions. What did your mother have to do with it?"

"Oh, she had her two cents in there," Jon said in disgust. "Ran it up into a couple of million before she was through."

"She's rich, then."

"Yes, she's rich—we're all rich."

"I knew she would be. That's what she wanted. I didn't have the drive. I just packed my bags and took off. I thought at the time it was the best thing to do—I know it was the easiest. She just didn't understand what I was all about."

Jon tempered his anger for a moment and listened.

"Now I want to give you permission to do the same thing—take the same risks. In fact, after looking at this place, I insist on it. Do you want to spend the rest of your days here? Who cleans it, anyway—the Englishman?"

"There is a staff."

"Big place to clean."

Jon shook his head adamantly. "What you did was wrong. You won't convince me it wasn't. You've got me mad now."

"I guess you've got to work that out of your system. I know in my gut that what I did, I had to do. So any way you cut it, I was right."

"Well, what did you find when you ran out on us?"

"A woman who respected me and didn't push me to do what I couldn't do."

"Does she know about us?"

"No."

"That sounds honest."

"By the way, where's the woman in your life?"

"That's too difficult to explain."

"Not as hard as you might think. Look at this place, Jonny. How much energy it must take to get things like this! But you've lost what's important, and that's what we've got to talk about tonight. I'll bet all you do in this place is drink and whore up a storm."

"What of it?"

"Where is it getting you? Up here, alone. You've got to find yourself a woman."

"That's not what I want."

"What do you want?"

"I don't know."

"All that push and drive is making you as blind as a bat."

"And you're happy, I suppose."

"I missed you kids a lot in the beginning. Sam was all pep and vinegar—too bad about him. Is there any helping him?"

"We're not in touch."

"What's this guy like who married Diana?"

"His name is Jack. He's under mother's wing. They're making money together."

"Diana was such a pretty little thing—still pretty?"

"Beautiful."

"And happy?"

"She has lovers."

"You rich ones. You say that as if you're buying soapsuds. She has lovers. Is she in love?"

"Yes, but it's been difficult for her."

"Tell me when it isn't difficult. There are no shortcuts there. And another thing. You'd be fooling yourself if you thought my leaving made it any rougher for you kids. Your mother forced me out of the picture before you were born. She knew exactly what she wanted from me and from each of you. I know she saved all her hopes and dreams for you, Jonny. I see she damned well got what she wanted. Sure, she'd like you to be a decent human being, but she always wanted the approval of the crowd. Like this place, she wants everyone to look at it and tell her what a great job she did to have you go out and get it.

"I guess that goes back to something else. I had all these stiff German aunts who looked down their long noses at your mother. Your mother always wanted their approval, even though she said she hated them. They made her feel inferior, so she set out to one-up them. Seems like she did it with you getting this place.

"Did she tell you what to do once you got things like this? That's why I'm here now. Not out of guilt. I just want you to know that you can walk among the rest of us mortals. See how people are making out with this life. It's not so bad on the other side of the Gates of Eden. Or is this hell I've stumbled into? You tell me."

"I don't know any more."

"I'll bet you don't. With all your money, you haven't lived a tenth of the life I have. Sure I've got some job I go to every day, but I've got people close to me. I put my emotions on the line, and that's enough excitement for me to contend with."

When the end comes, we'll see how much of a life you'll squeeze out of all this artifice. See, I know all the big words, too, I'm not missing anything. I'm sorry I hurt you and your mother, but not enough to go back and undo it." Abe reached out. The canary diamond flashed in the firelight that danced on his face. "I love you, Jon. That's a risk, isn't it? Coming here to tell you that. But I'm not scared you'll turn me away. I came here for you. If you turn your back on me, it'll be your loss."

Abe had warmth to impart; it didn't seem to pain him to give it, and it was nothing Jon had to pay for or regret having gotten. He inched closer to his father's lap and took his hand and held it to his cheek. Abe cradled him and smoothed his hair. "I'm just satisfied to have seen you, to have laid the cards out on the table for you. I won't even say, turn your back on what you've already got. Just get the hell out of here and go out into the world."

"I'm scared," Jonny said.

"Go and run with life, Jon. You disappear on *me* this time. That's all I've come to say."

"But I'm scared."

"Who isn't?"

35

I had no idea what had transpired out at the Pine Key place, so you can imagine my astonishment when, one day, as I was leafing through the *Miami Herald,* a headline caught my eye: "Jon Willig to Sell Circus to Maytime Toy Company." I was shocked, to say the least. I knew he'd been through some pretty rough times, but I'd just heard from Diana, who told me Jon was doing well.

"You're sure he doesn't need any help from me?" I asked.

"No, George, he's going to be all right. When I first arrived, he had that Treach woman and her friends sponging around, but I think he's had his fill of them."

"So you *were* able to help."

"Suzanne says I did." That was her strongest frame of reference for everything. If Suzanne confirmed it, then it made sense. "Jonny and I had a long talk one afternoon," she was saying. "I think this is the first time in his life that he's ever been willing to look at himself."

"Now what does that mean?" I found myself becoming increasingly irritated with her desire to have all of us scrupulously investigating our emotions and motivations. It was becoming something of a religion for her.

"What I mean is that he's willing to scratch the surface of his problems this time. Of course, he'll need some structure for what he finds. There is this marvelous analyst in Geneva I'd like him to see, but that will have to wait until he straightens out the business."

"Is he talking about the fire at all?" I asked quickly, wanting some footing in reality before getting lost in analytic theory.

"In a perverse way the fire may help him in the end. He's becoming introspective. I think that's good."

"You're sounding introspective yourself."

She laughed. "Are you making fun of me, George?"

"Wouldn't dream of it."

"How have you been, my love?" she asked lightly.

"Please don't call me that."

"Oh, George, we've been through that. I thought everything was settled between the two of us."

"It's not as easy as I thought it would be."

"Is that why you never came over to stay with Suzanne and me? We invited you so many times."

Why is it that everyone generally agrees that men cannot see beyond their egos? Diana had intuited something about herself in relation to me that settled the issue about loving me, so she assumed that I had done the same. I find women's intuition to be a very convenient mechanism. Unfortunately, it doesn't extend to anyone outside themselves.

"I can't compete, Diana. It's not my battlefield or ball game or boudoir."

"I don't follow you, George."

"Perhaps that is the problem. You're not following me at all. You've left me in the dust. I'm not all that civilized."

"George, are you having a difficult day?"

"See what I mean. Yes, a very difficult day. Well, I'm glad you called, and it's good to hear that Jon is on the road to recovery."

"Let's hope so. Will you come over to Europe and spend a holiday with us?"

"Perhaps."

"Plan on it. Jon has my address, and I know Suzanne would love to see you."

That had been a month ago. Now there was this new development. Something had prompted Jon to chuck everything he ever wanted. I was about to place a call to him, but before I could reach the phone, it rang. I could have guessed who it was.

"Did you see the newspaper?" Bea Willig asked.

"I did."

"What's going on at Pine Key?"

"I was about to call."

"So was I."

She really was off balance if she was willing to make the first move.

"Why don't you do that, Bea?"

"Do you think he'd want to talk with me?" Her voice sounded deliberately and elaborately carefree. "After all, he hasn't asked me for help in a long time, and I don't want to butt in where I'm not wanted."

"He might want your help now."

"I'll call. Will you be home?"

"All day."

"Good. I'll get back to you after I finish with him. We'll decipher this thing together."

I went upstairs to take my morning shower, and when I came back to the living room, the beach door was wide open. I saw something on the mantel I'd been expecting—another poem/epistle from Sam. I opened the envelope.

> For them who stole the birthright of the King,
> For them who trample over a lowly thing,
> For them who turn off lights in a star
> For them who steal my Shalimar,
> I sing one ditty—
> the chorus of which is my unflagging enmity.

Well, at least he was finishing them, although his style still left a lot to be desired. I read the letter that came with the ditty.

> Dear Friend George (that is if we are still friends),
>
> I cannot bear to think that you had anything to do with this dreadful plot to steal the land out from under my feet. It is easier for me to think that you had no part in it because you are the only friend I have left, so even if you had something to do with it I'd prefer you to lie to me and say that you didn't. Wasn't I right about Jack Chason? I told you he would get me. Now he and my mother have bought Shalimar. They got what they wanted all along. Too bad I never learned how to fire a gun the right way.
> Your friend, Sam

Maybe you can guess that the dreaded "deed" to which he referred and which was causing all this mental backsliding, was none other than the deed to Shalimar, which Bea and Jack had recently purchased. Actually, a corporation they formed called Miami Resorts had purchased about fifteen acres of what had been Shalimar. If the truth were known, I did have something to do with the incorporation, and the closing, but if Sam wanted me to, I would be more than happy to oblige him and lie about it.

A couple of hours later, as I was setting the table for brunch, a creamy white Cadillac convertible pulled up. The entire family was showing up on me that day. Albert and a blonde girlfriend. (Albert specialized in natural blondes with snub noses—his version of the Jewish/Wasp revenge, I suppose.) They were sitting out front talking, staring up at the house. It had been some time since I'd seen him, but I'd heard rumors about how he was moving up in the Jawitz operation. He was now operating two "supper clubs" on the south beach. He looked as flush as a nine-to-king run in spades—sharkskin suit, silk shirt, slicked back hair. Not just anyone's hired thug. He was trying to pass himself off as another young businessman on his way up, and while some people were buying it, I certainly wasn't. Bea wasn't, either. As I said before, she'd crossed him off her list years ago. Now, as I stood there looking at him, I decided that she'd crossed him off too hastily. I guess she thought this hoodlum thing was another one of his stages, but he didn't seem to be growing out of it.

Leaving the blonde in the car, he came up to the porch.

"Sloate, I want to talk with you."

Still the bully. Didn't he know there were dozens of ways around me?

"My friends call me George, Albert, and you and I are old friends."

He stared down at the sand self-consciously and then softened his approach with an almost avuncular grin. "Sorry about that, but I've got some trouble I got to talk over with you."

"If it has anything to do with you and your business associates, I'm not—"

He interrupted me. "Now hold on, damn it. It has nothing to do with that. My father, your friend, he's gone wild over this Shalimar thing—just gone nuts."

"I got a letter from him today. I know all about it."

"How could they have done it to him?"

"What are you talking about, Albert? He doesn't own that land any more. It was a business deal, pure and simple. They weren't out to get him in any way. You know, the more you feed that nonsense back to him, the worse it is for him."

"So you're in it, too. Well, we want that land back!"

"Oh, please!"

The phone rang. "Hello!" I said roughly.

"What's wrong?" It was Bea.

"Nothing. Did you speak with him?"

"George, the strangest thing is going on over there. I'm

worried. Jonny confirmed the fact that he's selling the circus, but doesn't really want to talk about it.

"That's interesting," I said, shaking my head, watching Albert pace around my living room.

"Who's there with you?" Bea asked.

"What do you mean?"

"Your voice sounds funny—what's going on?"

"It's your grandson. He's here to see me."

"What does he want?"

"Would you like to talk with him?"

"Don't be a damned fool, George. If he wants to talk with me, he knows where I am. What's wrong? Is he all right?"

"I don't know—let me call you later."

"Do that. Tell me everything after he's gone. By the way, Jonny said he wants to talk with you. He'll be in touch. Does Albert look well?"

"Yes, fine," I said, irritated.

"Good, well tell him hello for me. And, George, tell him to get out of that restaurant business or whatever it is he's into and get into something—"

"Goodbye, Bea, speak to you later." I hung up.

"What did she want?" Albert asked.

"Ask me what I can do for Sam, ask me anything, but don't one of you ask me what the other one wants any more, okay?"

"Calm down, will you?"

"No." I sat with a thud. "Okay, Albert, shoot."

"I want that land, and I want to get my father back on an even keel. He's like a wild man."

"That's why he is where he is."

"That's not too funny, George."

"What do you want me to do?" I yelled. My nerves were near the breaking point, and the damned phone was ringing again.

I picked it up and heard the crackling of long distance wires.

"Mr. Sloate?" a woman asked.

"Yes."

"One moment, please. Go ahead, Mr. Willig."

Jon came on the line. "George?"

"Jonny—what's going on over there? I read about it this morning, but I can't even pretend to understand it."

"Can you fly here tomorrow? I've got to talk with you. I'll have the plane pick you up."

"I don't know."
"It's very important, I'll tell you that much. Just come tomorrow. The plane will be there by noon. See you for drinks. Bye."
"My uncle?" Albert asked quickly.
"Your uncle," I said, still staring at the phone. "Okay, where were we?"
He stood and stretched. "I'm gonna go ditch that blonde I'm with. Then I'll come back here to pick you up. Get some clothes on, and we'll go talk with my father. You'll do it, won't you?"
"Oh, hell." I shrugged in disgust. "Old easy mark George. Yeah, I'll do it."

Albert's ill-gotten Cadillac was the perfect vehicle for the postwar era. It was a deluxe machine with a white body, bone steering wheel, rich walnut leather, and doodads and gizmos for all sorts of things.
"You seem to be doing very well yourself, Albert."
"I make out all right."
"You dealing with Mort Lister now?"
He looked over at me suspiciously. "Never met him."
"I'm surprised. Nice young ambitious man like yourself. I'd wager you are a credit to any organization."
"Come again?"
"I'm not out to scold you, Albert, but Stanley Jawitz is getting a lot of mileage out of that good name of yours."
"What are you talking about?"
"Oh, nothing—just seems to me that you are a perfect front for them. You add a dash of class. It looks like they pay you well enough to front. But I wonder, don't you ever want to get out there and play real ball with them? Start your own place?"
He tapped his hands nervously on the steering wheel. Obviously, I was bringing up something he'd already thought about.
"Let's can it with this business talk," he said.
I shut up.

Sam was on one of his rampages by the time we got out to La Hacienda.
"I want to know how you let them steal that land from me, George. Why didn't you protect my interests?"

"Sam, may we be reasonable for just one short moment? That land has not been yours for twenty years."

He looked over at Albert. Obviously, I was the only one not seeing the injustice. "Albert and I have been talking about it, and we're going to make a move on that land ourselves."

"With what?" I asked.

That was Albert's cue. "I can get my hands on some money. If we can't get the acreage Jack and my grandmother bought up, then maybe we can surround them."

"If that's your plan, then I don't know why you're telling it to me. I work for your mother, Sam, or have you forgotten that?"

"But why work for her?" Sam finally asked. "Why not kick in with Albert and me?"

"See, I'm gonna get my hands on enough money to buy that land around them and spring my father out of this place," Albert chimed in.

"Don't count on it. I know where you're getting your money from." Albert shook his head at me, cautioning me not to utter another word, but Sam had already gotten a whiff of what I was talking about.

"What money, Albert?" he asked. "I meant to ask you that. Where *are* you getting the money?"

Dead silence.

"Tell him, Albert."

"Jesus Christ, George. I got problems enough. I didn't need this."

"Albert's okay," Sam added. "He works with Stanley Jawitz. I used to work with Jawitz, George, you know that."

"And Jawitz is owned by a man named Mort Lister—that name ring a bell, Sam?"

Albert locked eyes with me, as Sam lumbered around the room mumbling Lister's name to himself. "Seems I heard of it."

"You shouldn't have done that, George."

"Mort Lister, Mort Lister." Sam's eyes were closed. "Seems I heard it or read it somewhere."

Albert got out of his chair. "I think we should leave now."

"Lister, Lister," Sam mumbled. Then his eyes opened. "Holy cow! You work for him?"

"Now hold on a minute, pop. I work for Jawitz."

"And Jawitz works for Lister. Always did, Sam, even when he was involved with you. He fronts for that hood."

Sam was furious for a moment, then he sank into a chair looking utterly defeated. "This is no good at all."

"Hold on a minute, pop. Money is money. What the hell difference does it make to you, anyway? I'm going to get you out of here and get that land back."

"Not good at all. What do I do, George?"

"I don't know. I tried to reason with him once, but he went out and did it. You got yourself one strong-willed kid, Sam."

"Will you listen to this crap!" Albert yelled. "Who do you think you're talking about—some kid you can kick out of the alley when you're through playing with him?"

Sam shook his head sadly. "Albert, you don't understand. Those guys, Lister and the rest. We never had anything to do with them. Even that bastard Jack wasn't into them."

"Not much. He was playing footsie with the S and G."

"That's over now," I said. "Anyway, the S and G were small-time compared with what you're into."

"Old men." Albert sneered. "Business is business. What's the difference? S and G or Lister. He'd just make it a smoother operation."

"There's got to be another place to get money," Sam said.

"Where? You tell me. Grandmother would get me frozen out at the banks. Where else do people like me get money?"

"There's always Jon," I said quickly.

"Sure, he's got lots of money," Sam said. "He'd help me. Hell, I've never asked him for a thing, have I?"

Albert was startled. "He doesn't even know me."

"It's worth a try."

"Sure, you listen to George, Albert. You go to Jon and tell him we're starting a land business again. We need a loan to get going. He'll do it. He must owe me for something. Hell, all of them owe me for something."

"But I don't know the guy."

"Damn it, he's your uncle. He'll do it. Won't he, George?"

"Tell you what. I'm flying over there tomorrow. Why don't you come along with me, and I'll see you get some time with him."

"He'll be there," Sam said.

36

Albert stood, his head craned back, staring up at the ceiling and at the gem-colored sunlight shining through the windows in the Pine Key place. Never before had he seen such opulence, and never before had I seen such hunger in anyone's eyes. It was difficult to comprehend the sort of wealth that Jon had amassed. His house was a palace fit for European royalty, and that it was here in America made it all the more spectacular. Corporations rose and fell around it. Taxes tried chipping away at it, but it stood imperiously.

Jon had lived there for years, and I don't think he was ever completely comfortable in it. Ruppert certainly had been trapped by it, but this new generation—Albert fresh from warfare, fresh from his hoodlum buddies—stood there, seeing it for what it was: spoils he could win if he knew how to bully his way into it.

"So you see, Albert," I said to him as we stood there, "not all the riches of this world are in the hands of the Commander Mosses."

All he said was, "How much did it cost?"

"I don't think you can put a price tag on a place like this today," I said.

"A million, you think?"

"A far sight more than a million."

"But how did he do it? How'd he wind up with something like this?"

"If you're not born into it, then you wait for the nastiest quirks of fate to get it."

I could hear Jon's voice coming from the office beyond the upper gallery. He had not met us at the airstrip; now we were waiting for him to finish his business.

"You're double-talking me, George. I don't like it when you do that."

"I didn't mean to. I was merely trying to explain the circumstances. Jon was taken in by the man who built it, Simon Ruppert. The man liked him, and Jon wound up with it. I wonder if your Uncle Jon thanks him for that now."

"What do you mean?"

"I don't think he's been too happy here."

"Poor bastard," Albert said smuggly. "I'd be happy here."

"I'm sure you would be."

Raymond came in carrying a tray of drinks. We helped ourselves, and then I watched as Albert started sweating, wondering how he would approach Jon.

"How we gonna do this, George?"

"Don't look at me. I brought you over here, but I want no part of your dealings with him. Remember, I work for your grandmother. Sometimes I work for your uncle, but *your* business with him is your business."

Just then, Jon appeared at the railing and stared down. He smiled at me, then stared incredulously at Albert.

"Who is that?"

"You surprise me," I said, rising. "This is your nephew."

"Albert? Albert Willig?"

Albert nodded.

"Why did you bring him here?" Jon asked, padding silently down the staircase.

I chuckled nervously. "What a pleasant first thing to say to your nephew."

He was wearing a raw silk jumpsuit, espadrilles, and a silk scarf knotted at his throat. His face had lost some of its youthful tightness and looked less masklike. But he did have that same florid skin that tanned so beautifully. As he walked up to us studying Albert, he extended his hand.

"Pardon me, Albert. I was surprised to see someone with George. I thought he'd be alone." The sentence fell out of his mouth as if it were a pair of false teeth. He turned to me with a tight little smile neatly in place. "How nice of you to bring him over, George." His words froze as they hit the air. "A family reunion—a very nice thought, George."

Well, this looked as though it would go less smoothly than I thought.

"You look like your mother," he finally said to Albert.

"That's what I've been told."

"We'll have lunch outside. Are you hungry?"

"I can eat," Albert said.

Jon tugged the bell pull. Raymond appeared.

"We'll be three for lunch, Raymond."

"Whenever you are ready, sir."

Jon appeared disoriented for a moment. "I've had a series

of unexpected visitors lately," was all he said as he led us out to the rose garden.

"What do you do with yourself, Albert? Are you working with your grandmother?"

"No."

"Are you one of those fortunates who doesn't work at all?"

"I'm getting into the real estate business."

"How ambitious."

Just as Albert looked ready to launch into his sales pitch, I interrupted. "You're looking well, Jon."

His eyes flashed. "I've never felt better."

"This is quite a place you've got here," Albert chimed in.

Jon said nothing. He led us out of the garden to the dock, where servants were putting the finishing touches on the luncheon table.

"Is your father still in that place?"

"I'm trying to get him out."

"But he's still in your grandmother's custody, isn't he?"

Albert nodded as we took our seats at the table, elegantly set with a large basket of hydrangeas in the center and tiny vines extending from it to our places. Servants reappeared behind us offering beluga caviar, cold salmon with a sauce *verte,* and a cheese soufflé, and a duck *ála pêche.* It was Albert's turn to feel uncomfortable, and he looked up at us every now and then to see if he was using the correct utensil or drinking from the correct glass. Jon was suspicious of Albert's presence from the first moment he saw him in the gallery. Every time Albert tried to broach the subject of money and business, Jon veered off his course and continued on with some mild, mindless badinage. As the meal ended, Jon looked up at that colossal house and smiled nostalgically.

"I never had many large parties here. I always wanted to, but I was too busy. I'll wager that you would have wild parties here if you owned it, wouldn't you, Albert?"

Albert looked up embarrassed, as if he'd been thinking about just that before Jon interrupted him. "I don't know. It must take a lot of money to run this place."

"Yes," Jon said flatly. "Tell me, do you see your grandmother at all?"

"She and I had a falling out."

"We all do sooner or later. She's a difficult woman but a

very successful one. I'd think that an ambitious person like yourself would stay pretty close to her."

"I want to go off on my own. I've got this plan for a real estate development on the north beach."

"Sounds like the old days, doesn't it, George," Jon said. He was starting to annoy me with his contained little asides. "I mean it sounds like your father talking, Albert."

"He wants to get involved with it as well, but he's not in a financial position to help out."

"No, I don't imagine he's in any position at all. Will you two excuse me for a moment? I have to check on something. Please remain seated." He got up and went into the house.

As the glass doors closed, Albert threw his napkin on the table.

"Goddamn it, who does he think he is? He may have wound up here, but I know he started out running booze. He treats me worse than he treats the niggers in this place."

"Just calm down. He's got a lot on his mind. Just go slow and easy with him."

"That's not my style. I don't know what the hell I'm doing here in the first place. He treats me like a kid. Back home, Jawitz and the rest of them respect me. I don't have to sit still for this. I don't care how much money he has."

The glass doors opened. Jon reappeared, and I was sure he had heard Albert's last remark.

"Sorry to have kept you waiting."

"Listen, Jon," Albert said, getting to his feet, index finger stabbing at the air, "I came here to talk business with you. My father needs help, and he thinks you're the one who can help him. Tell you the truth, I got my doubts about that."

Jon stood where he was, his smile still in place. "Well, don't let me stop you, Albert."

"We want to go into the real estate business, and we need some capital to start it with. I got sources for it, but my father thought I should go to you first."

"How generous of him—and you're here."

"Yeah, I'm here. I want to know if you'll do some business with me. If not, then I can disappear."

"Let's take this step by step," Jon said evenly, sinking back into his chair. "What does your father have to do with this? He's in the hospital, isn't he?"

"You've been out of touch. My grandmother and Jack have gotten hold of Shalimar again—about fifteen acres of what my father used to own. They want to develop it. My father wants to buy up the rest of the acreage and get back what's his."

"And where do you come in?"

"Where do you think I come in? I'm gonna help my father."

"What are you going to do with the land?"

"Build a hotel."

"I see." Jon sat there pensively for a moment, then looked up at me. "Where do you fit into this?"

"I'm not involved. Sam wanted Albert to talk with you, and I volunteered to bring him over."

"Why come to me at all if you have sources in Miami?" Jon asked Albert, who blushed. I answered.

"Sam didn't like the sources. I don't, either."

"You stay out of it," Albert yelled. "Jesus, all of you give me a goddamn royal pain." He walked out to the edge of the dock and stared at the water. "My friends in Miami wouldn't put me through this crap. They can buy and sell you, Jon, but my father wanted me to come here and by God, I'm here."

I inched closer to the table and whispered. "He's involved with Jawitz and Lister. Sam's scared."

"I thought as much. We've all had our turn being wined and dined by them."

Albert turned angrily. "Naw, you're real white sitting out here, aren't you? You're as clean as the damn roses."

"You sound like a very angry person. Albert, and angry people aren't trustworthy. They jump the gun. Let me tell you something, Albert. For all I know, you're the same bungler your father was."

I interrupted. "Ease up, Jon."

"What for? This is the big time he's stumbling into, isn't it? Why shouldn't he take it to get what he wants. Your father blew a lot of money up there in Shalimar. He took a lot of people down with him. Why on earth should I trust him with my money? Answer me that, Albert. Why should I?"

"Because Jack and Bea Willig screwed him, that's why, and I want that land back!"

Jon shook his head in disgust. "This never ends, does it? My sister is the only one in this family who has her head screwed on correctly. She just leaves all of you to fight it out." He stood and walked back to the glass doors. "You and Sam want to use my money to fight my mother and brother-in-law. I've run from all of you my whole life, and I'm going to keep on running. You take your plans and schemes and eat them with the mousse, Albert."

He opened the doors and disappeared inside. I stood there pointing an accusing finger at Albert. "You've got a lot to learn about dealing with people."

"Don't give me your crap. Let's get off this island."

I followed Jon inside, running across the length of the gallery to catch up with him. He was already on his way upstairs.

"Jon, wait. The kid is hot-tempered, I'll admit it—"

"You always wind up in the middle of everything, George. I can't for the life of me figure out what you see in this damned family and why you're forever shoving yourself into it. Can't you see it's useless? I want nothing more to do with it."

"Be fair, Jon."

"What do you want from all of us? Does this tension get your heart going? What is it? Are we all that different from what you grew up with? I guess so. I can just see your scrupulously pious family sitting in the front parlor, not uttering a word above a whisper. It's our fighting that gets you, isn't it? The hope of passion, the tantalizing insanity lurking there waiting to spring out to devour the world. Isn't that it? Tell me, George."

"Listen to me, Jon. I'm sorry this made you uncomfortable, but Sam was worried about the kid. He's getting further and further into Lister. You know what that means."

"More insanity. Who cares any more? But you're not answering my questions, George. What are you getting out of being in the middle of it?"

"I never thought about it."

That stopped the fusillade of abuse. I was shaken to the core by his questions. He made me feel as if I'd trespassed one too many times. He was also asking me to justify a lifetime of actions that had entwined me in their lives. What *did* I want? Did I feel superior to them because I was the one who possessed control and enough rationality to put their lives back together for them? I know I felt needed by them. Maybe it was as simple as that—they needed me.

Now he looked sorry that he'd needled me so. He rushed down the stairs and put his arms around me. "I'm sorry, old man, I didn't mean to push you that far."

He stared out the window at Albert pacing furiously. "I'll

have Raymond tell the pilot to fly Albert back to Miami, and then you and I will have a final dinner here—just like old friends. Would you like that?"

"I suppose," I said sadly, not comprehending what he meant by a 'final dinner.'

Albert was gone in an hour. Jon and I stood at the deserted airstrip watching as his plane took off. Albert had refused Jon's handshake at the end, and he wasn't talking with me.

"You're really worried about him?" Jon asked, shielding his eyes against the sun, watching the plane climb higher. "I find him totally disagreeable, but I suppose that's not completely his fault."

"He's had a rough time of it."

"But there does come a time when you've got to realize that no matter what has been dealt, it's your own hand."

"But these people he's in with—"

"I know all about them. They'll be running the country soon. They're taking over Miami, aren't they?"

"Yes. They're not in complete control, but it's just a matter of time."

"What's stopping them?" he asked as we walked over to the bay.

"Something called the S and G Syndicate."

"Out of Chicago, are they?"

"That's the one. They're just bookmakers—but Lister! Good God, he's Murder Incorporated. Drug traffic and pimping. He sees a gold mine springing up out there on the beach, and he wants it."

"He'll get it," Jon said intently, but his mind was elsewhere. He was studying a stretch of water midway between the Key and the mainland. "That's where I ran aground. That's where my life changed."

"The hand of fate, you once said."

"With a dubious touch." He turned to me, smiling. "And I don't want it any more, George."

"That's why you sold the circus?"

"I'm selling everything. Ruppert will get his wish granted. I'll give the house to the state. Let them deal with it. It's perverse—the workers who built this place will be paying for its upkeep with their tax money. Let them pay admission to see the way I've lived. The funny thing is that I realize it was never mine. It was Simon and Georgia's dream, not mine. I'm tired of trying to live their lives."

We strolled across the lawn to the bathing pavilion. Jon suggested that we change into trunks and swim out in the bay.

He was standing near the water in his briefs by the time I came out of my cabana.

We didn't talk as he lowered himself into the water. I followed. It was like the night we'd gone on the rum-run together with him there in front of me, smiling so confidently, tumbling off the shoal, turning every now and then to make sure I was all right. Back then, he had the world in front of him. Now he appeared to be less hungry for it. He was taking long, measured strokes, his brown body gliding quietly through the water, hardly disturbing it. I remembered thinking the night of the run that he and I would remain friends all our lives. We'd come close to that now. My friendship had mellowed into a deep and abiding love for the friend who had set out to create his life.

He reached a sand bar and climbed up on it, strolling along in about a foot of water, staring back at the house. I joined him up there.

"Look what I did, George. Look what I got for myself."

"Can you turn your back on it?"

"That's where you and I are different, my friend. I can turn my back on all of it and walk away. You must stay with what you know. That's why you stay with my mother. It's comfortable for you. I'm sorry for taunting you about it. I just didn't want you involved in the insanity I see coming up again. Sam and my mother—it will never end."

There was a heron stalking in the reeds near us. We followed behind it for a moment or two, but the bird felt our feet rippling through the water, and it swooped up in a long, lazy circle.

"My father came to visit me here."

"What was that like?"

"Damned if the son of a bitch didn't change my life."

"How?"

"He wants me to go out and find myself. So, I'm disappearing for a while once I get all of this unloaded. The newspapers will probably say I'm dead, but you and I will know the truth. You must tell my mother that I'm all right. I've salted away a lot of money in Europe and out West, enough to live on for the rest of my life, so no worries there."

Appropriately enough, the sun was making its slow descent—a fiery ball showering the clear sky and white clouds with a tawny glow.

"I'm running off again and not asking you to join me this time. I'll probably find myself in the arms of some sweet young man. My father would be shocked." He laughed, but there was something else bothering him. "I made peace with you. Made peace with my father. It's my mother I don't know what to do with. At first, I thought I'd leave her to work it out for herself, but I don't know. I don't know how to reach her, don't even know if she wants me to."

"She loves you."

"I suppose, but I'm my father's son." He shrugged. "Oh, I'm taking this too seriously. I'll pop up when I decide what to do with my mother."

Two months later, he disappeared, and the newspapers speculated about his death or a kidnapping. I told Bea he was all right.

"I don't understand. Doesn't he want to be in touch with me again?"

"In time, but he still needs the time to find himself."

"Just like his father," was all she said.

37

Albert had come home from the abortive meeting with Jon refueled with indignation. He demanded Jawitz's help, and when Jawitz balked, he arranged a meeting with Mort Lister.

That took place one weekend in May, 1948, in Lister's rather unpretentious stucco house on the outskirts of Broward County.

As Albert sat in the modest living room with its rattan furniture and chintz curtains, he felt he was on more solid footing. He wasn't staring a palace in the face. No butlers or maids, just two Irish hoods who stood guard near the windows. The air inside was hot and damp. Somewhere in the background was a record playing—Frankie Laine singing

"Désirée." Albert looked out of place in his sharkskin trousers and silk shirt. He rose as a group of men walked in. The shortest of them was wearing plaid bermuda shorts and a flowered shirt that had "Miami, the Winter Playground" printed over one of the breast pockets. The short man cocked his head to one side, studying Albert, and then told the goons to leave. He sat down and spoke in a thin, raspy voice.

"You wanted to see me."

"You're Mort Lister," Albert said, sitting self-consciously, laying his large hands in his lap and then dropping them at his sides.

"That's right. I hear you wanted to see me."

"I'm Albert Willig."

The older man smiled benignly, looking like anybody's uncle or grandfather. Albert laughed to himself. This would be a piece of pie.

"I know who you are," Lister said. "I don't know why you're here."

"I have a business venture I think you'd be interested in."

"You do, do you?"

"A real estate venture."

"Stanley Jawitz has told me a lot about you. And, of course, I've heard about your family. Very nice family you've got."

"They've got no part of this real estate idea of mine."

"I been waiting for you to come around to introduce yourself to me. I been hearing how well you run the clubs. I'm very impressed."

"I'm glad you're getting good reports, but that's not what I want to talk about."

"Take it slow, kiddy, you got lots of time," Lister said. "You want a piece of fruit?" He pointed to a bowl near him.

"No."

"Why not? Fruit's good for you. Have a piece."

Lister placed the bowl under Albert's nose. Albert chose an apple but merely rubbed it against his shirt.

"So you got a deal for me. I like deals. Deals have made me a very rich man. What kinda deal you talking?"

"Put up a big hotel on the beach."

"I got hotel deals going right now. Not here, of course, but I got them. You heard of Las Vegas?"

Albert nodded.

"Got a nice deal going there, and you want to put one up here?"

The room suddenly seemed to be claustrophobic. Lister's voice was quiet, but it filled the corners with a premeditation you could cut with a knife.

"Big hotel up on the beach here, you say. That's a nice deal. You think you got the right timing for it?"

"What do you mean?"

"You think you'll fill this hotel of yours?"

"There is going to be a new boom down here."

"Sure, I heard about that. Heard your grandmother and Jack are going into a big hotel up on the beach. You been forced out of that deal?"

"I don't have anything to do with them."

"I'm surprised."

"I've had a falling out with them."

"But they're smart people. Your grandmother announces it, but I notice she doesn't want to build it for a while. She's gonna wait for them to start piling in here. Why do you want to go running off like a hothead?"

"If I beat them to it, I'll be the one on top before they even start theirs."

"*You* will, huh? I thought you were coming to me with this deal?"

"That's what I mean. We'll have it built—"

"Who cares who's first? If it goes, there will be money for everyone. If not, why not let them take the fall?"

"But why wait? Your gambling joints are making money hand over fist. The real money is going to be in the hotel business again."

"Smart kid. But you got to think about the timing part of it, smart kid. You know what that means?"

"I don't follow you."

"But that's what I want you to do. Follow me. We don't own the whole works yet. You know that, don't you?"

"You mean the S and G."

"Them, yeah, sure—we got them. We got to see how Las Vegas goes. We got to see how you play ball."

"I've proved myself. I make a profit for you out at the Palm."

"You do real nice, kiddy, I been watching you. You keep yourself nice and clean, and you got a nice education, don't you?"

"Yes."

"Sure, you talk like a real classy kid. I like what I see."

Lister got up as if the meeting were ending.

"But what about what I'm offering you?" Albert asked.

"You ain't offering me nothing. I'm offering you a chance to learn about the timing thing, kiddy. You're doing a nice job for me. It's good to know you want to get into the hotel business, but you got to wait it out. So go back to your job at the Palm, and I'll let you know when I'm ready to talk deals with you."

"I don't know."

Lister was walking out of the room, but he turned suddenly.

"What's not to know? Trust me, kiddy. I got my eye on you. I hear what you're saying—you just let me do the thinking. I want all you want, but you'll have to wait along with me. I want the whole town, kiddy—everything—then we'll talk deals again." He smiled. "Don't worry. And take another piece of fruit on your way out, it's good for you."

Old men, Albert muttered to himself as he gunned his Cadillac along a deserted stretch of beach on Collins Avenue. Where Shalimar had once stood, there was now a sign tacked onto a post:

> LE PALAIS—THE LARGEST RESORT HOTEL IN THE WORLD—WILL BE BUILT ON THIS SITE BY MIAMI RESORTS, INC.
>
> Owners: Beatrice Willig
> Jack Chason

Albert cursed as he read it. Then he forced the pedal down to the floor, showering the sign with sand as he sped off.

He was impatient all right, but he didn't have much to worry about.

Almost a year to the day after he met with Lister, a banner headline appeared in the *Miami Herald*: "MOB MUSCLES IN ON RICH S & G SYNDICATE."

Lister had gotten all he wanted, and that precipitated a final, bloody installment of the Willigs' story.

V

Empires in the Sun

38

Men and women.

I have a tendency to believe that just the mention of certain words like "men" and "women" is enough to evoke all sorts of emotions in you that will naturally correspond with mine. Like number paintings, you do all the work. I post the numbers. You draw the lines that lie between them.

The Willig men needed their fathers, but their fathers disappeared. Have I stumbled upon some question of twentieth century social dynamics? We no longer live on farms. Fathers have gone off to work in the city, leaving the women and children to fend for themselves. Everyone scrambles around doing the best he or she can until the father returns to restore order. Not that the fathers are capable of doing that, but there is a history of sturdy farm fathers, and just the image of them will suffice: sleeves rolled up against the noonday sun, sweat-streaked arms struggling with a plow. To hell with images—just the mere presence of a father would suffice.

After all, what did Abe give Jon but the mere notion of his presence, that he existed, that he was fallible but lovable, irresponsible but loving.

Poor Sam missed out; he became a father without knowing how to be one. No wonder he wound up in a loony bin; no wonder Albert had nothing but his temper left to cling to.

And the women. My God! Did Bea want all the power thrust on her? Was Abe right in assuming that was what she was after from the very first? Of course, Abe is lovable after all, but I think he only scratches at surfaces. In a better of all possible worlds, Bea would have liked to have been taken care of, but she didn't have the father to do it. Oh, yes, there was that saintly mother of hers who traveled across the ocean and raised her family against great odds (her own husband, to name one), but I think Bea's mother was nothing more than some source of retrenched anger and disappointment. When the older generation left the old country, the patriarchy disappeared, and nothing took its place. The women were scared. So there was Bea and her mother and "the beauties" alone in a new country while their father went off to his Polish men's club to drink the night away. Have I told you about him? Frieda once filled in the pieces for me. Bea's father skipped out of Poland on a freighter before being conscripted into the army. He went to Palestine but wound up in Ohio. He sent for his saintly wife, who came and in short order gave birth to three daughters. That was the last the women saw of him. This man, who'd seen the disillusioned remnants of a dying European century before coming to Ohio, went to work and got drunk. The mother brought the girls up until her strength gave out and Bea took over; she moved into that gentile girl's house, got the family into better quarters. She was quite successful as earth-mover and shaker, but she did not want the responsibility. She knew that with her drive unleashed she could have the world, but she didn't want it at first. She held her drive in trust for the right man. And along came Abe, always disappearing, who did not even bother to read the trust agreement. And where did that leave Bea? You think she coldheartedly set out to shape her children's destinies? Wrong. She was frightened. She hid behind her children. Yes, she wanted things, but she wanted the boys to get them for her. She wanted to remain in the wings, prodding them, perhaps, but she did not want to step out front to give the performance or take the bows.

Was Jack subservient? Did Bea make him that way? The easy answer is, yes. But the difficult question is: what did *she* need him for? She led him around by the nose, not to torture him, but because he was some male presence who hadn't up and run away. As for me, she told me countless times that she needed me there to reassure her and to share the responsibility of managing her wealth. She didn't want to usurp my power. She wanted me to usurp hers. All she wanted was the illusion that she could be able to traipse off to her mirror and play with the perfume bottles on her vanity in a bona fide cosmetic advertisement's vision of a woman's life. Leave me alone, she kept saying. Sail away—life on a ribbon of water surging out of a garden hose, no less. Leave me alone!

And now I am Bea's apologist. At least I can be fair and make a case for her. She had no choice. So I beseech you to love her for all her frailty, in spite of her inability to express love, in spite of her calculations and manipulations. I want you to love her because like me, like Jon and Sam and Albert and Diana—like all of us—she was left to fend for herself. So love her and know that what we have been dealing with all along is a child who did not grow up.

At age seventy-four, however, she did decide to grow up, to come out of hiding and take full control. She did it by building a stupendous hotel, which she called Le Palais.

The seeds of its great success were planted at the earliest planning meetings. Jack would start off in a huff. Always a great starter, he'd go on about his dream of a hotel on the beach; five hundred rooms, as well as pools, nightclubs, and cabanas.

"Too small, my boy," Bea would say to this fifty-five-year-old man. "You're not thinking big enough."

This was 1953, and she was beginning to understand the change sweeping across Miami. Hotel row was booming on the south beach. A new crowd was starting to show up in the winters; people whose parents had landed in the ghettos of New York a scant fifty years ago were now suddenly rich, and Bea saw thousands of them flooding into town.

Jack placed his renderings at her feet, but she merely stared down disdainfully.

"It looks like a gasoline station with flags," she sniffed. He flipped to another; this one was more of a towering slab.

"You don't understand," she said to him. "You don't even remember where you came from, Jack. Just because you make the buildings large, they still look like the damned tenements these people crawled out of. A hotel is no place like home. Get the car," she snapped. "I want you to take a look at what we are dealing with."

Off we went with artist in tow to the south beach along hotel row. Two men named Muffson and Novak had made a fortune with a hotel called the San Souci, the first of the glitzy postwar palaces. After it came the Saxony and the Versailles. We drove past them, walked into their lobbies with Bea leading the way, pointing out the sights. Platinum blonde grandmothers sat in the air-conditioned lobbies, wearing minks and diamonds in broad daylight. At the pool others dozed, rows of bottle green, mother-of-pearl sunglasses raised to the sun. Men were drinking and gambling. Women sauntered by in capri pants, walking poodles. Pink lipsticked mouths talked and clacked. Mah-jongg tiles clicked on sea-salt coated tables. Canasta games bustled. People tanned themselves toasty desert colors, roared with laughter, gossiped maliciously.

"Do you see what I mean?" Bea asked me.

"I think I'm getting your message."

"They've got more money than they know what to do with, and, believe me, this crowd doesn't know what to do with it first. Let's go out to our hotel site."

Off we trotted behind this seventy-four-year-old woman. Mr. Novak saw her and ran across his lobby to say hello to her, but she merely smiled tightly and breezed past him.

"He'll hate me soon enough," she said. "After I take his people away from him, he'll never talk to me again."

We filed into the car. Jack sat there trying to outguess her. "So we need something vulgar—something splashy."

"More than that," she said impatiently. "We have to outguess what they'll want to come down here to find. They've been brought up on those Norma Shearer overstuffed movies. That's what they think being rich in America is all about."

By God, she was a visionary. This was the postwar era. The American Empire. Money for everything. A house in every pot, then two cars shoved in there with it. Money for vacations, and soon thousands to be thrown away. Industry surging after a glorious breast-beating war. Suburbs starting their midnight creep. Steel thrown away on emerging car fins. My God, to have been white and middle class in fifties America—what pink-and-gray Formica promise the day held, and I refuse at this moment to feel guilty about any of it, because I refuse to look beyond DeSoto car fins and silver blue mink stoles and spike heels and golf clubs and bermuda shorts and Rockwell's dallying, cherubic faces or Molly and Sunny Jim in the backyard swinging from jungle gyms, whirling hoola hoops. Luci and Desi—thank God for them all—such calm, blue white TV tubes glowing with a reassurance that surely cave people felt sitting around their own fires. To be home—slippers and pipe and the dog and the mother in the kitchen with an apron cinched around her waist. I tell you they loved it, and they wanted more of it. They wanted color TV. They wanted additions to the house and patios and fantasy vacations. And they wanted Eisenhower to put In God We Trust on the currency, so they could spend it and feel blessed by the spending.

Bea held it all in the palm of her hand.

She and Jack and I stood with our backs to the water, staring up at the beach and Collins Avenue beyond it. There were still remnants of Shalimar scattered in the sand, but Bea didn't notice them. She was staring into the future.

"We've got to design it from this vantage point," she was saying.

"But hotels are designed from the road," Jack argued.

"No, we'll have gardens out there, but we have to make them feel as if they can't see it from the road—that they have to come into it to actually be a part of it. Once we've gotten them inside, then we have to pamper them."

She walked over to the artist and repeated what she'd just told us. He studied the site and began drawing.

"It's got to be a circle," she said.

"It can't be a circle. Half the rooms will lose the view of the ocean."

"Right," she nodded. "Then a half-circle. I want them to feel enveloped by it. Do you know what I mean? I want them to feel as if they're being hugged by it."

"Like a mother's arms enfolding them," I said lightly, but she took that to heart.

"Exactly, just like a mother's arms."

"What about inside?" Jack asked.

"French all over the place. Anything French and as far from the Bronx as possible."

After a little while the artist walked over to her with a couple of sketches. One was exactly what she wanted! A mammoth half-moon rising ten or fifteen stories flanked by lower structures that fanned out on the beach.

"Yes. That's it. All in white. Everything outside will be white."

"What are you talking about here, Bea?" Jack asked. "How many rooms you think you're gonna have?"

"One thousand."

"You're crazy. We'll never get financing for something that large."

She disregarded him and began walking back up to her car. "If you can't get it, Jack, then I will personally go to the banks and get it. Do you understand? You and George work up a prospectus. Hire an architect who'll do what I tell him to do, and don't come to me with excuses or whines, telling me I can't get what I want." She stopped for a moment, staring north at the deserted stretch of beach adjacent to her property. "They tacked a sign up there, George. Did you let that land slip through our fingers?"

"The bank is still holding onto it, Bea. I spoke with them last week."

"I want that land," she said. "Walk over there with me." She had the chauffeur follow us on the road.

"I'll tell you something, Bea. With what you've got planned, I don't think you've got the money to buy more land."

"You and Jack—a bunch of old maids."

We reached the property. A sign was posted saying the land had been sold, but the buyer was not named.

"We were damned fools to let this slip away from us."

"Bea, you haven't gotten the first one built," I said.

"You just keep watch over Jack. I'm not going to make any compromises with this hotel."

"This going to be your monument?"

"Monument? Hell, no, we'll make a fortune on it and pull out at the end of the fifth year!"

Final renderings were submitted within a month, and she finally got what she wanted: a marble half-moon. When you stood by the pool or beach and looked back at it, it was lying there, arms outstretched ready to cradle you. Teams of engineers and architects put the final bill at sixteen million dollars, and after I scraped Jack off the floor, he and I set out to find the money to finance it.

Generally, Miami hotels are run like any other syndication. Seed money is brought in with the first renderings; you sell investors all the hoopla implicit in a four-color picture of a fifteen-story half-moon. Then another syndication is issued to start construction, and then more shares are sold off to decorate, etc. Bea wanted to hold on to as much control as she could, so we approached banks who were willing to take large chunks of it, with Bea putting up the largest chunk (about five million), mortgaging almost everything she owned to do it. When the deal was completed, it was the largest real estate loan in the history of the South, and we managed to get it with the participation of only two banks, the Miami Federal and the Atlanta First.

I think it would be best here for me to reel off some statistics to give you an idea of the enormity of our undertaking. Twelve hundred workers broke ground for Le Palais in January, 1954. Eleven months later, it was completed, using 49,000 square yards of carpeting; 76,000 square feet of windows; 2,000 mirrors; 22 carloads of furniture, including antiques and not so very antiques; 100 miles of pipes; 150 miles of wiring; 2,000 telephones; and 850 full-time staff. At one point during the construction, one of the designers flew off to France to loot the flea markets. He hired twenty French copyists from the Louvre to copy almost every well-known statue in the museum.

It was garish, outrageous, and outlandish, but it took your breath away. Frank Lloyd Wright called it an "anthill." Jack Benny said he loved it but thought Bea had gone overboard "to have put a ten-piece orchestra in the men's room." People poked fun at it, but they seemed more than willing to pay the going rates: $180 a day for a suite, and a cabana rental of $40 a day.

The interior design could have been called "oh, what the hell, do it" moderne.

"You've got to understand these people," Bea would say. "People who come to luxury hotels have escaped to somewhere else so they can be someone else. Everything has to be an illusion, so we mix a little French with a little Hollywood and add a dash of the tropics."

"The tropics?" I asked.

"Sure. Bird cages and plants."

"Who is going to take care of tropical birds?"

"Who's talking birds? Just the cages—you're not thinking fast enough, George."

She was right. I was dumbfounded, while she sailed off with more energy than all of us. In her lobbies she designed huge sweeping staircases that went nowhere, because, she said, people love to walk up and down grand staircases. She designed oversized railings for the staircases so that a woman's hand would glide down them. She had pin spots put into the ceiling above the rails so that the jewelry on the woman's gliding hand would sparkle all the way down.

It was a hodgepodge. A mess. But it simply reeked of money, and by the time opening day arrived, it was sold out through December of the following year. Bea had not underestimated the taste of her clientele; she simply matched their talent for spending.

On opening day, however, Bea wanted nothing to do with it. I'd gone over to the Coconut Grove place early that morning to fetch her, but her maid said she was going to stay at home. She was sitting in the gazebo, staring out at the bay. Off in the distance La Palais's crescent-shaped tower rose above the beach. She smiled slyly when she saw me.

"I know why you're here, and my answer is no."

"But why?"

"I'm not going over there. You and Jack run the show. I don't like crowds."

"You can't be serious."

"I am. Why would I want to see all those people? My sisters will be there. I hear that even Tildy Schultz is showing up. I don't want to have anything to do with them."

"Who cares about them, Bea? The entire state of Florida is turning out for this."

"Did you give the final orders to the publicity people?"

"Of course."

"The planes and everything?"

I looked at my watch. "The planes are set to take off any minute now."

"Good, then I'll watch it from here. You go over there and make sure everything runs smoothly."

"I'm not moving."

"Don't be a damned fool, George. There's work to be done."

"I'm not leaving unless you come with me."

"I can't go."

"Give me one good reason."

She turned away from me. "Should we have gotten Sam out for this?" she asked. "Would he have come?"

"I don't know. I've been too busy to see him."

"None of my people will be there. Jonny's gone. Sam's gone. And Diana—where is she, George?"

"I don't know."

"Albert won't be there. None of my own people. Why on earth have I built that damned thing?"

"This is one hell of a time to be asking yourself that."

Just then the sky filled with a dozen small airplanes circling over the city. Each made a pass over the bay near her house.

"Everything is running like clockwork," she said rising, waving up at the planes, which were now heading north toward Le Palais.

When they reached the beach, they swooped down and began showering the sky with thousands of pearl white balloons. I could hear cheers filtering across the water.

"You go inside and get dressed. I refuse to let you miss this."

She stared quizzically at me.

"I'm serious. Either you get dressed or I'll drag you over there now."

"Listen to you."

I grabbed her hand roughly, jerking her to her feet. "Okay, if this is the way you want it, I'll drag you."

"Okay, okay. Calm down. You win. But I don't want you waiting around here while I dress. You go over and keep your eye on things. I'll take my time and join you."

"If you're not there in an hour, I'm coming back for you."

"I heard you," she said, sauntering back to the house. "Give me two hours. But I'll tell you one thing. You better keep those sisters of mine away from me—keep all of them away!"

"To hell with them!"

"That's what I've been saying my whole life, but it doesn't work."

39

Le Palais's opening . . .

Women carrying bathing towels trimmed with baby seal . . . Men with pinky rings flashing, cigars smoldering, shooting craps, anteing up for poker. Thousands of people were there. Hands were coming out at me, congratulating me. Jack was in the center of it, taking most of the credit, overseeing the newsmen and managing the bellhops, which was okay as far as I was concerned. All of them swirled around me as I stood staring at the useless staircases. Bea had been right; women were sailing up and down them in *grande dame* fashion. Everyone loved it; the bird cages and Louis XIV furniture; the Versailles-like mirrored halls and baroque statues.

"If this is Americana, then we lost the Revolution," someone whispered in my ear.

I turned. Frieda took a long drag of her cigarette.

"How are you, Frieda?"

"Jack's got a perverse sense of humor. He sent me a free ticket, and he's putting me up in this—this—what would you call it?"

"Hotel?"

"Is this a banana republic or is this a banana republic?"

"This is obviously what they want," I said, indicating the crowd.

"War profiteers." She sneered.

"On which side did you wind up in the war? The Hitler-Stalin pact must have thrown you for a loop."

"You're still so clever," she chided, plucking a glass of champagne from a waiter's tray. "How well are you fitting into this era of loyalty oaths?"

"Damned messy business."

"And you're still so civilized and accommodating. Where is the lady of the hour—playing Marie Antoinette or Lady Du Barry?"

"Bea will be here soon, and I think you should steer clear of her. You frighten her."

"What doesn't?"

"Just behave yourself and go get quietly plastered. Tell me something. How have you been supporting yourself?"

"I'm up in New York," she said, depositing her empty glass, plucking another from a passing tray. "I'm a salesman for a printing firm. It's a living."

"That's the spirit that made this country great. We'll have Communists in Cadillacs any day now." I turned and gasped. Barreling toward me was Tildy Schultz Willig with husband number two in tow. The years had not been kind to her. She was weighing in at about one seventy-five and had persisted in wearing tight-fitting dresses and elaborate make-up. I wanted to hide behind Frieda, but rat that she was, she disappeared.

"George, my God, George Sloate!" was Tildy's opening line. Then she thrust her husband into my chest. "Meet Henry Finkelstein, my husband. Where's Sam? I been lookin' all over for him." Her head bobbed up and down as Henry Finkelstein and I exchanged quick handshakes. "Oh, forgive me, George, you deserve a great big hug." She lunged at me, planting a slobbering kiss and about a pound of lipstick on my cheek. "George and I go back a long time, don't we, money?" She made that sound a bit more heated than I recollected.

"We certainly do. Sam is still in the—"

"Is he still out there? Poor baby. I really did him in, didn't I? I've told you he just went nuts after I left him, didn't I, Henry?"

"Constantly," Henry said. I was glad to see he had a sense of humor.

"Poor Sam. Have you seen my baby, George?"

"Is Albert here today?"

"Well, of course he is. He wouldn't miss his grandmother's opening day—now would he? Although I understand she's been just awful to him. Saving grace is that he's got my ability to swallow a craw-full and come out punching. You know what I mean?"

"He swallows along with the best of them," I said, trying to extricate myself from her ever-tightening grasp.

"We all wanted to be here, although I was hurt that I wasn't invited directly."

"Be serious, Tildy," I said.

"Well, I heard about it, and I said to Henry, 'I'm not gonna miss this for anything.' Didn't I say that, Henry?"

Henry was watching the behind of a comely blonde girl, although he had the presence of mind to nod in Tildy's direction.

"If this place doesn't beat all," Tildy gawked. "I'm just waiting for my baby to build one just like it."

"Is that what he's planning to do?" I asked lightly.

"Albert's got all sorts of plans, but he told me that he's gotten a hold of the rest of that Shalimar land, and he and his partners are gonna put up a huge place right next to this one."

"Albert bought that land?"

"Did I open my big mouth again? My God, I always do that. Sure he bought it. Well, his partners did—that Mr. Lister, a very fine man. I understand, although I haven't met him personally. Lister and Jawitz—you remember Jawitz, don't you, George?"

"Very well. Are you sure it was Albert who bought it?"

"Well, of course I'm sure. You all will have to come to our opening, now, won't you?"

We had been damned fools to let that land slip through our hands. Now Mort Lister would be our closest competitor. That scared the hell out of me.

"Would you please excuse me, Tildy? I've got lots to do around here."

"I will not let go of you until you tell me where Bea is. I'm dying to see her."

"She'll be here soon."

"Well, do tell her that I'm here and that I'd love to see her."

"Do yourself a favor, Tildy, and keep your distance. I don't think you'll get much of a reception."

I pried my arm loose, and as I walked away, she turned back to Henry Finkelstein. "Well, of all the nerve. Didn't I tell you these Willigs were jealous of me?"

"Oh, yes," Henry said.

"Of all the nerve, but isn't George Sloate the most gorgeous gentile man you've ever seen?"

I was out of earshot for the answer.

I started grabbing champagne glasses myself. Just as my eyes were glazing over, Stanley Jawitz threw his arm around me.

"You son of a bitch," he said, looking around at the lobby

"You should talk."

"What do you mean?"

"You got Albert Willig to front a hotel for you."

"You heard? That mouthpiece mother of his no doubt."

"No doubt."

"Business is business, my boy. We're gonna be neighbors."

"I don't like it, Stanley."

"What's wrong with a little competition?"

"I don't like your brand."

"You always were a bit of a tight ass, George, but I like your style."

"I'm sure I should thank you for that."

Jack Chason was bearing down on us, all smiles; his day was obviously coming off without a hitch.

"Stanley, how are you? George, where's Bea?"

"Does he know about your plans?" I asked Jawitz.

"What plans?"

"We're building a hotel right next to yours," Stanley said.

Jack froze; his mouth was caught somewhere between a pliant grin and a dying gasp. "You what?"

"They bought that land, Jack. Albert is going to run the show."

"Well, not exactly," Jawitz added nervously. "He's got partners, you know. We were just waiting to see how you people did, and it looks pretty good. Close your mouth, Jack, you look dumb enough as it is. I'll leave you gentlemen alone to contemplate the future."

"I don't like this at all, George," Jack said.

"Who does?" I polished off one champagne, then reached for another. "Oh, hell, who cares? We're going to do just fine, and, anyway I've been dealing with the banks for months, and I haven't heard about any development loans for a new hotel."

"Those people don't need banks."

"That's true, too—forget it, Jack. We're a smashing success."

I started walking away, but he tugged on my sleeve.

"Do you know the people who've rented the Versailles Suite for the season?" Jack asked.

"No."

"The Amusement Company—something like that—they want to see me up there, but I haven't had the time. I've got my hands full. Why don't you go up there and take care of it?"

"I'll circulate awhile longer, then head up."

"Where's Bea?"

"Stylishly late."

"Keep her away from Diana when she comes in," Jack said before taking off.

Dear God, all of them were going to crash this party. I was beginning to feel too old for it, too tired to keep this faction away from that one and too drunk to deal with Diana again. What was left between us? I forgot to look the last time we'd been together. Too old, too tired, and too drunk. I decided to disengage completely. I'd get blotto and sit on the sidelines to watch them fight it out.

Planting myself in an oversized gilt chair, I snagged a passing waiter and had him deposit three more glasses of champagne at my feet. I polished them off, closed my eyes, and waited for a drunken sleep to overtake the buzz and scream of the crowd floating around me. But when sleep came, it was unmercifully short. I awakened smelling the lingering scent of gardenias.

"Not you," I said behind my tightly shut eyes. "Not today."

"Don't treat me as if I were a leper, George," Diana answered.

"I'm having a dream," I said, still refusing to look at her.

"Do I figure in it?"

"No, I've rid myself of you—or you of me—I've forgotten which. No, you're not in this one at all."

"Who is?"

"No one, none of you, you've all gone away somewhere," I slurred drunkenly, not knowing where this conversation would take me. I felt her hand on my forehead brushing away strands of hair. I remembered her tenderness the last time we made love. I thought I'd start crying again if she didn't stop touching me.

"Open your eyes."

"No."

"George, you're a grown man, dressed in a blue silk suit, sitting with your eyes shut in the middle of what looks like the largest whorehouse on earth. Not very becoming." She paused. "Mother sure has become tacky in her old age."

"You forget, Diana, that I knew all of you before she was called 'mother'—when she was called 'mama, mama, mama' by Sam, who stood under her window wanting, wanting, wanting."

"You are drunk."

"All of you wanting something. It exhausts the rest of us."

"Will you please look at me!"

"You sound nervous. Is Suzanne here with you?"

"Upstairs. I thought it would be fun for us to see this place, now I don't know."

Slowly, my eyes slit open. She stood above me, Diana at forty-nine. Although her hair was much straighter and laced with gray, although she was doing her best to deny her femininity, dressing in loose-fitting gray slacks and a man-tailored shirt, she was radiant. Her face was tanned, her eyes were a deep blue complement to the rich color of her skin. When she looked down at me, I closed my eyes again. She sank to her knees and hugged me.

"I saw you peeking. Come on, George, I don't look that bad."

"Where did you get your tan?"

"Morocco. We've been there all autumn."

"Diana, do I look old and worn?"

"George, how sweet. Vanity—who would have thought it possible? No, my love, you look beautiful."

Those hands again, stroking my hair, my cheek, bringing my hand to her lips. I had no choice but to look at her.

"I'm wasting my whole life waiting for you," I said.

A look of mild disappointment crossed her face. "You are drunker than I thought."

"You're the only woman who can excite me just by touching me. I'm a mess. I sit here with an erection, and all I want to do is cry at the sight of you."

"Write this down, George, it's sheer poetry."

"And your husband is staring at us across the room."

She did not even raise her head.

"Well, it's out in the open now," I said.

"Don't be silly, I'm a lesbian."

She kept kissing my hand. Her enigmatic smile, perhaps now less enigmatic than it once had been, flashed up at me. I groaned.

"You in pain?" she asked.

"Let's go make love."

"But my Aunt Sunny was just telling me that the place is booked up."

"She's here, too?"

"The whole world is here. Come," she said standing, tugging on my arm, "I've got a surprise for you."

"No surprises—just make love."

"Maybe we can in the Versailles Suite. Who thought up those names, anyway?"

"The Versailles Suite? Something called The Amusement Company is renting that for the season."

"Is *that* the name he used to register?"

"Who?"

"Jon. The Amusement Company." She laughed. "I get it—it's for his own amusement."

"My God, he's here, too. Maybe I should have let Bea stay home."

"But we're all so anxious to see her," she said. "Let's see. There's Jon and his lover. Me and my lover—or should I say lovers?"

"When do you grow up, Diana?"

"Treach once told me not until my sixties."

She had me by the hand, steering me through the crowds. Tildy appeared from nowhere.

"Don't you two make a lovely couple."

"Hello, Tildy. Goodbye, Tildy," Diana crooned, sailing past her.

"Diana, I'm surprised at you. Want you to meet my new husband."

"Tildy, you've got some set of balls," was what Diana said as Tildy dissolved back into the walls she'd crawled out of, balls and all.

"You are on edge, aren't you?" I asked.

"Either that or truthful."

We got lost in a maze of coral-colored halls. I was toting a bottle of Dom Perignon I'd made off with from the bar. Muzak was playing something disgustingly poignant as Diana talked nonstop: about Suzanne's serenity and the pressure that created for Diana; about Suzanne's sense of adventure, which did not match Diana's; about the poet who'd taken her to France and how she'd felt compelled to be so normal for him, to take care of him; how she always forgot to take care of herself. It all had a familiar ring to it.

We climbed the fire stairs to the roof, where I plunked my body down and began guzzling the bubbly as she walked near the edge and buried her feet in the white pebbles covering the tar paper. Diana spread her arms out to catch the ocean breeze that swept across the crescent-shaped roof.

"Remember those gypsy outfits I used to wear? All my feminine clothes. I don't know where half of them are any more. I dress just like Suzanne now."

"Something *is* bothering you."

"Quite the contrary. How little you know me," she taunted. "I feel full of energy."

I stared suspiciously at her down the length of the champagne bottle.

"You're nervous because you're going to see your mother!"

"You're wrong. I was happy all the way from Morocco to Miami waiting to see my mother."

"Happiest in transit."

"That's right. Happy from Florida to Paris, then from Paris to Morocco, then from Morocco to Miami—"

"But it doesn't go well once you settle in."

"That's not my fault."

"That's very convenient."

"It's the going to or coming from that I love. I can't abide staying put. That's what I love about you and me. The freedom—"

"You're free, I'm not."

"Don't interrupt me. That's why I love you. When we have time together, then it becomes a different story. You become just like the others. All of you want to change me. You want to save me, and I don't want to be saved." Her arms stretched out in the wind again. "You're always saying that you'll wait for me. That's what Suzanne says. Waiting for me to do what?" She turned to face me. "What are you all waiting for?"

"For you not to lay the blame at my feet. To merely accept my love and then go on about your life."

"But you never tell me what you want from me."

"That, my dear, is a load of manure."

"Well, then, George, you be clear with me. Tell me what you want."

That stopped me in my tracks, although the answer was on the tip of my tongue. I'd spent so many years protecting her from what I wanted because she always accused me of trying to change her. Now I realized that I'd protected myself from getting what I wanted, and I'd be damned if I had the patience or the years left to do that any more.

"I want you to learn to live with yourself and then come live with me."

She kicked the pebbles and then sank down on them.

"Quite a declaration," she said bitterly. "Sure, 'Diana, come live with me, but go fix yourself up before you do.' Like a dressmaker, George, two inches in here, an inch in there. You're all the same!"

Now it was my turn to be angry. "I don't think you heard me," I yelled. "Let me try again. I love you, but I don't care a damn about changing you. I don't have the time any more. You decide what you want, but just don't accuse me of pressuring you. You've lived your entire life blaming other people. I ask you now, man to woman, to declare yourself, goddamn it! I don't want to hear about pressures from me or the others. Stand on your own two feet. Come after *me* for once. Try and win *me* over. But I'll tell you something. I won't be such an easy lay any more!"

That broke the tension. She giggled nervously.

"Let's get off this roof." She stood quickly and walked back to the fire stairs.

I stood there watching her—Diana Willig Chason at forty-nine, still running off. And George Sloate at fifty-one, still chasing after her.

40

When we climbed down the fire stairs from the roof, we were in another maze of coral-colored halls, standing opposite a set of double doors marked Versailles Suite, Diana stood staring at them for a moment and then opened them.

Jack was standing in the center of the room glowering at us. "George Sloate, every man's best friend."

Suzanne was pacing nervously—the first time I'd ever seen her do that. She did not look particularly relieved to see me with Diana.

"Where have you been?" she snapped.

Diana took a seat and stared off into space. Albert came rushing out of the bedroom. He yelled out over his shoulder, "Great! Now you've got everyone here. Can I leave?"

He'd been talking with Jon, who walked out of the bedroom and smiled when he saw me. With him was a young, neatly dressed man. I knew in an instant that this young man was Jon's lover. He looked like Jon when Jon was nineteen or twenty. He had fierce eyes, but a calm face. He said nothing. As a matter of fact, I don't think he uttered a word the entire time we were up there.

I was disturbed by Jon's appearance. He'd aged badly in the past five years. His hair was long and unkempt, and he'd lost too much weight.

"Don't look at me like that, George. I'm not a ghost—not yet, at any rate. Have you met Michael?"

Michael walked over and shook my hand, then retreated to a chair in the corner.

"Michael is a good friend," Jon said, "or some such euphemism."

"I don't have time for this family reunion," Albert piped in. "I've got business to attend to."

"One hell of a business," Jack added as they both headed for the door.

"Now the least you can do is wait for the mother of us all," Jon said evenly, going over to the bar to pour himself a drink.

"If it's a family reunion, then I don't think I have any reason to be here," Suzanne said. "Diana, let's head back to our hotel."

"But you are family, Suzanne," Jon said.

Jack was staring at Diana, who looked numb.

"Is this your doing?" he asked her. "It's not enough that you've brought that woman here, you have to be carrying on in my lobby with him." His finger pointed directly at me. "I keep thinking that I don't care any more, but this is the limit."

"Why don't you divorce me now, Jack, you finally have what you want. I don't think my mother gives a damn any more."

"Children, children," Jon said lightly. "Please. This is a historic day, isn't it? No wonder there is a flutter of nerves in the air."

"Which you can cut with a knife," I said.

"And no doubt someone will offer to do the job," Jon added, "but I have not gotten you all together under one roof for murder."

"What *did* you have in mind?" Albert asked.

"I'd like to talk with you, Albert. I only wish Sam could be here with us."

"Don't you start in on my father."

"I have no intention of doing that. I'd like to talk with you about your future, dear boy."

"Don't patronize me, either."

"I'm doing nothing of the sort, but inasmuch as I'm the oldest blood-related male in this room, I feel it is my duty to talk with you about certain things."

Suzanne snapped to attention. "Jon, What kind of a game are you playing?"

"A game called Mafia."

Albert stalked across the room. "You had your chance to help me, but you turned your back on me—the whole lot of you did—and if you don't like the business I'm in, eat it. Weren't those your words, Jon?"

"Let's forget about that for the moment, Albert. I've already apologized to you for that."

"What else should I forget? My father is still locked up somewhere because of that man." The finger was leveled at Jack this time. "There's no forgetting that."

Jon lost his temper. "There is some benefit in forgetting things too old to recall or things you have no power to change." He sat down. Michael brought him another drink. "You're posing great problems by getting yourself involved with a very sinister bunch of people, Albert. A very dangerous move—not just for yourself but for your family as well."

"Don't make me laugh."

"I've no intention of doing that. What I want you to understand is that these are killers you're dealing with, and if you don't watch out, they'll turn on you one day. We've all heard the rumors about your involvement with them. You're going to build a hotel on a site just up the beach. You get your revenge and right your father's wrongs, but the truth is, he hasn't lost Shalimar. It is still in the family where it belongs. We are sitting in a room in a hotel on that very land. This is where you belong, Albert."

Jack interrupted him. "What do you mean by that?"

"What I said. This is where he should be working, and it is your job to make room for him."

So this was Jon's grand scheme. He had popped up to right wrongs—to help his family, more to the point, to help his mother. The family was speechless.

"That's very noble, Jon," I said.

Suzanne left her chair. "You know, I've never met the infamous Beatrice Willig, but I can't help feeling that you're all still playing in the sandbox, and you've still got to wait for her to tell you when to come in for lunch."

"It's true," Diana said, laughing. "She'll come marching in here and ruin all your nicely laid plans, Jonny."

Albert's anger exploded to the surface once again. "Listen to all of you—pulling me back and forth as if I don't have a thing to say. Well, I don't give a damn about your plans." He rushed to the windows and pointed down at the beach north of the Palais. "Come here next year, Jon. Stare out your window and you'll see a hotel—my hotel."

None of us heard the front door open or saw Bea standing in the doorway.

"I'll run the whole lot of you off this beach before I'm through. So don't talk about family to me."

"Is that what you want to do?" Bea answered. Everyone turned. "Who are these people?" she asked, pointing to Michael and Suzanne.

Jon rose and walked over to her. "This is your family, dear." He tried to hug her, but she shrugged him off and walked into the room alone.

"Have you heard about it, Bea?" Jack asked. "Albert wants to put us out of business—and on our first day." He laughed nervously.

She merely stared Jon down. "You and Diana ask your friends to leave," she said disdainfully, staring out the window.

Diana bolted from her chair. "How dare you come into this room and say that! Suzanne is as much a part of my family as you are."

Bea shuddered. "Get her out of here," she said to Jack, and Jack, good lap dog that he was, sprang into action.

"Perhaps it would be better."

"Oh, shut up!" Diana shot back. "If Suzanne leaves, then I do."

"Suit yourself," Bea said coldly.

"Don't feel badly on my account," Suzanne said, gathering up a sweater and purse. "Michael and I will be having drinks at the pool."

"Don't leave," Diana pleaded.

"And don't you be ridiculous. Will you join me, Michael?"

Michael looked over at Jon, who told him to run along. The two of them left.

"You think I'm as easy to be rid of?" Diana asked.

"Not easy at all. None of you is. My beautiful children. How nice of you to come to see me."

"Is she being serious? I don't understand." Diana tore around the room, looking for her purse. "I can't stand this."

Bea shook her head mournfully but said nothing as Diana headed for the door and angrily slammed it behind her.

"Now, what was that all about?" Bea asked.

"It's just Diana, you know how nervous she is," Jack said, placating her.

"And how would you know that, Jack? Such a good husband who knows his wife so well."

"I'll go after her and bring her back."

"And with such great timing—only twenty years too late," Bea said.

Jack left the room.

Bea was staring at Jon, seeing what I did, I suspected. He looked as old as she did that day.

"You don't look well, Jonny. It's all catching up with you, I suppose. All that running around."

"I haven't been well."

"I've got to be going." Albert said. "It was nice seeing you again, grandmother."

"Not so fast."

"We don't have a lot to talk about."

"I've heard all the rumors. Your mother was kind enough to throw them in my face on my way up here."

"Good. You know. I'm glad. What else do you want to know? Are you wondering if I'll take that offer Jonny made? Will I come to work for you? My answer is no!"

"So it's Jonny who's been making offers for me? How nice. I hope you didn't put them in writing, Jonny." She covered her eyes with her hands for a moment and then sighed. "The whole lot of you makes me sick. Jonny's offer. What a laugh. I haven't seen him in five years, and he's doing business for me." She rose slowly and stood in the middle of the room. "You see the place we're standing in? You see all of this? It's mine. I built it! No one says what goes on around here but me. Do you understand that, Jon? Listen well. You cannot come in here and make any decisions at all. You lost your right to do that by running off the way you did. And as far as *you* are concerned"—she dismissed Albert with a faint wave of her hand—"you need to be taught a lesson. I don't care what scum you wind up with —I couldn't have hired better to do it if I tried."

As Albert stalked out of the room, Jon said, "Don't do it, mother. Now is the time for you to act. Don't dismiss all of us this easily. You'll regret it."

"Is that what you've come back to say to me?"

"Please, mother, they need you—bend just a little."

"It's too much responsibility for me, don't you understand that? I'm too old. I want all of you to leave me alone."

Jack came back into the room. "Diana is upset—you know how she is—maybe you two can talk later."

"You know, before I walked into this room I was standing in the hall, listening to you. I heard what Diana said, Jack. Why don't you divorce her?"

He stammered, "I—I—she didn't mean—"

"Just get my driver and have him meet me out front. I've had enough of all of you for one day."

She walked to the door, then turned and looked at Jon.

"Will I see you again?"

"You've disappointed me, mother."

"And what am I supposed to do with *my* disappointment?"

"Hold on to it. It's all you have to protect yourself from us. This family is still your responsibility. That's all I came back to say."

Bea turned and left without saying another word.

Later that afternoon, Jon and I sat drinking on the terrace outside his room. Michael sat near us sketching in a large pad. He still had not uttered more than two words.

"Perhaps I should never have left this town, George. I could have wound up owning all this with my mother. Maybe I could have helped her run it and kept everyone in line for her." He turned in his chair, and I noticed that he winced in pain. Michael dropped the sketch pad and walked over to him, brushing Jon's hair back.

"Do you want another pill?"

"Yes," Jon mumbled. Michael walked inside. "That boy loves me, George. I'm lucky to have found him."

"What's wrong with you?"

"Cancer."

"Oh, God. Are you sure?"

"It was diagnosed in Paris. Then another opinion in Switzerland. Then one in New York. I've been all over, and they play me the same tune wherever I go."

"Isn't it operable?"

"Lymphatic system. It's not very good."

My stomach twitched. I felt queasy and sick—such a strange, immediate sensation. His news had made me feel so human and vulnerable. His hand reached out and touched mine.

"You okay?"

"Just the champagne. Excuse me for a moment, will you?"

"Sure."

I went inside, passing Michael in the living room, and then I ran through the halls until I got to the bathroom. I locked the door and sank to my knees, clutching the bowl as I vomited.

Afterward, I stared at myself in the mirror, washing my face with cool water, which did not put out the fire in my brain or wash away the tears streaming down my cheeks. What was it someone had once said to me about the dead? Do we cry for them or for ourselves? It had all taken place just an instant ago—the rum runs, the midnight swims, those Indians on the water, that palace of his, and Simon's death with me huddling there in the corner, cringing from death yet the smell of it closing in on me. It was all going too quickly.

He was banging on the door.

"George, are you all right? Let me in, dear boy. Let's talk a little while longer. George?"

Oh, don't take these people from me. I don't want to lose them yet.

"George, please let me in."

My hand reached for the door. As soon as he saw me, he hugged me to his chest. Michael was standing behind him with tears in his eyes, too.

"We're still so young, aren't we? We're still so young."

"It's going to be all right, George. Remember what Simon said. 'There's no time for tears. There's too much to be done.' "

"I don't know if I'm crying for you or me."

"Don't cry for me, my dear friend. Look at that sweet boy in the doorway. He loves me, George. I found someone."

But my tears would not stop.

"I had a dream once," he continued, "a premonition. Ruppert was there leading the way. I saw Georgia. She had cancer. They're waiting for me." He laughed. "I've got friends and lovers on both sides. There's no need to worry about me. I may even have years left. Please don't cry for me. Here," he said, taking a damp towel and washing my face with it, "stop now, no need to cry for yourself, either. You're fine and good and strong."

"Why did you come back today, Jonny?"

"I tried to reach my mother. I feel very good about that. I did everything I was supposed to do. But come on now, let's go back outside and talk again. Everything is all right."

We walked back out to the terrace. Jon took another pill, and in a little while he started feeling drowsy. He kept on talking, rambling on as if he could talk death out of existence.

"We are living in a world of women, aren't we?" he was saying. "And I suppose there is no satisfying them. I've left the race, I suppose, bundling off with this young man. Gave up the race. I suppose that's why homosexuals are so thoroughly despised inside and outside our ranks. We've said 'up yours' to the propagation of the species. And then there are men like you, George, who never marry, who chase after the likes of Diana. She's crazy, you know. Diana with all her freedom is as crazy as a loon. Will you continue to chase after her?"

"I don't know."

"Well, she's certainly beautiful, and she'll give you a good run for your money. Her freedom. Freedom to do what? I wonder. I suppose she wonders, too."

We sat and talked awhile longer, and then he grew tired. I said I'd see him tomorrow.

Michael walked me to the elevator.

"How long have you been with him?" I asked.

"Three years."

"When did he find out he was sick?"

"About a year ago."

"I see." I was hedging with this young man, and I think he knew. I wanted to find out why he was there. Was it the money? "Jon cares a great deal about you. I've never seen him this open with anyone else."

"Don't worry, I won't disappoint him."

I was embarrassed. "No, it's not a matter of that."

"Of course it is. You're a friend of his. You're concerned."

"He says he's found someone to love. That is going out on a limb for him. He's very cautious."

"I know. Perhaps that's why what you said before is so important. He cares for me. Sometimes that is more important than love. I care for him, too."

"He has my address and phone number. I don't imagine he'll want to stay around Miami much longer. This family business depresses him. But you must tell me when it's getting bad. I'll want to be there to help."

The elevator doors opened. Michael nodded and walked away.

41

The day after the opening, Albert drove out to La Hacienda to see Sam, who was in one of his ferociously lucid states. He'd read about the opening, and he was railing against his mother.

"Damn big success, wasn't it?"

"Dad, listen to me for a minute."

"They'll make a fortune out there, and that money is rightfully mine."

"Dad, just listen."

"Listen to what?"

"I want your blessing to go ahead with my plans."

Sam's hand pounded on the stucco walls of his room. "I want to get out of this place!"

"I can get you out of here, but you've got to understand that, in order to do that, I'll have to deal with Lister."

"With Lister? What's this again?"

"Lister owns the rest of the Shalimar land. He wants me to build a hotel for him right next to Bea's."

"You'll get trapped with that Lister."

"Don't worry about it. I know how to handle these guys. They need me as much as I need them. I'm legitimate, you understand?"

"I won't stick around this damn town once I get out of here. Maybe I'll go up to live with Frieda. She and I were always good friends. She's a damn good woman, Albert, you should talk with her."

"You don't understand at all, do you?"

"Of course I do. Damn it, you think I'm as crazy as they say I am? You're gonna build some hotel, and you don't care about where you get your money. Who the hell cares where you get it. Just get back what's ours."

"Then it's okay with you?"

Sam stormed out of the room. "Don't keep stalling, damn it. Do what you have to do."

What that entailed was a little dirtier than even Albert suspected. It was all laid out for him at his next meeting with Lister, which took place in the same little stucco house off in the boonies. The same Irish hoods were hovering near the glass doors, the same record player crooning in a back room. And Lister, as inconspicuous as ever, slipped into one of the chintz-covered chairs without Albert noticing him.

"You look good, kiddy," Lister said. "Sit down. Why so jumpy?"

"You talked about timing the last time we met. I think the timing is right. My grandmother's hotel is going to make a lot of money."

Lister sat back, appraising Albert. "We came through some rough times back there, but we came through."

Lister was refering to what Jawitz used to call "Senator Kefauver's Crime Circus," which had started in Miami in 1950 and from which Lister and the organization had emerged unscathed. Perhaps it had come out even a little more powerful than before, because the local boys and the S and G had been thrown to the lions. Sheriff Jimmy Sullivan had been fed to them as well. Some of the Italians had fallen, but Lister, the master builder, remained in the background with a governor, half the cops in the state, and Las Vegas in his pocket. Jawitz had once said, "Let them talk Mafia, Lister doesn't care. Let the Italians cover for us, they need us. We're big business, Albert, and business means loopholes and lawyers and legitimate operations. That's where you'll come in."

And there he sat with Lister, this decidedly unmenacing little man.

"We came through fine, and I like your ambition, Albert."

"That's nice, but I want to talk turkey with you."

"Talk turkey, that's cute. Well, talk turkey, kiddy."

"Bea developed a formula we can follow. Build it big, give it a French accent, and pour money into it so the suckers think they're getting their money's worth. I've even got a name for it, the Antibes—it's a classy French resort on the Riviera."

"Antibes, cute. How big a place?"

"Just like Bea's. A thousand rooms."

"You think big."

"That's what they like."

"And where do you get the money to pour into a place that size?"

The question threw Albert for a loop. Why else was he there talking with the man?

"I don't understand. That's why I'm here."

"You think I'm a bank?"

"No, but you see a good opportunity faster than most. I tell you, this will be a gold mine."

Lister nodded skeptically as Albert continued. "Why else did you buy up that land on the beach? You're not going to sit on it forever, are you?"

"No, I like your idea, but it's an expensive one."

"You said it once yourself, you got Las Vegas pumping money. You got the whole town here."

"But I got partners, Albert. I got to make an accounting. You see the Italian and Irish boys hanging around me? They represent my partners. Nasty tempers, those boys, they can't read a balance sheet, but they got real twitchy hands."

What did he want, Albert wondered. Just what the hell was he after?

"Financing a hotel, that's a big money operation you're talkin', Albert."

"But you've got it, don't you?"

Lister sat up suddenly and whispered. "Just how far you want to be into me, kiddy?"

"I don't understand."

"How dirty you want to get your hands?"

"I've been doing a good job for you all these years, haven't I?"

"Let's walk outside."

There were no goons hanging around out there, only pink plaster-of-paris flamingos and a wading pool surrounded by date palms and acacias.

"You think you know something about my operation, but you don't know anything about the plans I got for this town. I always liked your hotel deal, kiddy. I told you that, and I want to keep it our little operation. Don't want my partners in on this one, you get what I mean?"

Albert nodded.

"So that means I got to raise the money myself. I got plenty of money, you understand, but it's got to become usable. Listen up, kiddy, because that's where you're gonna come in and help me. Then we'll build your hotel for you."

Lister poked his way around the trees, smelling blossoms, checking over his shoulder to make sure none of the goons was listening.

"I got a lot of stock certificates. Millions of bucks worth. Bona fide companies—Bendix, General Motors, real stuff. Got 'em in Europe now sitting in vaults not doing anything for me. I want you to clean 'em up."

"They're stolen?"

"Five years ago. Like cash in the bank, but you gotta be patient with 'em, gotta know when to let 'em come back into the country. I put 'em away for you, kiddy, for your French hotel idea."

"How do you sell them? Aren't the numbers on file?"

"You find an agreeable banker to clean them. Don't kid yourself, they're around. You talk to Jawitz, he knows who to go to. We can build a lot of hotels with the money I got. We let the banks clean it—we use the stock as collateral for a loan. Some of what we get we invest in your hotel, and the rest we use to become bankers ourselves. Not everyone can walk up to Mr. Chase and get money from him. We lend money at high interest rates, but there are plenty of guys around who need us. It's business, you know what I mean, kiddy?"

"What do you want me to do?"

"You smell good, Albert. You look the part. You want your hotel built? Then you clean up my money, and we'll get it built."

"And Jawitz helps me do this?"

"You seem eager, kiddy, I like that. Yeah, Jawitz knows who to go to. That's enough talk for now. You talk to Jawitz. You keep smelling good, Albert. You play it right, we'll build a lot of hotels together."

Albert nodded and then started walking away.

"But, Albert, listen to me. We're *landsmen,* you know what I mean? We don't need a kiss of death or any blood oath to sign a deal. Leave that to the wops, Albert. But don't kid yourself, you go in on this with me, and you're mine. Do you understand?"

"Sure, I understand. We'll make a lot of money together."

"Mine, Albert, there's no running out on me. You wanna think about this, go ahead, but there's no leaving once you start in with me. You'll know too much. You're mine, kiddy."

A few nights later, Albert and Jawitz cruised the streets of Miami Beach in Albert's cream white Caddy.

"What's he talking about, Stanley? Doesn't a bank know if they're dealing with stolen certificates?"

"Banks don't have to know if you deal with the right banker. I got one picked out for you. Take a left here at the light."

Albert swung the car into a deserted street. At the far end of it was a bar with a dimly lit sign above it that read Wilde's.

"What's this?"

"Another one of Lister's operations. A fairy bar. Pull up there near the phone booth. I gotta check something out."

"Are we going in there?"

"Shmuck, hold your horses," Jawitz said, walking to the booth and dialing. "Hello? Yeah. Is Murray around? Hello,

Murray? It's Jawitz. He in there? Yeah. Okay. I'm parked near the phone booth opposite the bar. Number is Neptune 4-1584. You got that? Ring me once when he leaves."

"What's going on?" Albert asked when Jawitz reentered the car.

"Want you to meet your local friendly banker. This bar is supposed to be a private club. We only get the highest class of faggots. We stock the place with hot and cold running boys. Take a nice piece of the action. They go for Cubans down here. Your banker has a real thing for Cubans." Jawitz turned and smiled. "Lister told me to give you the keys to the kingdom, Albert. You're gonna learn the whole thing from now on."

The phone in the booth rang twice and then went dead.

A tall, blonde man wearing a blue blazer and gray slacks stepped outside with a dark *cubano,* who was no more than fifteen. The *cubano* laughed nervously as the large blonde man grabbed his arm and took him into the parking lot behind the bar. In a minute a maroon Buick pulled out of the lot and disappeared down the street.

"Who's the blonde guy?"

"Your meal ticket." Jawitz laughed. "Franklyn Petrie, President of the Federal Bank of Miami."

Jawitz and Albert worked the plan out about two nights later. It was a simple affair involving two *cubanos* and a camera with an infrared lens. Around midnight, the boys showed up together at Jawitz's house. Jawitz got them drunk, and then he told them what he wanted them to do. The younger would go after Petrie in the bar while the other waited in a hotel room.

"Snap, snap," Jawitz said. "Money in the bank."

Wilde's, named after Oscar, had a premeditatedly sinister atmosphere. It kept the element of danger alive. Sex on the sly. It kept patrons hopping and hoping. Boys of all ages were lolling under amber spotlights, flexing their muscles, practicing their petulance, preening all the while, waiting, dismissing the fat patrons, dismissing the old ones, an implicit teasing in the dismissal because any of them could be had for a ten spot.

Albert and Jawitz were twitching uncomfortably at a back table when Petrie walked in for that week's second helping. Jawitz said, "Go," and his Cuban lover-boy went into action, his *café con leche* skin shimmering in the amber light. Petrie approached another. The Cuban looked back at Jawitz self-consciously, momentarily defeated, but he knew his trade. He ordered another rum and sipped it slowly, almost decorously, his lips wet, pouty, his jaw set firmly, aggressively. Petrie turned back to the bar and ordered a drink, striking up a conversation with the lover-boy, who now looked pleased with himself but maintained a distance, stringing Petrie along with a measure of mockery and innocence until he had him salivating. The connection was made. They took off.

Albert and Jawitz kept circling the motel until Petrie was finished.

"Two goddamned hours," Albert complained. "What can he come up with in two goddamned hours?"

"Pull over to the curb and wait until he drives off," was all Jawitz said. "Then we'll pick up the Cubans."

Petrie finally got into his car and left. Then the Cubans appeared in the doorway of the motel room. Jawitz leaned over and flashed the car lights twice. They laughed like two nervous birds.

"Where to now?" Albert asked.

"We stop back at my office to pick up a friend; then we take them out of town—up North Kendall."

"Who are we picking up?"

"Just a friend. Keep your mouth buttoned. You follow instructions from now on."

The Cubans jumped into the car. Albert rammed the gas pedal to the floor and headed over to Jawitz's office.

A goon was waiting for them, a big swarthy Italian goon, a bouncer from one of Jawitz's clubs.

"Get in," Jawitz said.

The goon got in back with the two boys and sat there silently as Albert drove out North Kendall to a deserted stretch of land.

"You got the film?" Jawitz asked, smiling, reaching in back for the camera.

"We got it," the younger one said. "You got bucks?"

Jawitz reached into his pocket but held onto his roll of cash.

"Big money, amigos. Don't get too drunk on it," Jawitz said. "Was he good?"

The younger one laughed again. "I had him before."

That really cracked them up. They roared with delight.

"Pull over here, Albert."

Albert swung the car into a field as Jawitz and the goon got out, followed by the two boys. Jawitz checked the film to make sure he'd gotten what he wanted. As he held the money out to them, the Italian goon pulled a gun with a silencer out of his pocket. He aimed it at their heads and fired twice. The boys fell.

"What the hell is going on?" Albert screamed, rushing from the car. "What is this?"

Jawitz patted Albert's shoulder. "You can't trust those *cubanos*, Albert. They'd blackmail him before we got the chance."

Albert stood there dumb with fright as the goon got back into the car.

"Come on, baby, today you are a man. Didn't even get your hands dirty, did you?"

"What?"

"The keys to the kingdom, baby, and now you're signed, sealed, and delivered. Didn't Lister give you that little speech? 'You're mine.' " Jawitz mimicked Lister's raspy voice. " 'You're all mine!' "

42

It was not as if Franklyn Petrie hated Jews, he merely had trouble warming up to them. He liked stringing them along with icy stares and locked-jaw manners that usually made them uncomfortable. Exclusivity was what he coveted. He wanted Jews to pant to gain entrance to his club or his bank; more importantly, he wanted them to appear to be thankful that he'd granted them an audience in his mahogany-walled, green-carpeted office. Bea Willig had been so put off by him that I was forced to deal with him whenever business warranted it. Now Albert sat with him as Petrie went over Albert's proposed development plans: the costs, the prices, and the loan request for the Antibes.

"A very ambitious project, Mr. Willig," was all Petrie was prepared to say at the moment.

Albert was put off by him, too, but he had an ace tucked

up his sleeve, and he thought he'd relish stringing Petrie along with it.

"More than ambitious, Mr. Petrie. I think it's a lucrative investment opportunity."

Petrie smiled broadly. "We here at the bank have been following this latest land boom. There have been so many of them in Miami. It's enough to boggle the mind."

"But this investment should be worth serious consideration."

"And how kind of you to bring it to us first," Petrie offered. "Tell me, is your grandmother involved in it with you?"

"No, I represent another organization."

"Which one?"

"Molister, Incorporated."

"I don't believe I've heard of that one. It doesn't by any chance have anything to do with Mr. Morton Lister, does it?"

"A subsidiary of his."

"I see." Petrie tapped his fingers nervously on Albert's proposal. "Ten million dollars is a lot of money."

"Hardly something I expected to hear from a banker."

"Yes. You represent Mr. Lister's interests, and yet the proposed loan agreement is with you alone. If your grandmother is not involved with it, I wonder how, Mr. Willig, you intend to put up collateral for a loan this size."

"Securities."

"Come again?"

"I'm prepared to put stocks and bonds up as collateral."

"Your securities?"

"Mr. Lister's."

Petrie's tapping fingers picked up tempo. "We do use securities as collateral. Which companies are we talking about?"

Albert reached into his briefcase, bringing out a certificate for five hundred shares of General Motors stock. A crude move at best, but when he placed it on the desk, Petrie had the audacity to hold it up to the light to check its water stamp. Then he smiled and passed it back to Albert.

"A loan of this size would require infinitely more than five hundred shares of GM," Petrie said politely, looking at his watch.

"I have more than enough to cover what is required."

Although he'd never been approached in this manner, Petrie knew exactly what was being offered, and he'd be damned if he would put up with it for another moment. His bank was a bank, not a laundromat.

"I'm afraid I have another pressing engagement scheduled, Mr. Willig," he said rising from his chair, extending his hand. "Perhaps we can discuss this some other time."

"Sit down."

"I beg your pardon."

"I said sit down."

"Perhaps I haven't made myself understood. I don't think our bank wishes to be involved with your venture, but, again, thank you for thinking—"

Albert interrupted him. "But I want your bank involved with this venture," he said, leafing through his briefcase again and pulling out a folder with some photographs in it.

"That, I'm afraid, is impossible."

"Nothing is impossible, Mr. Petrie. As a matter of fact, the older I get, the more I realize that everything is quite possible. Who, for instance, would have imagined that a bank president, a highly respected man in his community, a highly visible, polite, and conservative man, would have such highly visible but not terribly respectable, polite, or conservative sexual appetites?"

Petrie blanched but remained on his feet.

"Who would think that a very tall, very blonde man would have such a predilection for such short, dark boys?"

Albert took out one of the photographs and slid it across the desk. Petrie stared down. It was dark and blurry, but there was no mistaking the face of the tall blonde man engaged in fellatio with the short, dark boy.

"How dare you." Petrie sank back into his chair.

Then something peculiar happened—perhaps Albert didn't have the killer's heart he presumed he had. He started sweating, and his fingers twitched beyond control.

"My back is to the wall, Petrie, there's no telling what anyone can do in that position. It seems to me a contagious disease, and now your back is to the wall as well. Would you like your secretary to cancel your next engagement?"

Petrie's voice was quivering. "This is a terrible thing to take advantage of—for one man to do to another."

Albert stood and stretched, trying to relieve himself of his tension. "I agree, but I've seen worse. I have other photographs if you'd like to relive that night."

"Oh, stop it, please!"

"And now the rest of our conversation finally gets down to basics. Man to man. I'm a businessman who has a proposal. It's a good one, too, so you won't be getting any raw deal. You simply have to look the other way while you recirculate some securities that have been abroad for a while."

"How long have they been out of the country?"

"About five years."

"But ten million dollars. I can't commit the bank to a ten-million-dollar loan."

"Are you playing with me, Petrie? You can do whatever you damn well want to do."

"You're wrong. I have committees to report to."

Albert took out more photographs and shoved them across the desk. "But you've got the incentive to get to work on that, don't you?"

"This is a terrible thing to do," Petrie said again.

"Oh, please, Petrie, you think it's easy for me? It's got to be done. That's all there is to it. We're both stuck with it, don't you understand?"

Of course Petrie did not.

That did not stop the loan from being approved, however; nor did it stop Albert from getting his hotel built.

The Antibes was the smashing success of the next winter season. That was back in the years when each winter brought a new lavish resort opening. Although each hotel owner tried to outdo Bea's grand splash, only Albert came close to doing it.

The Antibes was a huge, starkly modern white tower, and what Bea had not looted from the antique markets of Manhattan and Paris, Albert made off with, filling his lobbies with statues and mirrors, immense chairs, and gilt tables. In the middle of the main lobby was a huge terrarium in which designers had created a tropical rain forest. Another eclectic mess, the critics complained, but during that first season, and for the first time in his life, Albert was able to thumb his nose at everyone.

He built the Antibes close enough to the Palais so that it rose majestically above it, with nothing more than a large swimming pool separating it from Bea's French extravaganza. That precipitated a final break with his family because not only had he built this hotel on his own, and consorted with known criminals to do it, but in so doing he had ruined the Palais's northern view.

He and Jack became Miami's most notorious rivals, causing havoc whenever the two happened to show up at a restaurant or nightclub at the same time. Maître d's went out of their minds trying to keep them apart, yet give each the best table in the house. Bea's response was infinitely more primitive. And effective.

She and Jack and I stood near the water's edge staring up at the Antibes one early morning before it was completed. Jack was cursing under his breath, but Bea looked positively aglow.

"He still needs to be taught a lesson."

"What can we do? It's too late," Jack muttered.

"A spite wall."

"I think you'll need a mighty big one," I offered.

She pointed at the Antibes's swimming pool. "You see where he put the pool? Right under our windows, but he still gets all the midday sun he wants. I want to build an addition."

"What?" Jack shrieked. "We can't."

"Who says I can't? I own the most successful hotel in the world. I can do anything I want. And I want to build an addition above the northern wing."

"But why?"

"To block his sun. Call in the architects and tell them that I want his guests to freeze all winter long when they swim in his pool."

A magnificent gesture in the tradition of Marie Antoinette —in this version, however, Bea made no reference to anyone eating cake. It was, "Let them freeze their asses!"

Surely the Great Wall of China and the Palais addition must stand on record as being the largest spite walls ever constructed. By the following winter, Le Palais's new set of rooms successfully blocked Albert from ever getting the winter sun on his swimming pool. And I imagine that if you've ever stayed at the Antibes during Christmas, you've suffered through a morning dip, but did you know that you had Beau Willig to thank for that?

Capricious whim, spite, or shrewd business move—how was one to know? Beau's addition brought more business down during those booming fifties, and Albert did not suffer all that much. He still had one of the most successful hotels on the beach, but he never did manage to get himself out from under Mort Lister's thumb, and because of that the Antibes developed a certain reputation. . . .

Not only was it reputed to have the coldest swimming pool on hotel row, but, rumor had it, it was the watering hole for every major member of organized crime in America. Albert complained about the reputation to Mort Lister, but to no avail.

"They're partners, kiddy. What's the matter? Don't you like their money any more?"

"I'm being mentioned in crime investigations. Do you know that? I've got my name to protect."

"Some kid. You've got a hotel booked up two years in advance, and you're whining like a brat. You can't turn people like that away at the door. We're in business with them. By the way, Jimmy Benno from Detroit got his eye on you. You know Jimmy?"

Benno was a racketeer who'd set up winter residence at the Antibes.

"Jimmy says the FBI knows too much about the Vegas cash operation. He says there's too much money staying in the country. He thinks we should drop more of it off down in the Bahamas or Latin America. So I got a job for you."

"What are you trying to do to me?"

"Albert, quit your whining. You still smell like roses. I want you to go talk with this guy Trujillo. He wants to set up an arms deal with us, and I want to use his banks."

And so it went. Albert got in deeper. His name began appearing regularly in Hank Messick's crime columns. He got richer and dirtier and more frightened. He was inextricably caught.

Through it all, another more unfortunate soul languished in a cell, becoming more disillusioned with each day. Poor Sam was left to rot out at La Hacienda. Albert never managed to get him his reprieve, and Sam's poems took an angry turn:

> Who would have thought any son of mine,
> Would leave me to worry, to mourn, to pine,
> Scientists say that when a person is mean,
> He gets that way by being passed a gene.
> So let his grandmother claim him,
> If I had him in this room with me, I'd maim him.

43

While her children drifted further away from her and her grandson drifted deeper into entanglements with the underworld, Bea thrived. If she had any lingering doubts about her ability to stand alone and master the world, all she had to do was drive out to the beach, stare at her colossal hotel, and gloat. I often wondered how she pulled it off without going mad. Where and when did it hit her that everyone around her was drowning? I fantasized violent scenes of self-reproach or grief enacted in the sanctity of her home. At the end of the day, did she run around Coconut Grove cackling like a lunatic or wailing like a Sabine?

While this was pure fantasy, the reality was maddening. She was becoming interested in knowing all the sordid details of her children's lives. Was she choosing to compare her success with their failure? I don't know, but she began asking me probing questions about them, and my angry reaction surprised us both.

She asked me one day, "Will you show me some of Sam's poems? I wonder if he's as mad as everyone says he is."

"What do you think his poems have to do with that?"

"I'd like to see it documented."

This struck me as being somewhat akin to necrophilia. I shut up, but that did not stop her. Off we went to the next topic.

"Diana has had quite a life, hasn't she? Leeching onto café society, emotions always spilling all over the place. I'll tell you a secret that you must promise to keep."

"What's that?"

"Sometimes I envy her."

"Envy Diana?"

"That girl has done everything she's ever wanted to do. Of course, she's broken my heart in the process, but she certainly runs headlong into things—or should I say heart-long?"

"You should talk to her about that. I'm afraid she's not as happy as you imagine."

"But she's had every opportunity to travel and see more of the world than I ever dreamed of seeing. If she's not happy with that, she's a damn fool. My God, all my children are fools. Albert so entranced with those hoodlums, and Jon turning his back on everything. Why did he do it? How much happier is he?"

"What I'd like to know is why are you so interested in it now?"

"I'm a seventy-seven-year-old woman, George. Can you blame me if I want to know more about life?"

"More about life," I said sarcastically. "Not about your children per se, but about life."

"You certainly are in a bad mood this morning."

"Am I? I hadn't noticed. Ask me more questions, Bea."

"What's wrong with my asking questions?"

"It's the clinical way in which you ask them. It's perverse."

"Those are rather strong words."

"Oh, never mind—let's follow this through to the end. Ask me something else."

"Well, Jon, for instance." She stopped and looked at me. "You're baiting me, aren't you?"

"No, go ahead. What about Jon?"

"He never married, and I've often wondered why."

"Ah, that's a good one. Jon never married because he chooses to spend his life with other men."

"That I do not want to hear—it makes me sick to my stomach."

"I thought you wanted to find out more about life."

"Why are you acting this way?"

"That's the question I should be asking you. What is that, Bea? Why do you want to know about them? You crossed them off your list years ago. They were labeled and filed, arranged neatly in little packages and placed out of your reach where you wouldn't have to see them."

"George, how dare you talk to me this way!"

"Damn it, Bea, I don't like being used."

"I'm not using you."

"Of course you are—you always have. These are your children we're talking about. You know who they are, know them intimately, in fact. They're suffering along with the rest of us. What more is there to know?"

"Perhaps if I understood them, I could help them."

"Don't make me laugh. You've consistently turned your back on them. At least remain consistent. I can bear that, but don't pretend that you want to help them or that you envy them."

"This is so unfair."

"No, it's the truth. You want to know more about them so that you'll know how better to control them. Keep them at that safe distance. Preface this question-and-answer session with that much truth, and I'll tell you anything you want to know."

Her face was so filled with surprise that I knew I had hit the truth smack on the head.

"How dare you judge me in this way?"

"You say that as if I've committed some crime, as if judging another person were an unnatural act. Of course I judge you. Fault me for not saying it sooner, but don't imagine that all of us are not judging each other all the time."

"And what do you expect me to do with your judgment? Do you think I'll change? I'm too old. And what's more, I don't want to change. I've got too much to hold on to, and I won't listen to this for another moment."

"Do you think you'll fall apart if I slip a judgment in with the pap? Will you fall apart if you accommodate yourself to your children—if you allow for just the slightest bit of change? Will you crumble?"

"I'll be damned if I'll risk finding that out. I've had enough talk for one day. You must have other things to do—business matters to attend to, or something."

"Of course detachment is the easiest way out." I left.

Utter detachment must have been in the air that year, because even Jack Chason caught the bug. He and I had steered clear of one another since that episode with Diana at the Palais's opening day. But one Sunday in June, 1956, I believe, he showed up at my house. He seemed friendly enough, although a bit uneasy. I asked him to join me for brunch.

"You know you'll be able to sell this house for a pretty penny some day," he was saying, pointing south, where hotel row was beginning to encroach upon my privacy.

"I've got some time before that."

"Well, you've got a nice view of the Palais to keep you warm. You keeping an eye on business out here?"

"I've always left that to you, Jack."

He'd been stirring his cup of coffee for about five minutes.

"Did you come out here on a Sunday to talk business with me?"

"Sort of."

"Would you like me to pry it out of you?"

He dropped his spoon on the table. "You're always so damned sharp with me, George."

"Am I? Just a case of nerves. We haven't been on the best of terms lately."

"We've never really been friends, have we?"

"Not really."

"And you've always thought I was a bit of a fool."

"About some things. But if you're talking about my feelings about you and Diana, I've never thought you a fool. Actually, I empathized with you."

"You were always in love with her."

"I suppose so."

"Did you want to steal her away from me?"

"That is a sad question, Jack. You never had her, but it doesn't matter. Diana is not capable of loving anyone."

"My staying married to her is a joke."

"I'm sure you've had your reasons."

"I know what you think. I stayed married to keep Bea happy. Well, maybe that's true, but I loved her, too. I just never knew what to do with her."

"A lot of us have spent a good many years trying to figure that one out."

"I'm going to divorce her."

I was speechless for a minute or two. "Have you come out here for my blessings? Or to tell me that the coast is clear—I can go out and bag her like a deer now that you've left the forest."

"No, it's nothing like that. I had a long talk with Bea. She and I decided it's the only thing to do."

"What is going on inside Bea's head these days? I tell you, Jack, I'm worried about her."

"She's having the time of her life. She thinks this is the best thing for Diana and me. She wants you to handle the divorce."

"That is the final perversity," I said, throwing my napkin on the table.

"I think she'd like you to marry Diana."

"Get out of here, Jack. I've finally had more than I can stand." I stood angrily and went into the living room.

"But, George," he said, running after me, "it's what Bea wants. There's nothing to worry about."

"I gave you an order, lackey. Leave my house immediately!"

"What should I tell Bea?"

"First, go get yourself another lawyer to handle your divorce; and secondly, tell Bea that I think she's in grave trouble. I'm not sure I'll be sticking around to help her out this time."

Jon had been right all along. I'd gotten in so deeply with them that now my life was being bandied about along with theirs. I had embraced it and asked for it, and I didn't care why any more. It drove me straight into my bed with only a bourbon bottle for comfort. I stayed holed up like that for a week, refusing telephone calls, drinking myself into a stupor. One night, after I'd passed out fully dressed on my bed, I heard the telephone ringing. The sound of it was so urgent that I had no choice but to answer it.

Long distance lines crackled. Someone was whispering on the line, a voice I did not recognize at first.

"Who is it?" I yelled.

"This is George Sloate, isn't it?"

"Yes, who is it?"

"Can you hear me?"

"Yes, I can hear you. Who is this?"

"It's Michael. We met in Jon's suite in Miami about a year ago."

I bolted out of bed, my head suddenly clear.

"Is it Jon? Is he ill? Michael, what's wrong?"

"It happened very quickly. We should be thankful for that. There was no time to call. The pain was very bad last week. We got him into Sloan-Kettering in New York last night."

"He's gone. We've lost him."

"It was very quick. I was with him. They drugged him so he didn't feel anything at the end. He was sleeping."

"Poor Jon," was all I could say.

"It was a good year, this last one, we had a wonderful year."

"I'll be up there in the morning."

"No, there are other things for you to do. He wanted to b

uried out at the Pine Key place. He said you could arrange hat. Can you do it?"

"Yes."

"George, there's something I must know. I'll arrange to ave the body shipped down there, but if you think my resence would disturb his family, then I won't stay around or the funeral."

"He'd want you to be there."

"But his mother—"

"You just be there. Are you in touch with Diana?"

"We saw her in Paris last spring. I have a number for er."

"Good. Michael, will you be all right?"

He stammered for a moment. "I didn't want to lose him, ut it was quick," he said again. "He was asleep one minute, nd then he died."

"You get some rest. We'll talk in the morning. I'll arrange verything."

I hung the phone up and walked downstairs. I could see the ights from the hotels twinkling in the distance as I sat on ny porch. My mind drifted through the years. It kept settling n that last evening he and I had spent out at Pine Key.

We'd eaten on the dock. I know we talked about many hings, but somehow time erased most of that conversation. What I remembered most clearly was the image of the two of is standing on that sandbar in the middle of the bay. We ooked as though we were stranded out there, locked in a ime tempered with sweet-sounding talk and friendship. One noment in a lifetime of moments that appeared to be more eal than the others.

"Am I crying for you or for me?" I asked Jon. Now his life vas diffused in the dark sky, in the sand and water, in those ights twinkling on and off in the distance. Why was I asking uch questions? Surely his answer, like the sound of my own voice, would have merely dissolved in the damp air of that till night. Only the image of us remained, and after awhile, I ell asleep, wrapped in its comforting warmth.

44

His death had finally brought them together. Bea did not loo at any of them as she stood near his grave in the rose garden Sam was there, keeping his distance from his mother and son Poor Sam could not comprehend what he'd lost—a brothe he'd never really known. Albert shifting awkwardly fron one foot to the other, was as uncomfortable with grief as h was with joy. Jack, although he had been a part of the famil for thirty years, now looked like an outsider. Michael stoo silently at one end of the garden away from the others; h didn't cry or say a word to anyone. Diana was shakin spasmodically. I think it was the sight of her mother, s distraught and isolated, which frightened her. I half expecte to see Abe there, but he didn't make an appearance.

I offered to deliver a eulogy, but Bea declined. She walke over to the grave and whispered, *"Shema y'srael, adon elohaynu, adonoi echod."*

Sam touched my shoulder. "Hear, O Israel, The Lord Ou God, The Lord Is One," he whispered in my ear. "It's not th prayer for the dead, but it's supposed to be the last thing yo say before you die. I haven't heard those words since I was kid."

He walked away, and the others followed him.

Bea turned to me, her eyes hollowed by a grief that seeme trapped inside. "I did not want to live to see this." Sh watched the others walking away. "Let them leave," she sai "Thank you for staying here with me, but I want to be alon now. He never invited me over to this place. I'd like to wal around it. You'll go back to Miami with me, won't you?"

"Of course."

"I'll just walk around."

"Is there anything else I can do?"

"That's very sweet, George. You've been a better son to m than my own."

I put my fingers up to her lips; I didn't need to hear tha "Please don't go on. I'll wait for you. You tell me whe you're ready to leave."

Diana was watching her mother. She and Michael were preparing to leave, waiting on the dock for the ferry from the mainland.

"I don't think I can help her," she was saying.

"She might need you."

"I can't do it. I'm sorry."

Albert and Jack joined us on the marble path.

"Will you see that Bea gets back safely?" Jack asked. "I'll go home with Diana."

Albert began walking away, but I reached out and stopped him. "Don't leave your father alone here."

He stared up at the house. "He's sitting in that big room with all the pictures. What do you suppose he's thinking about?"

"Why don't you ask him?"

He shrugged sadly.

"You know, Albert, there has been very little you've done with your life that I've respected, but I always told myself that at least you were the one who stuck up for Sam. You've been a loyal son. He still needs you. Don't disappoint him."

The others were boarding the ferry.

"Albert—you coming?" Jack called out.

He stared nervously at me, then shook his head. "No, you go on without me."

"Thank you," I said. We walked back to the house together.

"I study art books in that place they keep me," Sam was saying as he inspected the paintings in the gallery. "All these look genuine to me. They are the genuine thing, aren't they?"

"The best money could buy," Albert said.

The state museum people had put ropes up to keep crowds from touching the paintings and furniture. Sam had shimmied under one.

"Just think, Jonny bought all of this."

"He didn't buy them. The man who built this place did. Jonny just lived with them."

"What was the guy's name who built the house? I forgot."

"Ruppert—Simon Ruppert."

Sam laughed. "Remember those camels I rented for Shalimar? I got them from Ruppert. You remember those camels, Albert?"

"Sure."

Sam shook his head mournfully. "Guess there's no reason for laughter today."

"There doesn't have to be a good reason for laughter, Sam."

He giggled mischievously. "You're right. I laugh all the time without reason. Part of my mad act."

Just then the glass doors on the bay side of the gallery opened, and Bea walked in. Surprisingly enough, she seemed relieved to see Sam and Albert waiting there.

"Well, at least some of my children have the decency to wait for me."

"Mama," Sam said softly.

Bea stood there as if she were measuring herself against the immense proportions of that cavernous room.

"Just look what your brother turned his back on."

"You've never been here before, either," Sam said.

"No. Maybe he was embarrassed by his old mother."

"You're not embarrassing—you're impossible."

Albert laughed, then I did, and the tension dissipated for an instant.

"Maybe you shouldn't have stayed behind, after all," Bea said. "What are all these damned ropes for? How does a human being sit in this place?"

"The house is a museum now," I said, undoing one of the ropes, helping her into a chair.

"You impressed, mama?"

"It's humbling, I'll say that for it."

"Well, if you're humbled by it, then it must be impressive."

"Did you stay behind to hurt my feelings, Sam?"

"I'm in no position to do that, mama. I wanted to talk with you."

Bea turned away from him and stared at Albert. "How have you been?"

"I'm all right."

"Did you know your uncle at all?"

"Not very well."

She buried her head in her hands. "Why have I lived to see this?" she sobbed. "He was always running. He never grew up. He was never satisfied. If he'd come to me, I would have helped him." She looked up suddenly at me. "George there thinks I'm a monster."

"You just never got to know who he was. He was restless for most of his life, but in the end he was satisfied."

"With what? With more running? With living with that degenerate? Who invited him here?"

"I did."

"How could you, George?"

"He was with Jon when he died. He stayed with him for years when Jon knew he was dying. He took care of him. Can you understand that?"

"Did you know about Jon's illness?"

"Yes."

"And you never told me."

"What difference does that make now?" Sam said.

Silence hung in the room like a shroud.

"What's the use of talking," she finally said.

"Perhaps we should start back to the mainland, Bea."

"No, not yet," Sam interrupted. "There's something I want to talk about."

"I've had enough talking for one day."

"No, there is something I must ask you, mama. I want you to let me out of that place."

"Sam, please, haven't I been through enough today?"

"Doesn't Jonny's death show you anything at all? It's goin' faster now, mama. We're all gettin' older. There's no time left for you to put me off."

"What would you do? Come back to live with me?"

"No, I don't want to hang around Miami any more. I thought I'd go up to New York. Frieda has always been nice to me. I can live with her."

"And how would you live?"

"My son's got money. He'll help me."

Bea interrupted before Albert could respond. "It's not up to Albert. Don't you forget that."

"How can I, mama? I may be crazy, but I'm not stupid. Okay, so you hold the cards. You always did. I'm not askin' you to give up your control. You can keep on feedin' me if you want. Just get me out of that place. You give me the money. You're the boss, aren't you? Lend me some money to buy somethin' of my own up in New York. A little roomin' house or somethin'. We'll keep it in your name. I don't care any more. I don't even want to get out from under your thumb. Just give me a chance."

For the first time, I realized why Sam had embraced his

lunacy with such devotion. It gave him leverage and comfort—he could say what he wanted, do what he wanted, without any restraint or fear of being judged.

"I'm the boss, am I? What about the law, George? Am I free to do what he wants?"

"You know you are."

"I see. You've all talked about this, haven't you? You've got this plan all worked out very neatly. Well, we'll see if I'm the boss. If you want your freedom, then a deal has to be made."

"You name it," Sam said.

"Involving you," she said, pointing at Albert.

"What about me?"

"If I give your father what he wants, then you must make a deal with me. I want you to join forces with me. We'll run the two hotels together, and you get yourself untangled from those thugs you're involved with."

"It's not that easy," Albert said, walking away from her, his hands fidgeting at his sides.

"What do you mean?" Sam pleaded. "Listen to her, she's offering me my freedom, and you're saying it's not that easy."

"You don't know who I'm involved with. They won't be bought off so easily."

"We've got the money," Bea said. "I can help you with that."

"It's not a matter of money."

"Then walk away from it. Run the Palais with Jack."

Albert looked astonished, but Bea mollified him.

"Jack does what I tell him to do. He won't stand in your way. I'm giving it to you, Albert."

"Please, Albert, I never asked you for anything in my life. Please do this for me," Sam said.

Bea rose abruptly.

"That's my deal. You want to see your father get what he wants, and I want you back with us, running our hotel, not being a messenger boy for a bunch of criminals. It's an easy matter to decide."

"You'll make good on your word, won't you, mama?"

"Don't insult me. Of course I will."

"This will take time," Albert said.

"I know that. I'm in business. You give me your word that you'll start negotiating with them, and I'll give Sam what he wants."

"He'll do it, mama. Tell her you will. Say it, please."

What choice did Albert have? He nodded his assent.

"Thank God," Sam yelled. I don't think those halls ever heard a more joyful sound.

Bea suddenly began crying again. "Now, all of you help *me*, damn it! I lost my son today."

Sam put his arm around her. "I'm here, mama, I'm here."

She stared at me. "I know what you're thinking, George Sloate. I'm not such a monster, am I? I'm giving Jonny what he wanted."

She stayed true to her word. When we got back to Miami, she had Sam released from La Hacienda, and within a month's time, he and I went up to New York to hunt for real estate.

Against my better judgment, he chose a broken-down rooming house near the theater district on West Forty-fifth Street. He was as excited about it as he had been about Miamiland that first day I met him. He went on and on about how he'd fix up this old dump, how he'd lease rooms out to starving actors and writers.

"Me and Frieda will live on the top floor," he said excitedly, pacing back and forth in front of it. "I always wanted to try my luck in New York. I'll get myself a study, and I'll write like mad."

"But why this one, Sam? I know your mother. She'll buy you anything you want."

"You're talkin' with a man who's been in a nut house, George, but I'm not crazy enough to think I can run some fancy place. I want this one—that's all there is to it. Gonna call it Shalimar, too What do you think of that? Gonna have the time of my life."

I wasn't about to be the one to deny him that. Bea wasn't either. When we returned to Miami, she arranged to buy the property.

He told us that he wanted to go up to New York in style, on the only express train still running.

On the day of his departure, he and Bea and I stood on the platform waiting for Albert to arrive.

"The kid knows I'm leaving, doesn't he?"

"He'll be here," I said.

"Frieda will be waiting for you at Pennsylvania Station, won't she?" Bea asked.

"She'll be there. Don't worry about me, mama. Contrary to

what those psychiatrists always told you, I wasn't half as crazy as I made myself out to be."

"Don't talk nonsense, you'll be fine. You'll come down to see me every now and then?"

"I'll be back," he said, his eyes studying the parking lot. Albert's cream white Caddy pulled up to the curb, and Sam ran toward him.

"Got myself a fine son, don't I, mama?"

She nodded silently.

"I know what's worryin' you, mama. You want Albert to make good on his part of the bargain. Well, he won't disappoint us any, will you, Albert?"

Albert couldn't look any of us in the eye. "I told you it isn't easy."

But Sam wanted to hear none of that.

"You'll make good. That's a promise I make for the kid, mama. You kept your word, and he'll keep his."

That's all there was to it as far as Sam was concerned. He and Bea kissed each other goodbye. Albert embraced him.

When Sam walked over to me, he whispered, "You make sure the kid does the right thing."

The porters made their final call, and he was gone.

As we were leaving the station, Albert stopped Bea. "I will keep my part of the bargain, but we won't wind up with two hotels."

"I don't care about that."

"I'm going to make a clean break, but it won't be easy."

"You do what you have to. I'll take care of the rest," she said, looking as satisfied as I'd ever seen her.

45

Nothing but imagination will be of any use in describing the following events. What follows is my reconstruction, you should remember that, but I think I have gotten to the truth about Albert Willig.

Albert was pacing the floor of his suite at the Antibes waiting for his meeting with Lister and Jawitz to begin. For once in his life, he was risking his neck for someone else.

Jawitz came in first, still the nervous puppet. He smelled something in the air.

"What's up?" he asked. "You got something to drink around here?"

"The bar is stocked."

"You look like you got a bug up your ass, Albert, and I don't know why. Money's rolling in, Lister's got nothing but good to say about you, baby. You're not pissed off at anything, are you?"

"We'll talk when Lister comes—where is he, anyway?"

"On the way up. Don't make me nervous, Albie. I don't like the look in your eye."

The front door opened, and Lister walked in slowly. He'd suffered a heart attack about a year before, and he moved through the room like an old man.

"Kiddy, you drag a sick man out of his house."

"I thought it would be better if we met here."

"I hope it's worth it. Get me a glass of water, Stanley."

Albert walked to the windows and stared down at his grandmother's hotel.

"So you got me here, kiddy. Now, what's this all about?"

"I've come to a decision. I want to bow out of our partnership."

Lister's expression didn't change, but Jawitz nearly jumped out of his skin. "You're not making sense. You want to repeat that?"

"You heard me. You've got me running cash down to the Bahamas and dealing with the likes of Batista and Trujillo. You pushed me too far, and now I've had enough of it."

"We *pushed* you!" Jawitz screamed. "Where were you when all the pushing was being done? Look what we got for you!"

"Shut up, Jawitz," Lister said, his lips tightly clenched. "Let's hear the kid out."

"The 'kid' wants to call it quits."

"This sudden attack of morals," Lister taunted, "this sudden streak of cowardice. I don't get it, kiddy. You came to me with a deal. You wanted backing, and I gave it to you. Is this any way to treat a partner?"

"Partner? You call me a partner? You act as if you own me."

"I do own you. Paid a very handsome price for you, too, Albert. That was part of our bargain, kiddy."

"No, I wanted to build a hotel—nothing more."

"I notice you're looking over at your grandmother's place. She have anything to do with this?"

"You leave her out of it!"

"She want to buy you out of a bad thing?"

"I want to make a clean break. I don't want any money from you, and I don't want to buy my way out."

"That's very generous of you. Well, this is some thanks I get. Some treatment."

"You think you can get out so easily. Think about what you know. We trusted you," Jawitz said, but Lister held his hand up to stop him.

"You threw in with me, Albert. You trusted me to get your hotel built for you. I trusted you. Jawitz here runs off at the mouth, but he talks the truth. I didn't treat you so badly. Look what I bought for you."

"You're not listening to me."

"I'm listening. Stanley, get me the water."

Jawitz handed it to him, and Lister popped a pill in his mouth. "I'm a sick man, Albert, you've got to talk sense with a sick man."

"But I am talking sense."

"Be reasonable. You don't want to get involved with the cash operation, you don't have to be involved. You want to stick to the hotel business." He began to rise. "That's what you want, that's what you get. Case closed."

"No, the case is not closed. I want out. No concessions. No arbitration. Nothing. I want out!"

"Stanley, help me downstairs. We'll leave you alone now, Albert. You must have a lot to think over."

"I don't have to think it over. My decision is final."

Lister continued walking toward the door. "Sleep on it, kiddy. You've got the world, don't lose it without thinking about it. We'll talk again."

Albert stood there speechlessly as the two men closed the door in his face.

Lister put his hand over Jawitz's mouth as Jawitz started ranting in the hallway. They walked to the elevator in silence and then rode down to the lobby.

When they reached Lister's car, Lister looked back at the hotel. "The young man gets himself wrapped up with us, then cries like a baby. I'm sure you'll know what to do, Stanley. I've always trusted you."

That night Albert could not sleep. He took one Seconal at about 11:30 and a second one at 3:00. Finally in the early morning, he drifted off to sleep. He could not have heard the front door of his suite open.

A tall figure darted from the door to the windows to make sure they were locked. He put on a pair of white gloves; then he made his way to the bedroom. Albert lay snoring on the bed. The tall man stared down at his scarred body, then nudged him.

"Willig. Willig. Get up!"

Albert's eyes opened, but they couldn't focus. A hand slashed down across his face. He was sent reeling. Then a glass of cold water hit him. He saw the tall man and the gun clutched in his hands.

"Put some clothes on," the man said.

"What is this?"

"Put some clothes on."

"What do you want with me?"

"Mr. Lister wants to talk with you."

"What time is it?"

The man jammed his gun into Albert's right temple.

"No more talk. Get dressed."

Albert went into his closet and put on a shirt and a pair of trousers. Then the tall man shoved him roughly across the room.

They made their way down to the hotel garage and got into Albert's car.

"We're not going to Lister's house. He doesn't want to meet there. Drive west. I'll show you the way once you get out of the city."

Albert did not have to be told anything else. He knew where this would end. Probably at the site where the Italian hood had gunned down the two Cubans. He knew it in his bones, but he drove on. He waited to make a move, waited for the dull thudding in his head to subside.

They drove on for about an hour. Then the man told him to pull off the road in a deserted field. As soon as Albert rammed the stick shift into park, his hand reached for the door, which snapped open. The tall man fired a shot above his head, but Albert had already hit the ground and was scrambling in the damp brush.

"Nowhere to run," the man said, jumping from the car.

Albert got to his feet and stared ahead at the flat, scrubby land. Lister's last words rang in his ears. "You've got the world." And now the world had come down to this. Scrubby flatland for as far as the eye could see, no sign of life, brush burned out by the deadening heat of summer. Some crickets rubbed their dry bodies together—eerie sounds of the early morning. Scrubland, his world. Another shot was fired, hitting him in the left leg just below the knee. He fell to the ground, not wanting to close his eyes on what was left of his world. He held onto the pain, because as long as he felt it, he was living. Is it true, he wondered—does it all flash in front of you before the end? He prompted his mind to flash backward—to his father sitting in an alley, to his buddy dying on that forgotten hill in a forgotten battle for a seaport. Kill me, his buddy had said.

The tall man stood above him with a rope in his hands. He tied it around Albert's neck and began dragging him back to the car.

"Tie you in a web, was what Lister said he wanted. You know what a web is," the man said, his hands wrapping the rope tightly around Albert's throat, around his hands, shoulders, waist; hoisting his knees, pulling them into a fetal position. Over and over again, the rope spun around him and held him so that each time he squirmed, it held him tighter.

The man picked him up and dumped him in the car's trunk. Then he shut the trunk and locked it.

He rapped on it three times.

"Lister wanted you to know that this is your web."

The man laughed.

Another car came from out of nowhere. A door opened and closed. The car took off.

Albert panted. Beads of sweat flooded over his face, saturating the ropes, swelling them until they twisted more tightly. If he remained very still, he could have saved himself, but the urge to free himself was too strong. He stretched his neck, the rope bit into it. He flexed his calves, the rope tore into the gaping leg wound. His hands twitched, his windpipe jammed. His feet kicked out. His breathing stopped.

I rode out to the site in a county sheriff's car to identify the body. It was noon by the time we got there. The stench of death was trapped in the brush, in the unrelenting glare of the sun. Albert's cream white Caddy looked so cool stranded out there in the flat field. That flashy car that had meant so much to him—a symbol of a world he'd set out to bully into line—was now a white coffin, dazzling in the summer heat.

I remembered the first time I'd seen this land, flat as a table top, engineers measuring it. Negro field hands working it. This is what Miami was built on, I had told myself, and now as I looked at Albert's contorted body lying inside the Cadillac, I knew that this was what Miami had become: chrome dazzling in the middle of nowhere, bodies strewn in its wake, all those passionate dreams just perverse deaths baking under the sun.

A hot wind blew across the field. Its harshness almost delivered me from making a myth of his death. His eyes were wide open. I wondered if he had ever grasped a truth beyond the aggressive assault he launched on the world. Those frightened eyes. I suppose he knew in the end that the world will bend under your sway one moment, and its chaos devours you the next.

I bent over his body to deliver a final benediction: "It was only life," I said for the benefit of my soul as well as his.

46

Albert's death was a blow Bea could neither comprehend nor cry about. I suppose that was the worst part of it. She did not attend his funeral. Sam requested that Albert's body be sent up to New York, and he and Tildy buried their son. Bea mourned alone, and her grief turned in on itself.

She reasoned that she had reached out once in her life, and this was how it had ended. She felt the curse of her love, but nothing of its repentant kindness. She withdrew completely and would only allow me to come see her when business necessitated it or when she was in the mood to talk with someone other than her staff.

She spent most of her time sitting by the water, staring at the waves or the towers of hotel row glistening in the distance. Sometimes when I turned the corner of that huge place of hers, I'd smell the jasmine she had planted everywhere, and thirty years would melt away.

"George, is that you?" she called out as I made my way across the lawn.

"Your friendly solicitor. How are you, Bea?"

"Feeling old and awful. I look awful, don't I?"

Her eyes were beginning to take on a gray cast, and her skin was terribly wrinkled.

"You shouldn't spend time in the sun. It's not good for the skin."

"The wrinkles are bad in this light, aren't they? I used to see them when I looked in the mirror in the morning, but I avoid mirrors completely now. I don't like this aging process. It's so unfair."

I pulled up a chair. "You've been spending a pensive morning?"

"Thinking about this and that. Do you still think I'm a monster, George?"

"I never said that, Bea."

"Sometimes I feel like a monster."

So there were finally scenes of self-reproach being enacted in the privacy of her home.

"My children," she sighed. "So restless. I mourn for them, but I do not feel responsible for the mess they managed to make of their lives."

"Is anyone asking you to do that?"

"Of course. Sam writes me letters, but I send them back to him unopened. And Diana is in town again, did you know that?"

"No."

"She's here, pestering me, calling me all the time. I can't face her. Tell her that if you see her."

"I'm sure she's gotten your message."

She shrugged in disgust. "Helpless brats."

"Bea, I don't think you're doing yourself much good sitting around this house all the time. Why don't you get out, go over to the hotel?"

"No. I got what I wanted. Look at it." She pointed at the Palais. "I don't have to leave my house to see it. Money, George—money and more money. It isn't doing me much good. Even my mother was happier than I am, and she worked her hands to the bone. She had something to hold on to."

"What's that?"

"What I turned my back on to build an empire in this

country of yours. My religion, George. I heard what Sam said to you at Jonny's funeral after I'd said the *shema.* It was the first time he'd heard it since he was a kid. That was my doing. My mother kept kosher. She kept the Sabbath, taught us who we were. Then I forgot and produced such a soulless bunch of children, with such anger and such disrespect. If I'm responsible at all for what happened to them, it's because of this. And if you are wondering how I pay for what I've done, I'll let you know that I'm aware that it's too late to change a thing."

"You're judging yourself too harshly."

She stood with some difficulty and walked to the edge of the lawn, dismissing, with a shrug of her shoulders, what she had confessed to me. "Oh, I bear up under it all right. I've got my strength, George. That's all I need. I never expected too much from other people, anyway."

I took that as my cue to change the subject. "Do you want to talk business?"

"No, not today."

"Would you like me to leave you alone?"

"Yes, please."

"Call me if you need anything, Bea. Anything at all."

"George?"

"Yes."

"There is one thing I'd like to know."

"What's that?"

"Something I've been thinking about. You won't think I'm being silly?"

"I don't think so."

"It's about Abe, my husband. There were always stories."

"What stories?"

"People said he ran away from me, that he didn't die down here. Have you ever heard those stories?"

"Just talk."

"But have you ever heard anything definite? Do you think it's true, that he's still alive?"

This was the secret Jon had carried to his grave. It wasn't mine.

"No, I've never heard anything."

"You think he's dead?"

"Yes, he died down here in 1919. Wasn't that it?"

She whispered, "1919," as I intoned the gospel and truth according to Bea Willig:

"He died somewhere on the road. A bad influenza that year. That's what got him."

She nodded, and I left her.

When I reached the front of the house, I saw Diana sitting in a car at the end of the driveway.

"Your mother told me you were back in town."

"She knows I'm here, but she won't talk with me."

"She wants to be left alone."

"And I want to beat my fists against her door and demand that she let me back in there."

I stroked her hair. "It's useless, Diana."

"It's my fantasy."

"And what will you do once you get in there?"

"I don't know."

"Perhaps you're not being truthful with yourself."

"Don't preach to me, George. She sees you. Why won't she talk with me?"

"I'm not one of her own. She's always been able to share herself with me because she's got nothing to lose by doing it."

"But I want to help her now."

"No, Diana, you'd like to change her. You'd like it to be entirely different. You'd like to beat on that door until it opens and you find some comfort and love. But it won't be that way. It never can be."

"What's wrong with wanting it?"

"Help yourself, Diana. It's too late for her."

"But if I could change her, George—for just one moment. I need it so badly."

"Please don't do this to yourself. Leave her alone. Come back to my house, spend some time with me again."

We stood there in silence for a long time. Then she shook her head.

"That's another fantasy, isn't it? Like a mother's love. No, George, I will not come back to your house with you."

She turned the car on, shoved the gearshift into drive, and left me standing there.

Some weeks later, I ran into Jack, who told me that Diana had gone back to Paris alone. There were no more lovers to hide behind. Suzanne was now out of the picture. The blonde poet was gone. Jack and I were gone. She'd used all of us up, and although I regretted her leaving, I was glad she'd finally gone off to live by herself.

EPILOGUE

1960

Left With Ourselves

Here I sit, approaching my sixtieth year. Through most of my life I've kept myself bottled up, contenting myself with private visions and unspoken observations. Now, finally, I'm able to tell all, hopefully without morbid histrionics. I am finding such comfort at this age, but don't get me wrong: I am still struggling, and I am still naive enough to wonder if all will end happily.

Jack finally did divorce Diana. I don't know what the exact grounds were, but I suppose they were lack of will, lack of initiative, lack of everything. He still owns an interest in Le Palais, and he's building condominiums up in Lauderdale. He lives with another woman up there. I suppose he's happy, although I think he's one of life's fortunates who doesn't think too much about happiness or unhappiness.

Sam is alive and well and still living in the Shalimar on West Forty-fifth Street, which did become a home away from home for struggling actors, writers, Puerto Rican immigrants, and stray Marxists. He was fortunate to have that lunacy of his to escape into; it's made his life bearable, and when things get him down, he merely pops off into what he calls "banana-land," where he can be as crazy and irresponsible as he wants. He's become quite a good writer. I'd like to share something of his with you. It's long, but I think you'll enjoy it, and I'll let you decide whether or not Sam is really crazy or if that matters at all:

Shalimar: a Rooming House on 45th Street
by Sam Willig

The Landlord comes to get the rent,
his face is hard and mean
A face like what the Landlords got
you never, never seen

Manyana, Manyana

The toilets broken every night
the hallways flooded high

I'm sure I know who done this job
I'm sure I know the guy
Manyana, Manyana

The plaster on the ceiling is falling every day
the tenants all have lawyers and the landlord's got to pay
Manyana, Manyana

The lady in room sixty-six has five children all her own,
she is ready for another one
the Father is unknown
Manyana, Manyana

The burglars are so busy, they have broken every lock
they are looking for some radios
that they can put in hock
Manyana, Manyana

The super cleaned the yard today and left his helmet out
but soon he got a shower of spaghetti, fish and sauerkraut
Manyana, Manyana

The Reverend on the other block
that's East of this here place
would like to tear the building down
He calls it a disgrace.
Manyana, Manyana

It's raining very hard outside
the sporting girls are sad,
They cannot walk the streets tonight
the business is too bad
Manyana, Manyana

On the third and eighteenth of each month
the welfare checks come in
the liquor stores are crowded
the house is full of sin
Manyana, Manyana

The lady up in eighty-four
is Alabama born
She calls us un-American
looks down on us with scorn.
Manyana, Manyana

The children coming home from school
have learned of bees and birds
and also mark the hallways up
with big four-letter words

Manyana, Manyana

The police hate the landlords
and blame them for the slums
They claim the greedy landlords
rent rooms to all the bums.

Manyana, Manyana

The children are so happy
and they sing the whole day long
but grown-ups are not children
and they know the world is wrong.

Manyana, Manyana

The cost of living in this town
is going up, never down
if welfare doesn't give more aid
we'll fight behind a barricade.

Manyana, Manyana

In 1959 Bea suffered a series of strokes. Although her doctors insisted she be moved to a hospital, she did not wish to leave her house.

Near the end of her illness, she asked me to find Diana for her. Diana was living in Paris, and when I reached her, she told me she'd be on the next plane.

I met her at the airport and was surprised to see how wonderfully well she looked. She was herself again with her gypsy skirts and her hair a tangle of silvery curls. There was finally an inner contentment in her eyes.

When we got to the house, Bea was awake. Her hair was shockingly white. Her skin had a deathly pallor, but a fire still burned in those half-moon eyes. She offered Diana her cheek, and Diana bent over her and kissed her.

"Thank you for coming," was all Bea said that first day.

Diana went to work, ordering the staff around, preparing meals, and serving her mother herself.

When they talked, Bea seemed eager to find common

ground with Diana, but there was always her pride and that wall of distance between them.

"I was thinking this morning that age has a way of leveling the differences between people."

"How so?" Diana asked, arranging the pillows on her mother's bed.

"I'm eighty-two and you're almost fifty-five—what are twenty-seven years any more?"

Diana smiled. "That's very generous of you, mother."

"I don't mean that we are the same sort of person."

"No, we're not."

"I've been driving George crazy all these years. Had him draw up a dozen wills, but I've finally gotten it all down on paper."

"Let's not talk about that now."

"Don't be silly. There is a great deal of money at stake. We have to talk about it."

"If you say so."

"Well, sit down. I can't concentrate while you're walking around dusting things or whatever it is you're doing."

Diana sat down.

"I've left Sam an income that should be more than ample for him. He lives like a ragpicker, anyway. I'm leaving George this house. He's family, and he always liked it here. I've left the bulk of it to you. You'll be a very rich woman, Diana. You'll own most of that hotel. You didn't make a go of a marriage with Jack—let's see if you can run a business with him. We'll see what we will see. The rest, and believe me it's sizable, I've left to you outright—no banks or trustces, so you must handle it yourself. You'll have George to help you out if you need it.

"Well, don't start building my coffin. I'm not dead yet. I merely wanted you to know how things will be. You'll have a lot of responsibilities—with all that responsibility, you'll wind up cursing me in my grave."

"I don't think so. Would you like to sleep now?"

"Yes."

"I'll leave you alone."

Diana rose, but Bea's hand stretched out and stopped her.

"There is something else I want to say. It is not easy for me. I know you're a very restless person. You've always led with your heart. I think that's a very brave thing for you to have done."

"Thank you," Diana said softly.

"But you'll have to learn about strength, and I'm too old to teach you. Now leave me alone. I'm tired."

I don't believe the two women ever again shared the degree of intimacy of that conversation but I don't believe they had to.

Bea died in her sleep about a month after Diana's arrival.

After the funeral Diana and I went back to the house and walked in the garden.

"Is it sad, George? I don't know any more. Is this the saddest thing that could have happened?"

"How do you feel about it?"

"Relieved, in a way. She was old. She had a long life."

"But not a very happy one."

"Who's to say?"

"That's true. Why are you relieved?"

"Because she allowed me to help her die, and I came through it intact. I think there were more things she wanted to tell me about herself, but she wasn't able to. By God, she held on tenaciously, didn't she? If I could only learn how to do that, I'd have everything."

I smiled sadly. "Burying people, building hotels—it comes down to a lifetime of rather mundane activities."

"George, you suprise me. You sound so cynical."

"I'm getting old."

"Thank God for that. It means you're still alive. What a miracle it is that we are here at all. I thought you understood that."

A year has come and gone since Bea's death. It has taken me that long to put all of this in perspective, to see what all these people meant to me and how I affected their lives. The writing of this got me through that year. It overtook me completely, and I surrendered to it. Each day I'd awaken and walk into this library in Bea's house to write. Now it is the dead of night, and I know I'm writing myself out, yet I stay hunched over my desk.

Diana has just walked into the room. She's peering over my shoulder.

"I thought today was the final day," she is saying. "Just put a period where a period belongs, and that will be that."

"I can't do it."

"Oh, George, just say, 'and most of them are dead.'"

"No."

"Did you include Sam's poem about the rooming house?"

"Yes."

"Good, I like that one. What's the problem?"

"I don't want to let go of all of you."

"Well, you don't have to let go of me, that's certainly true." She's bending over me now, nuzzling my cheek with her lips. "Tell your readers that we're facing the world unafraid and aware."

"I don't like that."

"Oh, hell, tell them any damned thing you want, but just come to bed—it's late."

So it ends happily after all. Diana and I will climb the stairs and get into bed. Sometimes we stay up all night telling each other stories. We laugh until our sides hurt or weep over things we've lost. It doesn't seem to matter, because we are finally together, tucked away in our bed, waiting for the night to end.

George Sloate
Miami, Florida

Note

I created the Willig family and their attorney, George Sloate, to tell you the story of Miami in as dramatic a way as I could. Many of the incidents that take place in this book are factual, however, and there have been a number of historical works written about Miami that I used to tell my story.

My basic historical reference was Samuel Eliot Morison's *The Oxford History of the American People.*

Basic Miami reference books: Nixon Smiley's *Knights of the Fourth Estate* and *Yesterday's Miami*; Frank S. Fitz-Gerald-Bush's *A Dream of Araby*; Polly Redford's *Billion Dollar Sandbar.*

Period Research: Time/Life Series *This Fabulous Century;* Condé Nast's *Vanity Fair* (for Havana in the 1930's), *Vogue* (for fashions).

Crime research was gathered from *Life* magazine's extensive coverage in the 1950s and 1960s; Hank Messick's *Lansky*; and the stories that appeared in the *Miami Herald* for all decades covered in this book.

Occult matters: Ralph Metzner's *Maps of Consciousness.*

Circus detail: Henry Ringling North and Alden Hatch's *The Circus Kings.*

Wonderful anecdotes: Jane Reno.

My uncle, Samuel Chamson, for the use of his poem, "Rooming House."

John Maccabee

Acknowledgments

I would like to thank the Miami Historical Society for the help it provided me during the research of this book.

The following people also offered invaluable assistance: Becky Smith, John Huddy, Jill Chamberlin, Fred McCormick, Jim Savage, Arthur Tietlebaum, Marcia Kanner, Jane Reno, Robert Reno, Thelma Peters, Hope Moss, Rhea and Bowie Arnot, Robert Weissler, Hortense Potter, Morris Lapidus, Paul Bruen, Alvin Malnick, Sydny Weinberg, Richard Parks, and Rena Wolner.